WRITING ON THE EDGE

An anthology of contemporary Alaskan stories

WRITING ON THE EDGE

An anthology of contemporary Alaskan stories

David A. James

∿∿∿ Epicenter Press

Kenmore, WA

ᴡᴡᴡ Epicenter Press

6524 NE 181st St., Suite 2, Kenmore, WA 98028

Epicenter Press is a regional press publishing nonfiction
books about the arts, history, environment, and diverse cultures
and lifestyles of Alaska and the Pacific Northwest.
For more information, visit www.EpicenterPress.com

ISBN: 978-1-684920-47-1 (Trade Paperback)
ISBN: 978-1-684920-48-8 (Ebook)

Library of Congress Control Number: 2022939437

Cover and interior design by Scott Book & Melisssa Vail Coffman

*To Lael Morgan, who gave me the idea
and then helped kick it over the finish line.*

"Alaska, by dint of geography and persistent mythology, is the place of far, far away. The people who go there for redemption, resurrection, or a place to hide forever make sure that critical part of it never changes. They make sure the Last Frontier stays at the end of the farthest road.

"For all their own reasons, they need it to be that kind of place."

—Colleen Mondor
from *The Map of my Dead Pilots*

CONTENTS

INTRODUCTION

ALASKA ISN'T A WILDERNESS, MY NEIGHBOR Rosemary McGuire once told me. It's a homeland. She was speaking to the popular conception of Alaska as a vast expanse of unspoiled land, where the human presence is barely measurable. The reality, as she explained, is that from the moment people first arrived after crossing the Bering Land Bridge into what is now called Alaska, people have called it home. Their stories are where Alaska's story is found.

This book was largely finished when Rosemary told me this, but it captured what the anthology had evolved into as I worked on it. The seed of it began several years ago when Lael Morgan of Epicenter Press called me one day and suggested that, as a book reviewer in various Alaskan publications for over twenty years, I write a book about Alaskan literature. This quickly turned towards the idea of compiling an anthology of more or less contemporary Alaska writing. And as I chose selections, I found myself drawn to pieces that explore what it is to make one's home in Alaska.

The problem, of course, is that there is no one way of making a home in Alaska. This is because there is no one Alaska. There are many

Alaskas. That's what I hoped to convey with these selections. Drawn from a range of authors, many of whose work I have written reviews of for the Anchorage and Fairbanks newspapers, the pieces included here wander all over the state. There are stories and dispatches from the rainforest of the Southeast Panhandle to the tundra in the remote Arctic. The writers found within these pages wander from absolute sea level in the waters beyond our shores to the peaks of the tallest mountains in North America, and from the Yup'ik village of Gambell on St. Lawrence Island, a quick boat ride from Russia, to Fairbanks, which lies in the state's geographic center, and onward to the capitol city of Juneau, which is significantly closer to Seattle than it is to Gambell. From places offering complete solitude far from the road system, to small towns where neighbors are a constant presence, to Alaska's largest cities, beset with the same urban woes as nearly every metropolis in America.

A book about life in Alaska would be incomplete without touching on such iconically Alaskan topics as mountain climbing, dogsled races, and solo backcountry jaunts. But it would also be incomplete if it overlooked urban Alaska, where most of us live. Riding a mountain bike on the Iditarod Trail in winter is a challenge far beyond what most of us have experienced. But the same is true for living homeless on the streets of Juneau. Driving a dog team over Eagle Summit during a raging storm while racing in the Yukon Quest tests one's endurance. So does driving a cab in Fairbanks on a forty-below-zero January night in Fairbanks. Bush pilots in rural Alaska face dangers on a daily basis. So do residents in low rent apartment buildings in Anchorage's roughest neighborhood. A Yup'ik teenager can find his life threatened by White environmental activists on Facebook after taking his first whale, following an ancestral tradition that dates back centuries. A woman from his village can find her life threatened by a White serial killer simply by walking home in Anchorage or Fairbanks. Alaska can be a treacherous place, regardless of where one lives.

Alaska can also be deeply rewarding. It's a place where people test themselves. Where they pursue dreams of physical prowess, seek gold from the land, find solace in the wilds, make their homes in imperfect communities, sustain themselves through the hard labor of hunting and fishing, or strive to convey Native cultures and values to the world beyond the state's borders.

Alaska is also a place where people come to reinvent themselves, often to find that the self they hoped to have left behind when they came north has followed them. Yet they keep trying. "I've got this friend Newt," one of Brendan Jones' characters states, in a line that can apply to many of the pieces found here. "He has this idea that the state's on one continuous wash cycle. The Alaskan laundry. That's what he calls it. Everyone coming north to get clean of their past." Sometimes they succeed, as Christine Cunningham learned in her journey from vegetarian to hunter. Sometimes they fail spectacularly, as Tom Kizzia explores in his book about the sad fate of the Pilgrim Family. And sometimes, as Seth Kantner tells us, they are simply swallowed by Alaska's vast landscape, never to be seen again.

The selections I chose for this anthology draw from both nonfiction and fiction, perhaps an unusual choice for a book of this sort. But what I looked for while assembling this collection were stories that are accurate to what Alaska is. Sometimes fiction tells that reality better than actual fact, something Tanyo Ravicz, Stan Jones, Rosemary McGuire, and others excel at. Sometimes reality can seem too impossible to be fact, as we learn from Julia O'Malley, Colleen Mondor, and Nancy Lord. Whether writing fiction or nonfiction, however, all of these authors tell us truths about Alaska.

Most of the writings in this book predate the pandemic that has upended the entire world for nearly two years as I write this. Alaska has been no exception. In the early days, as the state went into a brief lockdown, I felt that the spirit of camaraderie that pulls us together when temperatures plunge and snow and ice consume our existence would pull Alaskans through. That we'd look out for each other. Instead it's divided us as bitterly as it has any corner of the country. Alaskans pride themselves on being different from other Americans. What the pandemic has shown us is how much we are like the rest of the country. We aren't very good at getting along with each other. It hasn't been an easy time to be an Alaskan. It hasn't been an easy time to be human.

Perhaps what is found in these pages tells us why. Being Alaskan and being human requires constant work. "So we're all tumbling around in the Alaskan laundry out here," Tara Marconi says in Brendan Jones' novel *The Alaskan Laundry*. "If you do it right you get all that dirt washed out, then turn around and start making peace with the other shit. Maybe even make a few friends along the way."

When I first read those words in 2016, I felt the offered the perfect metaphor for the place I've called home for more than three decades now. They're only more true to me today. This collection of writing is, in essence, Alaska's laundry. Some of it clean, some of it dirty, most of it a bit faded and worn from too many trips through the washing machine. That's why it fits so well.

NED ROZELL

NED ROZELL FIRST CAME TO ALASKA IN 1981 when he was stationed at Eielson Air Force Base near Fairbanks. A year later he was sent to Mississippi where he finished his service, but he'd been bitten by the bug. In 1986, after being discharged, he climbed in his truck and drove from his home state of New York back to Fairbanks, where he had enrolled at the University of Alaska. It's where he's made his home ever since.

In 1994, Rozell took over the long running Alaska Science Forum column, a weekly article published in newspapers around the state that is provided for free by his employer, UAF's Geophysical Institute. In most of these columns, Rozell introduces readers to a researcher doing work in Alaska, tags along as this person goes about their job, explains what is being studied and why, includes key quotes that shed further light on the science while providing insight on the researcher's personality, and presents it all in a form that reads like a good story and runs a mere 800 words or so.

It's like taking a weekly field trip from your living room. What he does might seem simple, but to pack as much as Rozell does into such a brief space requires considerable skill.

Rozell's job has taken him to nearly every corner of the state, and when he's not out exploring for work, he's doing it on his own. A hiker, climber, cyclist, paddler, skier, runner, and more, he's written columns, blog posts, and books about his own adventures—including his two hikes along the full length of the Trans-Alaska Pipeline—and always does so with an endless curiosity about where he is. His warm writing style and quiet voice leave readers feeling like invited guests.

Explaining how his job provided him with a dream life, Rozell said, "I have found the best way to get to Attu and Iditarod is to hitch a ride with scientists and write about their work. It's been a great way to turn a trip into a mission and learn even more about a place."

This essay, a letter from an Alaskan raven to author Edgar Allan Poe, has long been one of my favorite pieces of Alaska writing. For all the wildlife Alaskans live in the midst of, ravens are the most common, and as Rozell points out, they tell us a lot of things about ourselves. A second piece by Rozell will close the book.

— Letter to Edgar —

Dear Edgar:

I was poking around in a bin of opportunity ("Dumpsters" to your type, with a capital D for some reason) the other day and came across a newspaper that said you died in October 160 years ago. Bummer. I had seen your famous poem about us, in another bin (you wouldn't believe what people throw out), and I wanted to chew your ear for a minute.

First of all, thanks for calling us "stately" on first reference. I'm with ya. In fact, we're the real state bird of Alaska, no matter what those place-mats say. Willow ptarmigan—whose idea was that? You ever see a willow ptarmigan with personality? Take a poll of Alaskans, Eddy, they'll give you their state bird, the same "ebony bird" you made famous in 1845.

No other creature has the guts to go where we go. Climbers on Denali try to hide their food from us at 17,000-foot high camp, but it doesn't work. We wait until they throw a bit of snow over their food and stagger away. Then we dig it up and poke away. Easy money.

And the oilfields around Prudhoe Bay—no trees, blowing snow, about a gazillion below in winter. Those big-money workers up there do a Christmas Bird Count every year, and they record just one species. You know which one it is, baby. Biologists up there have seen us nesting in drilling rigs and feeding our chicks when it's 30 below. Thirty below! Know where the robins are then, Edgar? Florida! One biologist named Stacia captured a few of us up there to fit us with wing tags. She had trouble re-capturing us for her studies, so—get this—she wore a fake moustache to fool us! But we still know it's her.

We only hang out in Prudhoe because your type is there, Edgar. Don't take this the wrong way, but you guys are slobs. You don't finish what you eat. Today, humans are what wolves were 250 years ago. Once, we were all over the Great Plains, and today we're not. It's not that we don't like wide-open spaces, it's just that there's no more bison there, and there's no more wolves, who, like furry can-openers, would open the buffalo for us.

It's kind of odd you lived on the East Coast, Edgar. It's hard to find a raven in Baltimore, except for those ones on the football helmets (Purple ravens?! C'mon guys, black is beautiful!). Today we prefer the West Coast and the far North, from Baja to Barrow. We really like caribou and other prey species, and in Alaska there's more caribou than people, and there's lots of wolves and bears left to scatter carcasses around the landscape for us. Ever picked at a fleshy backbone on a hot summer's day, Edgar? Heaven.

Back to your poem. Let me see if I remember it: Once upon a midnight dreary, after rapping on a chamber door, a raven stepped into a dark parlor, perched on a bust of a Greek goddess, and terrified a bereaved lover by answering all his questions with the word "Nevermore."

I heard that a University of Alaska Fairbanks English professor once picked apart your poem like we do a road-killed red squirrel. He suggested your narrator's ingestion of opium might have given the raven its voice. That's baloney. We talk all the time. We squawk, we knock; we make sounds like rocks thrown into water. A Fairbanks scientist who followed us around with a recorder came up with 30 distinct phrases in the raven dictionary. Lucky for him he couldn't translate them.

The farther I read into your poem, the more you punch up the descriptions. You describe the raven as ghastly, grim, ungainly, gaunt, ominous, grave, a devil, a thing of evil, a fiend and a demon. I'm flattered, but others have held us in pretty high esteem. In Norse mythology, for example, the god Odin employed two ravens with the names Thought and Memory to fly the world and inform him of what was happening out there. We were less dependable for Noah, when a pair of us failed to return to the ark after he sent us to search for land. We probably found some carcasses out there; why go back for hard-tack and scurvy?

In Alaska, we're treated as we should be. Every Native group has raven stories. In many stories, including those of the Tlingit, Haida, and Koyukon, Raven is the god who created the sun, the Earth, the stars, the moon, and humankind. We are also the tricksters who deceive others in our endless quest for food. True, all true. And tell me, Edgar, what has the moose created? Nothing but moose nuggets.

BRENDAN JONES

FOR OVER A CENTURY, THE MYTH of the Last Frontier has drawn desperate people to Alaska. Beset by problems with families, finances, the law, or more, they come seeking refuge and a new start. This tendency has provided fodder for a number of authors who have turned their characters loose in Alaska, people running from their pasts, only to find that they can't escape themselves. No book I've read makes this point better than Sitka novelist Brendan Jones' *The Alaskan Laundry*.

Set in Port Anna, a fictionalized version of the city Jones lives in, the story follows Tara Marconi, a daughter of Italian immigrants who flees north from her hometown of Philadelphia after a pair of traumatic incidents. She arrives penniless to take a job in a fish hatchery and slowly builds a new life amongst the seasonal workers, burnouts, Tlingit Natives, and others who toil in canneries and aboard fishing vessels.

As the novel progresses, Tara charts her path through the local fishing industry, establishing her bonafides, but with numerous setbacks along the way. The world Jones sets her in, and which he knows well from his many years working in it, can be unforgiving, something

Tara quickly and repeatedly learns. But still she presses forward, because quitting means failure, and failure is what she came to Alaska to overcome.

For Jones, writing the book itself was a process of overcoming obstacles and refusing to accept failure. Reflecting on how the story emerged and why he chose to place a young woman at its center, he told me, "*The Alaskan Laundry* came about after many fits and starts, attempts to write about my experience as a teenager tendering sea cucumber boats, working in the fish processor and deckhanding on tenders and salmon trollers. After growing up in a family of women, raised by a single mother, I wanted to write both a celebration of strong women, as well as a love letter to the state that gave me my rites of initiation, for lack of a better term, that I could not find at home."

The two brief excerpts that follow are the scenes that give the book its title. It's a phrase Tara picks up from her one true and dependable friend among Port Anna's transients and hard working fishermen.

"I've got this friend Newt," she tells the captain of the boat she's working on. "He has this idea that the state's on one continuous wash cycle. The Alaskan laundry. That's what he calls it. Everyone coming north to get clean of their past."

Originally from Philadelphia, Jones, like some of the characters in his book, came north for a summer, never intending to stay. More that twenty years later he still hasn't left.

— From *The Alaskan Laundry* —

ON THE TWENTY-THIRD, SHE PULLED HERSELF out of her sleeping bag. Newt bought beers and told her to meet him at the channel marker. On impulse she swung by Fritz and Fran's to see if Keta was there. At first the dog seemed to ignore her, hardly looking up as she pet him. Then she knelt and whispered in his ear.

"Hi, sweet you," she said. "I'm so glad you didn't leave with those people. I thought you might have forgotten about me."

When he didn't move she turned his head toward her, pressed her forehead against his skull, and stared into the dog's unblinking eyes. *Funny, I was thinking the same thing,* the dog seemed to say back. She switched tacks. "Hey, monkey. I'm sorry. I've been busy. Okay? But I'm here now. I promise I won't abandon you. My resolution for the year."

After a few seconds he freed his head, gave her a quick look, then trotted out in front. When they got to the breakwater, he wouldn't go out on the rocks until she was there beside him, her fingers trailing along his back.

"Dog likes you," Newt said as Keta picked his way among the boulders. "See how he keeps making sure you're okay?"

When they were arranged in their usual spots, Tara leaned against a steel post, calmed by the rhythmic flashing of the light, Newt handed her a beer. Keta sat on his haunches, the sun reflecting gold off his white fur. Clouds swam like fish across the sky.

"Any word from Plume?" Tara asked.

He looked up at her, veins blue beneath his pale skin. "Not a word."

A whale exhaled toward the end of the landing strip at the airport. Keta watched the white funnel of mist come apart in the breeze.

"You know, my old man called me at the processor, just before I went out with Jackie."

"That right?"

"He said there was something he wanted to talk about."

They drank, watching the clouds for a couple minutes. "What's he like, your dad?" Newt asked.

She stroked Keta's silky head. "You know, today was the day she died."

Newt said nothing. She felt her stomach heave, then took a breath.

"Right before I left, like six months after my mother was killed, I'm coming back up the stairs late at night, sandwich in one hand. And there he is, favorite mustard cardigan tucked into his sweat-pants. I'm standing there holding my cheese sandwich. He asks me something, like if I was planning to start giving him a hand at the bakery anytime soon. I must have looked down for a second, because then I hear this crack, and he's got his fist through the plaster, hollering that it was my fault my mother died, that I never lifted a finger around the house, that all I did anyway was watch TV and eat his food. Spoiled good-for-nothing brat, that's what he called me." She swallowed. "I told him he could go fuck himself, ran out of the house in my pajamas, then spent three months at Connor's. That's when I called Acuzio, who got me the job with Fritz."

Keta whined softly. She was petting him too hard. The breeze blowing through the hemlocks along the coast made a brushing sound.

"Well, all I can tell you is—"

"I know, Newt. Do what you can, and let the rough end drag."

"Well, that too," he said. "But I was gonna say he sounds like a prick. Maybe he's calling with his tail between his legs."

Tara shook her head. "Urbano Marconi doesn't do tail between his legs."

"Well, then here's another one. We're put on this green earth to learn to love honestly and cleanly. Simple as that."

"So?"

"So we're all tumbling around in the Alaskan laundry out here. If you do it right you get all that dirt washed out, then turn around and start making peace with the other shit. Maybe even make a few friends along the way." He winked at her.

"I'm trying," she said.

"I know you are," he said seriously. He stood and slap-boxed on the rocks with Keta, who bared his teeth and growled. "It's pretty damn obvious."

EARLY THE NEXT MORNING, ON A BLOWY MONDAY, Tara woke to the sound of Zachary unloading groceries.

"Ready to catch some fish?" he said.

A hearty, upbeat nature was exactly what she didn't want to deal with now.

"Got some good reports at Fulton Island, and some at Dos Santos Bay, near the southern tip of Archangel. Salmon are like the rest of nature, I guess," he said, arranging milk, butter, and eggs in the icebox. "Hard to predict." He held up a package of bacon. "Don't tell my wife."

The dog stepped onto the docks, stretching, keeping a wary eye on Zachary.

"Whoa! You didn't say you were bringing a wolf on board."

"He's chilled out. Doesn't bark."

"You look like you could use another five hours of sleep."

"I'm fine."

She ignored his raised eyebrows as she brought more groceries into the galley. He climbed the ladder to the flybridge, then hoisted up the roof so the chute from the processor could drop into the hold. Their ice appointment was for five a.m. He gave her the job of inflating the buoy balls until they made a hard knocking sound against her knuckle.

"Cut her loose there, partner," he shouted down. She undid the bow, stern, then the midship line, and stepped aboard.

"Forgetting something?"

"Shit," she said. The dog watched her, standing on the end of the dock. With a pulse of the engine Zachary pushed them back.

"You might as well undo our shore power while we're at it."

"Shit," she repeated. The boat swiveled, tilting the blue dock post where the yellow cord was attached. She hopped back onto the dock, threw the breaker, and swung the cord over the bow.

"C'mon, love. Hop hop!"

With a surprising nimbleness Keta leapt over the gunwales onto the deck, giving Tara a quick lick when she leaned down to kiss his cheek. Again Zachary backed out, then swung the boat around the breakwater of Crescent Harbor and cruised beneath the bridge. Cars passed above, the sound of tires over the joints echoing off the water. Tara leaned against the hold, watching the sun rise behind town, jealous of Keta snoring away on the galley bench. Seasons were made or broken by salmon openers, she knew. She needed to get on with it.

When they approached the pilings of the processor, Zachary threw the engine into reverse and a backwash kicked out from the stern. She waited with a line in one hand, then leaned against a piling, caked with barnacles and scallops and a few starfish, to make them fast.

"The tide's pulling us," Zachary said as she seized the rope and began to tie a clove hitch. "Just come right on back to the boat." Unsure, she looked back at him.

"Here. Always go from bow to stern when you tie off to pilings. And leave some slack so the hull doesn't rub."

A voice came from above. "Holy shit, is that Tara Marconi you got on board?"

It was Trunk, peering down, earphones around his neck. "You stealin' my employees, Sachs?"

"What can I say?" Zachary shouted back. "She was ready for some real work." He turned to Tara. "Tie her off at the bow, then come and help me with this hatch cover."

Trunk lowered the hooped cylinder of the ice chute. "Tell me when!" Zachary dropped into the hold, caught the chute, and shouted up.

"All right!"

There was a rumble, and then the familiar bang of Trunk hammering on the chute with his wrench, followed by the scurry of ice chips. Zachary filled the stern hold, then the two sides.

"One minute!" Zachary hollered. Trunk hit a lever and the ice slowed. Zachary pushed the chute over the side of the boat.

"Y'all stay safe out there," Trunk shouted down. "And you take care of yourself, my lady."

She leaned over the gunwales. She liked how he said this, as if she were some aristocrat. "I will."

The hatch cover slid home with a whomp. The sun broke through the clouds, lighting the volcano a rusty red as he motored out past the breakwater. "You get seasick?" Zachary asked.

"I didn't on the tender."

"That old scow doesn't bob up and down like this one. If you need to throw up, just go right over the side. You wanna lie down?"

"I'm good, just hungry."

"Make lunch."

She smeared peanut butter and jelly onto a tortilla while he checked the tide tables. The RAM of the autopilot made barking noises as it shifted, the system keeping the boat oriented west-south-west, just off the volcano.

"You bring food for the dog?"

Keta's ears perked up. He looked between them.

"Nope."

Zachary shook his head, turning the knob on the VHF, adjusting the volume. "Well, I hope he eats fish."

Southeast Alaska waters, Cape Decision to Cape Edgecumbe, small craft advisory. A weak trough will dissipate over the panhandle Monday. A high-pressure ridge will build across the panhandle and eastern gulf Monday night. A weather front will move northeast into the central gulf by Saturday morning, with southeast gales up to forty knots diminishing to fifteen knots late. Seas sixteen feet.

Zachary grimaced. He opened the tide book again, and looked toward the volcano. A green-tinted line of clouds moved east off the ocean. The teapot on the Dickinson clattered against its railing. She handed him a sandwich, which he ate in large bites, holding a paper towel to catch loose jam.

"You ever take wheel watches on the *Adriatic*?" She shook her head. "Just keep an eye on the radar, and ahead of you for deadheads — floating logs. If you see one, go in the other direction. Red channel markers on your right, green on the left. I'll be right back. The other day the bilge was pumping oil. I want to make sure we're okay."

She stood in front of the wheel, keeping one hand on the dial. It was like a video game, making sure the image of the boat remained between the red and green points on the screen, and out of the light blue shallows. Glancing up at the radar every now and then, watching the blobs of islands and boats shape and reshape every few seconds. There was an intermittent whine, and she stayed quiet, trying to hear what it might be, until she realized it was the dog.

"You need food, don't you?"

When Zachary returned, Keta was eating the second half of his beef stew. Zachary lit a cigar, the wheelhouse filling with its odor. "That's good beef. Coming out of your crew share."

"I'm new at this taking-care-of-another-creature thing," she said, moving over so he could take the wheel. "Sorry."

He smiled to show it had been a joke. "So why didn't you finish out the season with Teague and Jackie?" One thing she had come to appreciate about Alaskans: when it was clear you didn't want to talk about something, people laid off. So she felt confident he'd let it drop when she said, "It just didn't work out."

Except he didn't.

"It gets squirrely on the water, especially in these small boats," he told her. "I like to have a sense of who I'm working with, where they've been. That's why I put you on that safety course. So if there's anything I should know, tell me before we put gear in the water."

She stared out the window. They were rounding the far side of the volcano. Ravines, still filled with snow, swirled off the rim. "We had a misunderstanding, and I left."

"And you hit her."

That was another thing about Port Anna. No secrets. "Yeah, I hit her, okay? If you had some guy getting up in your face, what are you going to do? Smile back at him?"

He drew on his cigar, exhaled out the window. "Depends on what the guy was in my face about. I also heard you were in a scrape up in Hoonah."

"'What the fuck?" she said. She felt a wetness on the back of her palm, Keta nudging her hand with his nose. "If you don't want me on the boat, drop us on the next island. We'll figure it out."

He pulled back on the throttle. For a moment she wondered if he was actually doing it. Then she saw they were coming into a cove. Small waves looped over themselves, breaking onto a narrow strip of beach.

On the flybridge he hit the kill switch on the generator. The silence echoed off the rocks. Back inside he said, "Listen. Like I said back at the docks, honesty is boat policy. I need to know who I'm working with."

"Should I get dinner started?" she asked.

He waited.

Fuck, Tara thought. This was a mistake. It was always a mistake to go anywhere with a guy you didn't know. Things never ended well.

"Tara," Zachary said. "Just be up front with me. That's all I'm asking."

She exhaled. "Okay. In Hoonah I was on the phone with my father, trying to talk to him, and this guy kept harassing me. It was my fault. I hit him. And with Jackie it was worse. Things got really weird in Tenakee. And she deserved it."

He picked at his beard, thinking. Finally, he gave a small nod. "Okay. Let's get dinner started."

Cooking calmed her. She sliced potatoes and onions into browning bacon while Zachary picked up the radio station, blues of some sort, and set to repairing his glasses, one arm held to the frame with a shred of electric tape. Gray wafts of smoke rose in the still air as he soldered. He put down the glasses, fed a handful of chips into his mouth. Flakes caught in his beard. "This bruiser over here keeps a good eye on you. Watches your every move."

She kissed Keta on his bony snout. "So how'd you end up in Port Anna?" she asked. This was the standard Alaska opening gambit, she had come to learn. She wanted to break the awkwardness. Thankfully, he went along.

"Well, I was going to a yeshiva in Kew Gardens Hills, in Queens, New York City, and I met a beautiful woman outside a synagogue. We married, everything was fine, then her parents were stabbed in a mugging.

And she decided that, if we were going to raise children, we would bring them up in a place where they would feel safe. I had read about this half-baked idea in the 1920s of Roosevelt's to send ten thousand Jews a year to Southeast. So I thought, why not check it out? We hitched up to Bellingham, caught the ferry, bought a boat, and I started fishing. Thelma found a job as a dispatcher at the police station, while I learned the charts, the pinnacles." He held his glasses away from his face, then slipped them back on, eyes large behind the lenses. He wiped his fingers with a wet cloth. "And that's my story."

"I've got a friend, Newt —"

"Guy on the *Spanker*? One eye? Works like a demon?"

"That's him."

"Yeah. I like that kid."

"He has this idea that the state's on one continuous wash cycle. The Alaskan laundry, that's what he calls it. Everyone coming north to get clean of their past."

Zachary looked toward the islands. "I've seen some folks get pretty dirty in the process. Take Newt, for example."

She set out plates and silverware. He had a point. "So how'd you get hooked up with King Bruce?"

"The crab guy? You know him?"

"I know *of* him. He's down an eye as well."

"You're kidding."

"I am not. Comes with the territory, I guess. You feel ready to work those volcanic reefs up there in the Bering Sea? That's a whole different game."

After dealing with Fritz, living in the woods, navigating her way through Jackie, Petree, and Betteryear, she felt like she could deal with anything.

"What happened to his eye?"

"As I heard it, he was stepping into a crab pot to change out a bait jar. The boat took a wave, the door shut, and the pot went overboard with him inside. He was on his way to the bottom until he kicked open the door, swam up, and whacked his head against the hull. Knocked himself out cold. His boat circled back, and some deckhand trying to save him hooked him in the eye with a pike pole. When he woke up he was half blind."

"Man."

"Coming clean exacts its price."

"I guess."

She scooped food onto the blue enamel plates. What would her price be? Had she already paid? The other night with Bailey? With Betteryear? The platform burning in the woods?

"One thing I can tell you," he said, "it's no country for a *nebbish*."

"What's a *nebbish*?"

His reached out to scratch Keta's chin. The dog seemed to smile, showing his long teeth. "Everything, as far as I can tell, that you are most definitely not."

SHERRY SIMPSON

INITIALLY ENCOUNTERED SHERRY SIMPSON WHEN SHE tagged along with a raven researcher who studies Alaska's most ubiquitous bird in its natural habitat, the dumpsters around Fairbanks. The story of this experience, which appeared in her debut essay collection, *The Way Winter Comes*, hooked me in immediately with her combination of informative reporting, lively prose, and sly humor. I've been an admirer ever since.

Simpson moved to Juneau as a child and remained in Alaska for nearly five decades, living in Petersburg, Fairbanks and Anchorage. Along the way she became a widely published essayist, exploring the interplay between her own internal narrative and her external surroundings.

This combination is in full bloom in one of her finest pieces, "Turning Back," which appeared in her second collection, *The Accidental Explorer*. It tells the story of her failed attempt at hiking the 58 mile long Circle-to-Fairbanks trail, accompanied only by her aging dog, Jenny. Neither of them, it turns out, is up for the effort.

Simpson expertly weaves the trail's history into the narrative of her aborted journey, while coming to terms with her not entirely noble reasons for taking on the challenge. The route was initially traversed by Athabascan traders, she explains. Then, using imagery characteristic of her skills, she writes, "prospectors wandered through, frisking the creeks for gold" (what a marvelous passage—an entire historical era captured in just eight words). Today it's a recreational route, and traplines and litter serve as reminders of the most recent visitors.

Yet despite its close proximity to Fairbanks and extensive use, Simpson learns on the trail that even heavily traveled routes can turn dangerous for those who go under-prepared. In this instance she hadn't thought things through as fully as she should have. But she has the wisdom to know when to turn back. Because Alaska, as she writes in another essay from the same book, is always prepared to throw hazards in the path of those who set out to explore it.

Live here long enough, and you'll learn that every moment spent admiring endless vistas or wandering the land is a privilege, accompanied by plenty of other moments evading mosquitoes by the millions, outlasting weather, avoiding Giardia, negotiating unruly terrain, and thinking uneasily about the occasional predator. Walking cross-country through alder thickets or muskeg may be the hardest thing you do all year, as you fight against the earth's tendency to grab hold of you for itself.

Simpson was the author of three books, and her work has appeared in numerous magazines, journals, and anthologies. She taught creative writing through the University of Alaska Anchorage and Pacific Lutheran University. Following a path taken by many former Alaskans, she moved to a place that is warm and dry (New Mexico), where, she told me by email, she was happily able to say "Oh, good, it's raining."

Sherry Simpson passed away in October of 2020.

— From *The Accidental Explorer* —
TURNING BACK

AT FIRST I THOUGHT OF THE hike along the old Circle-to-Fairbanks Trail as a walking meditation. For at least a week, maybe more, I would walk with only my blue heeler Jenny for company. I would spend all day, every day, quiet with my thoughts. For 58 miles I would hike through heat and rain and mosquitoes on a hilly route I didn't know. On the other end, seven or eight days away, my husband would greet someone different from the person he left at the trailhead. Of this I was sure.

For weeks I practiced with map and compass. I bought a GPS and learned to use it. I did girl's push-ups twenty at a time. I filled my pack with the heaviest items—tent, sleeping bag, pad, clothes, stove, fuel, water filter—and marched along the first two miles of the trail to remind my feet and back of the task ahead. At the path's high points, I looked across the domes, patchy with snow, and imagined myself walking toward the horizon, soon.

I told all of my friends about the trip. It was a way of not chickening out. Some of them told me stories. One friend said, "I feel I should say that the worst mosquitoes I've ever encountered were on the Circle-Fairbanks Trail." Another described following the footprints of a solo hiker near the White River in the St. Elias Mountains until the footprints disappeared into the river, which is what happened to the hiker: he disappeared into the river after trying to float it in a small raft.

I could not help myself; I looked up news stories about him, and about other solo hikers, too. There was the 36-year-old man who vanished in Glacier Bay National Park, leaving behind his tent, food, and most of his gear. The rangers decided he "strolled away from his camp, got lost, suffered hypothermia, and in his confusion fell into the water or crawled out of sight beneath a rock." What they meant was: "We have no idea what happened to him." There was the young woman who lost her way during a birdwatching dayhike on one of the most popular trails near Fairbanks. Three days later, searchers found her but not her little dog, which had wandered off into the woods, to be eaten by bears or eagles or who knows what.

This was not the first time I would be alone out in the woods somewhere, but it was the first time I would hike such a distance by myself, relying on my own judgment, strength, skills. I would have to be brave. That's why I wanted to do it, I suppose. At home I am the sort of person who is afraid to answer a ringing phone because a stranger might ask for something that I can't refuse, such as a donation to a suspiciously obscure charity or a subscription to a magazine I don't want. I spend long moments each day worrying about things that can't be changed, such as what I should have told the person on the phone instead of "yes." I vex myself with imaginative dramas about things that haven't happened but could: falling elevators, mysterious diseases, wrongful criminal accusations. To a person who frets herself through daily life, it comes as a relief to lie awake nights and think through real problems: getting lost, falling ill, dying alone in some ravine.

Other, less definable worries occupied me, including how to keep a clear head no matter what. Never mind about losing the way—what about losing *it*, the all-important it that must be kept intact? Now and then I would stir restlessly and reach my hand toward my sleeping husband, trying to soothe that jumpy feeling in my chest. It was a familiar sensation, the fear of being afraid, of being so swamped by uncertainty and dread that I wouldn't know what to do. It was a feeling that had texture, dimension, weight.

The night before I left, I gathered the gear scattered about my living room and stuffed it into my big blue pack. When I hefted the load onto my back, I pitched backward a step, then forward, struggling to remain upright. My husband laughed. I took everything out and ditched whatever seemed excessive: extra bandages, a mini-disc recorder, rope. The pack lightened by perhaps nine or ten ounces. Surely this was the heaviest weight I had ever borne.

I did not know what else to leave behind. One person has to carry everything.

SCOTT DROVE ME TO THE TRAILHEAD on a cool June morning. We climbed toward Cleary Summit on the Steese Highway, then turned onto bumpy dirt roads and ricketed toward the trailhead. Jenny paced back and forth across the back seat, smearing the windows with her muzzle. She was a dog who lived in constant anticipation. The radio repeated a news item about a 30-year-old Alaskan killed the previous day when his truck rolled over. He had been a top athlete and a two-time competitor in the winter Wilderness Classic, an arduous 125-mile race through the Wrangell Mountains. Any day of the week, a person could die. A person doesn't have to slip down a mountainside, or get mauled by a bear, or disappear into the wilds to die. A person could drive to work and be killed, just like that.

Mosquitoes hummed in a thick fog at the trailhead. I grunted as I struggled into the pack and buckled myself to it. Scott attached a tinny bell to Jenny's collar. He sprayed me front and back with bug dope. He photographed us standing by the sign that said "Circle-Fairbanks Historical Trail," and the traitorous part of my brain wondered if that would be the picture they'd put in the paper once the search started. Scott had never once tried to dissuade me from this hike; he just assumed I knew what I was doing. He held my face and kissed me good-bye. "Be careful," he said, and I nodded mutely and turned up the trail. The next time I looked, he was driving away, and Jenny and I had no choice but to keep going.

THE CLOUDS EVAPORATED AS THE DAY HEATED, and the mosquitoes dropped away in the sun. The pack's straps rasped against my collarbone. I leaned against a rocky slope and gulped water, letting it slop down my throat and chest. I offered Jenny a slurp and glanced at my watch. We had been walking for approximately thirteen minutes. Twenty minutes later, I trudged up a small slope to a rock outcropping, marked by beer cans and cigarette butts as a scenic overlook. Posts indicated each passing mile, but I hadn't seen the first marker yet. I was terribly afraid we hadn't reached it yet, because if it was going to take me an hour to walk a mile, then I might not get home before the end of summer.

A breeze stirred the creamy blooms of grass of Parnassus around our feet. "Thirsty?" I asked Jenny. She wagged her stub. A ridiculous tail for a dog. "Your tail is ridiculous," I told her. I could see I would be spending a lot of time talking to my dog. I missed Scott already. I heaved off the pack and poured water into Jenny's fold-up bowl. Then I sat on pointy rocks and drank deep draughts still cold from my kitchen faucet. Finding water would be a problem out here, but I could not stop gulping.

The hills roller-coastered around us. New leaves of aspens and birches riffled in the slow sea of air. A massive hard-rock gold mine named Fort Knox ground away in the distance, hidden from view. It was the newest quarry in a country that had been mined top to bottom for a hundred years. The maps are strewn with tiny Xs, hash marks, and crossed picks that symbolize prospects, mines, and tailings on every creek. Around here entire gold rush towns have long since eased back into the brush, leaving only names: Cleary, Gilmore, Golden City, Olnes. Pictures of

Dome City, not far from the trailhead, show a thriving community built by former luminaries of the Klondike. The town included three banks, police and fire departments, a mayor, a stage company, and plenty of hotels and bars. Today—nothing.

The Circle-Fairbanks Trail is a narrow four-wheel drive road at the start, muddy and rutted with tracks from all-terrain vehicles, motorcycles, horses, moose, wolves, and bears. It is said the Athabascans originally used it, or some version of it, as a hunting and trade route. Then prospectors wandered through, frisking the creeks for gold. After diggings proved rich, lots of people suddenly had reason to travel from Circle City on the Yukon River into the Birch Creek region. When a scruffy Italian prospector named Felix Pedro panned colors from a creek not far from this dome, hopeful people poured in from the Yukon and the Chandalar country to a new gold camp named Fairbanks.

Mail, cattle, sheep, passengers and supplies crossed the country between Circle City and Fairbanks. So much gold traversed this route that the "Blue Parka Bandit" shadowed the trail, politely but firmly robbing stages and lone miners of their fortunes. In 1928, the Steese Highway borrowed some of the trail, and then there wasn't much reason to use the rest. Most of the roadhouses closed, and the route lapsed, used only by dog mushers, snowmachiners, hikers, horse riders, and off-road riders. A few stubborn miners drive the trail to their claims, but the rest of us use it for fun.

I rolled my pack over and loosened the shoulder cinches. In a process that seemed to grow harder each time rather than easier, I hoisted it to one bent knee, wormed my right arm through the strap, twisted my left arm behind my back, and, stooping over, tugged it onto my back. Involuntary sounds emerged from my mouth that I thought I wouldn't be making for another 20 or 30 years. "Mother of God, why is this pack so heavy?" I groaned. Jenny stared at me, ears perked, pink tongue dangling wetly. "Why aren't you wearing a pack?" I asked. "You could at least carry your own food."

Recently I'd begun to wonder if her sharp eyes—eyes that could spot a bread crumb falling onto the floor from 10 feet away—had clouded a little. Sometimes I had to clap my hands to catch her attention. Her muzzle had whitened, and she no longer made wild, acrobatic leaps to catch Frisbees. In dog years she was 91. Bringing her along seemed a bit like dragging your grandmother on the Appalachian Trail. Nevertheless, I assumed Jenny would like walking with me, and of course, at first she did. What a grand creature a dog is.

UNTIL NOW, I HADN'T GIVEN MUCH THOUGHT to the actual hiking. Mostly I'd concentrated on simply getting here. Several weeks earlier I had spent three days in the hospital when outpatient surgery had unexpectedly become in-patient surgery. For a time, the diagnosis had been vague, and alarming words had been bandied about—"growth" and "malignant" and so on. I'd signed papers authorizing the removal of any suspicious tissue, up to and including entire reproductive organs—not that the doctor expected such a thing, he kept saying. During the procedure, the surgeons discovered I was suffering from endometriosis, a fairly common problem in which uterine tissue colonizes new territory, but they had been forced to abandon the minor procedure of a laparoscopy, with its modest nick through the belly button, and instead had slit open my lower abdomen and mucked about in my internal organs, leaving me with a six-inch scar and a sore belly.

I had shared the hospital room with an 80-year-old woman who'd had an abdominal tumor the size of a basketball removed, a tumor she hadn't known was there until she'd undergone a scan for back problems. She was proud of a Polaroid documenting her remarkable tumor, a photograph I repeatedly fended off. My doctor, though, ambushed me in the follow-up exam with Technicolor pictures of my body cavity with organs splayed out during surgery. I wasn't sure which was worse: actually seeing my own innards, or knowing that total strangers had been photographing them while I was as insensible as I ever hope to be this side of death.

I spent a good part of the spring huffing at crunches, scratching the red scar that embossed my belly, trying to regain a feeling of wholeness and strength. This hike would prove my health, my vigor, my endurance. Still I couldn't seem to shake the red truth of that photograph.

I SANG. IT SEEMED EARLY IN THE trip to holler spirit-bolstering songs, but I sang anyway. I stepped among the tracks of all who had passed recently—horses, people, wolves, a moose and her newborn calf—and I sang lullabies and hymns, love songs, and ditties composed entirely of nonsense. Jenny paced and panted just behind me. Usually she insisted on leading any expedition. When she was younger, it drove her to distraction on berry-picking expeditions if any of us wandered about; she spent all her energy trying to herd us into one safe, compact group. Today the heat seemed to have dulled her usual energy, and she lagged. Whenever we paused, she flopped in the dirt and waited, eyes half-closed.

Jenny didn't like me when we first got her as a repo dog, thirteen years before. Scott's boss had bred heelers, also known as Australian cattle dogs, and he had retrieved Jenny from her new owners when he discovered that the puppy was living night and day in a garage lined with Visqueen on the floor. He next sold her to a man who never asked his wife if she wanted a dog. She didn't. A week later, I was visiting Scott at work when the embarrassed man returned with a gray-and-red puppy that rocketed around at near the speed of light, ears flattened, tongue curled. We took her home.

She was four months old and had missed crucial time being socialized. She bared her teeth and rolled her eyes suspiciously whenever I tried to pet her, no matter how much I complimented her fine markings, the black that circled her eyes like kohl and tipped her ears, the silvery sheen of her coat and her ruddy belly, the white streak on her fawn-colored face. Within a few days, she decided to be my dog after all, a job she took far too seriously. It was years before she would let anyone else in the house without terrifying them, though once she did warn me about a man I was too stupid to realize was dangerous. Most of her attitude problems I attributed to chronic underemployment. Lacking cows to organize, she bossed around our two cats and the other dog, a male husky-Lab who was much larger than she was but who had the intelligence of a sharp-witted pet turtle. Jenny had not only brains but opinions she couldn't keep to herself. We called her piercing yap the "Vulcan Death Bark."

Unfortunately, she did not see me as the alpha female so much as an outsized littermate who occasionally made irritating demands and wasn't particularly accommodating about sharing the bed. But everywhere I went, she followed, even from room to room in the house. "Mind your own beeswax," I chided her one day, and Scott said "But you are her beeswax." Out here, it was comforting being somebody's beeswax.

AT EVERY MILEPOST I STOPPED AND entered the position in my GPS. It tracked my progress, but the satellite readings told me nothing my feet and back didn't know already. Mile two, uphill on a wooded slope. Mile three, along a forested straightaway, passing a leghold trap on the trail. Mile four, curving upward against the outside of a dome, where a runnel of clear water dribbled from the thawing tundra. Mile five, alongside two fresh sets of bear tracks pressed into the mud.

We passed an explosion of white-gray fur, and I panicked briefly when I saw Jenny nosing a caribou leg near the trail. For all I knew, that pair of bears lurked nearby protecting a kill. A prickly, urgent feeling quickened my steps. "Let them in, Peter. They are very tired," I bellowed tunelessly. "Give them couches where the angels sleep, and light those fires." But I didn't like the trend of that song, rooted as it was in the afterlife, so I switched to love songs. It's my belief that bears like love songs best.

The mucky trail turned toward the summit, and so had the bears. I labored on, sweat tracking my face as we rose above the treeline. Just below the dome's crown, I dropped my pack with an oof. For lunch I tired my jaws on jerky as I studied the ranks of black, dense clouds drifting in from the east and searched the tundra for dark shapes nosing through the vegetation. Jenny waited at my feet for the wads of jerky I couldn't conquer. Bear sign didn't alarm her. The possibility that I might not share lunch did.

On the downhill, my left foot slipped, and I toppled over in slow motion, gravity pulling the pack onto me. Jenny sniffed at my face pressed against cool mud. I laughed, but this would not do. On my top five list of things I did not want to go wrong: sprains, breaks, or twists of any sort. Pay attention, I scolded myself. Every moment demands attention.

THIS WASN'T ALL ABOUT OVERCOMING FEAR. I didn't know how else to see the world more clearly than to walk through it. I could not think of a better way to be quiet for a while. True, now that I was here, for long minutes I did not look any higher than my own feet, step by deliberate step up and down those long hills. It was also true that I felt compelled to announce our approach to the wild animals of the country in song and chant, and to speak often to my dog, and to offer a few encouraging words to myself.

But there were these moments, too, when I stopped for no reason that could be named, and stood silently in the middle of trail, head back, one more person on the way to somewhere that can't be mapped.

A GNARL OF THUNDER FOLLOWED FLASHBULB PULSES of lightning. Fog and darkness cloaked the distant hills—the hills we headed toward. The only thing I know about lightning is that there's nothing good about being the tallest object on a treeless dome. I walked faster until an upward thrust of shale appeared and offered shelter for the tent. Rain pecked against the fly, and Jenny snorted as she slept, ears twitching whenever thunder ripped close by. The nylon flapped in the wind but the structure held. A few inconstant drips rolled into the dog's water dish, the pot, and the water bottle. All this rain and we'd harvest but a mouthful. I pulled on long johns and rain gear, leaned against the pack and dozed.

At 5 p.m., as the storm drifted southward, I screwed the stove together outside the tent while I crouched inside. Flames shot toward my face as I twisted the fuel nozzle the wrong way. Fire lapped at the tent door before I could turn the stove off. My face still warm, I moved the entire setup to a nearby rock and tried again. The pot had just started bubbling when it slipped, spilling stroganoff fixings across the rocks. "This is why we won't sleep where we eat," I told Jenny, who began industriously licking up lumpy sauce and crunchy noodles. So far, a few hours into our trip, I had narrowly avoided twisting my ankle, searing my face, and setting our shelter on fire.

THE TRAIL LURCHED DOWNHILL THROUGH A BOGGY black spruce forest until it crossed a dirt track headed toward the Kokomo Creek mine. Jenny waded into a muddy yellow pond to drink and cool off. I dug out a water bag; as dirty as it was, the scummy pond represented the most water we'd seen in four miles.

An empty five-gallon bucket lay beside the trail, and I wondered about bear-baiting stations. Most any bear would run from us with enough warning, but a bear accustomed to slumming around mine camps, digging freebies out of trashcans, and being deliberately attracted by rotting food was exactly the kind of bold bear I feared the most. My thoughts ping-ponged now between sore feet and the bear tracks we'd crossed. All I carried was the pepper spray, a small flare for scare value, and an arsenal of Carpenters' songs, which I now grunted, one word per step: "On . . . the . . . day . . . that . . . you . . . were . . . born . . . the . . . angels . . . got . . . together . . . ."

We passed a sign lying in a ditch: "CAUTION. This and all trails are being trapped. Traps and snares in and along trails. Use with caution." The words "Trap Theives" were lettered within a circle and slash mark. The misspelling made it seem more ominous. Marten sets appeared periodically along the trail, with diagonal poles nailed to a tree, and some shiny trinket—a few inches of tinsel garland, can lids, or even CDs— hanging above the set to mark it.

I revisited my list of top five worries. Perhaps more than injuring myself, I feared that Jenny would get hurt by wandering into an abandoned trap or snare. I carried a small first-aid kit jammed with a wire splint, cold pack, gauze and Band-Aids, antibiotic ointments and antiseptic wipes, pills for diarrhea, urinary tract infections, runny noses, and miscellaneous aches and pains. But I was not sure I could do anything for an injured dog.

AT MILE 9, I STOPPED TO SET UP THE TENT in a gravelly clearing, proud to have exceeded my daily goal by a mile. Jenny snoozed on moss among the trees as I struggled with the tent, which was actually a tarp with a mesh insert for sleeping. Hiking sticks acted as the poles.

I filtered muddy water and filled her dish and my bottle, dosing mine with lemonade crystals to help me choke it down. She licked the dinner pot of leftover rice and beans. She was a terrible chowhound. We had stopped storing cat food cans on the pantry floor when Jenny began shredding them open with her teeth.

I dragged the pack into the bushes but took the pepper spray and signal flare into the tarp. It was hot in there, the black mesh amplifying the sun's rays. A violent hum of mosquitoes and buzz-sawing of wasps enveloped the mesh like a force field. The night would never grow dark, only dim, and for this I was glad. Now and then my mind circled around the game trails emerging from the trees, picturing moose bursting out and trampling the tarp, or a bear moseying into the open, sniffing after my pack, but there was no profit in those thoughts. Every couple of hours I stirred long enough to peer outside. Close to dawn, the quiet was liquid, something you'd have to push against to move through. Even the mosquitoes had disappeared. A fine dew misted the tarp and the sleeping bag.

At 8 a.m., the dog and I yawned in each other's faces and then stiffly sat up and stretched. There is a certain kind of earned pain that feels good, that reminds you that your body can almost always do more than you think it can. She looked at the kibble I poured into the pot lid and then looked at me. I sighed and spooned some of my oatmeal with brown sugar and raisins onto her food. Then she ate.

AT 10 A.M., WE TOOK OUR FIRST TENDER STEPS ON THE TRAIL. Blue sky. No clouds. Not enough water. Already I was hot. And thirsty. I was very thirsty.

Ahead the trail climbed and dropped over the 2,000- and 3,000-foot hills. Today we'd be hiking hard if we wanted to cover eight miles. I occupied myself thinking up new songs, taking that old chestnut "Bingo" and improvising verses to flatter my dog: "There was a doggy I called my own, and Jenny was her name-o. J-E-N-N-Y, J-E-N-N-Y . . ." I hoped no one would hear. It's the kind of thing saps do with their dogs, like giving them nicknames for any occasion: Jennifer Dogifer, Flufferbutt, Pigger Dog, Doodlebrain, Miss Bossy. Her ears radared my way as she wondered why I kept calling her when she was standing right there.

As the trail started rising even more steeply, I switched to army chants: "We are climbing up this hill. We will make it yes we will. Won't be the first, won't be the last. We are going to kick its ass. Sound off, one, two, sound off, three, four . . ." I was my own sergeant and recruit, song leader and chorus. Basically, I was doing all the work.

In some ways, traveling with no one but a dog for companionship was ideal. I could stop whenever I wanted. The dinner menu required no polite consultations. Nobody would drop helpful little hints about better ways to erect the tent or build fires. I could pee wherever I wanted. Acting cheerful when I didn't feel cheerful was not required. But a partner who could talk had advantages. It would be nice to say out loud, "Man, this hill is a bitch," and have someone pause and wipe his or her forehead and say, "You can say that again."

By noon, only a few mouthfuls of tea-colored water remained in the bottle. I stopped at every trickle, pumped brown sludge from pools gathered in moose tracks as Jenny slurped away. I couldn't afford to be picky;

no streams bubbled merrily along the route, no crystalline ponds waited, no rivers rushed by. There were only potholes and a few patches of stale snow in the shadows.

I had already used my compass to correctly divine the proper direction at a confusing fork. Now wayfinding depended on the trail itself and a vague, faint pencil sketch that I had transferred from a trail brochure to my map. At the next fork, I studied the rougher uphill path to the left. The thick dashes marking the trail on the wrinkled brochure were dismayingly ambiguous. They could signify either route—over the dome, or just below it. I turned right to continue on the well-used route we had followed successfully so far. It dipped down and seemed to round the dome just below the summit rather than crossing over the top.

A fire had swept over these slopes several years back, leaving blackened aspen trunks twisting out of the greenery. I kept on, unease growing as I failed to pass milepost 14 or 15. We stopped for lunch and more water filtering as I studied the map and worried. When the trail dropped downhill abruptly, I stopped and pulled out the GPS, compass and maps again. "You're not lost if you know where you are," I told myself fiercely. I sighted on the hill below. The trail should head northeast. This route was now clearly trending southeast.

A little while before, I thought I might cry if I discovered we had taken the wrong route. But now I did not feel like crying. I felt tired and mad at myself. Why didn't I pause at that fork to think things through? Why had I been so sure? This was when having a human partner would be good—someone to argue with, to help you think through problems, to blame. But now I had done something stupid and there was nothing for it but to retrace our steps two miles backward and uphill. There was no one to scold me, either, so I called myself a dumbshit just to make me feel better.

My legs ached as the hill steepened. It was almost 4 p.m., and now our mileage lagged behind schedule. After a mile we plodded past a rough mysterious track that jolted upward. I paused to consider. As steep as the path was, I felt certain it headed to the ridge top and intersected the Circle-Fairbanks Trail in a shortcut. I braced my trekking poles in the mud and pushed.

Every few steps, we stopped so I could suck air. The route was not perfectly vertical; it only seemed that way. I mumbled songs to create a rhythm. Hike for a verse, stop. Hike for a verse, stop. Water trickled through ruts. The alders thinned, but I blew my whistle now and then in case bears idled unseen. The sky blackened above the ridge as the daily thunderstorm approached. A solid wind pushed against us as we took the last, struggling steps onto the ridge, where low alpine flowers shuddered. Ahead, the saddle dropped sharply into a spruce-draped valley. Greening hills, hummocky and mottled from cloud shadows, rolled out before us, and the Crazy Mountains surfed in peaks. To the left, a bald dome. To the right, an even steeper hill. I strained to see if the lump on top was a cairn, or trail marker. I couldn't tell for sure. Now I regretted leaving binoculars behind just to save a few ounces.

I dragged the pack behind a rocky bluff and pitched the tarp against the coming rain. My feet ached, and the skin joining my big toes to the footpad was raw. Jenny flopped in the lichens and watched me with her head on her paws.

Inside the tent, I fell into the pleasurable daze that comes when your feet don't have to move. Every time the wind lifted the tarp's nylon edges, I studied the dome behind us in brief glimpses, searching for a trail. Perhaps there was no obvious route because people could cross the dome's bare flanks any way they pleased. I imagined faint trails through the lichens and low brush. Tomorrow we'd leave early to make up for wasted miles.

When the wind failed, the mosquitoes rose up, a hidden wave of attackers that had discovered the only warm-blooded creatures for miles. I decided to shift the tarp to face the sun, and rather than walking around to tug out the stakes, I yanked at the taut ropes. A heavy plastic stake snapped from the ground and smacked against my face before I could react. My lip went numb, and blood oozed down my chin. In the compass mirror I studied the welt splitting my lower lip. *Dear Diary: I am one grand adventurer. On Day One I almost set my eyebrows and the tent on fire. On Day Two I took the wrong trail and then belted myself in the face and dripped blood all over the tundra. On Day Three, a bear tracked the scent and ate me up.*

IN THE TENT, JENNY CURLED AT MY FEET, but every few minutes she sat up and licked at her right hind flank. "Mosquito bites? Poor doggy," I said. My commiseration meant nothing to her. Tomorrow I'd rub a little bug dope over her fur. Tomorrow I'd be much more careful about fire and maps. Tomorrow we'd be in the alpine, high above the world, and well on our way to serenity.

Through the night, Jenny's licking became so frantic and compulsive that I woke several times as she shook the tent, jarring loose hundreds of mosquitoes attached to the mesh, intoxicated by the carbon dioxide. I surveyed the tundra each time I woke. A cotton-candy sky rimmed the horizon, and dawn's sparrows lilted in the brush. Low twists of willow and dwarf birch and berry bushes glowed with a faint green haze as spring settled in the alpine.

In the morning, when I sat up, cramped and sore, Jenny was still lapping at her hindquarters. Animals in pain have a glazed, unfocused look; I recognized it in her. She had licked her leg until the fur was sopping, and drool puddled on the tent floor and soaked the sleeping bag. I groaned aloud. "What? What is it?" I asked. Clearly something was wrong, but all she did was eye me and then return to nibbling and licking. She showed me her teeth when I reached toward her leg.

Jenny didn't seem to limp, but she dropped into the soft tundra after we climbed out of the tent and occasionally nosed at her trembling flank. Bugs settled on her nose and on her eyes. In the old days, backcountry travelers simply shot crippled animals and moved on. If she lamed up, I could not possibly carry her to the trail's end, nor could I leave her. I looked out across the hills where green laid upon green, to the southern horizon and the white illuminati of the Alaska Range.

The reasons for making this trip now rose clear and hard before me. One was pride, the ego boost of being able to mention casually that once I had hiked by myself for a week, just me and my dog, through the backcountry. I had announced this trip widely. How could I return now having walked only 15 miles?

Part of it, I admitted, was the hope of encountering some kind of inner peace, maybe even an epiphany, which was the very thing I criticized others for seeking in the wilderness. Probably that was because I desired it so much myself. The last time I had spent a week alone in the woods, fear and loneliness had dropped me to my knees, and then a calmness had fallen upon me, as cool and needful as the wind moving through the crowns of ancient trees.

Out here, by myself, I could be honest: Hadn't I made this journey as a way of finding that peace again? After this spring's frightening surgery, didn't I count on some kind of spiritual transformation as a reward for walking a week by myself, for facing my fears? Wasn't I expecting to be struck like a gong sometime along this trail, to vibrate with all the meaning and intensity possible when one climbs a lesser mountain, under a pale sun at midnight, alone? And I had learned nothing so far except all the foolish things of which I was capable.

But now I did know about something else: the pain of turning back. This was the mildest of journeys, and yet for the first time I understood a little why explorers sometimes made such excellent liars. Frederick Cook stood on a minor ridge of Mount McKinley and took the photographs that he hoped would fool the world. He had to; how could he again fail in his quest to summit? Few things are sadder and less interesting than someone who turns back before reaching the top, the pole, the end of the world, or the end of the trail.

Companion and journalist Robert Dunn mocked Cook's pretensions during their first unsuccessful attempt on Mount McKinley. But as they crept up the most dangerous slopes, unroped and weak with hunger, he found himself admiring the doctor's steadiness and cursing his own fear. "As for me, is the doing of a thing to be no longer its end, as was in the old adventurous days?" he asked. "The telling of it the end instead?" And here I was, on my little jaunt over well-trod ground, with neither a doing nor a telling to show for it.

How much easier to be a prospector than an adventurer. Looking for gold was a solid reason to roam around these hills. But looking for glory, or looking for God—that's just asking for failure.

Jenny watched as I melted snow by the potful. This is your decision now, I thought. Just make it and don't second-guess yourself. Just live with it.

I cried. This is something wilderness is good for: crying as loudly as you want, letting tears and snot run down your face as you shake and sob. I cried because this was not the summer I would walk alone after all. I cried because I hate retracing my steps. I cried because the shadowed hills ahead would not reveal their mysteries to me.

And I cried because every time I looked at my old dog's face I could see death in it. I knew she would die some day, of course. We all will. You know it and I know it, but we know it as dispassionately as a memo, as formally as a warranty that we glance at once and then tuck away in a junk drawer. There is no gut truth in such knowledge. But in that moment I knew that my dog would die before long, and soon enough, I will, too. I myself had seen the red and slick tenderness of my own organs. I had seen the future in a lonely old woman holding out a Polaroid of a tumor the size of a basketball.

This was my only discovery: that I had reached the place where middle age tips into loss, when everything worth caring about begins to disappear—not just my beloved dog, but relatives, friends, my husband, time itself and all its possibilities. For two days I had walked just to arrive at this place, just so I could recognize that in life there is no turning back.

I looked at my dog, lying quietly in the tundra, dark eyes fixed upon me, ears flicking away mosquitoes. There was no dishonor in attending to her. I thought of all the accounts I'd read of people and dogs in the north. For every act of indifference or cruelty, there was some old miner or explorer who valued his dog above any person, any gold. Only history remembers the husky named Mose, owned by a Klondiker who told an admirer: "Mister, don't ask me to place a value on my partner. I couldn't think of it! Why, if I should lose my poke of dust, rather than to part with Mose, we would hit the trail back and try for another raise."

I could always take this trail again, add my steps to the long procession of Athabascans, stampeders, freighters, bandits, thru-travelers, all of us collaborating on keeping this passage open across the landscape. This trail was older than I was, and no doubt would persist long after my passing. So few people anymore know the country this way, step by step, hill by hill. Someday I would return. Just not with my dog, who was moving faster than I toward what awaits us all.

I DRANK DEEPLY OF MELTED SNOW FROM THE WINTER PAST and washed myself clean with what remained. I collapsed the tarp, and shook out my sleeping bag, and arranged my pack carefully, for we had a long way to travel. I sat on a rock and inspected my feet and babied my blisters and pulled my boots back on. I climbed the bluff to sit and memorize the hazy wash of green in the valleys and the silver gleam of unknown mountains. With every step I crushed perfect alpine flowers flecking the tundra like confetti.

Jenny followed me, as is her way. For this little while, we were high above the world, pausing on a path each one of us travels through life.

Then, finally, I tied the bell back onto her collar so I could always find her and I hoisted the pack to my shoulders. It had not lightened a bit. I looked northward once, thinking, *It's not too late to keep on. You've been wrong so many times already. You could take a chance that she'll be all right.*

But even as I turned back, I could feel the sorrow and beauty of the world sinking through me, settling into my flesh, as firm and necessary as the bones that would have to carry me along this trail.

TOM KIZZIA

IN THE EARLY YEARS OF THE NEW MILLENNIUM, curious stories began to appear in Alaskan newspapers about a family that called itself the Pilgrims, who had recently taken up residence in the tiny town of McCarthy, an independent-minded community located inside Wrangell-St Elias National Park.

The family had arrived with their fifteen children in 2002 and in short order purchased an abandoned mine where they began homesteading. Their patriarch, Robert Hale, looked and talked like an Old Testament prophet. An ex-hippie with a back story stranger than fiction, he had experimented with drugs and eastern religions before meeting Kurina Rose in Los Angeles in the seventies. The couple ran away together, adopted a deeply fundamentalist and apocalyptic form of Christianity, and in 1979 headed for the mountains of northern New Mexico to raise their children in isolation from the world. Along the way they became Papa Pilgrim and Country Rose.

Things went sour in New Mexico, and in 1998 the family packed its belongings and headed for Alaska, looking for their promised land. Four years later they arrived in McCarthy and decided they had found it.

For a man who by that point despised the federal government and wanted to live independent of the world beyond, McCarthy was a natural fit. Located at the foot of the Wrangell Mountains, the town had originally been established to serve the nearby Kennecott Mine in 1906. It was never large. In 1980, after passage of the Alaska National Interest Lands Conservation Act, the town was swallowed by the newly established Wrangell-St. Elias National Park. Residents were allowed to keep properties lying within the park's boundaries. But a way of life ended. Accustomed to doing as they pleased on the surrounding lands, they suddenly had to follow rules set by the National Park Service. Resentment took years to cool and lingers today.

An even greater trauma struck the town in 1983, when a recent arrival killed six of the roughly two dozen inhabitants in a mass shooting.

When the Pilgrims arrived two decades later, they were initially welcomed into town. Papa Pilgrim was an oddity, but his fiercely anti-government views aligned him with many in the community. After the family purchased the mine site, however, they struggled with getting supplies there since there was no road to it. So Papa Pilgrim did what any self-reliant backwoodsman with no use for rules would do under such circumstances: he bulldozed a thirteen mile access road across National Park property. He claimed to be maintaining a historic right-of-way.

The result was a standoff and more publicity than McCarthy probably wanted. Park Service demanded the disturbed land be restored to its natural state. The Pilgrims claimed to be victims of an out-of-control government. Supporters in McCarthy claimed they were a good Christian pioneer family being persecuted. It wasn't long before the press got a hold of the story.

Right-wing groups, religious fundamentalists, and property rights advocates in both Alaska and the Lower Forty-Eight rushed to the family's cause. For a brief time, Papa Pilgrim was Alaska's leading political celebrity.

But having the light shown on him was his undoing. The story shifted when Pilgrim's oldest daughters escaped the homestead on a snowmachine. The older brothers followed, and a kind Christian family reached out to help them. It eventually became known that Papa Pilgrim had been abusing his children, especially his eldest daughter, for years.

Tom Kizzia was a reporter for the Anchorage Daily News at the time, and, along with his wife, a property owner in the McCarthy area. He began reporting on the family shortly after their arrival and covered events as the conflict boiled up, visiting the remote homestead before the ugly details emerged.

Kizzia's recounted the family's saga in his book *Pilgrim's Wilderness*, a *New York Times* bestseller that was also ranked #5 on Amazon's Best Books of the Year for 2013. It's a sometimes surreal tale of the many forces brought together and into conflict by Papa Pilgrim during his brief time in the limelight. Old time Alaskan values of independence and open land use clashed with modern day efforts at wilderness preservation. Religious fundamentalism found itself hemmed in by modernity. The line between family togetherness and family terror was exposed. The role of the federal government in the lives of people who want nothing of it was debated. And McCarthy itself was divided as the Pilgrim Family's antics forced a tiny community to choose sides. But mostly the book is about the madness of one man, and the damage he wreaked on his own family and others around him.

Kizzia, who lives in Homer, knows the state well, having traveled through and reported from many of its remote locales. Because he was a part time resident of McCarthy, Papa Pilgrim trusted Kizzia for a brief time, which allowed him access to the family and its homestead that no other reporter gained. He also grew close to the Pilgrim children, who shared with him their experiences.

Reflecting on the events, Kizzia told me, "Alaska was going through a major historical transition in my generation, and as a reporter I was always on the lookout for stories along certain political fault lines that captured the conflicts of the era. The Pilgrim Family story was perfect from the start. When I finally learned what was going on inside the family, what lay beneath the community conflict and my own suspicions, the story deepened. The wilderness was not the family's sanctuary after all. The innocent children had to escape a prison built of faith."

In the excerpt that follows, all the factors in this complex and ultimately tragic story collide as the battle between the National Park Service and the Pilgrim Family takes shape and the residents of McCarthy struggle with the confrontation's impact on their town.

— From *Pilgrim's Wilderness* —
GOD VS. THE PARK SERVICE

IT WAS ONCE A POINT OF LOCAL PRIDE that no government ranger ever slept overnight in McCarthy. For the first few years of Wrangell-St. Elias National Park, staff made diplomatic visits, as if to an independent principality, but kept them short. Over time, however, this strict policy eased in face of the elements and the local custom of hospitality. The first rangers to sleep over arrived one dusk in a winter storm, wet and shivering, and even then had to be talked out of riding their snowmachines another two hours in the dark to reach their trucks. Eventually, the Park Service bought a cabin to house its traveling employees. By the start of 2003, when the three park rangers made their reconnaissance run up McCarthy Creek, the government had finally decided to base a full-time ranger in the park's only town.

They had somebody in mind with just the right mix of local credibility, backbone, easygoing nature, and federal work experience. He was a young man with a neatly groomed beard and wire-rim glasses who lived with his girlfriend in a tidy cabin two woodsy blocks from the McCarthy Lodge. The only problem with hiring Stephens Harper was that he lived right next door to the Pilgrim Family's camp in town.

Stephens Harper remembered running into the Pilgrims for the first time at the mail shack by the airstrip. In their Davy Crockett fur hats and prairie dresses, they were buttonholing locals to ask where they lived and how they got their land. People grumbled at the time about the family's presumption—it seemed the complete opposite of the painstaking process by which Harper himself had been vetted, interviewed, and admitted to McCarthy three years earlier.

At that point in Harper's life, a decade of rootless seasonal work around Alaska—part-time park ranger in summer, remote lodge caretaker in winter—had drawn to an end, along with his first marriage. He had looked for a place to put down roots and begin again. He was intrigued seeing McCarthy on a map, a wilderness town at the toe of a glacier. After a visit to look around, he focused on a log cabin built by a longtime resident, a local seamstress and dog musher, who had been one of the few survivors of the murders back in 1983. One of her dogs had been in heat that morning so she hadn't waited by the runway with her friends. She moved away afterward, saying the place never felt the same, but she had kept her cabin.

Careful about who took her place, she had already turned a number of prospective buyers down. Stephens Harper seemed to have the right values, but in light of past events she had concerns about a single, bearded, bespectacled young man fleeing a broken marriage who would choose to spend his winters in one of the most isolated communities in Alaska—a pretty fair description of the mail-day killer, Lou Hastings. To his credit, Harper found these concerns reasonable. He agreed to fly out on the mail plane in winter, stay at her cabin for two weeks, and visit a dozen people whose names she wrote down. When her McCarthy neighbors reported back that Harper seemed all right, he was allowed to buy her cabin.

In the summer of 2002, Harper was away working as a seasonal ranger at Katmai National Park when he got a letter from his renter saying a big family had moved in right next door. Their cow was blocking the path to the outhouse. Harper knew it had to be the Pilgrims. He recalled that Walt Wigger had parked his wanigan trailer in a clearing near Harper's house. Wigger told the Pilgrims they could use the wanigan when they came to town on mail-plane days once he removed the old dynamite stored inside. The family didn't wait, taking over the wanigan as their in-town base camp. What happened with the dynamite, they never said.

The cow was gone when Harper returned home in the fall. His new neighbors had moved themselves and their livestock up to the Mother Lode. Harper settled in with his girlfriend, Tamara, a Peace Corps veteran with a master's degree in resource conservation. That winter, they traveled in South America. But when they returned in March 2003 to get ready for Harper's new full-time job with the Park Service, they discovered rusty trucks parked around the wanigan, a bus that had been pulled across the river, horses, goats, stacks of recycled construction materials, and a swarm of busy Pilgrims.

Elishaba and her brothers were friendly. Harper introduced himself to their father, who described his family's joy at completing their first year in McCarthy. The two spoke pleasantly regarding plans for the material strewn in front of Harper's cabin. Papa Pilgrim assured him that by mid-April they would be hauling everything by bulldozer and sled up the road to their land. Then Pilgrim asked Harper what he did for a living. Harper said he was going to be a ranger for the park.

Pilgrim turned on the spot and disappeared into the wanigan. Moments later he returned, with a small daughter at his elbow, and launched into an angry tirade about government snooping.

Within days, the Pilgrims had posted notices around town accusing the Park Service of planting a spy next to their camp.

Harper realized it was not going to be easy to separate his new job and his home life because the Pilgrims were going to be part of both—morning, noon, and night.

Compassionate neighbors were the last thing Papa Pilgrim expected when they moved deep into the Alaska wilderness. The citizens of McCarthy were not their friends, Papa told his family. The way the community pulled together in times of need, helped one another out, and wanted to get to know the Pilgrim children better—these things might seem like good Christian behavior, but in fact they were dangerous temptations. He warned his children against becoming man pleasers. They needed to turn their attention inward again toward God. His old fighting instincts were aroused. Once he finished bulldozing open the road along McCarthy Creek, he said, his family would see how nosy and angry and unsupportive the people in McCarthy really were.

The government had certainly responded according to plan. The Park Service was aghast, the family under a state of siege, the children inspired and indignant. Papa's dramatic unmasking of a police spy on their doorstep helped raise the level of tension. Any lone impulse to mutinous dissent could be more easily suppressed during wartime. When Elishaba suggested God might be opening a door through Stephens Harper, Papa accused her of selling the family out.

But news that the Pilgrims had started using the old Green Butte Road to travel back and forth from the Mother Lode had not riled people around McCarthy, not even those who might have considered themselves environmentalists. The family struck some neighbors as passing strange and grandiose, their defiance of the Park Service oddly petulant for a cabin full of avowed pacifists. But the use of a bulldozer to clear a grown-over mining trail did not register locally as a flagrant environmental crime.

For some people, in fact, Papa Pilgrim was now a local hero. And Pilgrim didn't seem to mind his new stature one bit.

On the morning of April 11, 2003, a community meeting was convened at the lodge to talk about the McCarthy Road, the footbridge, and the latest bollard extraction. Joining via teleconference were state transportation officials and the local state senator, an Athabaskan woman from the Yukon River village of Rampart, whose sparsely populated legislative district, extending north to the Arctic Circle and west to the Yukon and Kuskokwim River deltas, was the largest in the United States. State officials agreed not to replace the bollards at the footbridge.

Two park rangers were in McCarthy and listened quietly at the lodge. After it was over, they walked around town and stapled up a public notice on the public board at the lodge and on a tree by the trail leading out of town:

No MOTORIZED VEHICLES ARE PERMITTED TO USE the illegal roads bulldozed on federal lands located in the McCarthy Creek Drainage, connecting the state land around the town of McCarthy with the Marvelous Millsite private property. This notice does not apply to the use of snowmachines on adequate snow cover.

THE GOVERNMENT NOTICE HIT McCARTHY like an artillery shell. The decision to close a historic road threatened to undo two decades of peaceful coexistence with the park. Maybe it was true that no one had used the road in recent years—but no one had needed to before the Pilgrims. In a few days, the family planned to bring a bulldozer down from the Mother Lode to get supplies. There was no other way to haul so much material—lumber, insulation, hay for livestock. The sudden road closure seemed cold and heartless. Park critics called it a government blockade.

And why had the two rangers skulked through town, not telling anyone what they were up to? The notices were torn down and burned.

Two days later, Stephens Harper was roused from bed on a Saturday morning. Peering out the cabin door in his underwear, with Tamara watching curiously from behind, he saw two neighbors: Keith Rowland, with a rifle over his shoulder, and Rick Kenyon, brandishing a microphone. They told him they were about to take their four-wheelers up the McCarthy Creek road to go rabbit hunting, in violation of the road closure—did he want to arrest them?

Harper told them to seek their redress of grievances elsewhere: His job didn't start for another week and they were trespassing.

McCarthy Annie retold the incident in the next issue of the Wrangell St. Elias News. The cover photo showed Bethlehem and Lamb perched endearingly on a set of bull-moose antlers, with the title THE PILGRIMS—NEIGHBORS, FRIENDS.

The story did not name Harper except as a local "parkie" whose voice was a "low, menacing growl."

CURIOUS THING, HOW THAT DOOR KEPT SLAMMING SHUT. Hopefully he'll get it fixed, or I'm afraid that, after a while, the good folks here in McCarthy may begin to think him an unpleasant sort of guy . . . Desperately, the parkies tried to calm the situation, protesting to one caller, "We didn't mean for the notice to be aimed at your community. It was really just meant for the Pilgrims!" Well, fellas, this was the wrong thing to say, because if there's one thing that will unify a small, close-knit community in a hurry, it's this: Big, Bad, Powerful Government Men singling out a peaceable, law-abiding family with lots of adorable, defenseless children, and doing illegal and mean things to try to force them off their land.

THE NATIONAL PARK'S ROAD CLOSURE BOILED into a full town meeting a few days later.

The park superintendent, Gary Candelaria, showed up with Hunter Sharp and Marshall Neeck to explain the decision. Candelaria was not especially well liked in McCarthy. Critics found him inflexible. Even locals sympathetic to the park's goals had not warmed to this superintendent during his four years at the Copper Center headquarters near Glennallen. A few previous park bosses had fared better, showing more of a common touch. They had been hunters or fishermen who considered the Alaska assignment a storybook job. Candelaria had been a surprising choice. Officious and slightly pudgy, he was nearing the end of a government career that had concentrated in smaller park units: Saratoga National Historical Park, Ozark National Scenic Riverways, Fort Laramie National Historic Site. When Candelaria arrived to take over the system's biggest national park, the government's press release described him as an aspiring bookbinder and an amateur historian.

It was his interest in the past, perhaps, that led Candelaria to conclude he had come to Wrangell–St. Elias National Park at a crucial moment in American history. He knew this would win him no popularity contests. But from now on, Alaskans were going to need permits to do certain things on federal land. He arrived in McCarthy that April day in 2003 ready to argue the point.

More than a dozen McCarthy residents were waiting in the lodge dining room. Some were eager to challenge the federal overlords, some merely curious. The Pilgrims refused to participate. The children stood across the street from the McCarthy Lodge with Papa, holding protest signs before their horse and wagon. One sign said IF GOD IS FOR US, WHO CAN BE AGAINST US? Another, held by blond, blue-eyed four-year-old Lamb, said PLEASE LET ME GO HOME TO MAMA. There was defiance, too: A sign on the family bulldozer read MCCARTHY CREEK TRAIL RIDES.

The Kenyons and Rowlands led the argument. They demanded to know how the Green Butte Road up McCarthy Creek could be declared illegal, since it had been used for much of the century. Candelaria said the road had been erased by time and nature. The new road, rebuilt illegally, wandered off the original route.

For more than two hours, temperatures rose in the lodge as the sides hammered back and forth. Kenyon had been researching the issue in fine detail. The discussion turned on technicalities involving legal access rights under two laws: the 1980 Alaska conservation act and a Civil War–era law regarding historic trails known as Revised Statute 2477. The Pilgrim supporters said the family had just been doing road maintenance on a legal historic route. Candelaria said access to inholding properties required a permit. No one had ever sought a permit for the Green Butte Road and the Mother Lode.

Every time the park officials looked into the street, they saw the Pilgrims standing in front of their bulldozer. Candelaria finally pointed out the window and said, "Do you know who created your problem? Those folks created your problem." The crowd hooted in protest, Kenyon wrote later.

McCarthy Annie, in her more pungent account, said the parkies showed up for the community meeting "with their trademark park green bulletproof vests, and packing Sig-Sauer handguns and pepper spray." She said the park rangers added insult to injury when they called the

McCarthy residents "inholders." It was another way of asserting control, she said—"Let me tell you, Control is the name of their game!"

But, she said, the local folk had a measure of sweet revenge when the meeting broke up and a protest parade of vehicles started up the Pilgrims' road: "After all, we mountain folks know our history and law . . . . When you're on the right side, there's no need to hide, apologize, or give in." And there was no question who else was on their side—she pointed out that another of the Pilgrims' protest signs said GOD IS BIGGER THAN THE NPS. WATCH OUT, HE'S GETTING MAD!

AFTER THAT, NO ONE IN MCCARTHY COULD AVOID getting drawn into the Pilgrim drama. Not even the flinty homesteading elder of the area, Jim Edwards, who had stayed away from the protest meeting at the lodge. He could never hear much of what people said on such occasions, for one thing, having spent most of his life around bulldozers and airplane engines. More important, he had no wish to take sides in a contest over who was tougher, God or the Park Service. He had always preferred to engage Nature in the Wrangell Mountains directly, without interference from either of those meddlesome outside parties.

But one morning, as spring gave way to summer, Papa Pilgrim showed up at Jim Edwards's door, clutching his cowboy hat to his chest, with two small children clinging to his coat. He had come to ask a favor.

A bemused indifference toward the religious ferments of his neighbors had served Edwards well in McCarthy for fifty years. He had never been a churchgoer, not even after his wife, Maxine, was killed in the mail-day murders. His personal religion remained pretty much the same as the day he first flew a small plane into the country as a twenty-four-year-old and saw the Kennicott Glacier spilling off the mountains. You could call it nature worship, he said: the trees, the animals, the summits migrating all the way from South America. It about killed him to cut down two perfectly healthy spruce on his homestead so he could see through to a television satellite.

On the other hand, he held no great affection for the Park Service. He remembered how things were before. Despite promises in the 1980 Alaska conservation act, the park had pretty much confiscated Edwards's part-time placer gold operation on Dan Creek. They told him they didn't have one thousand dollars to buy him out but could spend unlimited funds flying helicopters across the Nizina River valley to inspect his operation and explain the latest regulations.

Edwards was a soft-spoken man with the shambling demeanor of an accountant, though his diffidence was misleading—he had a ropy strength, strong opinions, and unstoppable energy. He had ties as strong as anyone's to McCarthy's mining past. His gold claim had once belonged to a tough old Croat named Martin Radovan, a holdover prospector from the old days. Edwards had befriended Radovan in the 1950s and one summer led a geologist's crew out on the face of a cliff above the Chitistone River to examine a Radovan claim known as the Binocular Prospect because not even European mountain climbers hired by Kennecott Copper had been able to reach its turquoise stains. Radovan got there, however, and told people he might have found the greatest bonanza of all time. Edwards led the team along a ledge several thousand feet up, nudging scree with their toes to make steps. In places the ledge was ten inches wide. Where the rock bulged, they crawled on hands and knees. A hanging glacier hundreds of feet over their heads dropped blocks of ice that whistled like bombs. The survey crew got close enough to see the cotton mattress atop a boulder where the old prospector bivouacked, but rocks buzzing past the geologist's head convinced him to turn back without actually reaching the pay streak. Radovan finally sold his interest in the claims to investors and continued working for the new owners into his eighties. After he died, a mining company helicoptered in, looked it over, and turned the claims over to the new park. Radovan's lifelong dream of a mountain of solid copper blipped off the screen as a corporate tax write-off.

Radovan's placer gold claim disappeared next, a few decades, later, when Jim Edwards, using it mainly as a hobby, surrendered it to the government. Now there was hardly any mining left in the park. The man at his door, Papa Pilgrim, the new owner of the Mother Lode Mine, was not even a hobby miner. It wasn't clear to Edwards what exactly he planned to do with his hole in the mountain.

Pilgrim said the family's goats had escaped from the old millsite property and were scattered somewhere in the high country. Edwards knew the Mother Lode valley well, having led packhorses up McCarthy Creek for a prospecting crew in territorial days—a hell of a difficult trip, he recalled, given how the road was grown over before Wigger cleared it again.

Edwards always tried to think the best of people. Sometimes he lived to regret it. But he figured family cohesion like the Pilgrims' was to be admired in this day and age. And he was hardly one to hold the newcomer's bulldozing against him. Before Papa Pilgrim steered that Caterpillar D5 down from the Mother Lode, Edwards had been famous locally for the most audacious bulldozer ride in the history of the Wrangells.

Back in the winter of 1961, when there was still no road to McCarthy, Edwards left Chitina for home on a D4 cable-blade dozer. He crossed the frozen Copper River and rumbled along the old tracks, finding just enough room to move between the iron rails. He crept across wobbling trestles, built detours around washouts, dynamited broken rails, and at one point hiked back to Chitina and flew to Anchorage to get a replacement front axle, approaching each new obstacle as calmly as a mathematician working his way across a chalkboard. Finally he crossed the Kennicott River, pulled up at his house, and presented Maxine with her pale-green 1949 Chevy Deluxe sedan. He had pulled the car all the way to McCarthy on a sled behind his bulldozer. He had come sixty miles and it took him thirty days.

In his seventies, Edwards was still flying his kit-built plane off the grass strip he'd cleared on his homestead. He told the abjectly grateful Pilgrim he would fly up McCarthy Creek and have a look around.

The escaped goats were easy to find. Edwards landed at the Mother Lode and described their location high on a flank of the Green Butte. He was warmly thanked, and invited back for a visit any time. The next time he flew there, he brought a guest, a hardy young German who had bicycled thousands of miles to Alaska. The visit to Hillbilly Heaven seemed to go well. Elishaba served fresh bread, and Pilgrim regaled them with stories. But when they got back to Edwards' place that night, the German friend surprised him. He'd found the afternoon disturbing.

"That Elishaba really hates her father," he said.

THROUGH THE SUMMER, THE MCCARTHY CREEK SITUATION deteriorated. The U.S. Justice Department formally notified the Hale family of plans to seek an injunction against further bulldozer work in the park. A Park Service team was assembled to complete a summer assessment of the bulldozed road and prepare damage estimates. A second team would finally survey the Marvelous Millsite and other related Mother Lode properties to establish where the family's clearing activities had violated park boundaries. All steps necessary to assure the teams' safety would be taken, including dispatch of an armed Special Event Tactical Team.

People started to worry. Nearly everyone in town, regardless of their comfort level with the Pilgrims, felt deployment of a half dozen flak-jacketed government riflemen was more likely to escalate matters than to calm them. The more vehement government critics fastened onto this resort to arms with a mix of horror and relish. E-mails began to fly from remote Alaska to national property-rights and other conservative mailing lists, describing how the "NPS is hunting this family like a wolfpack stalks a pregnant elk."

"Bear in mind that these folks are pacifists, very akin to the Mennonite faith," Rick Kenyon wrote in one national alert. "We plan to evacuate the children from the property and send observers up to the property, but beyond that, we need help. What should we do? We feel like the Wrangell/St. Elias National Park has become 'occupied territory' and is being ruled by a dictator."

The Alaska regional director of the National Park Service, Rob Arnberger, called Kenyon to try to clear the air. Arnberger's exasperation was plain in a subsequent e-mail to several colleagues, reporting on the conversation: "[Kenyon] stated he felt the 'NPS was coming in to do its work and kill some kids.' I expressed my deep disgust with this kind of irresponsible comment as direct evidence of his intentions to inflame the process and that his assertions of fairness in representing the issue was a fallacy and fabrication. We both severed the call with a quick commitment to look for ways to better communications."

In midsummer, the park set out once again to close the last remaining tunnel entrance to the Mother Lode mine. It was an old ventilation tunnel that led from park land into forty miles of catacombs, where temperatures remained a few degrees above freezing year-round. The Pilgrims had chiseled their way in through the ice that blocked the entrance. A ranger flew out by helicopter and found a hand-lettered sign on the tunnel door: THIS ENTRANCE IS CLOSED TO ALL PUBLIC AND "PARK" OFFICIALS—LIABILITY LAWS ARE NOW IN EFFECT WITH THE NEW OWNERSHIP! WORKERS ARE INSIDE AT THIS TIME—AND THIS ENTRANCE IS PATROLLED DAILY—VIOLATERS WILL BE PERSECUTED TO THE FULL EXTENT OF THE LAW! "PILGRIM" FAMILY.

The ranger replaced the Pilgrims' sign with his own—a skull-and-crossbones above a list of generic underground dangers: rotten structures, deadly mine openings, lethal gas and lack of oxygen, dangerous animals, unsafe ladders, cave-ins and decayed timbers, unstable explosives, deep pools of water. He padlocked the door . Two weeks later, tipped off about paying customers headed to Hillbilly Heaven, three park rangers returned to the mountain and spent a night staked out with binoculars. They watched Joseph climb to the tunnel. When they scrambled over they found the lock broken by a pickax and ticketed Pilgrim's oldest son.

Then in August they sent an undercover agent posing as a tourist to book a horse ride to the Bonanza Mine. The rocky trail, a full day's hike on foot above the Kennecott ruins, climbs past abandoned timber tram towers and around ravines and rocky turrets that give the ridge a look of deep relief in the shadows of a long summer sunset. The trail leaves the state-owned roads around McCarthy and enters the park. At the end of the trip, Joshua was cited for operating in the park without a commercial permit.

Federal court dates in Anchorage were set for the Pilgrim brothers later in the year. Kenyon complained that the potential fines could ruin the family. Carl Bauman, the conservative Motorhead lawyer, agreed to represent Joseph and Joshua for whatever money Kenyon could get by passing a hat.

A crew of federal surveyors flew to Hillbilly Heaven, but the park backed down on sending a team of armed guards. The surveyors cleared a swath of trees around the Pilgrim perimeter, which turned out to be pretty much where the park expected. The Pilgrims had indeed been clearing park land, but from the air, the rectangular perimeter in the forest was a more jarring sight than the homestead itself. The logging was a tool of rough frontier justice. A line was drawn through the wilderness, and the Pilgrims had been told not to cross it.

The property line ran through the middle of the Pilgrims' kitchen.

WITH AIRPLANES AND HORSES THEIR ONLY OPTIONS for going home, the Pilgrims spent more time around town that summer. It was their second summer in McCarthy, and locals were starting to feel less charitable. One day the horses got loose and scattered across the runway. Natalie Bay, a formidable Australian who owned Wrangell Mountain Air with her pilot husband and managed the complicated logistics for dozens of backpacking and hunting parties every summer, lashed into Papa. It was bad enough that the horses left piles of manure by the community's drinking water spring, and that the family's horse-drawn wagon, competing for Kennicott tourists with the air service shuttle van, had now evolved into a rasping dune-buggy taxi. Cute little Pilgrim children were posted by the footbridge to direct tourists to their own "Jelly Bean" rig. Natalie had even heard reports of the children trying to solicit footbridge-crossing fees. She had put up with all this, in part because she appreciated having the Pilgrim girls around to play with her own young daughter. But endangering the pilots was over the line. She went up to the airstrip with a rifle and threatened to shoot the horses.

Pilgrim apologized. It wasn't long after, though, that he ignored Natalie's wishes one afternoon and snuck her daughter away to play with his girls in the wanigan. Then he tried to prevent Natalie from going inside to retrieve her. "There's nothing you can do about it," Pilgrim told her, blocking her way. He was wrong, it turned out. But the rest of the afternoon several Pilgrim boys followed Natalie and her daughter around town, taking videos.

At the Hardware Store, where the summer college program was again under way, Ben Shaine worried that the escalating antagonism might leave permanent scars in the community. Kenyon was blaming every problem not on the Pilgrims but on the Park Service blockade. It was brilliant political theater. Shaine marveled at Pilgrim's performance art the day Papa stopped by the Hardware Store and monopolized an open house, drawing the college students about him with his tales of bush living. The occasion left Shaine's daughter, Gaia, indignant. She had graduated from college back east and had come home for the summer to guide whitewater rafting trips. Gaia found it insulting to hear the Pilgrims, in only their second summer in the Wrangells, refer to McCarthy as "our town." They didn't understand that the town had always gotten along by common law and respect for neighbors. By forcing the park to get nasty about rules, she felt, they were changing the place in ways that would last even after the family's wilderness experiment failed and they moved on.

Neil Darish at the McCarthy Lodge continued to serve as the family's go-between with the park. But even he began to wonder whether the description of "colorful" was quite adequate. Pilgrim rejected his suggestion that the family manufacture copper wall hangings of salmon as a cottage industry, saying it would be idolatry to fashion the image of a living being. Pilgrim's source was Deuteronomy, in which Moses extended the commandment against graven images to cover specifically the likeness of any male or female, or beast on the earth, or winged fowl or fish or anything that creepeth on the ground. When they lived in Fairbanks and drove through the highway town of North Pole, Pilgrim made them look away as they passed the Christmas factory with the giant Santa Claus.

All that was fine with Darish, though he shared the estimable Ayn Rand's atheism—even charming in its eccentricity. But Pilgrim's attitude about law enforcement was another matter. The police never just come over and celebrate your birthday with you, he told Darish. They justify their lies with their higher purpose. He had grown up around law enforcement, he said. There's nothing you can tell an officer like Stephens Harper that can help you. They're only out to get you.

SOMEHOW IN THE MIDST OF THE COMMOTION surrounding his new park job that summer, Stephens Harper and Tamara Egans got married. Tamara's parents flew to McCarthy in July 2003, and Kelly Bay took everyone on a flight over the vast ethereal emptiness of the largest subarctic ice field in the world. They landed on a river bar and Bay read the essential words off a fluttering three-by-five card and took off promptly because the wind was picking up.

Back in McCarthy, the newlyweds had to cross a neighbor's yard to reach their cabin from the rear. The meadow out their front window was blocked by the dreary dark brown wanigan, along with old vehicles and oil drums, stacks of storm windows, pallets, batteries, saddles, and other tack hung in a shed built of tree poles.

Tamara had planted a little garden, and one morning she found the Pilgrims' goats finishing off the tender seedlings. Stephens told Joseph that if he saw the goats in his garden again he was going to shoot them. This was no longer park business, in his view. This was his hearth and bride. He checked with a state trooper acquaintance as to whether Alaska's law regarding defense of life and property, generally invoked when grizzly bears were shot out of season, could be applied to domestic goats. The trooper recommended trying anti-bear pepper spray first.

Harper was surprised a few days later when Elishaba came over with new seedlings to help replant the garden. It felt like she was trying to clean up the mess. When she asked them to say nothing about her visit to her papa, he felt a flicker of sympathy. He felt it again a few days later, as he was threading his way through the junk piles in the Pilgrims' camp— it was, after all, his legal access—and Joseph, following behind, picked up a hammer. When Harper turned around and stopped him with a practiced lawman's stare, Joseph set the hammer down and blushed.

Harper did some more legal research. This part of town looked like vacant woods. The old schoolhouse and other nearby buildings had burned or collapsed, the poplars and cottonwoods grown back. But all of it was platted town lots, and Harper found that Wigger never owned land there. The wanigan had been left on an overgrown lot owned by an elderly lady in Anchorage, an original McCarthy kid whose father had been the local U.S. commissioner. Wigger apparently assured the Pilgrims they could claim the land by adverse possession since his little trailer cabin had sat there for so long. This legal advice proved unreliable. The owner, contacted by Harper, said she wanted the Pilgrims off her land.

The Pilgrims checked the survey corners themselves and moved everything into the platted road right-of-way. Unable to move the material to Hillbilly Heaven, they had now used it to block Harper's legal access completely. Harper felt like he had been drawn into some eye-for-an-eye battle out of the Old Testament.

On the night they finished making their piles, the family lined up at the Harpers' property line and sang "Mind Your Own Business." They hung up blue tarps and surplus parachutes in the poplars to screen the view of their wanigan. Then they moved a twenty-kilowatt generator with no muffler to the edge of the property and ran it all night so that Stephens and Tamara slept with ear plugs.

In August 2003, the team of government specialists assembled at the park's May Creek outpost across the Nizina from town.

The post consisted of a remote cabin purchased by the park, and wall tents set in military fashion around a mowed-grass parade ground. It was used by firefighters and would provide a helicopter base camp for the next two weeks. The assessment team had been whittled to nineteen, including three cultural resource specialists, a plant ecologist, and rangers to keep the Pilgrims outside of the work perimeter. Stephens Harper would carry a video camera, to record the work and any confrontation that might develop at Hillbilly Heaven.

In Rick Kenyon's newspaper, McCarthy Annie described what came next. First she set the garden-like scene into which the government machinery came crashing: a little old-fashioned cabin, a curl of woodsmoke, a "chuckling stream" and "wildflowers on the breeze." Sounds of singing, children playing, doing chores, the faithful old dog. Amid forbidding peaks, this little piece of paradise that Country Rose called home.

SHE TRIED NOT TO LET HER MIND DWELL on how vulnerable she was—a woman alone on the mountain, with half a dozen of her youngest children to care for.

Far from help. Far from Pilgrim and her sturdy, capable older sons.

With a suddenness that made her head jerk up, the heavy wooden door flew open. An excited voice called out, "Mama! The helicopter! I can hear it coming! Hurry, come on!"

Alarmed, Country Rose left her bread bowl and scooted out the door.

THE RANGERS WERE "WARLIKE APPARITIONS." Little Psalms offered them a plate of cookies, "as trusting eyes the hue of faded bluebells searched earnestly for approval." She was pushed roughly away, the paper's correspondent wrote.

The Park Service saw things differently. The Pilgrims pushed up against the single ranger guard, trying to provoke something. One afternoon, Marshall Neeck was fending off the three oldest boys on the trail. At a signal they split, running in several directions into the trees toward the assessment team. Neeck retreated to join the others and they circled up, not sure what the Pilgrims, crashing unseen in the woods, would do next. They called in the helicopter and retreated for the day.

Stephens Harper was able to reach Tamara on the phone each night after they flew back to May Creek. She reported that the Pilgrims had put up protest signs in front of the blue tarps. The generator with no muffler was running again. They played loud recordings of old-time spirituals and pointed the headlights of two trucks right at Tamara's cabin.

It sounded to Harper like the Branch Davidian siege, except with the religious crazies on the outside.

On the night she finally moved out, she looked out the window and saw teen-aged Moses high up in a nearby tree, watching her. Hanging from a limb below was the butchered and skinned carcass of one of the Pilgrims' goats.

KRISTI MINGQUN MCEWEN

I'VE KNOWN KRISTI MINGQUN MCEWEN FOR AT LEAST TEN YEARS, both as the music teacher in the grade school my children attended, and as the wife of one of my longtime mountain biking friends. When I picture her in my mind, two things come immediately into view. The smile she welcomes everyone with, and the qaspeq she wears at work and elsewhere.

A qaspeq is a hooded overshirt, a bit like a hoody, with a front pocket. Qaspet (the plural of qaspeq) are commonly worn throughout Alaska, especially in the southwestern and western regions of Alaska, where McEwen was born. Handmade and usually quite colorful, they are a frequent sight in the state, brightening many public gatherings even in cities far from where they originated.

McEwen's mother is Yup'ik and her father is from Seattle. McEwen was born in the southwestern regional hub of Mamterilliq, also known as Bethel. At the age of ten, her family moved to Fairbanks, where she still lives, but her connections to her heritage run deep.

During the long year of 2020, when the nation was rocked by political turmoil and a pandemic, McEwen kept busy in part by posting to

Facebook recollections of her life. That's when I realized she has a hidden talent for writing that I had previously been unaware of. In the selection that follows, which began as a Facebook post, her abilities are on display. First she welcomes us into her childhood home, setting us alongside her as she absorbs from her grandmother the skills for one day sewing her own qaspet. It's a scene readers will be in no hurry to leave behind. But we soon follow her to Fairbanks, where she applies her grandmother's lessons to her broader life.

But there is also sadness. I had not known that McEwen wears the qaspeq I picture her attired in partly due to a harmful incident in her past, when a colleague mistreated her for speaking out as an Alaskan Native. She only briefly discusses the incident, omitting details that could identify the individual, and instead focuses on her response. Choosing to rise above adversity, she embraces, and is embraced by, her qaspeq as a symbol of who she is, and of the broader culture that she is part of. A culture both ancient and fully a part of the modern world.

When I asked her why she chose to begin sharing so many incidents in her life, she told me,

"I am fortunate to benefit from the example of so many brave, strong, and brilliant Indigenous women, who are both pulling us gently and lovingly forward, and challenging us to leap beyond what we perceive as our limitations. It is the empowered voices of so many others that gives each of us the strength to speak our own truths and create our own narrative. We all have a part to play in welcoming the stories and experiences of our Indigenous brothers and sisters, so that we can work together to build a better future."

As for where she learned to story tell so well, she replied, "Yup'ik and Indigenous people have been telling stories for tens of thousands of years, and we still continue today. We all have poignant and powerful stories to share. It takes the compassionate listening ear and heart of another to bring them to light."

McEwen is the only author in this collection who has not, as of this writing, been published. I hope this changes soon. She has a wonderful skill for storytelling, and her stories need to be heard. I asked her to let me include this sample because I was moved by her experience, because I learned something I had not known about a friend, because the piece speaks strongly and firmly to an unhealed racial divide in Alaska, and because I hope her stories will one day be collected into a memoir. She could easily have a second career as a writer.

— Qaspeq —

I REMEMBER AS A GIRL, SITTING ON THE EDGE of my grandmother's bed, next to what felt like a mountain of qaspet. As I tried on every qaspeq made by my grandmother, I felt rich! I felt like the richest girl in the world. And now I look back and see that I was surrounded by a richness that went much deeper than the cotton print of my qaspeq.

I learned to sew from my grandmother, who we all called Aan (mother in Yup'ik). I sat very still next to her, quietly observing everything she did. Without instruction or reminders, I knew that if I wanted to be near her and learn from her, I couldn't disturb her work. I had to remain silent and still. I did not ask questions, talk, or fidget. I knew that I was responsible for my own learning in how carefully I observed and remembered the motions of Aan's hands. While she worked, my grandmother knew that she was my teacher, and that she was equally responsible for my learning. Aan was an expert teacher while never speaking a single word.

As I sat with Aan, the room was full of the sound of the rhythm of her work—the needle puncturing the fabric, the thread as it was pulled then stopping at the knot, her fingers folding, gathering, and smoothing the material, the way she would wet the end of the thread before guiding it through the eye of the needle, her breathing, her gentle grunt at making an error, her deep sigh of satisfaction when her work was complete.

And then, also without an exchange of words, I had a needle, thread, and scraps of fabric to try to sew for myself when I was ready. And the evidence of my careful observation was proven in how my fingers could do what my eyes had taught me, after watching Aan's skilled tasks repeated again and again, hour after hour.

Just as my sewing skills were burgeoning, my mom, sisters and I moved away from Bethel and Aan. And though the following times I was able to watch her sew were rare, I know that still today, my hands work the same way that Aan's hands modeled for me.

My love for working with my hands turned to music. After graduating with a degree in music education, I became a music teacher in Fairbanks. Because of the way that I learned all throughout my life, I relied so much on the experts around me. I watched, I observed, and I listened to other teachers. And today, I still try to apply what those generous and adept mentors demonstrated.

Just like many of you, my schooling was full of racism. The daily stings and deep bruises caused by words spoken and unspoken, and the actions and inactions, fueled by hate and ignorance, still feel like fresh wounds. But the racism I experienced once I became a teacher hurt in a different way. It is a different weight to bear those same insults and violations as a professional, especially as an educator. Because as a child, I once looked to my teachers to correct, condemn, and protect me from the racism that flourished in my schools in Fairbanks.

After a particularly awkward and hurtful encounter with a racist colleague, I made a decision, an oath, a promise, that I would wear a qaspeq to school every day of my teaching career. I wanted every person I encountered to see me as an Alaska Native woman, as a Yup'ik, first. I wanted my students, particularly my Alaska Native students, who were learning in the same racist environment that I was working in, to see their teacher as an Alaska Native woman, as a Yup'ik, first.

When students and colleagues ask me why I wear a qaspeq every day, I often cheerfully respond with, "It's so fun to wear clothes that you make," and I recall those who shared their precious qaspeq patterns and secrets with me, as well as the hours of trial an error of creating my own designs. Or sometimes I answer, "They are so practical - look at this pocket!" This garment is the predecessor to the hoodie and parallels the design and function of the anorak, or annuraaq of the Inuit, the atikłuks of the Iñupiaq, and the be'tsegh' hoolaanh or me'tsegh' hoolaanh of the Koyukon. Or I might answer, "They are so comfortable!" because one can dance, harvest, hunt, celebrate, work, and play in a qaspeq, especially in one that is made just for you.

While those are all true answers to the question of why I wear a qaspeq every day, they are not the true reason. I wear my qaspeq to remind you that Alaska Natives are thriving professionals, we are people deserving of dignity and respect, we contribute to our communities every day, our cultures are beautiful and alive, we are witness to the racism and injustice that goes unchecked, we are resilient and enduring, we are still here on Indigenous land. When you interact with me, you must do so fully aware that I am a Yup'ik woman, and I stand here with thousands of years of ancestors behind me. When I wear my qaspeq I stand testament to my grandmother, Aan. All her kindness and patience and courage and strength and knowledge and wisdom and power and love and dignity and righteousness runs through my blood, too.

My qaspeq is my armor, my shield, my protection, my comfort, my refuge.

What does it mean when you wear a qaspeq?

MARY KUDENOV

LONGSTANDING MYTH AND RECENT REALITY TELEVISION shows leave many non-Alaskans with the belief that residents of the Forty-Ninth State are rugged outdoorsmen who spend the bulk of their lives worrying more about bear attacks than muggings. It's an attractive vision for people living far from the natural world. It's also largely false.

Most Alaskans live in cities, many of them eking out an urban subsistence lifestyle working soul-deadening low-wage jobs instead of living off the land. They dwell in trailers or dilapidated apartments instead of snug cabins, and eat cheap processed food from Walmart instead of fresh moose.

In her remarkable memoir *Threadbare*, Mary Kudenov documents this Alaska from the perspective of one who has lived it. Raised in the small towns of Haines and Moose Pass, and not knowing her father was until shortly before his death, she grew up poor. Like many rural Alaskans of limited means, she migrated to Anchorage as a young adult hoping for a better life. Entering the University of Alaska, Anchorage, she eventually earned an MFA in creative writing and literary arts. But first she endured urban poverty.

Threadbare is a collection of essays drawn from her personal experiences. Kudenov weaves her own story in and out of the tales of others she encountered, creating a community memoir about the places she has lived and those she knew.

Kudenov told me, "I received consistent advice to turn the essay collection into a memoir. But a memoir demanded an attention to the narrator that stripped the other profiles of their power and forced those often underreported voices into the background in favor of the white, educated narrator's filter. I felt, and still feel, that the heart of these essays are the community profiles. And I am very much a part of that, not separate from it."

The first section of Threadbare focuses primarily on Kudenov's life in Anchorage's Mountain View neighborhood, known for high crime and low rents. Her neighbors in her apartment building live with all manner of abuse as a daily part of life: substance, emotional, physical, sexual. Yet most maintain a hard-won dignity despite having it assaulted on all fronts. Kudenov tells their stories with deep compassion that can only have come from having suffered many of the same indignities. Her depth of personal character, as demonstrated by her writing, is striking.

The second and third sections of the book deal with her time in Anchorage after graduating college. Unable to let go of the place she knows so well, and unwilling to give up on those still trapped in it, she goes to work at the Salvation Army helping addicts attempting to recover, and teaches creative writing to female prison inmates. She tells of two coworkers whose lives spin out of control and into crime. She explores her brother's suicide. Often she finds herself confronting horrible actions that the people she lives and works with have taken. She never condescends, she does not make excuses for the crimes of others, but nor does she dismiss their humanity. Their stories are her story. She was just more fortunate.

Kudenov, who now lives with her husband and sons in North Carolina, has received acclaim and awards for her work.

In the following selections, drawn from the first part of the book, Kudenov documents life in her Mountain View apartment. This is not the Alaska one sees on reality shows. This is one of Alaska's realities.

— From *Threadbare* —

I NEEDED AN AFFORDABLE PLACE, THE KIND OF APARTMENT that didn't have rules about smoking or pets. I drove east, toward the Chugach Mountains, with Basil nervous beside me in the passenger seat. Bart, the landlord, was to meet us at his south Mountain View apartment complex. He offered a "moving-in bonus"—a piece of paper saying he had collected a $450 security deposit, when in fact, he never would. Presumably, this meant I would receive a gift of $450 upon moving out.

Taku Drive ran alongside a chain-link fence that separated the residential street from the Glenn Highway, the road that led north to the Alaska Range. Denali, the state's most famous mountain, was out there somewhere, wrapped in fog and pulling tourists northward toward some ideal Alaska that they perhaps read about in an adventure magazine. While the promise of a mountain view might have sounded romantic to a visitor, mountains were the common backdrop. It was the foreground that spoke to the neighborhood. Plastic soda bottles, fast food wrappers, and malt beer cans lined the road. I pulled into the driveway of the apartment complex, where a tall man leaned against the driver's side door of the "rebuilt, 1996, green Ford Taurus" he'd given me as a landmark.

Bart was a handsome thirtysomething with John Kennedy Jr. looks: dark hair and bright green eyes minus the dapper quality. He walked toward me, hand extended. Not bothering with small talk, he launched into an explanation of the trash in the parking spaces: "This is all getting cleaned up tomorrow." He indicated the driveway and the yard with a hand's sweep. "I've got one of the Russians coming over to mow the lawn."

"The Russians?"

"Yes, ma'am," he said, his molasses voice warm with used-car-salesman ethos. "I've got some Russians working for me on an exchange program. They're great. It's all on the books. You'll like them."

The Craigslist ad Bart had posted didn't include any photographs or details that acknowledged the building's general disrepair—a broken window in one of the basement units, postal boxes missing doors, dumpster overflowing with loose trash. A piece of cylindrical glass glinted under the tire of my truck. I bent down for a closer look.

"Is that a crack pipe?"

"Damn it!" Bart fake-yelled. "I told them to pick this crap up." He explained that no one wanted to pick up the drug paraphernalia because other tenants didn't want anyone to think it was theirs. "I've got one problem tenant that I'm trying to get rid of, but I have to do everything by the books. We do everything by the books around here."

"Right," I said.

"How about I pick this up and you go look at your new apartment?" he said, slipping the key into my hand. "Top of the stairs. Number 3."

The efficiency's formerly blond wooden floors were gray with wear and water damage, and the linoleum in the kitchen was torn in several places. An ancient refrigerator leaked Freon and the smell overwhelmed the small space. I walked to the center and turned in a slow circle, making a note of what it would take to make the place livable: blinds, bleach, a throw rug or two. I would stick it out until I graduated or found something nicer for the same price. I told myself either was possible and to look on the upside, to find something to like. The walls consisted mostly of windows. The light would be a refreshing change. The windows faced Elmendorf Air Force Base and in time, I reassured myself, I would get used to the boom of the jets.

In the parking lot, Bart made a show of gathering trash and stacking it beside the full dumpster. I leaned out of the apartment door and yelled, "I'll take it."

"Great! I'll send one of the Russians over tomorrow to pick up the rent. Cash only, okay? I just can't take checks. I've been burned too many times." He wiped his hands on shopworn khakis and waved good-bye.

CHELSEA AND I SMOKED SIDE-BY-SIDE on matching green milk crates. She had moved into number 2 a year earlier, and our balcony habit made us fast friends. She didn't look like a smoker. She had a round Madonna face and a little frame swimming in big curves. With her porcelain-clear skin and lustrous blonde hair, it was no surprise to hear a strange man yell up to her, "Hey, gurrrrl!" as he drove by in a car thumping with bass.

Chelsea was a skilled maintenance woman. I called her when I had plumbing or electrical problems, or when I needed my oil changed or help with a flat tire. Her husband, John, was jumping out of planes somewhere above Afghanistan, and his tour wasn't scheduled to end for several months. They had married when John last came home. The cigarette Chelsea smoked was the last one she'd have for several months.

"I'm pregnant," she said.

"Congratulations. Are you sure?"

"I took three tests this morning." She inhaled slowly, eyes closed, and let smoke out in a long, even breath. "They can't all be wrong." The late Alaska sunset gave her features a pink hue. She looked like a painting. "I don't know what to do. We're always so damn broke. And his parents are Mormon."

"Is that bad?"

"No. But they'll probably think this is why we married. Not the best impression."

The music of an ice cream truck drew near. It was close to midnight, but children from the neighboring building raced toward the sound.

"How much you wanna bet there's a pedophile clown driving that truck?" I joked.

"How much you wanna bet he's not just selling ice cream?" she countered.

Taku Drive rests just outside of Mountain View, once considered Anchorage's worst neighborhood before city council committees "cleaned up" around the business districts. But gun crimes and prostitution never went away; they crept into surrounding areas, making our street the dark underbelly of the former underbelly. The first month in my apartment I had called the police often, any time I heard gunshots or arguing, but they seldom came.

"I hate to say this, but if you're going to have this baby, you really need to move."

"I think we'll move back to Wyoming," she said, stubbing her cigarette out on the side of an old coffee can. "I need to be able to count on having water and electricity."

Periodically the water or gas shut off. Once, when the electric company had turned off the lights, I called and begged for power to be restored for tenants who had diligently paid their utilities-included rent. In his most buttery voice, Bart later explained that his accountant had paid the bills with the wrong credit card, again.

Chelsea said goodnight. I stayed on the deck for another cigarette, wondering who would do the maintenance after she moved to Wyoming. Who would help me shovel snow? Who would clean up the litter after the bank finally took the building from Bart and his Russians? And who would move into the apartment next door?

One year later, Saturday, 10:00 p.m. I was a thousand words into a fifteen-pager due the following Monday. I had an evening shift the next day and needed to boogie on the homework. Basil curled up on my pillow, likely dreaming of the good old days when I used to let her outside to kill things. The place looked good and smelled like a fresh pot of coffee. I had torn up the dirty linoleum, reworked the original wood floors with a belt sander, and picked a cherry varnish. The new landlord did not reimburse me for the materials. Still, the apartment finally felt like mine.

I couldn't focus. Deng Ba Dang was home from a job on the North Slope and was partying with his payday friends. Something slammed against my kitchen wall and rattled the clock. Raucous laughter and generic drunk sounds echoed throughout the building. I stomped to the kitchen and pounded the wall.

They pounded back.

I had liked Deng when he first moved into Chelsea's old apartment, or at least I really liked his name, Deng Ba Dang; the phonetic pop of it thrilled me. Deng Ba Dang. Deng Ba Dang. The name bounced around your mouth. He even laughed when he said it out loud. He was a tall Sudanese man who smiled often, his white teeth flashing against his dark skin. He was quiet at first, seldom had company, but this changed once he passed the citizenship test and accepted a job cleaning asbestos out of old buildings on the North Slope where most remote communities are dry. He binge drank whenever he came home.

I checked the locks on my door before going back to my desk. We never locked our doors in Moose Pass, and I often forgot to in Anchorage. After a few minutes of unproductive work, I heard Deng knocking.

"Sarah," he slurred, "open the door."

"Name's not Sarah!" I said. I'd corrected this many times, but I looked like a Sarah to him. I grabbed my pepper spray and opened the door. Deng spilled into my kitchen. He used my shoulders to steady himself and kept his hands there after regaining his balance.

"Don't touch me," I said. He removed his hands but stayed uncomfortably close. I kept the door open so he would understand he was welcome to leave quickly. Basil alerted to the fresh air and looked like she wanted to run for it.

"You give me a ride to get beer, Sarah," he said. Deng had graduated past broken English but was not yet fluent. He asked questions without modals.

"Are you asking if I can give you a ride to the liquor store?" I felt his beer breath on my forehead.

"Yes, you can?"

"I don't want to, Deng. I'm doing homework." I put my hand on his chest and pushed him back toward the doorway. "Watch your step." I closed the door as soon as his face cleared it and headed back to the computer. Deng seemed harmless, but I was afraid of the predatory way his drunken friends looked at unaccompanied women. They stood blocking my door when I came home, forcing me to interact.

The work went well for a couple hours after Deng left. Party sounds muffled into the background noise of cars on the highway and the growling boiler. Around midnight, my door burst open and one of Deng's friends, a stocky man who looked to be in his late thirties or early forties, stood in my kitchen with a can of beer in his hand. He froze. I froze. I had forgotten to lock the door after Deng came over. I grabbed the pepper spray on my desk, but adrenaline muddled my brain, and I couldn't understand how to maneuver the safety feature in order to make the can work.

"Get the fuck out! Get out!" I screamed, my voice shrill and silly sounding. The man smiled. He said something, but his accent was too thick.

"What?" Behind him the door wasn't closed all the way. If I scream really loud someone might hear me and do something, I thought.

"Bang. You bang? Me?" he asked, laughing.

"You're asking me to bang you? I don't understand." He laughed at this too and put his arms up and started backing toward the door. Suddenly, I understood what he was asking me to do.

"I'm going to Mace your fucking eyes out. Asshole!" At this, he recognized anger and left quickly. After a few minutes of waiting on hold for the police, I hung up the phone and stomped over to Deng's door.

"I want to talk to you, Deng!" I yelled through the door. In a chorus, his friends oohed him, as though he were in trouble with the teacher. He stumbled out and gave me a sheepish smile.

"This isn't funny, Deng. If I had a gun, I would have shot your friend. My door is not open to you." I pointed at my closed door to emphasize the point. His smile dropped suddenly, and I thought I was finally getting through to him.

"I know, Sarah," he said. "I drink too much."

A FEW NIGHTS LATER, I WOKE TO POLICE SIRENS at 3:00 a.m. and lay in bed listening to radios and voices for forty-five minutes before curiosity finally coaxed me outside. Flashing red-and-blue lights blended with the orange glow of the streetlamp. A blanket wrapped tightly around my bare legs, I squatted to talk to a few of Rae's friends who stood below the balcony.

"Is someone getting arrested?" I asked, noting an array of cleavage and thongs, pants that needed pulling up. All across the parking lot, police officers were interviewing teenagers. The group below me had finished talking to the officers who, even in the dark, appeared irritated.

A skeletal brunette looked up at me, the black bags under her eyes so pronounced that I wondered if the cause was meth, lack of sleep, or mascara build-up. Pockmarks encased her mouth and nose and she moved in the jerky fashion I'd come to associate with hard drug users. It's meth, I thought.

The boy beside her tightened his arms across his chest. He looked young, probably still a teen, but drunk and surly, a budding alpha male. He gave me one of those what's-it-to-you looks that teenage boys fling around.

"My friend here," he pointed to the brunette, "was just chillin' on the trunk and some motherfucker got his panties all up in a twist and called the fucking cops, and they think she was getting kidnapped or some shit." He said this loud enough for the police to hear, emphasizing certain words to make his point. The brunette rolled her eyes and looked appropriately churlish.

"You were just sitting on the trunk of the car? Why would anyone call the cops about that?" I asked her.

"No, she was in the trunk," the boy said for her.

"Why was she in the trunk?"

"I don't fucking know. She wanted to be. Why you trippin'?" He scowled, pulling his low-hanging pants up by the crotch. His hand lingered there a moment.

What I wanted to say was "Really? You have to touch your genitals right now? Nobody wants to see that." But the day before, I'd spotted an empty box of .38 shells beneath the stairs.

Let the punk be a punk, I told myself.

When Rae's dad bought the building, he'd given me a card with his business motto spelled out in bold italics: Safe, Affordable Housing. I tossed my cigarette into the Folgers can and let the punk's question roll around my head. Why was I tripping?

When the last police car pulled away from the parking lot and Rae's friends dispersed, I slipped back into the relative protection of my apartment. The night had stretched into morning, and traffic whooshed past the chain-link fence that divided Taku Drive from the highway. I lay in bed wondering how many fences kept me and the people in my building in low-rent neighborhoods. There were so many unfulfilled needs, for good parents, education, treatment programs, decent wages. When the community task forces "cleaned up" neighborhoods like Mountain View, they failed to address what made them dangerous in the first place.

I wondered if hard work, education, and good luck would push me out into the great suburban sprawl, push me into some safer, wealthier place where I would forget my time on Taku and watch with half-hearted concern as crime moved from one street to another without ever touching me in the deep, intimate way that forced me to acknowledge its reality.

Deng Ba Dang was stumbling up the stairs, and I couldn't remember if I locked the door. I shot out of bed and ran toward it, slamming my full weight against the fiberglass material. Deng tried to enter. I managed to lock the bolt and the knob. He smashed against it with his shoulder, and I heard the wood of the doorframe splinter.

Adrenaline turns some people into action stars and others into Bambi. I was a deer-in-the-headlights type. My hand shook, and I couldn't remember how to use my fingers or dial 911. Concentrating mightily, I was finally able to connect with the emergency dispatcher.

Deng was yelling, "Open the door, Sarah!" I couldn't hear the operator clearly.

"I don't know why he's trying to get in," I said to the emergency dispatcher. Deng gave up on the door and started working on the window beside it.

"He's going to break my window!"

Before the glass shattered, he moved to the next door and began pounding.

"I think he's gone," I said. Another man began bashing my window and yelling Deng's name.

The dispatcher said the police would be there any minute and to lock myself in another room. The only "room" in the studio apartment was the bathroom and the door didn't latch, let alone lock. Nevertheless, I sat on the bathroom floor with my back against it and waited for the reassuring sound of sirens. The man stopped before the police arrived.

I stayed on the floor in the bathroom for a long time after the police came, smoking indoors, using my toilet as an ashtray. Later, Lou came to check on me. I learned that one of Deng's friends had tried to stab Deng in the neck. Deng caught the knife with his hand and ran from his apartment barefoot. When I didn't let him in, Deng went to Lou, who opened his door. The second man who'd pounded on my window was the one who had stabbed Deng and was hunting him down. The police caught and arrested Deng's stabber.

I slept late the next morning and didn't leave the apartment until after noon. The door was covered in blood. It dried on the handle and in rusty drops that led down the stairs and around the corner. Dark red handprints and smudges marked the doors of the neighbors who had turned Deng Ba Dang away.

I KNOCKED CHRISTOPHER OFF HIS FEET when I opened my truck door. I might never have spoken with him at all if he hadn't been directly in my path. By then I knew that the smartest course of action on Taku was to mind my own business. I had pulled into the parking lot of my no-bedroom, 450-square-foot "apartment" and lingered an extra few minutes in the driver's seat to finish listening to a song, something maudlin and angsty, I'm sure. I didn't want to go inside at all because it was March, a month that straddles winter and spring and brings with it a general irritability after a long Alaska winter. I was just so tired of being inside. We had that in common.

"Hi, lady," the boy lying at my feet said. He held up a hand, a cue for me to help him up. Instead, I stared down at him while he pushed himself back to standing position. Normally, I wouldn't have remembered many details about a child's appearance—I wasn't a mom yet, and children all looked generically cute, like puppies or kittens or any newly formed creature, and they invoked mostly fear and annoyance, emotions that I had neither the patience nor willingness to understand. But that boy was as classically memorable as a Norman Rockwell subject: blond hair, blue eyes, and a plate-round face as symmetrical as a Disney character. He wore Oshkosh B'gosh overalls with a windbreaker. No winter coat. I thought someone is missing him, someone close, but easily dismissed the pang of worry.

I said something like, "Hi, kid. Watch out," and turned back to the truck's cab to gather my things. He stayed close as I headed toward my stairs, close the way children do, so unaware of personal space that if I'd stopped walking, he would have bumped into me. I ignored this. I didn't want his parents, whoever they were, to discover me talking with their child and get the wrong idea. I should say here too that I was single and self-concerned (which might be a redundancy), and I didn't want to draw any attention from my neighbors, who I, perhaps unfairly, assumed were all armed.

"Do you know where I live?" he asked, still following. "I can't remember, and Jaden's mom said he can't play outside and I can't come inside because he's being mean to his sister."

I scanned the windows facing my parking lot. There were no overprotective mothers watching us. In fact, most of the curtains in the vicinity were still closed.

"He's in there somewhere." He pointed to the nearest building, four stories of rental units with dozens of doors and windows.

"Is that where you live?"

"No. I live in a yellow house with a brown roof."

So helpful, I thought. He stared at me with curiousness. I was not used to the frank appraisal of children. His cheeks were dark pink from the cold that had not yet lost its February seriousness. I might have been a little squeamish about the snot streaming straight from his nose and into his mouth (something I wouldn't even see now), but his vulnerability was grossly conspicuous and even I couldn't look away.

I DIDN'T KNOW WHAT TO DO WITH the boy following me up the stairs. I couldn't drive him anywhere—what if someone thought I was abducting him? I could have called the police, but I didn't think they would arrive in a timely manner. I had called them recently for a woman who lived alone in the apartment behind mine. She was trapped inside while one of our other neighbors, drug violent and wanting her, kicked in her door. She slipped past him and hid in my apartment. The police came several hours later, long after her door had been broken open, as though they thought a woman ought to know better than to live alone in East Anchorage. The police inspected her splintered frame, the door that would no longer close or lock, and advised her to make a complaint to the landlord. The woman didn't insist they arrest the man, as though she too thought she ought to have known better.

I hoped the boy didn't wander as far from home as I did when I was a child. Haines was a small town, population just over a thousand at the time. The long distances trekked in my youth were likely shorter than my memory recalled. The boy lived in a rough part of Alaska's biggest city if he lived anywhere near me, and I assumed he did but thought to ask if his mom had dropped him off.

"No. But I wanted to play with Jaden, so I came to get him, but his mom says he's in trouble and he can't play. She's mean."

At the door of my apartment I said, "Wait right here. Okay? I'm going to walk you back home." He nodded. When I came back out, he was trying to slip his head between the bars of the balcony.

"Which way is home?" I asked. He disengaged from the railing and looked around.

"It's somewhere over there." He pointed south. There were small houses a few blocks into the neighborhood, an elementary school where the District 22 folks voted, and softball fields beyond that, but I didn't think he came that far on his own.

"Let's trace your way back, okay? What is your name?"

"Christopher."

"All right, Christopher, did you come down this hill?" I pointed to Fireoved, a street I suspected was misspelled and then renamed, which ended at my driveway where it intersected with another.

"Yes," he looked up at me. "Do you think I'm going to be in trouble?"

I thought of the sorts of trouble he could get into in our neighborhood. I (just barely) had the sense not to scare him with stories of vicious dogs and pedophiles and men with guns. I told him I didn't know. We walked up the first block of Fireoved, past apartments with blankets for curtains, past a car on flat tires, past an overfull dumpster.

When we got to the first intersection, I pointed to a house and asked, "Did you walk by here?"

"Yeah. That dog scared me." Christopher pointed to an American pit bull laying in a chicken-wire enclosure. The dog watched us walk by without lifting his head, his eyes following our feet disinterestedly. Christopher was nervous, though, and slipped his hand in mine. His hand felt warm and soft as summer sand. He's so small, I thought. My concern about being accused of kidnapping lessened some, and I held onto him. After a couple blocks the houses appeared tidier, more like homes and less like rentals, but Christopher kept walking.

"What is your mom doing, Christopher?" I asked to make chitchat.

"She was tired, so she told us to play outside," he said.

"You and who?"

"My little sister."

His little sister. "Where is she?"

"I dunno."

We walked for about fifteen minutes, straight through a handful of no-light intersections. Christopher didn't show signs of stopping.

"Are you sure you came this far?" I asked.

"Yeah. I remember that house," he said, pointing to a two-story. "Guess how old I am."

"Eight." I estimated up, hoping to flatter him.

"No!" He said and laughed. He held up his one hand and one thumb. "I'm this many."

"Five?"

"Six!"

"Wow. Are you going to start school soon?" I asked.

"Yeah, I already did."

I told Christopher that I was in school too.

"No way!" he said. "You're way too old to be in school."

"I'm only twenty-seven," I said, my feelings a little hurt.

"Wow. You're really old. You're even older than my mom! She was in school, but she had to quit."

"Are we getting close?" We were almost to the elementary school. I heard children playing on the next block.

"Look, it's Tommy!" Christopher yelled, pointing with his whole arm to a boy in the distance. "My house is bigger than his!" He began pulling away, his feet itching to run to the other boys.

"Wait a second," I held his arm. "I need to talk to your mom. Where do you live?" He pointed to a yellowish duplex with a brown roof and leaned away from me, but I didn't let go. "Which door?"

A silver truck pulled out of the driveway Christopher had pointed to. I held onto his arm as he tried to wriggle out of my grip. The truck was coming toward us. It stopped in front of us, and the driver's side window rolled down. I let go of Christopher's arm and thought, I'm going to get my ass kicked now. But Christopher froze at the sight of the male driver, and I wanted, suddenly, to put myself between him and the man.

"Where's your sister?" the man asked. Christopher said he didn't know. And just like that, the man drove on. He barely looked at me. I asked Christopher if that was his dad.

"That's my sister's dad. Can I go play with Tommy now?"

"Go for it. I'm going to tell your mom you're with Tommy. Okay?"

"K. Byeeee," he said, stretching the last word into two syllables and already running.

I approached the door where I thought Christopher's mom might be and knocked. When no one answered, I knocked harder. As I turned away, the door opened and a woman around my age looked at me with sleep-crusted eyes. The house behind her was dark. She wore pajama bottoms, and her blonde hair hung in long tangles over a faded T-shirt.

"Hi," I said, hoping I didn't look like a crazy or a missionary. "I live by the highway, on Fireoved and Taku. Christopher walked all the way over there. By himself. I brought him home."

"Thanks," she said and shut the door. Firmly.

COWBOY HAD TURNED OFF THE LAWNMOWER and was crawling on his hands and knees in a patch of grass. This was awkward to watch: Cowboy was tall, maybe six foot two, had thick glasses and an ungroomed gray-and-white beard that blasted off from his face in all directions. He covered his male-pattern baldness with a crusty ball cap. He usually wore paint-stained work jeans and flannel, even on warm days. I'd come to think of the whole look as standard, blue-collar Anchorage. He kept a set of tools on his person—screwdrivers and pliers in his breast pocket, hammer in a belt loop, screws and washers in his pants pockets.

"You looking for rocks?" I called down to him.

"No, ma'am." He stood, walked up the steps, and handed over two four-leaf clovers. He then pulled a pack of Marlboro filters out of his overstuffed pockets and lit up. "I'm a lucky man," he said.

"Why do you say that?"

"Did you know I grew up on a farm? That's why they call me Cowboy."

"What's your real name?" I asked.

"David Boyton. Long story short: I got kicked by a cow right here." He pulled off his cap and pointed to the front of his bald spot. It looked like every other bald spot to me.

"So now you have an affinity with cows?" I asked.

"No. But I'm lucky. I can go down there right now and pick you ten four-leaf clovers with my eyes closed."

"Is that right? With your eyes closed?" Cowboy could make himself the hero of any anecdote.

"Yep." He reached into his pants pocket and pulled out a cluster of clovers, holding open his hand in front of me. All had four leaves.

"How do I know you haven't been collecting those all morning?" I said.

"Hold this." He handed me his lit cigarette and stuffed the four-leaf clovers back into his pockets. He went to a different patch of grass directly in front of the parking lot. "Watch me now," he said. With his eyes closed he put out his hands and started walking in circles like a zombie. After a second, he stopped, hands out still, and dropped to his knees. I saw him pluck grass but couldn't tell if his eyes were still closed. He pushed himself up and came back, taking his still-lit cigarette from my hand and replacing it with four more four-leaf clovers.

"You can keep those too," he said.

I looked at the clovers, thinking he must have done some sleight-of-hand maneuver and grabbed some that were in his pocket. But the clovers weren't crushed or wrinkled. I slipped them into my journal with the first two he'd given me.

"When I was a boy I got kicked by a cow, and it knocked me out. When I came to I was lying in a patch of clovers. Ever since, I can feel for them," he said.

"What does it feel like?"

"I don't know. Maybe like electricity or something. But it's not just that. I can feel when I'm going to get lucky."

What is so lucky about Cowboy? I asked myself. Almost sixty years old, living alone in a tiny apartment in a bad neighborhood, kicked in the head as a kid, and now he feels lucky. But I wanted to believe him more than I wanted to be cynical. I liked his good outlook, and now I had a journal full of lucky charms.

"Thanks for the clovers, Cowboy. I need all the luck I can get. I think I'm going to try to quit smoking. After this pack."

"Oh yeah? Well, if I could quit drinking, you can quit smoking," he said.

"How long you been sober?"

"Fifteen years," he said, then changed his mind. "Maybe five. It took me a few tries. It doesn't take luck, though. It takes balls. Big balls and hard work."

"So it's a lot like everything else."

"Pretty much."

Cowboy tossed his cigarette in the can and sat on the top step, looking outward or inward, I couldn't tell. It was a good silence, an easy silence. I smelled the coffee brewing in my apartment, and a sweeter smell wafting up from the rosebush. I'd read that the sense of smell is the first thing a body recovers in nicotine withdrawal. I arranged the remaining clovers into my journal and wondered if I could capture that luck—the essence of clover, green and fresh, pushing up and up and into summer.

HEATHER LENDE

H AINES IS AN OUT OF THE WAY COMMUNITY even by Alaska standards. Located near the northern end of the state's Southeast Panhandle, it's accessible by boat, small plane, and a single road that crosses an international border. It's a mere fifteen miles from the better known town of Skagway, but if you want to drive there, plan on a 350 mile trip that takes you through Canada.

Wedged between Chilkat and Chilkoot Inlets, Haines is home to fewer than 3000 year-round residents, including well known author Heather Lende. Originally from the East Coast, she and her husband Chip settled there in 1984 and have remained ever since.

In the mid 1990s, Lende began writing obituaries for the the local newspaper, the Chilkat Valley News, and soon attracted national attention for her literary style that seeks to capture the character of her subjects rather than simply list the events of their lives. To read one of her obituaries is to feel you have met the person being memorialized.

During that same period, Lende also established herself as an essayist, writing vivid sketches about life in a small town that capture the joys and difficulties of living in a place where everyone knows everyone else and also knows their personal affairs. Lende might have escaped the crowded Eastern Seaboard, but she didn't go hiding from people. A town the size of Haines doesn't permit such self indulgences.

Lende's first collection of essays, 2005's *If You Lived Here, I'd Know Your Name*, from which the selection here was taken, was a New York Times bestseller, and she has since then published three more books, most recently *Of Bears and Ballots*. Lende's stories of life in Haines are filled with quiet humor, quirky personalities, an underlying faith that's heartfelt rather than evangelical, and rich details that bring her little corner of Alaska fully alive. More than any other Alaskan writer, she focuses on the idea of community and how the people comprising it interact with each other and the land and water surrounding them.

When I asked her to discuss writing about Haines, Lende explained, "I came to Haines as a young mother with a husband and a three month old baby, and made a life here. My husband owns a lumberyard, we raised five children, and now have six Haines and Juneau grandchildren and one on the way. My writing, my soul, the people I live with, the stories I see and share, are so rooted in Haines, and it is all so much a part of my being, that I'm not sure where one begins and the other ends. I can't help but write about life here—and death too. I have written over 500 obituaries for the Chilkat Valley News, all for people I knew—and some for very close friends—that more than anything shapes my work and my world view. Love, loss, grief, and gratitude for all of it, is all mixed up in a place so beautiful that all I have to do is take a walk, with my dogs, or a friend, or both—to feel the universe tugging me toward goodness and mercy, even grace, and laughter too—there's a lot of crazy—in a good way, in Haines."

"Fire and Ice," the piece that follows, captures the elements that make her writing so encompassing. Her community and family are captured in a few telling moments that include mishaps, personal trials, the humor people turn to as a means of overcoming hardships, a narrowly-averted tragedy, a tragedy fulfilled, longtime friendships and the tests they can be put to, and a gentle spiritual lesson which, like all the messages she draws from her faith, is about striving to better oneself as a member of both the local and global human communities. All of it takes place against the backdrop of Haines over a few winter days.

— From *If You Lived Here, I'd Know Your Name* —
FIRE AND ICE

AFTER THE LAST FISHERMAN'S FUNERAL, I decided water around here is best when it's frozen. As I help my youngest daughters into their ice skates, I hum the old carol "In the Bleak Midwinter": "Earth stood hard as iron, / Water like a stone." The afternoon is so perfect; it's like a big exhalation, throwing off all that crummy winter-weather tension. The bowl that Chilkoot Lake sits in is protected by a rim of high mountains and tucked back into a valley. Although a north wind blows forty knots across Lynn Canal, icing boats in the harbor at the foot of Main Street, here on the lake it's calm. Dark spruce trees and white mountains reflect on ice as hard and shiny as a marble floor. Chilkoot Lake is so big that, although I recognized the handful of Subarus and pickups parked on the road, their owners are out of sight. Looking across the ice, I can't see a soul.

I learned to skate on an artificial rink on Long Island, the kind filled with organ music and people in rented skates all circling around and around in one direction. I still can do crossover turns only to the left. Skating at Chilkoot is as different from skating at a rink as swimming laps in a pool is from snorkeling in the tropical ocean. Instead of weaving in and out of other skaters, the girls and I quietly glide about a mile out, to where the rest of the family is already playing hockey. Chip and the three older children are crazy about the game. It's only a matter of time before the two younger girls join them. The games are so fast and rough that it's no place for cruisers like me. Every time I think about playing hockey, too, I'm reminded of the mother in *A Prayer for Owen Meany*. Instead of being killed by a Little Leaguer's foul ball, I'm sure a stray hockey puck will catch me right in the temple.

A safe distance from the game, a group of children my girls' age are learning to make figure eights. Leaving J.J. and Stoli there, I venture beyond the sounds of the game, beyond the voices and scraping of blades on ice. I am so far out I can't even hear a dog bark. The ice is absolutely smooth and clear and the air so cold that my breath makes frost on my eyelashes, scarf, and on the edges of my wool hat. I skate with my arms wide open, singing out loud: "I could have danced all night . . ."

Near the middle on the western side, I can see open water and an orange buoy ball floating way out in the distance, marking the danger. The best skaters, the oldest and wisest, have assured everyone that the rest of the ice is thick enough to hold a dump truck. Now I wish there were a dump truck here so I could see for myself. In places, the ice does look new, similar to the thin layer that appears overnight on puddles in September. The kind of ice that breaks like glass when children stomp on it. I slow down but keep moving across the stillness, hearing nothing but the *scritch* of my blades and the occasional muffled thud of a pressure crack under-foot. That sound makes my heart beat faster. What if the ice won't hold? Can I make it to the shallow end in time? I am about to turn around and go back when I see the tracks of a lone skater. Two graceful curves of white on the dark green ice, repeating in a simple pattern over the lake.

I catch up with Linnus and feel much better skating with a friend. We push and glide fast for fifty minutes in one direction, then slowly circle back to check on the children, Chip, and Linnus's husband, Steve, who is also playing hockey. Everyone is happy, so we leave them again and zigzag silently along the shore, back to the landing, looking for wolves in the woods.

ON THE WAY HOME, CHIP AND I TAKE THE KIDS to the museum in town to look at a traveling exhibit of blown-glass bowls, vases, and balls by world-renowned artist Dale Chihuly. They are beautiful, but they can't compete with the swirling patterns of frost and bubbles suspended in the clear green ice at Chilkoot Lake. I think I love those much more than the fancy glass because I know they won't last as long.

As if Mother Nature wants to prove the point, the day after our per-fect skate we wake up to whirling snow. Across town Tom Heywood looks out the window, too, and knows he doesn't have much time to enjoy the lake. Soon snow will cover the ice. Tom hasn't been skating yet this season and is in a seize-the-day mood. But the rest of his family isn't. His wife, Liz, has a cold, and the kids don't want to go. When his ten-year-old says he prefers his computer game, Tom leaves, alone.

Steve and Linnus, who also decided to get in one more skate before the heavy weather, come ashore as Tom starts out. They tell him the skat-ing is great. Tom follows their tracks in the thin coat of dry snow out into the white winter wonderland. He is alone, so alone, in such a beautiful place that he thinks, *This is unbelievable.* He is happy; skating makes him feel light and carefree. The same way it does for me.

Tom is a mild-mannered former midwesterner. A pilot, he has his own small plane. At forty-six, after teaching first and second graders for twenty years, he's retired and with Liz owns the Haines bookstore. He had children relatively late in life—two adopted Korean sons and a biological daughter. When he taught my kids, their favorite time of the day was when he'd play the guitar and sing with them.

Since no one is watching and he's in such a good mood, he dances. A few fancy moves, some curlicues, a swirl, and a loop on the white surface. He's left behind the other tracks now and skates toward a buoy ball. He wonders what it's doing out on the ice. He decides to go beyond it all the way to the end of the lake, something he can't do with the kids. It's a long way down and back, nearly ten miles. He's thinking that there is no place he'd rather be when suddenly, completely without warning, the ice gives out. One second he's skating, the next he's in the water. *This can't be happening.*Tom is incredulous. *I can't believe this.*

Hanging on to the edge of the ice, up to his neck in frigid water, Tom Heywood doesn't watch his life move before his eyes like a movie. Instead, he sees one still image of his wife and three children. *I am not ready to leave them*, he thinks, kicking to keep his head above water and gripping the ice with his left hand. He knows he can climb out, and he says so, out loud, to the fish below and the mountains above. "I can do this," he repeats, echoing the Little Engine in the story he's read so many times to so many different children. "I can do this, I can do this." Like an icebreaker, he moves toward his tracks, hoping he'll find the solid section that held him just moments ago.

It's so clear what he has to do; the challenge is so immediate that he acts without hesitating—almost. *This*, Tom thinks for just a second, *is how people disappear and are never found.* The snow keeps his hands from slipping; he has a good grip, but the thin ice caves in with each attempt to climb out. His long johns, jeans, sweatshirt, and down coat are heavy. He's working so hard he doesn't feel the cold. He almost gets his right knee up but the ice breaks, again and again. He's not a church-goer and knows he shouldn't expect a hand now, but he prays for help.

Finally, after almost getting up and crashing back in the water six or seven times, he pulls himself out and crab-scoots on all fours until he's sure he's on safe ice. With a shout he thanks the angels of Chilkoot Lake and skates back faster than he ever has. He sails by the patterns he made earlier and knows *that that was a different life*. He hears a cracking sound and his heart beats harder until he realizes it's the ice chipping off his coat, jeans, and ice-crusted skates. On the shore, arriving skaters help get him to his truck and take his skates off, but he waves them off and drives himself home. All he wants to do is get there. His family is at the kitchen table when he walks into the house. There's so much Tom wants to say, he is so grateful and loves them so very much, but all he can manage is "I had a bad experience." Later, he makes a sign warning of thin ice and drives back to the lake with it.

At the bookstore Monday morning Tom greets well-wishers, who all want to hear his story. We think it's a miracle he got out alive, especially with none of us there to help him. Tom says that isn't necessarily so. "I know people say you shouldn't go out alone," he tells us, "but I'm really glad no one else was there. If Liz was with me, we both would have fallen through, and I can't even imagine what would have happened if I had the kids." Then he says, quietly, "I'm certain that somebody else would have gone in, so if it had to happen, I'm glad it was me." I ask him if he'd skate again. "When I know it's totally safe," he says. "And I'll be real cautious if there's any kind of snow."

WHICH IS ALL THERE WAS FOR THE NEXT TWO WEEKS. As the third line of "In the Bleak Midwinter" goes, "Snow had fallen, snow on snow, snow on snow." It could have been making me temporarily insane. Although I don't think that excuses me from thinking vengeful thoughts or almost committing a crime. Maybe I was just so cold I wanted to heat things up. I had been having trouble coping after close friends of mine split. He'd left her for a woman twenty years younger. I'll tell you the story, but I won't use names; this is too small a town for that. The whole episode had left me feeling as if my heart was under a glacier. It was just enough pressure to cause permanent damage, but not enough for people to notice unless they looked closely.

When my friend who was left home alone asked me and another friend to help her switch around the bedrooms in her house, of course we said yes. We would do anything for her. How we got from simply moving her old bed to almost cutting it up with a chain saw, tossing it out the window, and burning the mattress in the new girlfriend's driveway at midnight, I'm still not sure. The three of us were playing a card game in my kitchen on a Saturday night when the question of what to do with the old bed made a spark that caught fire. Before we knew it, we were all excited and talking at once.

Chip has a dump truck. We could put the mattress in it, tip it off the back under cover of darkness, and light it before speeding away. We'd never have to get out of the cab. No one would know who did it, unless we passed Fireman Al on the way home. When Al was in college he burned his folk's cabin near Chilkoot Lake down to the foundation. It was an accident, and no one was hurt, but he decided to become a fireman instead of a biologist after that, so he could help prevent such a catastrophe from happening to anyone else. We agreed that Al would recognize us for sure.

"Then we'll wear ski masks," one of us said. "And dress in black," another said. "And light it with a Molotov cocktail," added the third, a librarian, who also mentioned that "you can learn how to make them on the Internet." I thought we were doing some heavy housecleaning, not starting a riot. Luckily, our friend with the bed said that we couldn't toss a bottle with fuel in it. The leftover shards of glass might cut a dog's paw.

As I served up warm apple pie and ice cream, I recalled the song "Alice's Restaurant" and all those eight-by-ten glossy photos at the trial, and I knew that while burning your own property in someone else's yard might not be arson, it would, at the very least, be littering. We could all end up in jail, as Arlo Guthrie had. When I said so, one of my friends reminded me that Guthrie's story did have a silver lining: "I mean, he didn't have to go to Vietnam, right?"

But she knew what I meant. It wasn't the law or government we were worried about, it was a higher authority. "If we burn your mattress this way now," she said to our friend, "the smoke will only soil your soul—and ours." We all agreed to a private bonfire on the beach, with just the three of us, the next day.

Still, I worried that the black smoke from all that foam rubber would attract Fireman Al and the volunteers. Chip came into the kitchen and put his pie plate in the sink with the others. "When they see who it is and what you're burning," he said, "they'll run."

Before we went to sleep, I asked Chip if he thought I was crazy. "Yes," he said, "but you were when I married you." I thought about our wedding, how happy we were, and then my friend's wedding, which had been such a fun day, too. I was suddenly dizzy with a grief that was worse in some way than the dying kind. I was so afraid it might happen to us, too, that I turned out the light and kissed Chip hard.

In the morning my friend canceled the burn. She'd heard that the wind had blown most of the snow off Chilkoot Lake and said she'd rather go skating. So instead of standing by a bonfire watching her old life go up in smoke, we started her new one gliding over thick ice.

A few weeks later, I went to see Father Jim. I was writing a story for the paper on his Catholic mission boat, the *Mater Dei*. We met over coffee in the rectory. When the interview was done, I told him I'd been having some trouble lately with forgiveness. I didn't tell him how we'd almost burned a man's marriage bed in his new girlfriend's driveway, but I did ask if you could still be a good Christian if you were thinking really bad thoughts. "Heather," Father Jim said loudly in his South Boston accent. (I think he used to work in big cathedrals.) "Heather," he said, warming up for the punch line the way he does. "Heather, when God taps you on the shoulder and says it's time to go, he'll ask you one question: *Have you been good to my people?* If you can answer yes, then you've got it made."

On the way home, I ran into Christy Tengs Fowler, a close friend of the Stuart family's, at the library. She asked me if I'd be writing Gene Stuart's obituary. I told her I would be, as soon as I finished Father Jim's story. . . and I needed to record an essay for the radio . . . and I had to write my column, too. I didn't have time to visit with anyone about anything right now, especially that obituary. It was terrible and sad and could wait—the weekly paper wouldn't be printed for six more days. But Christy needed to talk and I'm her friend, so I slowed down and we moved out of the doorway to a quiet corner. Gene had died that morning in Seattle from the burns he'd suffered in a fire at his remote cabin the afternoon before. He had been lighting a woodstove with diesel fuel and the fumes had built up and it had exploded. He was on fire when the friends who were out there with him pulled him through the window and then "dropped and rolled" with him on the ground to put the flames out, the way Fireman Al has instructed us all to do. A helicopter that usually transports extreme snowboarders and skiers saw the cabin in flames and radioed town. They flew Fireman Al and an emergency medical technician in to help Gene just as it was getting dark. Then a Coast Guard chopper flew him out of town from the airport. Doctors at the Juneau hospital decided to send him on to a burn center in Seattle, but there was not much that could be done. If that wasn't bad enough, Gene's dog, Willow, died in the fire, too.

Gene was a sawyer in the old mills; he ran the huge blades that cut logs into boards. When the mills were shut down, he became a fisherman out of necessity, naming his boat *Reluctant*. Mostly, Geno, as his friends called him, was a practical joker. He came up with electrician Erwin Hertz's slogan: "Hertz Electric—We'll Fix Your Shorts." Gene was a good man, and he was good to God's people. I told Christy what the priest had said about that, and I decided to take his words to heart. I promised Christy I'd start Gene's obituary whenever the family was ready, and asked her to let me know when they wanted to talk with me. My other projects would have to wait. Christy told me she felt awful for Gene's widow, all alone in her house. "She doesn't even have her dog," Christy said. She also couldn't help thinking about how quickly life can change.

WHEN I GOT HOME, CHIP'S BIG OLD BOAT with the blue tarp flapping on the deck looked as pretty as a white-sailed sloop in the harbor. The skates and boots all over the floor in the mudroom, the dishes in the sink, and my good old dog sleeping on the couch all seemed to shout, *A family lives here; they are busy and happy and a little messy but someday that won't be so and you'll be sorry.* A little joy has come from all this winter's sadness. After Tom fell into the lake and lived to tell about it, his wife, Liz, said she didn't care anymore what he bought her for her upcoming birthday; he'd already given her the best present ever—himself. My friend's divorce has given me a new appreciation for my own marriage. That doesn't mean I would want the bad in order to have the good, but I know that love and life are all mixed up with loss and death, just like beautiful bubbles frozen in the lake.

Robert Frost wrote that the world may end in fire or ice. Well, from what I've seen, heard, and imagined of both this winter, all I can conclude is that the world could end in any number of ways, and there's nothing anyone can do about it. The only choice any of us has is what to do if we're still here after it happens. Do we die a little death every day ourselves or do we reach for someone's hand and dance again?

JUDY FERGUSON

J UDY FERGUSON IS AN ALASKAN TREASURE who, Epicenter Press's
Lael Morgan once told me, is under-appreciated for what she does.
A self-taught oral historian, she has gathered hundreds of personal
narratives from across the state, conveying through her subjects' words
and experiences a diverse and wide ranging look at who Alaskans are as
a people.

Ferguson first visited Alaska during Thanksgiving, 1965, while
studying fine arts at the University of California Los Angeles. In 1968,
she moved north permanently and settled near Rika's Roadhouse in Big
Delta. In 1975, Ferguson and her husband, Reb, canoed the Yukon River.
There she began interviewing people she met along the way. It seems she
hasn't stopped. "I love to hear people's stories and to document who they
are. It helps me to better understand where I live," she said.

Beginning in 1996, Ferguson spent thirteen years writing a column
for the *Fairbanks Daily News-Miner* that alternated oral histories she had
gathered from others with stories of her own family's wilderness adventures. For two and half years, she also wrote the *Alaskana* column for the

Anchorage Daily News and for many years, she wrote for the *Delta Wind*. She has published eight books.

Thanks to her efforts, the memories of many Alaskans who have since passed on are permanently preserved. She explained, "It's abysmal that if no record is made, that when people die, their lives and their era drift into the abyss. We lose important parts of who we are as a people. After the grave, there is no retrieving of that information."

Ferguson, who is now semi-retired, always lets her subjects edit their stories, making them in effect coauthors. This has gained her both the trust and the friendship of people in every corner of Alaska.

While she always enjoyed learning about Alaska through its indigenous people, Ferguson decided in 2003 to focus almost exclusively on Alaska Native stories. "I lived through the era of ANCSA (Alaska Native Claims Settlement Act) and ANILCA (Alaska National Interest Lands Conservation Act). I remember the tug of war on both sides, but I wanted to know how it evolved, to learn from those who made our history."

The result is a sprawling, two-volume collection entitled *Windows to the Land*, in which she presents stories as told by dozens of Alaska Natives from every region of the state, as well a handful of whites who were closely tied to Native issues. The first volume explores the era leading up to and through ANCSA, while the second volume examines the broader scope of Native life, past and present, including a focus on the Iditarod, World Eskimo-Indian Olympics, and the indigenous use of land and water.

The stories found in the books are fascinating–and sometimes painful–personal histories that shed light on the struggles and triumphs that Alaska Natives experience while maintaining distinct cultures in a predominantly white society. Her subjects discuss traditional subsistence practices, art, spiritual beliefs, tragedies, the racial divide, substance abuse, maintaining land rights, rescuing languages from extinction, and cultural revival, all of it extensively illustrated with photos, timelines, and maps. These books tell the history of Alaska from each of its indigenous areas. It's a remarkable accomplishment, and an invaluable contribution to recent and contemporary Alaskan history.

Fred John, Jr., an Ahtna Athabascan from eastern Interior Alaska whose account is excerpted here, once told me during a newspaper interview that Ferguson "writes good stories for Natives. Good truthful stories."

John is the son of the late activist Katie John, who was the lead plaintiff in a court challenge against the State of Alaska over access to traditional fishing waters, which the state had closed to subsistence and other fishing activities. Katie John's case bounced back and forth between state and federal courts for three decades and exposed fierce conflicts between rural and urban residents, as well as Natives and nonnatives. It wasn't fully resolved until 2014, a year after her death, when the U.S. Supreme Court declined to review a Ninth Circuit Court ruling in favor of Native rights. Even so, new challenges to the decision have recently emerged.

The following excerpt includes small parts of Fred John's lengthy account of his childhood, and then tells the story of his own activism. His openness is a testament to John's determination to have the history of what Alaska Natives have endured be known and acknowledged, and to Ferguson's ability to build the sort of trust necessary to get people to share intimate and sometimes very traumatic parts of their lives.

Having probably interviewed more Alaskans than anyone else in the state, Ferguson gives credit to those she has come to know rather than to herself. "It's been my privilege to hear these people's voices, to know their stories," she said. "They have been my teachers."

— From *Windows to the Land, Volume Two* —

CHILD OF WRANGELL INSTITUTE, SON OF KATIE JOHN: FRED JOHN JR.

I WAS BORN JANUARY 3, 1943, TO KATIE SANFORD JOHN from Batzulnetas and Fred John Sr. from Mentasta. [Batzulnetas pronounced, *Bets'ulnii Ta'*, the "Roasted Salmon Place," was originally a camp of ten to fifteen Natives, seventy miles above Gakona, on Tanada Creek near the headwaters of the Copper River. Lt. Allen visited Batzulnetas in his 1885 historic exploration.]

WHEN I WAS YOUNG, WE NEVER SPOKE ENGLISH. We had to travel by dog team, sometimes walking, from Suslota to Mentasta. It took three days and we camped overnight. The only three "cities" we went to were Suslota, Chistochina, and maybe Tanacross. In 1949 Suslota died off. The last three women, Irene Johnson, Molly Galbreath, and her younger sister Helen John, along with their little kids, had to walk out of there alone.

In those days our whole world was the mountains and the valley of Mentasta. When I sat on our mountain, I wondered, "What are those things that white people tell us about? Big cities, high buildings?" My world was right here. These villages were big for me then.

WHEN I WAS ONLY SEVEN IN 1950, there was no school in Mentasta. A Bureau of Indian Affairs agent Mr. Valentine came to Mentasta and told my parents that we children had to be in school. They said that if we didn't go, they'd come and take us away. We didn't know what boarding school was. To avoid this, the Houston Sanford family left Mentasta and went to Chisana. They stayed away as long as they could. Cherry Nicolai's children also refused.

When we left, I remember Nancy at age five, me, Ben, and Nelson, dressed in our Ward's catalog clothes, waiting with our suitcases for the bus at Mentasta Lodge to go to Anchorage. From there, we flew for the first time to Wrangell Institute Boarding School in Wrangell, Alaska. We were driven to the school. When we pulled up in the car to the dorms, students lined up outside our windows, looking at us. They had bald heads and wore uniforms, which made their faces look round and chubby. They referred to us new students as "fresh meat."

The matrons took us to a place called the "rumpus room." On the way there, the older students sized us up and bumped into us. Nelson and Ben bumped them back so the students knew not to mess with them, but I was only seven and I was really scared.

They took Nancy to the girls' dorm and us brothers to the boys' dorm. They stripped us down, deloused us, gave us a bald head haircut so that our ears stuck out. Then they ran us through showers and afterwards female and male staff checked us, even our privates, to be sure we were clean. We were given a uniform: crimson shirt, blue pants, and brown shoes. There was a permanent number over the left pocket in front and under the neck collar in the back. That number was our name from 1950–1958. Anytime they called me, it was "77!"

We marched everywhere: to classes and to meals. We got demerits for infractions for which there were a variety of punishments. If we spoke in our language, we got beaten with a heavy belt. We had to learn English fast. My older brothers were eleven and thirteen and at those ages, they had to learn quickly. We had no say at all.

When I dropped my coat on the floor three times in one week, I got three demerits. When I wasn't in class, I was confined to my bed after lunch, in the evenings, and during the weekends for three months! Another punishment was the gauntlet. A naked boy ran through a gauntlet of fifty to a hundred boys who beat him with a heavy belt. Some were so angry that they flailed back the whole way. The brown-nosers supervised. Wrangell turned our own people on us. Saturday morning was spanking morning. Before breakfast, they called the numbers of those who were going to get a spanking. They'd get hit twenty times with their pants down with a heavy belt. Before the spanking, the little kids were already crying. Sometimes a family friend would take the place of a little kid; the older child's sacrifice would make the child cry all the harder. Smaller punishments included taking away a child's weekly twenty-five cents to spend at the candy store or disallowing him to go to the movie.

There were three types of kids there: those who conformed to every rule, of which I was one. Then there were those who rebelled and who couldn't be managed; those were sent home in the middle of the year. The third type was the brown-nosers, the tattletalers. I hated them. Much later at Tanana Chiefs Conference Old Minto Family Recovery Camp, a counselor said, "Did you know the brown-nosers were trying to survive as much as you were?" I had to forgive them. Myself, I survived by following every rule. The hard core ones survived by fighting, by knowing that they'd be sent home. My brother Nelson wouldn't conform and he was sent home.

That first stint in boarding school, we were there for two years. When the lights were turned off, we could hear other kids sobbing in their beds, then others would join in until we all fell asleep. We were ages five through nine in the dorm and we didn't know why we were there. We didn't know why our parents gave us away. We cried because we were lonely; we were homesick. Nobody hugged us or kissed us good night anymore.

We younger ones didn't know why we were beaten when we spoke the only language we knew. Why were the other students so mean? We didn't know that the longer we were there that we too would also become mean. Before the first two years were over, I only knew I was number 77. We became a number and not human anymore. Luckily my two older brothers kept reminding me that my name was Fred John Jr., but I still remember number 77. It never left me. I bet the prisoners in the World War II concentration camps never forgot their numbers either.

We learned to fight, to lie for ourselves, and for each other. We learned to survive the best we knew how. We lost our language and we became ashamed of ourselves.

FROM 1954 TO 1957, EXCEPT FOR THE SUMMERS, we were back at Wrangell, from the time I was eleven until I was fourteen. There was sexual abuse at the boarding school. Matrons would get boys. The woman who was in charge of the boys' gym enlisted some of the older boys who were just coming into their manhood. They were scared but they were also excited. Even when I was twelve to thirteen, a couple of nurses would make us make love to them. Even the dentist would have us watching a cartoon while he checked our teeth and fondled us. We were scared; we had no one to talk to about it. Those who reported it got put on long time restriction. I don't know what happened with the girls. They never told me.

Our people were broken: physically, emotionally, and spiritually.

Our family also began to change at home when a lady missionary, Auntie Mae, began living with my family in Mentasta. She began teaching them the principles of the Word, of living a life in Christ. She and my mom became good friends.

I REMEMBER WHEN BEN, NANCY, AND I returned home in 1952. Nancy was seven and I was nine. When we stepped off the bus at Mentasta Lodge, we saw our mother, Katie, sitting on a blanket with her dog Spike. It had been so long and we were scared. We were afraid that Mom and Dad didn't love us anymore. We were glad to get home but we were also scared because we didn't understand why our parents sent us there. We didn't know that they had no choice. For two years we had never been shown any affection. We were afraid our parents might have forgotten us. We kind of shuffled around the bus door and we didn't know what to do until Mom raised both her arms out to us. We dropped everything and our little feet ran into her open arms. We were hugged and kissed and cried over. For over two years, that is what we wanted and needed.

When we came home, we told our parents what had been going on. Our dad cried, "No more, no more, no more will I do this to my children."

RECENTLY MY COUSIN FROM COPPER CENTER who went to boarding school with me asked, "Freddy, do you remember those days at Wrangell Institute?" He had done well in life; a lot of them did. But a lot of them didn't: alcoholics who buried anything of meaning in their lives. You see them walking around Second Avenue in Fairbanks with no life in their eyes. I am a part of that generation. I don't want to pass on that generational grief to my kids. I'll do whatever I can to prevent that boarding school abuse from ever happening again. I talk for my sisters and brothers who died. For years I never talked about this but when I began with good Christian counselors at Old Minto Family Recovery Camp during the early part of the twenty-first century, it hurt, boy, did it hurt. At that time, I wondered, "Why do I drink? Why? I know it hurts me."

Since we weren't raised by our parents, we didn't know how to raise our own children. We lost so much of our ways that we didn't know how to support our family. We turned to drinking to hide our shame and our grief. Many never made it back to wholeness. With the love of my family and the Old Minto Recovery Camp, I volunteered to give my all to share what I have learned. It took a long time and after many second chances, I learned to appreciate my new life, to give instead of take. I thank God, my family, and friends for forgiving me for hurting them.

MAY 23, 2013 I LOST MY MOTHER, Katie John. I began to think about a way to honor her, to give back, to be a voice for the voiceless and in this way, Walk for *Tsucde* (Grandma) was born.

[HERE FERGUSSON TAKES OVER THE STORY, telling of John's activism.]
One day after his mother, Katie John, died, Fred said, "I feel I am supposed to walk from Dot Lake to Anchorage to raise awareness for Alaska Native subsistence rights. As I looked down at his injured ankle, I wondered if at his age he could manage such a beating, hiking from Dot

Lake to Anchorage, a journey of 411 miles. Fred John not only surprised me but he elicited great admiration statewide. He had a vision, he shouldered the burden, and he set a fast pace. His hour had come.

Unbeknownst to Fred, the U.S. Interior Department announced on May 1, 2014 that it would consider taking Alaska tribal land into trust. On that same day Fred was starting his month-long walk to support the indigenous use of the land. Fred is a son of Katie John who was the late lead plaintiff in a series of lawsuits that were aimed at ensuring Alaska Native fishing and indigenous rights.

After Governor Sean Parnell saluted Katie John at the 2013 Alaska Federation of Natives (AFN) convention in Fairbanks, Alaska, Attorney General Michael Geraghty asked the Supreme Court to review a decision by the Ninth Circuit Court of Appeals that the federal government controls subsistence hunting and fishing on navigable waters owned by the state that are adjacent to and within federal land. However, the Supreme Court refused to hear the appeal with the state responding by saying they would continue to pursue the issue. AFN President Julie Kitka stated that the win was "not only a victory for Alaska Natives" but also protected other rural Alaskans who depend on subsistence to feed their families.

To BRING ATTENTION TO THE TRIBAL NEED to govern their land, Fred John, family members, and supporters from Delta Junction and Tanacross, along with residents of Dot Lake, gathered May 1 to help begin Fred's journey. After everyone danced, Fred saluted Dot Lake founder Doris Charles and Gene Henry for fighting the subsistence battle with his mother, Katie John. He read a biography, *Number 77*, written about him by his daughter Gwendolyne John Jenkins:

During the 1950s, when I was taken from my Mentasta home and sent to boarding school, I was called number 77. I hated myself because of who I was and because of the face that always looked back at me in the mirror. I learned from others that I would never be anything worthwhile, so I decided to change that.

I learned the language they taught me; I went to the schools they sent me. I played their sports. I even married the blonde who looked like the cover models. I did my best to fit in. Then came my kids . . .

One after another they came, till there were five little brown faces that filled my two-story house with its plumbing and its refrigerator full of groceries. They looked like me. I loved them. I began to want to love myself when I looked—in my own mirror.

Through them, I began to accept who I was and who I was always going to be, an Indian. My kids were confident and proud; I became confident and proud. They wanted to learn where they came from. I began to teach them. As my long ago memories began to surface, I began to heal.

At times they tried to force me to hurry with my journey, to regain my self-confidence. They were young and curious; they did not know the pain and humiliation, the scars I carried. But neither did they know that they were the ointment, the healing touch I needed to survive and to begin to grow again.

I slowly began to realize that there was one person who, all along, had known my struggles, the gut-wrenching fear, sadness, and anger I carried: my wife, Linnea. She knew and she watched. She waited until one day I could journey on my own and share my story.

I am Fred John Jr. I am part of the hidden secrets of the forty-ninth state, the last of the U.S. attempts to assimilate the owners of this land. I am no longer scared. I have regained my voice. I want to share my story.

After speaking, Fred was accompanied by his brother Harry John, and Harry's wife, Diane, and more family and friends as he left Dot Lake and turned down the Alaska Highway.

On day two, ninety-nine-year-old Emma Northway, the oldest living person in the Upper Tanana and a friend of Katie John's, met Fred in her wheelchair and accompanied him on his last mile into Tanacross. That evening Fred and Emma celebrated at her birthday party in the community hall.

On May 4, Fred, his brother Harry, and wife, Diane, walked nineteen miles and stopped seven miles past Tok. As they prepared to continue to Mentasta on May 5, Fred messaged, "Feet blistered but I am taking care of them. Tell Facebook followers on Walk for *Tsucde* that I am doing OK so far."

They suffered blisters, shin splints, rain, hail, and an occasional taunt, but were warmly celebrated as people joined them and gifted them in the villages. As they walked, they honored their late nephew Charles David III, the Fairbanks Four,[1] and gubernatorial candidate Byron Mallott, as well as saluting veterans, which included Fred and Harry John.

1 This case is discussed below.

In honoring his sister Nora David and Charles David II's late son, Fred explained, "The Athabascans have a matrilineal system in which children belong to the mother's clan rather than to the father's clan. Often the core of the family was the mother and her brother. The father and the maternal uncle became lifelong hunting partners. The uncle was responsible to socialize and train his nephews and nieces, teaching their clan history and customs."

On day eight, Fred walked six miles out of his way to salute the fallen state troopers Gabe Rich and Sgt. Scott Johnson, saying, "I have no words to say how my heart feels for their families." [2]

Fred and his brother made excellent time, frequently walking more than seventeen miles per day.

In every village, supporters wore shirts and sweatshirts designed by Fred's wife, Linnea. A classy black, the shirts have a portrait of Grandma Katie John with the exhortation, "May her legacy continue" and her Athabascan name *Ts' ikuni'aan*, a sacred name which means, "to highlight an issue." On the back is Katie's prayer over a map of Alaska,

May God, who created our world, send His Spirit to be in you. May he protect you from evil. May His blessing be upon the land. May the land be good where we walk. May the animals have enough to eat for winter. May the water be good. May the goodness of God dwell in you. Walk For Tsucde, May 2014.

Out on the open road, Fred messaged, "Over our campfire tonight, we cooked dried smoked whitefish from Tetlin smothered in melted moose fat and washed it down with campfire tea." He added, "Tomorrow if you see two raccoons walking down the highway, it's Harry and me without our sunglasses!"

In Chistochina, children who had prepared signs celebrating their culture came out to walk with them. That evening Fred was gifted with a beaded dance strap made by his late sister Nancy Craig. To unwind, Fred and Harry relaxed in a steam bath at Lena Charley's house. He messaged,

---

2 Alaska State Troopers Gabe Rich and Sgt. Scott Johnson were shot and killed in 2014 while responding to a domestic disturbance in the predominantly Native village of Tanana, which lies off the road system. Two years later, Nathaniel Kangas, who was twenty at the time of the shooting and whose father Arvin Kangas is a Native separatist, was convicted for the murders and sentenced to 203 years imprisonment. The elder Kangas received eight years for evidence tampering.

"I rested my feet, taking care of my blisters. Love and thanks for the support and encouragement."

After suggestions from online friends, Fred posted from Gakona, "My feet are pretty well healed thanks to all the 'doctors' on Facebook and prayer warriors. We are all in this spiritual walk together." Tracy Charles-Smith, granddaughter of Dot Lake founder Doris Charles, replied, "History is in the making. Our ancestors walked all over this country. Prayers for you." Fred said, "The people give us inspiration to go on."

By May 18 Fred, Harry, and Diane had visited Dot Lake, Tanacross, Tok, Mentasta, Chistochina, Gakona, Gulkana, Glennallen, and soon would be at Chickaloon.

After being pelted with cold, sleet, hail, and high winds on the Glenn Highway, Fred, Harry, and Diane were filmed by KTUU. The newscast said, "For brothers Fred John Jr., seventy-one, and Harry John, sixty-five, each step is a struggle ... Diane John and her friend Pamela run the support side of the planned walk, taking food and water to Fred and Harry. May 21, as they walked, enjoying views of the Matanuska Glacier, they said the walk is becoming easier."

Fred added, "I know our mother, Katie, is walking with us right now, approving all of this."

Celebrating his pilgrimage, the John family said on their Facebook page, "We want to educate the public that our Native cultures, although historic, are not confined to history. Our culture is our living story. We want ... that Native people always have a place to live here and to practice our customs as our ancestors did."

To salute the unofficial Katie John Day on May 31, the day that Ahtna shareholders put in their fishwheels, Fred arrived in Anchorage, and despite the rain, a crowd marched with him and celebrated in front of the Alaska Native Medical Center campus, one week before Anchorage's first hosting of the National Congress of American Indians conference.

On May 20, Fred had messaged, "Tonight we are camped at Caribou Creek (near a tall outcrop with a knob on its top) where a woman and her baby on her back were turned to stone. She was warned not to look back at her own country but she wanted one last look. She and her baby remind us how much our land and people mean to us. She is still there—longing for it."

IN 2015 FRED FELT TO CONTINUE HIS DEDICATION toward raising awareness for traditional rights for those without a voice. On May 3, 2015 he and his brother Harry began walking from their home village of Mentasta to Fairbanks, a 270-mile trek honoring grandmothers across Alaska and their mother Katie John. The focus continued to be about preserving culture and traditional rights, but it was also about being a voice in the dark. On May 2, Mentasta hosted a kickoff when an old friend of the John family, well-known Alaska photographer Roy Corral, and his band, the Whiskey Jacks (an old Alaska term for Canadian or gray jays), entertained by singing the *Ballad of Katie John*, a synopsis of the Katie John history.

On day one, for the first miles, the John brothers' feet were punished. Blisters and toenails came and went as their feet toughened up to the daily beating. Despite that, their spirits were strong. The brothers were greeted with dinners in Tok and Tanacross. People visited with them on the road. This past year Fred had prepared by making chief necklaces, choker necklaces, and earrings, which he gifted to supporters along the way.

Fred's wife, Linnea, and daughter-in-law Rachel John designed beautiful grey sweatshirts and t-shirts again but with a different photo of Katie, captioned, "May her legacy continue" and on the back, red salmon were leaping in an arc.

In an interview from his home in Delta as he rested May 16, 2015, Fred said they were walking for Alaska Native traditional life values, for wholeness.

Fulfilling a promise made earlier in the year, in support of voices unable to speak, they were also walking for the Fairbanks Four in the miles between Delta and Harding Lake. The "Fairbanks Four" refers to four Alaska Natives: Marvin Roberts, Kevin Pease, Eugene Vent, and George Frese who were sentenced for the 1997 murder of John Hartman of Fairbanks. The four pled not guilty.

In 2008 the Alaska Innocence Project under attorney Bill Oberly began assisting prisoners who could be proven innocent through DNA testing. The chairman of the University of Alaska Fairbanks journalism department, Brian O'Donoghue, and students volunteered to assist Oberly. "The Hartman case was largely circumstantial," O'Donoghue said. "I have never seen anything that persuades me that the person who killed John Hartman was brought to justice in this case. I believe their conviction was based upon witness misidentification, bad science, and flawed confessions. Courts have chewed over the things that have been flagged as problems in this case. So far, courts have not been persuaded. You can't reopen it without new evidence," O'Donoghue said. "And that sort of evidence is proving elusive."

However in 2011 a California prison guard wrote a memo that inmate William Z. Holmes, a former Fairbanks man serving a double-life sentence, claimed that he, Jason Wallace, and three other Lathrop High School students killed fifteen-year-old John Hartman in 1997. Holmes' supervisor personally provided the information to Fairbanks officials. In the hand-written letter included in the filing, Holmes stated that he and the others gathered at an apartment one Friday in October 1997, then piled into a car together and drove downtown to "have some fun" messing with "drunk natives." After chasing a pair of intoxicated men who got away, the group cruised another twenty minutes before happening upon the "white boy walking alone" on Barnette Street." All of the Fairbanks Four men have served nearly eighteen years. In October 2015 Superior Court Judge Paul Lyle will review the case.

On the invitation of the Katie John family, Marvin Roberts' mother, Hazel Roberts Mayo, and the stepmother of George Frese, Mona Nollner, drove from Fairbanks to Delta May 18 to walk with Fred and Harry John.

HAZEL MAYO SPOKE FIRST:
I'm happy it's finally coming out into the open now and we're seeing the end of the tunnel. I'm so grateful for the Innocence Project and what Brian O'Donoghue has done. To show our gratitude for Fred and Linnea John for including us and also for the freedom of the Fairbanks Four we drove down from Fairbanks today to walk with the John family. My son Marvin Roberts has lost seventeen and half years of his life to prison. He's positive about his freedom now and he's very grateful for his supporters. Of course from the beginning, he knew and I knew he was innocent. I don't know why the state has been so slow about responding since the confession of the murderer.

Mona Nollner, George Frese's stepmother and the wife of George's father, George Nollner, spoke:

Yes, for the first time in eighteen years, I have hope because we have so many more people joining us, believing in our cause. Our son feels positive about the judge's review this fall. But it's been so long, really hard.

As the family members of these boys, we've always believed in their innocence and have never given up.

I told George that eighteen years ago, it was only us, the family. Slowly, more people have gotten involved. Now we have such strong support from all areas and that gives him and the others strength.

When asked why these boys became the target of the Hartman conviction, Mona said, *I think something political was going on in the Fairbanks arena as well as there was dysfunction in the police department. There are so many unresolved deaths in Fairbanks history. This is the first time in my lifetime that they had such a fast arrest. I don't know if it was an election year but it was like they had to show results quickly. It's just my own thought.*

During the last eighteen years, the system moved our boys all over. For awhile, they were in Florence in Arizona, then in Greely, Colorado, and finally in the last two years, they moved them back to Alaska. It made it hard because a lot of the family members couldn't travel down there. George's daughter was only two when her father was imprisoned. After so many years of being separated, she said, "I feel like I don't have a dad anymore." Of course, George also felt the same way. I was able to fly her down to see her father.

Fred John said that there seemed to be an evil presence that settled over Fairbanks that night Hartman was murdered in 1997. Even Fred's brother, who was out playing a game of Pan, was beaten up on the street.

A poignant statement was made by inmate William Z. Holmes to a reporter, "People will never understand how much of an act of God this is [that he could come clean] because that night [of the murder] was going to my grave with me. God used that officer to minister to my heart and Jesus did the rest. I'm flattered that anyone thinks I could concoct all this."

In 2013 the editor of the *Fairbanks Daily News-Miner* wrote, "The Hartman murder case more than any other case in Fairbanks in recent memory continues to burn, maybe not outwardly every day but certainly deep within the soul of so many people in this community. It is particularly searing among Alaska Natives of the Interior."

As he rested at home, Fred continued.

This isn't unusual for Alaska Natives to be incarcerated unfairly.

I've never talked about this much before but before my sister Ruth John Hicks died in 1994, she told me a story about my birth. I was coming out of my own journey with alcoholism when Ruth thought it was time to share the story. She remembered when I was born in a little birthing house, that our grandpa Charley Sanford slipped a little bone swan necklace around my neck. He said that when I was mature I'd become a spokesman for the people, to open their mouth, ears, and eyes so that they could begin living again. That's what this walk is: a grassroots movement that spreads our message by word of mouth to remind us of who we are.

The message is our life, our power, and the freedom to choose a traditional healthy lifestyle. In my youth, the authorities came into our villages and forced us children away from our parents, sending us far away to a boarding school. They thought that our parents didn't know how to raise us and that it was best to assimilate us Indians through western education. Today, that is no longer the case. We are free to make healthy choices. If we surrender to alcohol, the authorities may come again into our villages and take our children away because we laid down our own power to raise them. That's alcohol way; that's not our way.

We should not have had our land claims (Alaska Native Claims Settlement Act, 1971) decided between oil companies and federal and state authorities behind closed doors. Urban Alaska Natives were more focused on investing capital in the corporation model while the rural Alaska Native wanted their village [tribal] land held in trust. Today we should not be the only indigenous people in the nation who are not called by the word 'tribe,' a village people who cannot have our land held in trust. In Alaska most Natives don't say they are tribal but they use a nontraditional word saying that they are shareholders. There is a division between both the state, the urban Alaska Native corporations and the rural Alaska Natives. It is time to wake up and to govern our tribal lands, to raise revenue, and to have our own means of taking care of our local tribal resources.

ANILCA [Alaska National Interest Lands Conservation Act, 1980] divided the rural and the urban Natives. ANILCA's rural subsistence provision was originally intended to be Native preference only but because there were non-Natives married to Natives in the Bush, both rural Native and non-Native became those entitled to rural subsistence preference.

Urban Natives while living in the city didn't qualify for subsistence pref-
erence. The corporation model, rather than the traditional use of the
tribal entity, and subsistence preference for rural Natives have polarized
Alaska Natives.

ONCE AT OUR CULTURE CAMP AT BATZULNETAS *(pronounced* Bets'ulnii
Ta') *some of the kids and I went to Mom, angry that some New York kids*
were at our camp. "It's an Indian thing," we said. "We don't want them
here." However, my mother said, "Don't tell anybody, 'No.' All are welcome
here." She said, "Freddy, your ancestors met the first explorers. When the
white people, Lt. Allen and his party, came, they shot up in the air to salute
us. We told them, 'We are the Copper people,' and we gave them the name
'the Iron people.' She told me, 'If you don't respect those people, you're dis-
respecting your ancestors.'" It was hard on us to do that because we grew up
in a Bureau of Indian Affairs school. There was a lot of bitterness as we lost
our language and our culture. But after a lifetime of a long, hard journey,
that bitterness and anger has slowly slipped away in me. Sometimes the
best way to get grounded is to sit quietly and reflect on what your Tsucde
has taught you. Reflecting is important.

The Walk encourages all cultures to remember and to share their his-
tories. Remember what your own Tsucde *said to you. Let your memories*
surface. Mine always encouraged me to be an ambassador to the non-
Native and to listen to others' stories. Katie John said, 'That's the ONLY
way they' ll know.

"Tell them the story about how we take care of each other, how we
share, how we don't have no poor houses, no jail, and no exercise rooms!
. . . No, we don't have no exercise rooms."

On May 27, Fred and Harry John with family and friends entered
Fairbanks, going from the Noel Wien Public Library to Doyon head-
quarters. Representing justice for the "Fairbanks Four," they walked by
Ninth and Barnette where John Hartman was murdered and also by the
Fairbanks Police Station and the Fairbanks City Hall. They arrived at
Chiefs Court at the Doyon headquarters, where they were welcomed
by Fairbanks Mayor John Eberhart whose greetings were covered by
KTVF's *Fairbanks Evening News.*

Listen to your grandmother, Walk for *Tsucde.*

Marvin Roberts of the Fairbanks Four was released June 2015 with supervision at a halfway house and with the provision to be able to seek work. As Windows to the Land, Vol. Two *was being prepared to print, December 17, 2015, Superior Court Judge Paul Lyle ordered the "immediate and unconditional release" of the Fairbanks Four.*

LEW FREEDMAN

L EW FREEDMAN IS ONE OF ALASKA'S most prominent sportswriters. He spent seventeen years as the sports editor and columnist at the Anchorage Daily News, and covered the state's most popular sport—dog mushing—extensively. He is also the author of over one hundred books on sports and Alaska, many of them focused on mushing. No single author has chronicled more of the history of dog mushing and the outsized role it plays in Alaskan culture.

Outside of Alaska, the Iditarod is the best-known sled dog race in the world. But within the state the scrappier, slightly longer, but less publicized Yukon Quest is equally renowned. Begun as a way of celebrating the historic Gold Rush era connection between Alaska and the Yukon, the race runs 1000 miles between Fairbanks and Whitehorse, capital of the Yukon Territory. The start and finish lines alternate between the two cities each year.

In his 2010 book *Yukon Quest: The Story of the World's Toughest Sled Dog Race*, Freedman provides readers with a history of the race, which began in 1984, interspersed with chapters drawn from his personal reporting on the 2009 Quest.

Freedman explains that among mushers and fans alike, the Yukon Quest is often considered more challenging than the Iditarod. Checkpoints are fewer and further between, temperatures can plunge to fifty below zero Fahrenheit or lower, and daylight hours are shorter. In the face of such difficulties, Freedman writes in his introduction,

The Yukon Quest is definitely a place to come if you have something to prove to yourself, or to the world. There will come a time and a place along the trail when the body is weakening, the cold is penetrating the bones, visibility is non-existent because of blowing snow, when the dogs and musher would prefer to lie down in the night. At such a time the musher must reach down to find out if he has the right stuff.

The best sportswriting is all about storytelling. A good sportswriter presents the backgrounds and personalities of the contestants, explores the personal challenges some are overcoming in addition to the hurdles they've willingly placed in front of the themselves by entering into competition, and tells how the character of each person responds when put to the test. A great sportswriter applies a novelist's use of language and sense of timing to compose a story that will keep readers turning pages.

Freedman has all of these attributes, as shown in the two excerpts from *Yukon Quest* that follow. The first introduces the mushers at the starting line in Whitehorse. The second details the decisive moment in that year's race, where extreme weather, treacherous terrain, and reluctant dogs led to a complete reshuffling of the frontrunners.

Reflecting on his experiences reporting on races in remote regions of Alaska, Freedman told me, "While exhilarating to cover, writing about long-distance dog mushing can sometimes be as challenging as the races themselves. The logistics of following a race are daunting, the risk of frostbite can be high, and it is not always easy to send a story back to the office of a newspaper. Call it reality reporting, but being out in the beautiful wild is just as much fun for a writer as a musher."

These days Freedman and his wife Debra live in Indiana and Wyoming, but his ties to Alaska remain strong and he returns often to visit and to write about its multitude of outdoor and athletic opportunities.

Owing to differences between the boards of directors on the Alaskan and Canadian sides of the border, the 2023 Yukon Quest will remain entirely within Alaska. Hopefully the dispute can be resolved and in coming years the race will return to its original route.

— From *Yukon Quest: The Story of the World's Toughest Sled Dog Race* —

AT AGE FORTY-NINE, HIS HAIR GOING GRAY, his face seemingly ruddy from the cold, William Kleedehn planned to make 2009 his final attempt to win the Yukon Quest title after a dozen attempts and two runner-up finishes since 1990. No musher or fan would begrudge him the overdue glory. The phrase "sentimental favorite" was attached to his name with glue. Kleedehn had long before earned the admiration of everyone who followed the race. When he was eighteen, growing up in Germany, Kleedehn lost his left leg below the knee in a motorcycle accident. So Kleedehn had done all of his racing, 12,000 miles worth of Quest trail, supported by an artificial leg. Without being able to run up hills next to his sled, this meant he couldn't help his dog team in the toughest stretches, as his competitors did. If there was justice in the world, many people thought, Kleedehn deserved to win the Quest just once.

Hans Gatt was one of those people. He said aloud that if he couldn't win the race, he hoped Kleedehn would. Gatt was originally from Elbogen, Austria and gravitated to the open spaces of Alaska and Yukon at first as a sprint musher. When he moved into long-distance racing, Gatt won the Quest three times. Gatt won the event in 2002, 2003, and 2004, but after skipping the Quest in 2005, he placed second in 2006 and 2007. Hungry to win the Iditarod, he skipped the Quest in 2008.

Gatt, turning fifty by the time of the 2009 race, bred dairy cows and raced motorcycles in Austria. As a young man he decided he wanted to make his living as a professional dog musher. That is akin to an American declaring he wishes to make his fortune in luge racing. "When I announced that I was going to be a professional musher, everybody thought I was crazy," Gatt said.

A fixture in the Far North for two decades, Gatt built a name for himself in Anchorage and Fairbanks, Alaska, with his success in the two-and three-day championship sprint mushing events conducted over 20 and

30 miles at a time. At the end of the day in sprint racing, dog drivers can sleep in hotels. In 1,000-mile races, tents are a five-star luxury. Sleep, when it can be grabbed, might be on the floor of a cramped building. Those three-hour naps are blessings breaking up twenty-hour days on the trail while often coping with minus 50 F weather. The average human being on the planet cannot comprehend being outdoors and dealing with the intensity of such temperatures.

"When I tell them it's 40 or 50 below, they have no idea what I'm talking about really," Gatt said.

Like his friend Kleedehn, Gatt was thinking his body had had enough of such challenges. A new lifestyle beckoned. "I'm thinking about retirement," Gatt said in the weeks leading up to the 2009 Quest. "I would definitely spend some time in a warmer climate. The big problem is what to do with the dogs. I'm just not one of those guys who can sell the whole kennel. I love them all."

Jon Little, forty-five, was born in England, went to journalism school in Chicago, and worked as a reporter for the *Anchorage Daily News*. When he began mushing, he lived about 75 miles from Anchorage, trained dogs in the morning, and worked a night shift at the newspaper. Later, he staffed a news bureau 150 miles from the newspaper office. In his hobby time, through patience and hard work, he grew a small kennel of dogs into a team that once placed third in the Iditarod.

No one entering the 2009 Quest faced a more daunting task. Little and his wife, Brie, had two children under the age of three. Recently he had been laid off from his job writing for an outdoors web site. A few months earlier, he had suffered the type of tragedy that preys upon the minds of mushers. Four dogs in his twenty-four-dog kennel were killed during a training run after being hit by a car in the fading light of late evening near his home.

It was late October 2008, just before Halloween. Little was driving one dog team and a friend another, riding on four-wheelers because there was no snow cover yet. At one point, they paused to cross the Sterling Highway, a main thoroughfare on the Kenai Peninsula. On the way back to the dog yard, it was growing dark. Traffic was heavy. When there was a break, Little waved for the other musher to proceed. However, Little's friend hadn't mounted the four-wheeler, so Little signaled again for him to wait. The musher did not see the second signal.

Coming over the hill was a Subaru Outback traveling 60 mph. The driver never saw the team and plowed into the front six dogs. Three huskies died instantly. Another was hurt so badly it had to be put down by a veterinarian. A fifth dog had surgery and was unlikely to compete again. Miraculously, the sixth dog was unharmed.

"It was horrible," a haunted Little said. "They were good dogs." Little borrowed four dogs from another musher, dogs that were new to him. He called them "front-end" dogs, but they were not as good as the leaders he had lost. Little was very emotional about the death of his dogs, but after flirting with the idea of dropping out, he decided to stay in the race. On top of everything else, he had lost his job that same week.

"I've got enough money to coast on fumes until the Quest is over," Little said. "After that we have some hard decisions to make." Dog mushing is an expensive sport with the rewards for mushers as much spiritual as aesthetic. With a young family to feed, Little knew that he might be forced to give up long-distance racing for a while if he did not do well. The accident made him more determined than ever to succeed in the 2009 Quest.

Top women finishers are rarities in the Quest. In 1985, when Libby Riddles won the Iditarod, becoming the first female champion, sourdoughs took it personally that a woman could best the rough and tough bearded, long-haired, fur-wearing Alaskan men at such a manly activity. T-shirts appeared overnight announcing "Alaska! Where Men Are Men and Women Win the Iditarod." Susan Butcher followed Riddles, winning four of the next five races and, if Riddles' triumph had been a surprise, Butcher's victories were expected. She had been the next hot musher in line for the crown.

Things were different in the Quest. Fewer women entered and fewer women contended. But in 2000, Alaskan Aliy Zirkle energized the north with a rousing victory. It was a milestone triumph, the first in the race by a woman. Yet Zirkle promptly transferred her attentions to the Iditarod, and the Quest once again suffered from a shortage of top-flight female contenders. That changed in 2008. Michelle Phillips, a Yukoner from Tagish, placed fourth in that year's Quest, injecting her name into pre-race talk about who might win in 2009.

Phillips, forty, and her husband, Ed Hopkins, operate a tourism business giving dog sled rides to visitors. She had shown improvement on the trail. It might be her turn. Phillips, it seemed, was beginning to think along the same lines. "You get to the point where you realize you can be competitive," Phillips said. "You think, 'Okay, if I did that I would have been up there with those front guys.'" Quest fever colored her thoughts.

As an aside to her own aspirations, Phillips carried the hopes of others tucked in her sled. Besides the mandatory gear, from an ax to a sleeping bag, she was transporting one-hundred handcrafted "Feelie Hearts" along the trail to benefit the Hospice Yukon Society. The objects are lopsided fuzzy hearts that are given to comfort the dying and their loved ones. A four-year-old girl who was grieving for her dying mother was given the first one. The story spread and demand grew. The Feelie Hearts riding in Phillips' sled were to sell for $100 each and be accompanied by a copy of her race journal and a photograph of her dog team.

Phillips said the fund-raising was important and personal. The death of loved ones in her own life still affects her, and she wanted to help others cope. "This has helped me acknowledge my grief and work through it," she said.

The least likely musher in the 2009 field, and under no stretch of anyone's imagination a contender, was Newton Marshall, representing the Jamaican Dog Sled Team. Marshall, twenty-five, who had been living and training with Hans Gatt, is from Chuka Cove, Jamaica. It is a place where beach-lovers bask in gentle breezes, not a place where the temperature is measured by the wind chill. For the previous four years, Marshall had given cart rides on the beach and nearby roads to those who wanted to sample the experience of a dog-sled ride without wearing a parka or traveling 5,000 miles north.

There is a glorious history of the contributions of Siberian huskies, Malamutes, and the current-day Alaska husky mix for transportation in the wilderness, hauling the mail, and for racing excellence. But Marshall's dogs in Jamaica were strays. They were street dogs, animal-pound dogs, and castaways that he picked up and trained to trot.

Sponsors, including renowned singer Jimmy Buffett, a regular visitor to Jamaica, seemingly taken with the whole notion of island mushing, made it possible for Marshall to live and train in the Yukon. Marshall's Jamaican dogs stayed in the warm climate, substituted with northern breeds. While Marshall speaks with a pleasant lilt, there is no mistaking his meaning when he says, "I'm cold."

Marshall was a toddler when another group of Jamaicans made a brief appearance on the world stage of winter sports. The Jamaican bobsled team was an entry in the 1988 Winter Olympics in Calgary and subsequently was the subject of a light-hearted movie called "Cool Runnings." There was great anticipation that Buffet might put in a supportive appearance, perhaps wearing a fur coat over one of his Hawaiian shirts, but Marshall put the kibosh on such speculation. "He says he can't make it," Marshall said with some regret in his voice.

Over the winter in the Yukon, Marshall had experienced the impact of a severe cold spell. This was just months after the latest Jamaican sports hero, Usain Bolt, set world records and won gold medals in sprinting at the Beijing Olympics. Marshall was asked how a victory in the Quest might be measured back home against Bolt's achievements. "Usain Bolt? He has no idea what I'm up against," Marshall said. The real question was whether Marshall did.

One new Quest face was a guy who had seen every type of weather in his mushing career. Technically, he was a rookie because it was his first Quest, but Martin Buser, fifty, four-time Iditarod champion from Big Lake, Alaska, was not a garden-variety newcomer. Originally from Switzerland, Buser took the oath of American citizenship at the Iditarod finish line in Nome in 2002. After twenty-five Iditarod runs, Buser had more long-distance mushing experience than anyone else in the race. Many top Iditarod mushers have done well in the Quest. Vern Halter, Charlie Boulding, Jeff King, Bill Cotter, Rick and Lance Mackey, Ramy Brooks, Joe Runyan, and Lavon Barve are all past Quest champs. There was no reason to think that Buser, with his formidable track record, couldn't be among them.

Buser was the wild card. He owned the Iditarod finish record of 8 days, 22 hours, 46 minutes, a blistering time, and the only finish in less than nine days. He said he always wanted to give the Quest a shot and it finally worked out. His wife, Kathy Chapoton, had retired from teaching and could join him on the trail. His sons, Rohn and Nikolai, named after Iditarod checkpoints, were away at college. "We're empty-nesters," Buser said.

Oh, yeah, and with two boys in college, there were school fees to be paid. Buser said he was going to enter as many races as he could during the winter of 2008-2009. "It's the run for tuition," he said.

For those who understand long-distance mushing, Buser's plan to raise tuition based on the uncertainty of race payoffs sounded as risky as someone jetting off to Las Vegas to raise money to pay the mortgage.

Another contender, a long shot, had inched his way up in the standings in recent years. He was not a favorite, but he kept improving. Sebastian Schnuelle, another transplanted German, with his unbrushable Harpo Marx hair, was a musher to watch. Likewise, Hugh Neff had worked his way up from being a competitor on a shoestring, literally begging for equipment, to being a generous helpmate in the sport. No one counted out Frank Turner, either. Turner was a past champion and Canada's most prominent musher. They all wondered if they could reach the finish line first.

WILLIAM KLEEDEHN'S HARDY DOGS LED the 2009 Yukon Quest to the base of Eagle Summit. If they could climb the steep pitch smoothly, his dreams might come true. At this late stage in the twenty-sixth annual race, Kleedehn could dare to hope that he might take command and capture his first victory in twelve tries.

Kleedehn had run well the entire way from Whitehorse. His dogs had sneaked past Jon Little in the night to claim the halfway gold prize in Dawson City and, although Little and Hugh Neff hung close, it seemed that Kleedehn's dogs were the ones to beat as they approached the final few hundred miles of rugged trail in generally benign weather.

Quest mushers were fortunate. In prior weeks, the entire region from the Yukon to Interior Alaska had been gripped by fearsome cold, the kind that made metal brittle. There were days of minus 50 F when mushers were wary of taking their teams on extended runs. Forget-about-it cold was one way to describe that intense air.

Yet, when the race began in Canada, warmer weather prevailed. There were no storms, only light snow occasionally. There were days of sunshine and temperatures even rising above zero. And, as promised by race officials, the trail was groomed better than it had been in recent races. Conditions were as favorable as they ever got on the Quest.

With 250 miles remaining to the finish line in Fairbanks, Kleedehn had a two-and-a-half hour lead. Not insurmountable, but if nothing went wrong, comfortable. Everyone thought so, until by cutting rest and calling upon an energized team, Neff slashed Kleedehn's team's lead to three minutes leaving Central with 160 miles to go. It was a risky move that could backfire, or a bold one that could win him the title.

Then abruptly, the race took a quirky turn.

Leaving Central, Neff got off the regular trail at Circle Hot Springs where the race briefly follows the road. But rather than quickly return to the trail, Neff mushed on the road for more than five miles. Kleedehn saw him and so did reporters covering the race. Neff did not believe that he gained that much of an edge, but race marshal Doug Grilliot slapped Neff with a two-hour penalty that had to be served at Two Rivers, the final checkpoint and a mandatory rest stop. Whether the mistake stemmed from brain-lock, fatigue, or something else, Neff would have been better off taking an extra two-hour rest rather than his tour of the highway. He said later that he had stayed on the road because he thought Kleedehn had done the same. Seeing "dog poop" was the trail sign he followed, Neff said. The poop alibi did Neff no more good than if he said he had been following Lassie.

The next challenge was Eagle Summit. Before tackling it, Kleedehn took a break at the Steese Roadhouse. He ate a steak and contemplated his place in the Quest universe. Neff and Kleedehn are friendly and share mutual respect. Kleedehn did not criticize Neff's *faux pas*, but instead expressed admiration for how Neff was keeping up with less rest. "His team is really amazing to me," Kleedehn said.

After more than 800 miles of racing, Kleedehn said he felt the trail physically. "I'm a little bit bruised and battered, but I'm still here," he said.

Kleedehn was wise to fortify himself with that steak. He had no idea how much energy he was going to need to get through the next day. Racing with the burden of the penalty hanging over his head, Neff reached the base of Eagle Summit first and his dogs charged up the hill.

Kleedehn trailed, but felt good knowing he had a two-hour time bonus on Neff. Then everything went haywire. Kleedehn's team of frisky dogs, so full of run until then, took one look at the steep grade leading to the 3,685-foot summit and declared "No way."

Kleedehn's response was something on the order of "What do you mean, no way?" only with much more colorful language. Worse yet, the dogs became distracted by one of the great wild cards of life—sex. Until then, female leaders Breeze and Marimba and male leader Fajita had been totally reliable for Kleedehn, but then Breeze went into heat and the males surrounding her lost their minds. It was like a singles bar on a Friday night. Common sense went out the window as the males attempted to impress a female that gave off obvious signs of being interested.

Eagle Summit is just about the steepest incline on the Quest Trail. It requires narrow focus, intense concentration, and physical stamina to climb over the top, particularly when its finicky vicious weather pops up. Kleedehn did not need the aggravation of dogs with sex on their minds. He needed them performing in other ways. He was coping with a sit-down strike. He wanted the dogs to run. They refused. The terrain and the dogs' hormones conspired against him, but the result was the same. Kleedehn said, "I couldn't go backwards or forwards."

Along came Little, and his dogs also mushed onto the mountain. Kleedehn tried to convince his dogs to follow Little. No go. Kleedehn pondered turning back to Central to drop Breeze, definitely a distasteful chore.

Now Neff and Little led, and in a race where the weather had been tame, they dared hope to have an easy passage over Eagle Summit. It was not to be. As they approached the summit the weather deteriorated, and a storm blew in accompanied by high winds. They halted.

In a matter of minutes, with Kleedehn stuck at the bottom of the hill, and Neff and Little stuck near the top, the entire complexion of the race changed. "It was blowing really hard and drifting," Little said. "We were cold and wet."

Neff said he figured it was too good to be true that a dog team could make it through the Quest without violent weather. "It was like living in a fantasy world for a week and a half and then came Eagle Summit," Neff said. "For six to eight hours we were in a raging blizzard with no markers. It was pitch black. The dogs didn't know where to go."

There are several mountainous high points along the Quest Trail, but Eagle Summit is the most notorious, with the worst track record of shattering mushers' hopes. In 2006, mushers had to be air-lifted off the Summit. Past champ Frank Turner had his biggest trail nightmare on Eagle Summit. Vern Halter recalled dismal circumstances during unexpected hellacious weather on the hill. In the 1989 race, Halter said, he, Sonny Lindner and Jeff King got caught in 40 to 50 mph winds and turned back to a shelter cabin. Later, he saw another musher passing by bundled in so much clothing as to be unrecognizable. "I don't know if I've ever seen anything more miserable," Halter said.

It was just Eagle Summit exacting its toll.

Neff and Little were in the front, leading the Quest, with Kleedehn, their strongest competition, trapped behind them. Yet, they could not move away from him. They were shut down, too. At the Mile 101 dog drop on the Steese Highway, race officials stood around in sunshine, with the thermometer miraculously inching up. When weather isn't a factor, the run from Central to 101 can be made as swiftly as five and a half hours. Quest officials were unaware of the drastic conditions faced by Neff and Little, and they wondered where everyone was. When nobody mushed in after twelve hours, a snowmobile search was organized. Kleedehn was spotted at the base of Eagle Summit, but no one else was in sight.

Back at the Central checkpoint, Sebastian Schnuelle took his time getting back on the trail. He felt there was no chance to run down the trio of mushers ahead. Kleedehn, Neff, and Little had too much time on him, and were running teams too fast to catch. Schnuelle was fourth and he was okay with that. Not bad, he thought. He mushed out of the checkpoint more than eight hours after Neff and Kleedehn had departed.

Later, reporters informed Schnuelle that mushers had told them they thought he was the one to beat. He was astounded. "They did?" Schnuelle said. "I guess they knew more than I did. In Central, I had given up. I wasn't even in race mode. The summit changed everything."

That it did. The three mushers ahead of Schnuelle were stymied. Schnuelle set out from Central and first caught the frustrated Kleedehn. Schnuelle attempted to coax Kleedehn's dogs to the summit. He led the team partway up the hill, but they would not go on. Schnuelle mushed ahead, resuming his own race as he realized how close he was to Neff and Little. "I said, 'William, you are on your own now,'" Schnuelle said.

Brent Sass, the young Fairbanks musher, was the next to encounter Kleedehn. "It was on the steepest of the steepest part where he was stuck," Sass said. The men teamed up and at last Kleedehn's dogs went over the summit. But not before Neff and Little had moved on.

At one point, Neff disembarked from his sled and became his own lead dog in a whiteout. At the top, all of the trail markers had blown away. It was impossible to tell which way to go. Little caught up, the two

men parked their sleds and searched for the trail for about ninety minutes in the dark, before declaring a rest break. They wiggled into their
sleeping bags and napped for about five hours until daylight.

By then, Schnuelle had made up much of the time deficit and was
close to the lead. After the news blackout on the leaders' whereabouts,
Neff arrived at Mile 101 first and Little and Schnuelle came through
within an hour. Sass and Kleedehn trailed by a couple more hours. Neff
and Schnuelle were moving well. Little fooled the competition into
thinking his team was just as strong, but his dogs were flagging. Eagle
Summit, Little said, "was the pivotal point."

It was a whole new race.

"It's luck," Schnuelle said of his timing as he took over the lead. "It's
pure luck. It wasn't even the wildest dream of my mind."

HOURS LATER, IN MID-AFTERNOON, it WAS sunny and clear on Eagle
Summit. The wind died down, visibility was perfect. Martin Buser, his
head filled with stories about the summit's past destruction of race
optimism, crossed over the same terrain with his dogs zooming like
race cars.

Far back after setting an early blistering pace, Buser was in a jolly
mood as his team perked up. He was coming hard and could even joke
about the conditions he faced on the summit. "I missed Eagle Summit,"
Buser said.

That's how easy it was for him. A little bit of cooperative weather
makes all the difference.

ROSEMARY MCGUIRE

ROSEMARY MCGUIRE HAS A CABIN A MILE FROM MY HOUSE that she stays in when passing through Fairbanks. Once while I was biking with my dog on the backroad where she dwells, we happened to cross paths and stopped to chat. She was driving and apologized for not shutting off her engine, explaining to me, "Alaska is a place where you sit in your car with the engine racing and your foot on the brake because you know it won't restart when it's warm."

One can imagine Laura, the protagonist in McGuire's fiction piece "Snow Night on the Richardson," understanding this dilemma. In this brief scene that McGuire sketches, drawn from her 2015 short story collection *The Creatures at the Bottom of the Sea*, Laura arrives at a roadhouse lying at the junction of the Richardson and Denali Highways, two long and largely unpopulated stretches of road that connect some of the far-flung communities of Alaska's Interior. "The highway split here at the gas station," McGuire writes, "there was no other reason for this place."

Roadhouses are a longstanding tradition in Alaska, small isolated businesses that exist to serve passers through. Originally built to provide lodging and meals to those traveling by dogsled, horseback, or foot during the Gold Rush era, they quickly adapted as roads took the place of trails, and cars and trucks began streaming through. Visitors could purchase gasoline, choose from a meagre selection of high-priced groceries, and perhaps sit down for a hot supper, a drink, and some conversation.

As automobiles have grown more fuel efficient, the number of such businesses has dwindled, and the one in Paxson, a fictional form of which provides the setting for this story, is among the casualties. It closed its doors in 2013, a vintage slice of Alaskana that is unlikely to be restored.

Laura, the woman who stops into the roadhouse in this story, falls into another longstanding tradition in Alaska: people who run north to escape failing lives, only to have their tragedies and shortcomings follow them. It's a theme explored in several of the fiction selections included in this volume. Laura's response to her faltering life is to run even deeper into the state.

This story nicely captures the feel of those vanishing waysides along Alaska's road system, where life slows down to a near standstill in winter. Traffic is sparse, highway conditions often encourage staying put, and locals gather at the only open business to keep the cold and darkness at bay, glad that the same cold and darkness keep the rest of the world far away.

This is an Alaska McGuire understands well, having been born into it. She grew up without electricity or running water on a homestead near Haines, acquiring skills and knowledge that would serve her well as she made her way in the North.

McGuire has traveled widely overseas and adventured far into northern wildernesses. A perpetual vagabond, she's worked as a commercial fisherwoman, research tech, builder, bartender, and other jobs one associates with someone who earned her master's in creative nonfiction.

A careful observer of people and places, she breathes life into everything she writes, be it fiction, nonfiction, or memoir. Her recent writings have focused on Alaska's Arctic, and the relationships between the people who live there, and the wilderness they inhabit and wildlife they depend on for sustenance. It continues her personal and literary exploration of Alaska, which has taken her from it's southernmost shores to its northern edge, and many places in between.

— From *The Creatures at the Absolute Bottom of the Sea* —
SNOW NIGHT ON THE RICHARDSON

AT PAXSON SHE STOPPED, TIRED OUT, short of her destination. She turned the car off and sat listening to the snap of metal cooling, the small creaks as it settled. Markers on the bridge caught the light, the last light as darkness seeped in from the east. In the roadhouse by the gas station, the Budweiser sign flicked on. Snow drifted along the gas pumps and up the stairs leading to the door. The highway split here at the gas station; there was no other reason for this place.

NO MAINTENANCE the sign read on the road leading to Denali. TRAVEL AT YOUR OWN RISK.

221 MILES TO FAIRBANKS the other sign said. There were tire tracks in the snow on the Denali side. People had gone there, but not many.

On the Fairbanks side, the road was open. It led up toward the Alaska range, bent north and disappeared. A semi truck blared around the curve, its jake brake grinding as it downshifted for the grade. A blast of noise, color, and it was gone. As it passed, a man jumped out of the ditch and ran along briefly in its wake, waving a fist. He stopped, almost out of sight in the light-shocked dark. Turned and shouted something inaudible. His face contorted.

"Mopping and mowing," she thought, a phrase from a nursery rhyme. He ran toward her. She slammed the car door and started up the steps toward the roadhouse. He stopped when he saw her go, yelling across the road.

"Tell them they can't fuck with me," he cried. "Tell them I'm gone."

She moved faster at the sound of his voice, almost skipping up the stairs to the bar. Inside, she paused, the habit of a lifetime, to kick snow from her shoes before she slammed the door. A habit so familiar it broke through even the numbness that had engulfed her since last week—numbness shattered now, and twisted by the blast of cowboy music from the bar.

THE BARMAID WAITED, WATCHING LAURA'S APPROACH. Laura had the feeling the woman had been watching ever since she pulled over on the far side of the road in her battered Toyota. "Who is that? Why are they parking there? She doesn't drive well," she imagined her thinking. And

Laura looked at her, dipping her head in apology for some behavior she hadn't yet discovered or acknowledged. *I'm sorry, it's me.*

"Come on in," the woman said. "You looking for someone?"

Is it that obvious? Laura wondered. "Do you know how the road is north of here?" she said.

"I hear it's bad."

"That's too bad."

Two men sat at the end of the bar watching TV. The debates running up to the election. Their faces were solid, hair over their collars. They looked like men she knew.

"It's bad out," one said. "You got four-wheel drive on your rig?"

"No."

"Well, be careful."

The other leaned in to the screen again. "I just can't figure how a black man could run."

"I hope he wins," the one said. "Hope those fuckers don't assassinate him." They looked at each other, then back at the screen. *There was a time,* she thought, *they would've looked at me.*

"Can I get you a drink?" the barmaid asked. "'If you wait, you'll have a better chance of making it."

"Maybe Coors Light?" It wasn't a place where you'd ask for coffee.

"I got it in a bottle."

"That's fine," she said.

The barmaid set down a napkin, a coaster, and, unfathomably, a plastic swizzle stick, as if moved by a desire to make her welcome. A glass and the bottle, cap ajar. "Cold night," she offered.

She was older than Laura, though she was dressed for work in a low neckline and broad red lipstick. Her eyes were dark, faded, kind; her skin pocked with acne. "Where you headed?"

"I need to get to Cantwell. But if I can't get down the Denali Highway, I might have to go on to Fairbanks tonight, stay there and drive down in the morning."

"I wouldn't try that highway in the rig you got," one of the men called down, authoritatively. He finished his beer and stood as if to go. She'd thought he was there for the night. It had that feel, a place that no one ever left. But when he reached the door, he only looked out and returned to his seat again.

"People've been turning back. People in four-wheel drive. I wouldn't try it," he said.

"Thanks," she said. "Yeah. I'll take it slow." But on the inside, she was running, and had been ever since the night six nights ago when Emmett had picked up his fork. Laid it down again. Looked at her and said, "I'm sorry, Laura. It's over."

The other man changed the TV channel. *Junkyard Trucker.* Cars crunching into one another.

"That weirdo still out there?" he said.

"Yes, he is," she said.

"Don't go near him. He was in here, earlier. Yelling about something. He's trying to get to Fairbanks," he said.

"Fucking stupid. No one's going to give someone like that a ride," the first man said, his eyes on the screen.

"I wouldn't want to give him a ride," the other answered.

Laura uncapped her beer the rest of the way, and poured it in her glass. Ordinarily, she wouldn't've asked for beer, but she'd wanted to fit in here, anywhere. The room was warm, the people solid and real. Coors Light seemed like something you would drink if you were from here and had never left. It shone in her glass, a yellow glow. The bubbles stung the back of her throat, leaving a faintly unpleasant aftertaste. The men were drinking Rainier. Would that have been better?

Stout, she thought. That was what Emmett drank. Thick and dark as motor oil. He'd never been past Canada. But there was something about imported beer he liked, that went beyond the flavor. It was a way of setting himself apart. Of saying, I come from here but I'm different. I could've left. I should've left. I could've gone to England.

He'd worked as a mechanic in winter when they needed cash, or else spent hours tinkering with his truck, not out of pleasure but to get it to run. His fingers were often caked with grease, lining the seams of his weather-weary skin. She loved his hands, the look of them. She always had.

The summer she first saw him, in Washington, he was mowing the grass at her father's house. She was reading in the yard. He sat down to apologize for the noise, leaving the machine still idling.

"Whatcha reading?" He touched the book with one big finger.

Half apologetically, as girls did then, she showed the cover. "It's for a class. I want to be a doctor," she said.

"That's good," he said. "That's a good job." It was hot, and the air smelled of fresh-cut grass. He took off his hat, wiped his forehead, and lay back on the uncut lawn, a shirtless kid no older than herself, his body already built for labor. A leaf blew down across his face; he blew it up again, it fell on his mouth once more and he laughed and moved his head away.

That August they fell into what might have been a temporary love, neither of them yet old enough to know. But that fall, she'd found herself pregnant, after some awkward gropings in the car, the kind where she knew she was no longer virgin but still wasn't quite sure she'd had sex. Because sex was supposed to make you feel like you were flying, and what they did, however eager, hadn't quite. Still, it was a summer to remember, something to warm her heart on in later years, as their partnership acquired its own momentum, independent of desire.

She told him at the drive-in in September.

He took a long drag of his cigarette. "You sure?" he said.

"I'm sure." He was quiet for a while, looking out the window. Then he turned and laid his hand on her belly.

They were married a month later. Afterward, his uncle offered him a place at a crab buyer on Bainbridge Island. She threw up all through the ferry crossing. He, already looking older, harder, bought her seltzer water but counted the change.

After Neva's birth, Laura was hospitalized for weeks. Her hips had been too small to bear a child, and the clinic waited too long to call in help. When she was discharged at last, her baby seemed at first a stranger to her, a small bundle of needs and wants already established as a person in her absence.

Through those first months, Neva would only sleep when Laura walked her, down the quiet streets and out to the beach on the rare days that it was sunny. Or in the packing plant itself, where they could see Emmett. The bubbling tanks amused them both; the wet floors, salt smell, and the forklift squeal. The crabs tumbling slowly over and over in plastic tubs.

"The man in the wilderness said to me, / How many blackberries grow in the sea. / I answered him as I thought good. / As many red herrings as grow in the wood," she sang, dancing Neva up and down to relieve the ache in her own back. Little Neva. That was before she began to show the first signs of her sickness. Or maybe Laura hadn't seen it yet, the bruises on her skin. Her listlessness.

In pictures now, of Neva as a one-year-old, Laura could see it already. But then, she didn't know. It took a stranger to tell her, someone who saw them playing in the park.

"How long has she had those bruises?" she had said. She'd looked at her, as if Laura ought to know.

Laura looked at her baby with new eyes and saw the deep, blue splotches on her arms. Her little legs, still soft with baby fat. That night, she pulled Neva's shirt up to show Emmett, and Neva, understanding something was wrong, began to cry.

"Hush, sugar, hush, it's OK," Laura soothed her. But Emmett's eyes met hers over Neva's head.

The soonest appointment they could get was for two weeks out. They took her to the hospital in May. What Laura remembered now was the warmth of that morning, almost too beautiful for spring. The puddles in the hospital parking lot, and how Neva tried to step in them. She had just learned to walk by herself. She held out her arm for the doctor, not afraid, not yet. There was still a while before they knew for sure. Leukemia.

After that first visit, the three of them took the skiff and went out on the water. Below the boat, in a little cove, they saw a crab walking along the sea floor. Near neutral buoyancy, it moved like a dancer in the water. Each touch of a leg to the bottom sent it tumbling gently up through the shallows, a part of the morning, of the stillness and clear water. A part, somehow. Of each of them.

"Cyab," Neva said. It was her first word.

Later, after Neva died, they left the island and moved up north up to Thompsen's Bay. Few people there even knew they'd had a daughter. They settled in to a pattern of life, one that sometimes seemed too empty, silent; and if Laura thought there might have been more, a life lived more completely somewhere else, she tried not to speak of it.

Until last spring, when suddenly, long after she'd given up the thought, she found herself pregnant a second time. She'd been so happy. That was the thing. A liquid happiness almost unmarred by fear. She walked home from the clinic—it was April—with a feeling as if she suddenly could blossom. "Keep it secret," she thought, "keep it for yourself," this sudden, strange primordial delight. But when Emmett came in, she told him at the door.

"A girl," he said. "It will be a girl." He leaned on the door, eyes lighting up, at an urge put aside for her sake, now gratified at last.

SHE FINISHED HER DRINK. It'd ended, of course. She lost the baby. It wasn't only the loss, but the way they'd each turned aside into their private grief. After a while they no longer held each other, and soon enough, they lived as strangers, the space between them in the bed too carefully calibrated for love. She thought now it wasn't her, only a sadness he couldn't share for a failure that had implicated both.

NOW ONE OF THE MEN AT THE END HAD LEFT. The barmaid drifted down the bar to stand behind the other man, watching the tube. Her hand rested on his shoulder in a gesture that could've been merely friendly or could've been more. What was their relationship? Laura wondered. Probably not lovers, though if the barmaid worked most nights, it was more than possible her boyfriend came here, too. If she had one—she might also be the only single woman in the area. Maybe it was just that most nights, that man was here, and most nights she was, too, and over the years they'd forged a bond that was enduringly familiar and yet could shatter in a moment if something happened. The essence of such friendships was their dailiness. It was what they offered—all they offered. If for some reason, he didn't come in; if he got another job, or she did, they wouldn't write. In a year or two, they might not even remember each other's names.

The barmaid relinquished her grasp with a last squeeze of her hand and came down the bar when she saw Laura's glass was empty.

"Dale says you oughta stay," she said. "He says you're nuts, out there in that rig, on these roads. You got chains, at least?"

"I've got everything." Laura said. "Warm clothes, a jack."

"We got rooms here, you know. I think it's eighty for a single. I could ask." The woman looked at her. "I ain't trying to be nosy. Just hate to see you wind up in a ditch."

"Thanks for that," Laura said. She rubbed her swizzle stick against the glass. "Could I get another? Maybe rum and Diet Coke this time?" It was good to let go a little while.

The waitress raised her eyebrows. Took the glass. When she reached to take the swizzle stick, though, Laura pulled it back. "I'll keep that," she said. Methodically, she began to crack it into pieces. Emmett couldn't sit without fiddling with things. He couldn't talk unless his hands were moving. By the time they left a diner, their table would be strewn with mashed sugar packets, fingered silverware, and shreds of napkin.

"I know these roads," Laura said. "At least to Fairbanks."

"That where you're headed?"

"No. My husband's in Cantwell." Laura was becoming lightly drunk, even after just one beer. "He took off last week. I guess that's where he went."

"No shit," the barmaid said. She set the glass before Laura. "Hope everything's all right."

"Oh, yes," Laura said. "It'll be fine." This new drink was better—punchingly sweet, with the sharp, familiar flavor of Coke and the sugary rum.

"Well, just as long as everything's all right." The barmaid set an ashtray next to Laura though she wasn't smoking, and, after a moment, hesitantly leaned on the bar. Laura seemed to make her uncomfortable. Like she might need a friend. "My name's Delia," she said, confidentially. "That's my man, Dale, at the end. We've been together six months."

"Pleased to meet you, Delia."

"So you say you're going to Cantwell to meet your guy?"

"It's a surprise. He called last week, and I didn't come. But I figured now would be a good time." She'd sat in the darkened apartment, on the bottomed-out couch she'd meant to replace, while upstairs the neighbor's baby ran back and forth, his small feet thudding on the hollow floor. It was cold. The lightbulbs had burned out one by one, in the nights when she wouldn't turn them out. The phone rang on the little table. Rang. Rang again. Rang.

After a while it stopped. Started again. She picked it up, and heard only the hollow roar of static, as if Emmett were breathing on the other end. "Listen," she said then. "Why don't you come back."

If she wanted to, she could pretend it had been him. That, for a little while, he'd changed his mind. She listened to the dial tone as the plastic surface of the phone grew sticky and damp against her cheek. *Your call cannot be completed. Please hang up and try again.* Then nothing but the sound of space, slipping quickly into make-believe.

"Delia," she said, slurring a little. "And Dale." Laura beamed at her, trying to make contact. "Is this your place?"

"No. I just work here. Owner lives down in Wasilla. We don't see much of him in the wintertime. Not too many people come by once the Denali closes, and the tourists trickle down. Not much snowmachining down this far. Just the long-haul guys going Valdez to Fairbanks, and they mostly wait until Delta Junction. We don't mind. It gets kind of quiet, but I guess that's why we live out here, right?"

"I guess so," Laura said. "I guess it must be nice." She pictured a different Delia now, not the barmaid but the woman going home with Dale. They'd have a small house with carpeted floors and a big TV, in the black-spruce forest not too far away. One of those driveways that occasionally cut off of the highway, up into the mountains. She'd sometimes wondered who lived up there.

"I love the mountains," Delia said. "Came here from Anchorage ten years ago. Never looked back."

"You got kids?" Laura asked.

"Two. One of my girls's ten, the other'n's twelve. The twelve-year-old's living with her dad in Anchorage. My ten-year-old's my joy. She and Dale get along so well. She's learning how to snowmachine this winter. Let her do what the boys do, that's what I say, and Dale agrees with me. Some folks wouldn't."

"That's right," Laura said vaguely. "So where's she go to school?"

"We get the lessons sent in from Anchorage," Delia explained. "We got our own school. But families are moving in. One of these days, we'll have a real school here, too."

"That's good," Laura said. "That's real good." She liked that thought, this little family in the house hunkered at the bottom of the lavender mountains. Idly, she stirred her drink with the wounded swizzle stick. "I like that."

Outside, the night had gone black dark. Only the faintest tinge of light beyond the panes reflected them endlessly, as if the warm room was repeated through deep space. The drink filled up her veins warmly, filled up her inside that had been empty.

"You got kids?" Delia said.

"No. No kids," she said, though she crossed her fingers.

Delia shook her head. "Sorry to hear it," she began, then stopped abruptly, remembering that might not be what Laura meant. She jerked her head in an indefinite motion that set her hair, frozen in place, stiffly bobbing. "Some people don't," she said.

Dale got up at the sound of their voices and came down the bar. He leaned on it, friendly, looking at her.

"So why'd you need to get to Cantwell so goddamn bad?"

"It's a long story."

Dale nodded. He tapped his empty glass on the bar. "Get me another'n, babe?" he said, and when she put it in front of him, he patted her arm. "Thanks, doll."

Laura looked away, embarrassed to watch. Outside, the promised snow began to fall more heavily now, drifting on the sill. She watched it flash blue in the Bud Light sign.

She thought about the man out in the ditch.

"How'd he get here?" she said aloud, looking back at the circle of light where Dale and Delia sat. Maybe he was off a truck, one of those who thought Alaska would save them.

"God knows." The woman shrugged. "Hope he goes, though. He was in here earlier, making a fuss."

She looked away again. Now that he was gone, she couldn't stop thinking about him, trying to reconstruct a man out of memory. Was he out there somewhere, looking in at them? It must look so warm in here. She shivered suddenly.

"You cold?" Delia asked. "I could turn up the heat."

"No," Laura said. "Goose walked over my grave, I guess."

She sipped the dregs of her drink, and licked the straw as if to make the moment last. She got up to go. "You got a phone?" she asked. But the lines were down. And anyway, she knew what she would find.

"You good to drive?" Delia asked as she made out the check.

"Yes," she said. "You take care now."

"You going to Fairbanks?"

"Yes," she said again. "I'm pretty sure he's gone," she said out loud. And though she spoke mostly to herself, Delia nodded.

"Thanks," Laura said. Delia finished ringing up the tab, took her money, and handed her the change. "You take care now," she said again. "Thanks for stopping by."

She saw them watch her as she stopped by the door, adjusting her hat and coat before going out. The door to the roadhouse swung shut behind her with a small, self-satisfied click, a place of artificial warmth and light where she would not go again.

She crossed the median and fumbled with the door of her car. It bucked in gear, ice cold, the snow blowing from the glass. She began to drive too fast up the highway toward Fairbanks. Behind her, the man had stopped moving. He stood by the roadside, shoulders slumped. Steadily the snow fell, whitening the hills, settling over the houses and the road, covering it all, closing them away. Like a scene in a globe, a child's snow globe.

Later, she thought. *It's still not time to cry.*

BILL SHERWONIT

BILL SHERWONIT ENCOUNTERED ALASKA'S WILDERNESS while working as a corporate exploration geologist in the 1970s. Trekking through the Brooks Range in Alaska's Arctic in search of exploitable minerals, he gradually concluded that the greatest wealth the region could offer lay in preserving its natural state. Over the course of four summers, he experienced the first stirrings of a wilderness advocate.

Originally from Connecticut, Sherwonit switched careers and entered journalism, returning to Alaska to stay in 1982. He took a job as a sportswriter with the conservative and staunchly pro-development *Anchorage Times*. Three years later he became the paper's outdoors writer and editor, a position he held until the *Times* ceased publication in 1992.

Reflecting on that period, when he worked alongside fierce industry advocates, Sherwonit told me, "I appreciated the opportunity to be 'a voice crying out in the wilderness,' one that celebrated wildlands—and wild nature generally—and championed both wilderness protection and wildlife conservation."

Sherwonit next turned to freelance journalism and essay writing, and has become one of the state's leading literary voices for protecting its lands. His work has appeared in numerous magazines and anthologies, he has written or edited more than a dozen books, and he mentors new writers as well.

Discussing his approach, Sherwonit said, "As I've come to define or imagine it, nature writing looks at the bigger picture, while weaving together elements that may include personal observation, natural history, science, indigenous wisdom, spirituality, and mystery; and it tells stories about landscape and the myriad other forms of life with which we share the world. Nature writing also raises questions about how we can live more decently on the Earth, our original—and ultimately, our only—home."

These ideas are displayed in the following selection. Drawn form his memoir *Changing Paths: Travels and Meditations in Alaska's Arctic Wilderness*, it chronicles a sojourn in Gates of the Arctic National Park, where Sherwonit catalogues the wonders around him. Even on the north side of the Brooks Range, deep into the Arctic, one of the harshest environments on earth, life abounds. Dall sheep and caribou are the obvious residents, as are bears, but any Alaskan will tell you it's the ground squirrels that are most abundant. A hoary marmot, gulls, long-tailed jaegers, and ravens appear. American pipits fly into his camp, as curious about the visitor to their home as he is about them. He even observes a spider. How many Alaskan backcountry essayists pause to watch a spider?

Sherwonit looks at the grand scale as well. His background in geology lends him the knowledge and language to convey the slow movement of the earth itself. Meanwhile, far more rapid movement is transpiring. The Arctic is changing, as is all of Alaska. Sherwonit is aware of his own role in this, acknowledging the inherent hypocrisy of bemoaning the burning fossil fuels, yet flying into a remote region to go hiking.

Deeply immersed in both the natural and human histories of Alaska, Sherwonit has been here long enough that his own history has become woven into that story, and that grounding keeps him from despair despite the challenges he sees lying ahead. In the end of this piece, which wanders from biology to geology, wilderness to civilization, philosophy to the hard facts of the here-and-now, Sherwonit concludes that all of it, even the mundane everyday life of modern America, is part of the miracle he finds displayed on a distant slope, far from any human habitation, where North America begins its final descent into the Polar Sea.

— From *Changing Paths* —

THE VALLEY OF SPIRES

MY MIND REELS IN DISBELIEF, MY spirits plummet. Less than an hour into a 10-day, solo wilderness journey I face a crisis of my own making. The problem may in fact be minor and easily resolved, but for the moment (and hours afterward) it feels huge and dreadful: one of the tent's three aluminum poles has cracked and splintered, making it appear—in my panicked state, at least—all but useless.

It doesn't help that wintry winter has settled on the Central Brooks Range. Though it's only Aug. 3, surrounding peaks are dusted with fresh snow and temperatures hover in the 30s. The cold complicates things. Right now scattered, gauzy clouds float through an azure sky and the landscape glows in far-north light. But a ferocious wind hurtles down this valley north of the Arctic Divide. And, I've been told, this summer in America's northernmost mountain range has been marked by plentiful rain and snow. How the hell am I going to get through 10 days of cold and likely wet Arctic weather with a damaged tent?

Staring at the pole, I wonder how I could have missed the crack during pre-trip preparations, even if then it was a hairline fracture. Now the curved, segmented pole is broken at the "joint" where one piece slides onto another. It dangles limply at the end, a broken limb. I accuse myself of complacency, recklessness. Custom-made by a company in Vermont, the tent has performed so well for so long that I've come to take it for granted.

I also curse my shortcomings as a jury-rigger and fix-it guy. The son of a talented carpenter and brother of a highly skilled craftsman, I've never been adept at building things or doing makeshift repairs. And until now I've given little thought to my dependency on properly functioning gear when deep in the wilderness.

Fighting panic—what will I do if I can't fix the damn pole?—I search through the first-aid kit, pull out a small wad of duct tape and wrap the break, but it's clear the mend is weak. The gnawing in my gut resumes and my racing mind picks up speed. I next craft a crude splint, first with a small willow branch, then the thin brush (much like those used in paint-by-numbers sets) that's part of the tent's repair kit.

Shell-shocked with worry, I wrap the splint with medical and duct tape. The rush job seems to stabilize the break, but the pole still bends at a frightening angle and I wonder how it would hold up in a gale. What if it snaps and rips the tent's fabric? Could the tent function with only two poles instead of three?

A reliable shelter is so critically important in these Arctic mountains.

I LATER MAKE A SECOND *OH-NO!* DISCOVERY: I've forgotten the stove's windshield. That will complicate its operation. But at least I've brought a high-tech tarp; it will provide a windbreak when cooking.

One more scare awaits me. When firing up my stove, I can't get it to light. This doesn't make sense. It worked fine during a pre-trip check. Inspecting the fuel bottle that connects to the burner, I notice a hairline fracture in its plastic top. Can that be the problem?

Again my spirits plunge, pulse quickens. What if I can't repair the stove? Will I have to abort my trip before it's even started? I've brought a satellite phone, so calling for help would not be a problem. But how humiliating, to get "rescued" right at the start.

After fiddling with the stove for several minutes, I figure out the problem: I simply forgot to turn the fuel-flow lever to the proper spot. When twisted to the "hi/light" position, vaporized fuel squirts into the burner.

Huge relief floods my body and I allow myself an embarrassed chuckle. Maybe I can blame this awful, clownish start to being out of practice. I haven't gone on an extended trip deep into the wilderness since 2001, the year before I became my mother's primary caregiver. Seven years later I'm still responsible for her, but this summer my sister, Karen, came north from Chicago to watch Mom for a couple weeks.

MY CAMPING WOES GET ME THINKING about legendary wilderness travelers I've met in person or through reading. Contemporary Alaskans Dick Griffith and Roman Dial immediately come to mind, along with historic figures John Muir and Robert Marshall, both of the latter remarkable explorers and staunch wilderness advocates.

Marshall has been one of my heroes since the 1970s, when I first read *Arctic Wilderness*, which documents his travels through the Central Brooks Range in the 1920s and 1930s. Marshall named hundreds of the region's landscape features, including many now within Gates of the

Arctic, an 8.4-million-acre swath of Arctic wildlands that's been called our nation's "ultimate wilderness" parkland. A founding member of The Wilderness Society, Marshall's passions for this mountain range and wilderness preservation have fed my own and I've relished following his footsteps in some of my Arctic wanderings.

I imagine Marshall and the others shaking their heads in amusement at my worried mind and fumbling antics and a voice whispers in my head: *C'mon Sherwonit, get your act together. You can do better.* Then, more calming, *Buck up, things are going to be OK.*

Wherever it comes from, that advice and a hot pasta dinner seem to settle me down.

Occasionally I look up from the meal to scan the surrounding valley and hills. Once I notice a large bull caribou prancing beside the lake where I'd been dropped off. There's no sign of other caribou and I wonder if this one is a straggler or simply off on his own adventure. Whatever the case, he's a welcome presence on a mostly fretful evening.

I enter the wind-whipped tent around 9 p.m. and settle in for the night while a light rain begins to fall. Now comfortably cocooned in my sleeping bag, with the pole holding up well, I'm more at ease, even content.

My plan is to backpack 7 miles and establish a camp near an unnamed valley of soaring marble spires that I visited in 1998 with four others, including Dave Mills, then superintendent of Gates. Their tight schedules allowed us only five days and I vowed to return for more leisurely explorations. Now, alone and with 10 days to play around, I have plenty of flexibility. Whether I move camp in the morning will depend largely on the weather.

My second day in the mountains is mostly rainy and gusty, so I stay inside the tent except to cook and, during the afternoon, stretch muscles on a short ridge climb. The hike is exactly the tonic I need. Step by step, my worries wash away while I gently slip into the wonder of these wild and ancient mountains. It's as if this harsh, rugged place somehow eases me into a more tranquil state of being. The shift is subtle, until finally a it hits me: *Wow, it's great to be back.*

Night brings a change in the wind from south to north, colder temperatures, and a snow squall. A skim of slush covers the tent when I awaken from a deep sleep. A quick look outside convinces me I'm not going anywhere yet. Mountains and valley are veiled in soupy grayness and sheets of wet, wind-driven flurries rush by.

The tent and its damaged pole have held up well during two nights of steady and sometimes fierce winds and I'm much more relaxed. It also helps that I've caught up on much-needed sleep. I'm not yet itching to pull up stakes and carry my heavy load across the tundra in wind-whipped wetness, so I allow myself the luxury of daydreams, reflection, journal writing, and naps.

Now and then I study my maps, though I know exactly where I'm going and how to get there. I'm curious to see how this area links up with other parts of "Bob Marshall country" that I've explored on previous trips into Gates.

The valley I'm in is nearly two miles across, with the classic U-shaped form of glacially carved drainages. Its many unnamed rivulets and creeks feed a clearwater stream that will eventually join the much-larger Colville River and empty into the Beaufort Sea. The bordering mountains rise 3,000 to 4,000 feet above the valley floor, their brown, gray, and black forms whiskered by green alpine tundra.

Enough plants cover those hillsides to sustain a large population of Dall sheep. Aided by binoculars, I've counted more than 30, including 16 in the hills above camp. All that I've seen are ewes, lambs, and adolescents, but mature rams also inhabit these parts, drawing trophy seekers to the preserve, which is open to sport hunting. Right now I'm camped near the park/preserve border, but for most of my visit I'll be in designated wilderness, where only subsistence hunting by residents of the region is permitted.

An afternoon lull in the storm again pulls me out of the tent for another tundra walk. The landscape has already begun its seasonal shift; summer's lush greens are patched and streaked by the faint but deepening reds of bearberry leaves, the oranges of dwarf birch and the yellows of various willows and wildflowers. Summer's wildflower bloom peaked weeks ago, but several late-blossoming species still brighten the landscape and my mood. I begin to make a list that will eventually grow to nearly 20 species.

The wildlife isn't nearly as varied, but their whistles, chirps, and chatter also liven the somber day. Ground squirrels are everywhere; they scold me while I filter water, cook my meals, explore their neighborhood.

A hoary marmot whistles a warning before ducking inside a pile of rocks. Ravens and mew gulls squawk and screech around the edges of the nearby lake, which is also patrolled by long-tailed jaegers, handsome with their black heads, white breasts and "collars," charcoal gray backs and wings, and long, streaming tails.

Even more abundant than the squirrels are American pipits, sparrow-sized tundra birds with grayish backs, beige undersides, and striking white tail feathers that they display when flying. A mix of curiosity and shyness, they fly in close as if to check me out and wag their tails while flitting from boulder to tussock to boulder, then rush off while talking among themselves with characteristic "pipping" calls.

MORNING BRINGS A HEAVY FROST and an early wake-up. Fog drifts through the valley but overhead patches of blue sky peek through the grayness. And the air is calm. By 9:30 I'm ready to go.

The pack doesn't feel as heavy as I feared, though it must weigh close to 60 pounds. Going light is not my thing. I'd rather carry extra food and clothes and suffer the pounds that they add. Plus there's the tarp, the satellite phone, a camera, water filter, pepper spray, on and on.

By the end of my day's packing—six hours, seven miles and a thousand feet of elevation gain—my body is weary and achy, my feet carry a few blisters, and I've been stung by a yellow jacket while picking blueberries. But I'm a happy camper, now within a couple of miles of the areas I've come to explore, especially the narrow, steep-walled amphitheater that 10 years ago I named the "Valley of Spires." Even from afar, it's clear that something extraordinary lies ahead. Some great force has compressed the landscape into a tight, chaotic mass. Jumbled towers and huge, overlapping plates of bare rock hint of a gateway to another world.

Another member of that long-ago group preferred "Tortured Rocks." Either seemed equally fine, because both the horseshoe-shaped basin where I'm now camped and the more constricted, partially hidden valley beyond it are unnamed in park literature and on maps of the region. They will remain that way forever or at least deep into the future, because the National Park Service has adopted a no-new-names policy for this Arctic wilderness.

Only a few miles beyond this anonymous valley are mountains, creeks, and rivers named by Marshall. I've often wondered what he would have called this remarkable place; and whether it, like the famous Arrigetch Peaks, would have become a popular visitor destination. Popular, that is, by Arctic standards, which means from a few dozen to a few hundred visitors during the brief northern summer. Even that many people takes a toll on the Arctic's hardy yet delicate plants. For all its spectacular beauty, the Arrigetch landscape shows abundant signs of wear and tear despite its remoteness and expensive airplane access.

This valley, by contrast, seems almost untouched by humans. The few trails fade in and out and are mostly traveled by bears and wolves, caribou and sheep. I followed one, heavily marked by wolf and bear scat, for a few hundred yards before losing it in the tundra.

MY HIKE TO THIS SPOT HAD ITS SHARE OF SURPRISES. The presence of tall fireweed, a tundra slump, dense willow thickets, and mixed songbird flocks that include robins, tree sparrows, and varied thrush all have me thinking about global warming and how it's changing this landscape. Recent research makes it clear that Arctic tundra is getting brushier and permafrost is melting in many northern areas.

It's difficult to say how much has changed here since my 1998 visit, because I wasn't paying close attention to such things then. And documenting changes would likely be just as tough 10 years from now, unless someone were to do baseline measurements. Maybe a series of landscape images? Perhaps this trip I'm noticing surprising details—patches of tall fireweed, woodland birds—I might have missed before because I know the Arctic landscape is shifting. The thrush, especially, seems out of place, because I associate the species so closely with forests. On returning home, a check of my Alaska bird guide will confirm that varied thrushes are rarely seen in the Arctic. Is that changing?

My awareness of human contributions to global warming is also heightened, yet I flew north anyway. Of course I can rationalize the trip, my first to the Arctic in seven years, but any nonessential travel—especially by an avowed Earth-friendly person—is open to criticism. I wonder what sort of guilt-assuaging carbon credits would adequately compensate for the series of flights that brought me from Anchorage to the Brooks Range, especially the air-taxi flight on which I was the only passenger.

Another surprise: a grizzly family. Not that grizzlies should be unexpected here. On my previous visit to this valley we didn't see any bears, but today I saw enough "sign"—mostly scat and uprooted tundra—to stay on high alert. Still, the presence of a female and two cubs shook me up a bit, especially while bashing my way through head-high willows. Fortunately, they were a good distance away, a hundred yards or more.

The bears must have seen me first, because mom already had her cubs on the move when our eyes met. The female paused briefly, which led to an *Uh-Oh* moment: will she charge or will she flee? Flee she did, after the briefest hesitation, which confirmed everything I've learned about Arctic grizzlies. In my experience, they steer clear of humans when given the chance; I've never known one to charge from a distance. It's only when humans and bears suddenly stumble upon each other, as in dense willow thickets, that a grizzly has to make the instantaneous fight-or-flight decision that sometimes leads to maulings.

Heading uphill, the grizzly mom barely stopped until reaching the ridgeline, pausing only now and then to check on her cubs. I watched enthralled while the family of bears ascended a thousand-foot slope in a matter of minutes, the female's muscles rippling as she climbed, the cubs only slightly slower. After watching the effort that female put into removing her family from danger, it is easy to understand the severity of attacks by grizzlies protecting their cubs.

The short trek toward the Valley of Spires has reminded me how much I dislike backpacking. A strange thing for a wilderness lover and sometimes-explorer to admit, perhaps, but backpacking just isn't much fun, especially hauling a heavy load across wet, tussocky tundra, with its unstable mounds of sedges and grass. I stayed on higher, drier, and more stable ground when possible but in places—both here and in other parts of the Arctic I've visited—it's impossible to avoid marshy areas without a lot of climbing. It becomes a pick-your-poison choice.

Even in my younger, more athletic, days, I was never a gung-ho backpacker. Instead of focusing on the landscape through which I'm passing, I find my attention going to bodily aches and weariness, where to place my feet, route-selection, and bothersome bugs.

Rather than go point-to-point on long-distance trips, my preference is to set up base camps and take day hikes in a variety of directions;

exactly what I'm doing for most of this trip. While I may not cover as much ground, I become more intimate with a smaller piece of the landscape. Less focused on the miles I must travel or a schedule to keep, I pay more attention to my surroundings.

AUG. 7. HAPPILY, I'M LOSING TRACK OF THE DAYS, but now and then I still check my watch for the time and date. Another inconsistency for one who wishes to be immersed in the wilds and "wilderness time." So it goes. I've learned to accept the fact that I, like other humans, am a bundle of contradictions.

It's a cold, frosty morning. And gloriously clear. Waking at 6, I'm tempted to rebury myself in the sleeping bag, but the cold—and memories of last night's opening of clouds to reveal blue skies—prompt me to peek out the tent's front flap. Lower body still wrapped in down-filled bag, I'm treated to a dazzling sight: early morning sunlight warms and brightens the uppermost reaches of the marble amphitheater I've come so far to see. I quickly bundle my torso in several layers of clothes, add wool cap and fleece gloves, and join the day.

Backlit by the sun, a dense and glowing fog bank moves up valley, though only a few faint wisps will reach this high. Still in shadow, the tundra around camp is white with frost, tiny fragile needles of ice growing on every leaf and limb and berry. It's hard to imagine these crystals grew in the hours I slept, transforming the tundra into a miniature, if ephemeral, world of ice.

I climb higher on the bench that is my temporary home, to gain a more expansive view of the marble spires and walls, which rise brightly into pale blue sky. A soft, diaphanous cloud grows around the front spire, casting shadows and adding depth and texture to the landscape.

I enter a "photographer's frenzy," something that rarely happens to me anymore, and take picture after picture. As much as anything, I want to capture images of this stunning place to share with friends and family, a photographic record to complement my journal jottings.

Wishing a different slant, I walk over to a neighboring knoll. The earth and mountains move, too, giving the sun room enough to flood nearly the entire basin with its light. The landscape now flashes with uncountable sparkles, ice crystals reflecting the sun even as they begin to slowly melt.

Though my attention has largely been focused on the bigger, more dramatic rock "drama" before me, I stop now and then to marvel at the equally wondrous frost crystals and the myriad plants they've grown upon, an infinity of shapes and textures hugging the ground. A person could spend hours, a week, a lifetime, meditating on those small beauties.

It's a blessing to be here for this morning's spectacle, one that's been repeated an untold number of times across the ages and yet never quite the same as today's. I think that's one of the things I love about this wilderness, the immensity of scale that's revealed, both across the landscape and through time.

I'm reflecting upon all of this and more, breathing in the light and grandeur of the place, when it hits me: the same sort of earthly wonders that once inspired me to become a geologist have now inspired my return to the Valley of Spires. And they're a big part of what keeps bringing me back to Gates of the Arctic. Not just the spectacular rock towers of this place or the Arrigetch, but the many landforms—the peaks and valleys, the rivers and ridges—I've explored.

I first entered the Brooks Range in the mid-1970s, working on a field crew that hoped to find mineral deposits in these mountains. Not long after, I left the field and have never once regretted it. Decades have passed since I mapped a landscape or tried to figure out its "history," since I collected rock samples or sought natural riches for their economic value. But now, once again, I've been drawn back by the complex and contorted nature of immense rock formations, and the unimaginable forces that have formed the steep-walled amphitheater that rises before me.

Through binoculars I look at some of the limy strata that were once deeply buried and are now thrust high into the air, revealed in all their magnificent complexity. Though the marbles are layered, it's impossible—at least for a non-specialist—to follow any one bed for long, while gazing upon the more vertical and deformed towers. The rocks have been squeezed and squished, fractured, slid along faults, uplifted and eroded, to now form fantastically curved and broken shapes.

How long have these spires stood here, revealed to grizzly, wolf, and human? How have their shapes shifted in the thousands of years that people have inhabited Alaska's Arctic? In the millennia that humans have walked upon the earth?

I love coming here as naturalist, writer, explorer, to revel in the landscape's mysteries and majesty, without having to "figure out" the geology. Or even try.

TAKING A ROUNDABOUT ROUTE to stay on the driest, firmest tundra, I reach the Valley of Spires' portal in a little more than an hour. Then I follow the one easy route into it, up a narrow chute that's regularly traveled by local inhabitants as well as the occasional visiting humans. Scat and tracks show that caribou, sheep, grizzlies, and wolves have all passed this way.

An initial steep ascent brings me to a small meadow, but there's still one passageway to go, a narrow seam between marble bedrock and a huge pile of rubble. Stepping out of that, I enter a place that has the feel of a hidden, magical realm.

Immediately before me is a lush marshland whose sedges, cotton grasses, and other plants form a bright mosaic of greens and yellows. A gently moving stream meanders through the marsh, connecting a half-dozen milky aquamarine ponds, their surfaces mirror smooth.

A delight in itself, this alpine wetland is made even more memorable by the stark, soaring rock walls that enclose it. Dark gray marble slabs form the valley's northern flanks; one stacked upon the other, they slant steeply and uniformly to the south, with huge piles of rock debris heaped at their bases.

While the north rim is eye-catching, the valley's south face is mind boggling. Still and lifeless by human standards, the towering spires nevertheless embody a strong sense of movement. Once-horizontal rock strata have been violently tilted until standing on end. Their precipitous faces rise 2,000 feet high from base to top. The tilted layers, in turn, have been folded crosswise, transforming the rock walls into sharply angular shapes with vertical striations. It's easy to envision giant fangs, dark and ominous. Or, like the Arrigetch, they can be imagined as the clawed fingers of an outstretched hand, clutching for the sky.

I've wondered if the magic of this place would be dimmed on a return visit. Though the surprise of my earlier entrance can't be repeated, the place continues to hold great power. Again I shrink in size, humbled by the landscape and the gigantic forces it suggests.

My first time here I stayed near the ravine's entrance, so one of my goals is to explore its upper reaches. The valley bottom is strikingly flat for several hundred yards, as a long-ago lake has been filled in to form the marsh. Gradually the floor begins to rise and the marsh gives way to wet tussocky tundra, then to an area that resembles a braided river, with multiple channels, gravel bars, and fields of dwarf fireweed, river beauties now largely faded. The fireweed fields give way to a rubbly outwash plain of gravel and cobbles and an occasional boulder.

I stop my wanderings near the tundra's upper edges, at about 5,000 feet, close to five miles from camp and 1,500 feet above it. Here the valley bends to the south; a quarter-mile away is a dark-brown "rock glacier." The map shows its icy parent to be higher in the basin, but all I can see is more rock debris, streaked in places by recent snow. If there's ice above, it's buried by thick deposits of rock and dirt. More evidence of warming.

Though the day has been mostly calm, a fierce wind begins to roar out of the north as I make my way back to camp. It smacks full force into the side of my tent, which I aligned with the east-west trending valley. Again I worry about the damaged pole, but again it holds up admirably.

I GO ON ONE MORE LONG HIKE, but for much of the next week I choose to take shorter forays and spend hours in camp or nearby. Initially I criticize myself for not being more ambitious. But in fact I'm enjoying this more leisurely approach to wilderness "exploration" and I gradually embrace my way of getting to know this part of the Arctic. And my place in it.

On one of my sleep-in mornings, the urge to pee finally pulls me from the sleeping bag. As I open the tent door I find myself looking directly at a bear, which is also looking at me. Fortunately it's a young grizzly, an adolescent, at least 50 yards from camp and headed away from me. In a couple of seconds, he's out of sight. If I'd been a few moments slower, I likely would have missed the bear's passing. I'm calm, but there's an inevitable surge of adrenaline to see a bear so close to camp. Did the grizzly hear me zip open the door? Or already know of my presence?

Eager to get a second, longer look, I quickly pull on my clothes, grab binoculars, and walk uphill. I scan the upper basin and its tributary valleys for at least a half hour, but the bear has disappeared.

Returning to camp, I put up the tarp and make myself breakfast. More like brunch, actually, since it's early afternoon. I love my flexible wilderness days, so different from the busy, often harried schedule I keep in town. Here I can sleep until midday or leap out of the tent in pre-dawn light to welcome sunrise, something I rarely if ever do in town. I have plenty of time to meditate and reflect on life's challenges and blessings. I can muse in my journal or read Loren Eiseley (more weight, but worth it when the book is *The Immense Journey*, in which Eiseley blends science and mysticism). I can sip coffee and nibble dark chocolate while studying the landscape or, when the spirit moves, grab my pack and go tramping around the countryside.

Time like this is good for the spirit, good for the soul. I know I'm blessed to be able to do this. And I've arranged my life so I can have these times of grace.

My RENEWED CALM AND ENJOYMENT of the Arctic is tempered one afternoon when I return from a hike and discover the tarp has been damaged. When leaving camp, I routinely pull the tarp tight against the ground and place rocks along its edges, to keep it from blowing around (or away). There's been no strong wind this day, yet two stakes have been pulled out and several rocks tossed aside and the tarp itself has been flipped over. Taking a closer look, I find two gashes, one about 18 inches long. Near the tears are a few small holes, suggestive of bite-puncture marks.

All the evidence suggests a grizzly has ripped the tarp, perhaps the same adolescent I saw earlier. I swirl around, looking for the intruder, but see no sign of bear.

Though rattled by the damage and what it suggests, I'm greatly relieved the tent remains standing. From a distance it looks untouched, but a thorough inspection reveals two small, parallel tears near one of its zippered entryways. I imagine the same bear swatting at the tent. I keep a clean camp, so I wonder what could have possessed the grizzly to enter it, then strike or nudge the tent and tug on the tarp. And what possessed it to stop before doing more damage?

Again I swirl around, consider other possibilities. Human? Wolf? Some mythical Arctic trickster? It had to be a grizzly. Young "teenage" bears are notorious for their curiosity. And sometimes, boldness.

Next I check my food, cached apart from both tent and tarp. It's untouched. At least the bear didn't get any reward. I whisper thanks, even while trying to imagine what must have happened. A part of me wishes I could have watched the bear, though if I'd spotted a grizzly in camp I would have chased it away. Or tried to.

Pulling out the duct tape, I again make temporary repairs. My senses remain on "high alert" for several hours and I periodically scan the area with binoculars. I doubt the grizzly will return; but I do keep the pepper spray close at hand when I settle into my sleeping bag. And I wake a couple times during the calm, quiet night, listening for footsteps or breathing outside the tent. All I hear is the soft, guttural growling of a willow ptarmigan somewhere on the tundra.

TOWARD THE END OF MY STAY, I realize it's no coincidence that I brought the writings of Loren Eiseley—a scientist who believed in miracles and embraced mystery—on this latest venture into the Brooks Range wilderness. No accident, either, that life's circumstances forced my girlfriend to bow out of the trip at the last minute, leaving me alone in the Arctic wilds for 10 days. That's not much when compared to Christ's 40 days in the wilderness or any number of contemporary solo journeys. But it's enough time, certainly, to do some serious soul searching and shed enough of my urban skin to more openly embrace the wondrous wild.

Going solo into the wild raises the stakes; it magnifies and intensifies experiences, whether unnerving (a broken tent pole, a bear in camp) or sublime (the Valley of Spires). There's nothing like a wilderness sojourn, especially when alone, to renew or enlarge one's awareness of life's mysteries and miracles.

Is it not a miracle to watch Dall sheep lambs gambol across steep slopes that would paralyze a human mountaineer? Or to watch a yellow spider, no bigger than a sesame seed, crawl across the back of the hand before disappearing back into the tundra, where it somehow survives Arctic extremes? And isn't it a marvelous thing to walk among huge, contorted, leaping, walls of marble, formed over great expanses of time and then squished, fractured, and thrust upward into the sky—all by unimaginable earth forces—and finally sculpted by glacial ice? Or to stand in a valley sparkling wildly as ice crystals are lit up by the sun?

I know: not everyone can go deep into the wilderness. Or would want to. But of course that's not necessary. While remote wild places may more easily open us to the miracles of this world, there's plenty of wondrous stuff going on around us—and inside us—all the time.

As Eiseley and other wisdom keepers have reminded us across the years, life itself is a miracle—as are the parts of creation that our western culture tends to consider "dead" or lifeless. And to be part of that spectacle is a miracle that needs to be regularly honored.

So while it's important that we be educated and warned about global warming, toxins everywhere, the dangers and potential cruelties of industrial farming (or industrial anything), we humans also need reminding that to simply be alive and part of this grand experiment—or whatever you wish to call it—is a mysterious and astonishing thing.

This matters because we behave differently in the presence of the miraculous. We act more respectfully and generously. We're more open to being joyful, playful, and, perhaps most importantly, hopeful, essential ways of being in these anxious, destructive, scary times, when it's so easy to be overcome by despair, hopelessness, and paralysis.

I'm not suggesting a retreat from harsh realities. We need to keep working for the greater good, a more just and peaceful world, a healthier planet. But we need to stop now and then to praise and embrace life.

First-hand experience of the miraculous is always best. But when that's impossible, we need reminders. I get them from people like Eiseley, Wendell Berry, Robert Bly, Matthew Fox, Terry Tempest Williams, Chet Raymo, Michael Meade, Scott Russell Sanders, Kathleen Dean Moore, James Hillman, Gary Snyder, Thich Nhat Hanh.

Above my desk is a quote attributed to the latter. In his own way, he says much the same thing that Loren Eiseley does. I return to it often, especially when things seem darkest: "People usually consider walking on water or in thin air a miracle. But I think the real miracle is not to walk either on water or in thin air, but to walk on earth. Every day we are engaged in a miracle which we don't even recognize: a blue sky, white clouds, green leaves, the black, curious eyes of a child—our own two eyes. All is a miracle."

Amen and hallelujah.

THE MORNING AIR IS DAMP AND CLOUDS HANG LOW over the mountains when I awake on Aug. 12, but there's almost no wind. And no rain, no snow. I wipe moisture from tent and tarp, eat a leisurely breakfast, then take down the tent and marvel, one more time, at the damaged pole that's held up so well, and pack my gear.

By 11 a.m. I'm ready to head back down valley to my pick-up spot. One more day of heavy packing, one more night of camping and I'll be headed out of the mountains and back to town, body lighter by a few pounds but stronger, spirit lightened and strengthened too. Journal and mind are filled with stories and ideas, heart carries renewed passion, and I intuit a refreshed sense of well being, a renewed sense of purpose.

The day is warm and still enough that mosquitoes harass me for the first time this trip. I douse myself with repellent, pull on my pack, and begin sloshing my way across the tundra, wettened by last night's rains. Coming to a thicket of willows, I start my bear chant. I will shout it, off and on, throughout the day.

"YO BEAR, HELLO, HELLO. HUMAN PASSING THROUGH. I MEAN NO HARM."

Hello . . . and goodbye. Ten days in the wilderness and the company of bears was just about right this time around. I'm ready to rejoin the world of humans, ready to go home.

CHRISTINE CUNNINGHAM

ALASKA IS ONE OF THE LAST PLACES where hunting remains deeply ingrained in the broader culture. While elsewhere it has come to be associated (often incorrectly) with rural conservatism, in Alaska one finds hunters from all walks of life. I've often said that at a potluck in Alaska you can find yourself in a conversation with a plumber, a university professor, and a doctor while enjoying chili from the moose they brought back from their annual group hunting trip. They've known each other for decades, and in Alaska, hunting, like numerous other outdoor activities, springs from a shared love of the land that transcends social divides that have grown nearly uncrossable in other parts of America.

Christine Cunningham was born in Alaska and spent most of her childhood here. She didn't start hunting until her late twenties, however, and this after a stint as a vegetarian. "My family did not hunt, but I grew up on salmon from the Kenai river and moose provided by family friends," she told me. "In Alaska, subsistence hunting has fed families for generations and many supplement their diet with wild game."

Cunningham embarked on her first hunting trip at the age of twenty-seven when her friend Steve Meyer was recovering from a life-threatening medical situation. He wanted to go duck hunting, which was his favorite childhood activity. She tagged along, and permanent relationships with both hunting and Meyer resulted.

A few years later, Cunningham wrote a humorous hunting piece and submitted it to Alaska Magazine. The editors printed it, and Cunningham soon became one of the state's most widely published outdoors writers. Her work appears frequently in the Anchorage Daily News, among other places. She also published a book, *Women Hunting Alaska*, in 2013.

Cunningham's essays generally spend minimal time on the kill itself. As a writer, she's more focused on relationships with people, with hunting dogs, with wildlife, and with the land. In sharing her stories, she told me, it's this connection to Alaska and the natural world that she seeks to convey.

"Many people live in urban areas and don't have a relationship with nature or the ability to obtain food from sustainable sources. Part of my desire to hunt was to learn responsibility for some of the realities of life - that eating meat means eating an animal that was once alive."

While most of Cunningham's writing leans towards bird hunting, in the selection that follows, she and Meyer travel hundreds of miles north from their Kenai Peninsula home into the Alaskan Arctic in search of caribou. They find what they're looking for, but the story is also populated with a ground squirrel, fish, mosquitoes of course, and the sound of wolves in the distance. It's a moment in Alaska, captured by an author who pays attention to the world she draws sustenance from.

— From *Horns on the Hill* —

AN ARCTIC GROUND SQUIRREL LIVES BELOW the highway sign near the Yukon River Bridge. He didn't want his picture taken, although he would have no way of knowing that's what I was doing. He didn't want me there, whatever the case. I backed away and watched him from a safe distance. His movement flicked between a scurry to standing vigilant. He was aware of me as a potential threat. What didn't bother him at all—and I know from watching him for an hour while he sat like a

Buddha at the base of the highway sign—was the rumbling, dust, and noise of semi trucks powering across the wooden deck of the bridge and hitting gravel at 50 mph.

The mostly gravel road is officially named the Dalton Highway, although to call it a highway rather than a road is somewhat like the difference between calling a particular stream a creek or a crick. My hunting partner, being raised on a farm, knew cattle alone could change a creek "where native brook trout make their living" into a crick "where cows and ducks do their business." The hunting regulations refer to the Dalton Highway in reference to a five-mile corridor on either side in which game may be taken by bow and arrow only. Hunters refer to the migration of caribou herds by locating them to the nearest pump station or milepost and call the highway the Haul Road.

In late July, the road is covered with potholes and metal with high odds of no visibility due mainly to fog and the haze from constant fires. Driving it requires extra fuel, food, tires and camping gear to account for the lack of services for hundreds of miles in grizzly country. It follows the northern section of the 800-mile-long steel oil pipeline that strikes the height of Alaska. The Haul Road got its name for its use by tractor-trailers hauling supplies and equipment to the North Slope for oil exploration and development and is the only road crossing the Yukon River in Alaska. The ground squirrel watched me unknowingly from the intersection of two streams: the longest river crossing all of Alaska and a man-made colossus.

His back was to the road surface as he closed his eyes and chewed the flowers from a fireweed.

"He's adorable," I said.

My partner, Steve, looked up from his book propped on the steering wheel. His leathered face always appeared to squint into the sun as though somewhere in the distance a field of wild horses must be wrangled. He looked to the squirrel. "The thing is, some asshole could come by and smack him with a rock and he'd be done."

"Should we just kill him now?" I said.

"Well I don't want to eat him," he said. We had not driven for two days to shoot a squirrel, and we had a loaf of sandwiches and another 300 miles of road left to travel before we reached the airstrip at Happy Valley. From there we would take a Cessna 185 to a fly-in only wilderness lodge on the Ivishak River, located on the northern slope of the Brooks Range.

Steve had invited me on my first duck hunt ten years earlier. The ground was cold and unforgiving that day, and the nearest escape from the misery of damp cobwebs and the flesh of rotting salmon was a 400-yard crawl away. Mascara dripped into my eyes as the sky opened up with rain. Life, at that level, was as foreign to me as anything I had ever experienced. The raw sludge of the swamp filled with spider webs and shrews was a kind of hell I wondered if I had the grit to bear. As I crawled through the marsh, each throw of the shotgun ahead of me was a decision to not stand up and leave. When I reached the edge of the pond, two widgeon glanced at me from the sides of their heads. Their bodies broke from the surface, shedding pond water and lifting into the rain-filled sky.

I had made enough mistakes my first season to clear the continent of ducks for the next century. When we left our home in South Central Alaska two days earlier, we left a family of bird dogs: three waterfowling chocolate labs and half a dozen ptarmigan-pointing English setters just before their season opened. There was no closed season for bull caribou where we planned to hunt. My only experiences coming close to hunting big game were a number of unsuccessful hikes into the Kenai mountains and a pig I'd shot for dinner on a ranch in Hawaii. Nothing beat bird hunting in my mind.

Steve had hunted big game in the years before we met. His weary look held every camp he'd ever left behind. To me, they could only be duck shacks, fishing sites, and tent camps in the mountains hunting ptarmigan. I'd flown in bush planes and floated rivers but never seen a wilderness lodge operating in the remote backcountry. This hunt was my first proper big game hunt. It was only natural, I told myself, that I would be nervous. The experience could forever change my perspective the way my first experience duck hunting had. It was only natural, I thought, that I would try not to overwhelm myself with the possibilities and fixate on a barren-ground squirrel.

We took the road as far as the gravel airstrip built as a former pipeline construction camp and now used by private guides and road crews. We had traveled just over 1,000 miles. The mid-day skies were blue but they could be fog to the deck or heavy rain by the time we left to set up our camp the next morning. I opened the glove box and ate my last store of chocolate. I usually lost as much weight camping as I gained on a cruise. "I'm preparing for the misery," I said, to explain my overeating. The sky couldn't fool me, and the mosquitoes would be hitting their stride. The temperatures could drop below freezing at night, and the caribou could make for the hills before we crawled out of the tent with our bodies hunched and frozen in our collars.

Despite what I knew about the unpredictable nature of the arctic, I'd watched the weather in Deadhorse for weeks and followed roadside reports on the movement of the herd. I ignored the pleasantness of the lodge and focused on the undistracted dread I would enjoy for the next week after we were left on a mountain with our minimalist camp.

Nothing at the lodge demanded my attention except the far off hills. I petted the two camp dogs and briefly missed my own. Steve left with the pilot for the first trip out in the super cub. My turn was next, and I sat at the table in the kitchen eating fresh baked cookies and drinking cup after cup of black coffee. As much as I missed my dogs, I wanted to hunt caribou in that wild country marked on a map as the northern front of the continent. I wanted to see the herd make its way through any of the varied peaks and shapes of summits in the range and see a big bull caribou grazing by himself, his white cape standing out against the backdrop of red lichen without a care in the world.

I heard the super cub approach and finished my coffee. The camp cook handed me a bag with the last of the cookies, and I said goodbye to the jarhead pit bull he'd brought to camp with him from the barrio district of Dallas. He was as unlikely visitor to camp as I was, only I was about to board a cub and camp in the wide open alpine without the benefit of snacks. "We saw a grizzly about a half mile off the airstrip," the pilot said. "And we had to wait for a good-sized bull to clear the runway coming in." We wouldn't be able to hunt until the next day by Alaska law. I knew enough to know predicting anything a day in advance was as dangerous as predicting the weather.

That evening the weather was perfect for flying. We followed the ropey teal blue and bright orange veins of the Ivishak, and the pilot said he didn't know why they got that color, and the water was unusually low for that time of year. Then he pointed to caribou as we came into view of the airstrip. Steve waved to us from below. He'd already set up the tent and poured himself a cup of blackberry brandy. It was a blue sky evening, and we watched the cub fly off and leave us in complete silence at the edge of the air strip with a small herd of caribou cows and calves watching us from a few hundred yards away. "There they are," Steve said. I wondered where the bulls were just as he said, "Let's go see if we can find the bulls."

As we walked around the edge of the rise, I glassed the surrounding valleys and hillsides. Every direction held groups of cows and calves feeding on lichen. The vast space of the blue-green moraines dotted in bright colored lichen would have overwhelmed me if it weren't for the warmth of the sun and the abundance of game. "Holy shit," Steve whispered. I pulled up my binoculars and looked the direction he pointed. A wide-set bull still in velvet was feeding about 300 yards away from us. It was my bull, I thought. That's my bull. "Let's not bother him," Steve said. "Will he be there in the morning?" I asked. "Let's go back to the tent."

It was getting late, and I couldn't gather enough information about what we should do first thing in the morning. "We can't hunt until after three in the morning, right?" I asked. "Right." "Do you think he will bed down there?" "I don't know." "Do you think the weather will hold?" "Hard to say." "But will he stay there all night?" Silence. "Well what do caribou usually do at night?" I asked. "Once," Steve said, "me and a buddy spotted a moose bedding down and we camped on him." "Should we do that?" I said. "It's not the same with caribou," he said. "You don't know where they'll be in the morning." "But what are the odds?" I said. But he was already snoring.

The light and silence outside while the rest of the country had gone dark was maddening. I could hear the click of heels as caribou passed by our tent throughout the night. It was worse than the night before Christmas when the reindeer weren't an imaginary flying team but game on the hoof. I fell asleep just before it was time to wake up. I knew it was amateurish of me to believe my bull would still be standing in the exact same spot we'd left him, but I thought it anyway. We went around the knob same as we had the night before. The herd was gathering up and stretched out as it made its way between two hills into the mountains. "All cows and calves," Steve said. "The bulls might be in back."

We followed the curve and were disappointed to find the caribou had vanished from the surrounding valley. There were more caribou higher up in the rocks than the valley around us and no bulls. Every animal that moved was a cow or a calf. We continued along, stopping to glass and then moving again. It was cold, but it looked to be another bright day. I thought about how we might hike into the higher country while still believing my bull would appear at any moment. "Right there," Steve whispered. I spun around and sat at the same time. "Is it him?" I said. "There's two of them."

Through the binoculars I saw the two bulls about 600 yards away—almost identical twins except mine was wider and the other was taller in the horns. We dropped into a depression as the bulls wandered our way until I could see their horns at 150 yards. The wind was quartering away from us as I chambered a round in my .300 Weatherby. I passed over the narrow bull in my scope and steadied myself. "The one on the right," Steve said. "They see us now." Both bulls lifted their heads. They stood straight at us with their heads turned, watching. "They're coming this way," Steve said. "Wait for him to turn." I watched as the weight in their bodies shifted the way slow motion allows all the muscles to flex and a bead of sweat to appear with microscopic clarity when nothing so small and far can be seen with the human eye. I could see hair and velvet horn. I pressed the trigger and heard the bullet hit without hearing the rifle fire.

The bull swayed back and was close to falling. I chambered another round and fired again. He dropped in a long and heavy fall. The silence was deafening, and my senses were lost so completely I wondered if I could do anything except fall myself. I shouldered my rifle. As much as I wanted to see the bull up close, the pounding silence was full of slow breath and my hands were shaking. I held them out in front of me to balance myself and seemed incapable of letting them fall to my sides. When we reached the bull, I dropped down on my knee, somehow lost a glove and felt the velvet of his antlers. "He's beautiful," I said.

If I said while we cleaned him two wolves howled in the distance and the second bull paused and watched us from high up on the hill, it would be true, but hard to believe. If I said we worried the grizzly bear would come back so hauled the meat to the edge of the super cub landing point just as the pilot flew over in his cub on his way from dropping off his guides and landed to pick us up just hours after I'd shot my bull, it would seem like too perfect of timing. But that's what happened, and I wondered as I flew away with the meat in the hold and the horns on the wing how it was possible to not have suffered the misery I had dreaded and wanted for its uncomplicated magnificence in a place that would haunt me until I saw it again. And just as it was behind me, my mundane senses rushed back.

We spent the afternoon bonus fishing and the next day weathered in at the lodge. It would rain for the next week, and the rivers would flood. According to another pilot, the Ivishak where we fished clear holes choked with Dolly Varden and a few bronze-colored grayling was col-ored like chocolate milk from the Sag (Sagavanirktok) River dumping in. "It is what it is," the pilot said. There's no predicting the weather or cari-bou, Steve told me as we headed down the road we'd left just three days earlier. I was never much of a realist, a fact which exhausted my partner on every hunt we'd ever shared. When thinking of hunting I envisioned chocolate Labradors with green-headed mallards hanging from their jaws, skies filled with every kind of wild fowl, English setters holding a point in a field of grass choked with game birds, and now a pair of horns high up on the hill.

COLLEEN MONDOR

COLLEEN MONDOR FLED NORTH IN 1992 after an unhappy experience working for an airport in her birth state of Florida. She intended to leave the aviation field altogether, but flying is something people have a hard time quitting. Within a year she was employed as a dispatch coordinator for an outfit she refers to in writing as "the Company," remaining there until 1997.

In *The Map of My Dead Pilots,* her memoir of this period, Mondor brings readers into the world of small time aviation in the country's largest state, where geographic immensity, difficult terrain for road building, and a widely dispersed population conspire to make light aircraft the only cost-effective means of travel between smaller communities.

It's dangerous work. Planes sometimes crash and pilots and passengers often die when this occurs. It takes a certain level of madness to be a Bush pilot, Mondor tells us, a madness that renders those who do it unsuitable for any other occupation. Mondor introduces us to her coworkers, memorable characters running from their pasts and flying headlong into the only life they're capable of living.

The pilots haul all manner of freight along with their passengers. Groceries, mail, sled dogs, human bodies, even a head in a box (the pilot never learned what kind of head). Whatever needs moving, the pilots load it, complain about it, and deliver it to its destination.

The early chapters of the book—including the first which is presented in its entirety here—have a hallucinogenic feel. Mondor forgoes a linear narrative in favor of scattershot imagery that jumps back and forth in time and airspace, repeatedly folding back to different scenes to add a few more details before scurrying onward to the next. It's an approach that contains subtle echoes of Jack Kerouac and William S. Burroughs.

Subsequent chapters narrow their focus more tightly to foibles and mishaps that pilots for the Company and its competitors experienced. Mondor, who wrote her master's thesis on the causes of pilot error accidents among air taxis and commuters, pays particular attention to this latter topic, detailing several crashes that involved people she knew. Bad decisions in split-second situations are the usual culprits, although sometimes bad decisions are what create these situations. One particularly cocky pilot was killed while looking for a wolf pack to harass rather than looking where he was going. A friend tells Mondor, "He flew into a mountain. You can't save someone who's going to fly into a mountain."

When I asked her what drew her to bush pilots in Alaska and why she chose to write about them, Mondor told me, "From the beginning, Alaska aviation has been about more than flying. The early bush pilots created a heroic myth that became part and parcel of the Last Frontier ethos and under its weight those who followed them have reckoned with far more than unpredictable weather. It is a common belief that flying in Alaska is inherently dangerous, but to understand why so many crashes still occur requires a hard look at the bush pilot myth itself. Risk-taking always exacts a mighty price, but why it has been willingly paid for so long here is a question long overdue for answering."

These days Mondor and her husband Ward Rosadiuk, both licensed pilots, own and operate Moro Aircraft Leasing, supplying planes and helicopters to customers in Alaska and the western United States. While the company is based in Alaska, she and her family divide their time between the Forty-Ninth State and the Pacific Northwest.

— From *The Map of My Dead Pilots* —
The Truth About Flying

Sam Beach went to Alaska seeking redemption, reflection, a rehearsal for the rest of his life. He told his family it was only for a year, maybe two, and he believed it when he said it. He believed everything about Alaska: the books, the magazines, the endless supply of cable TV shows.

Especially the TV shows.

He fell hard for the myths, even though he pretended not to. *Outside* magazine said that becoming a bush pilot was one of the fifty things you must do in your life. And because he couldn't stand the thought of one more day flight instructing for minimum wage, he read that article again and again. He read it a hundred times.

He didn't see himself as Ben Eielson, heading to Fairbanks in 1922 on his way to fame and glory as the first pilot to fly across the Arctic. By 1995 commercial flying in Alaska wasn't really about the bush anymore; it was about commuter schedules and hauling mail and building flight time to get a jet job. But he still had that same vision of Eielson's in his head: This time it would be different; this time the job wouldn't go away; this time he would make it. Sam had been in aviation long enough to know what Alaska meant; it was the place where pilots were needed, where they mattered. This is my chance, he told his parents, and he said it just like Eielson did so long ago, with promises to be smart and careful and come home again soon.

He said it like he believed it, and maybe then he did. Sam believed a lot of things in the beginning, and he learned to repeat those things every time his parents called, even after he realized they were lies. And he never told them Ben Eielson crashed in 1929. And of course they never thought to ask.

Some things never do change after all.

The things they had to know were endless. From their first day flying for the Company, they filled their heads with facts and figures of length and distance, knowledge of rivers and mountains, the location of a hundred landmarks, or a thousand. They learned when it was safe to drop down through the clouds, when they might continue forward, when they must turn right or left, when they absolutely had to turn back. They made sure sled dogs were tied on short leashes because one of them would jump on another and cause a fight at the worst possible time. They understood why they needed to strap down dead bodies extra tight after Frank Hamilton had one slip free on takeoff. (Frank was superstitious, although he wouldn't admit it, and the sound of that body sliding back and forth all the way in from Koyukuk sent him right to Pike's for a beer minutes after he got back to Fairbanks. His plan was to be too drunk to drive home as quickly as possible.)

No one liked flying with bodies.

They learned to respect the cold and then hate it. They became cautious or cocky, whatever worked. And in spite of themselves, they started laughing at everything, because it really was funny when they took the time to think about it. "We're just a bunch of damn bus drivers," Tony would say, "glorified bus drivers."

"Bus drivers in Mexico," said Sam, "a really lousy part of Mexico."

"Fuck that, more like bus drivers on the moon," said Frank. "No one does this kind of work anywhere else for the pay we're getting. Might as well be on the moon."

And they all nodded because he was right. Seventy years after the first bush pilots took a million crazy chances to get the job done, the Company might as well have been the moon for all that the rules applied. It was truly the ends of the earth, or even farther if you were making a living in the cockpit.

TO COMBAT BOREDOM, MOST OF THEM FLEW with reading material. There were magazines, paperback novels, the Fairbanks Daily News-Miner, and for the more ambitious, yesterday's copy of the Wall Street Journal. They packed their flight bags with flashlights and Leathermans, sunglasses and seatbelt extenders, gloves and extra batteries. Since state law allowed it and because most of them were pessimists, they also carried guns. Tony flew with a 9-millimeter and Scott Young a .44; Frank had a .45. Bob didn't have the money to buy a gun and Casey didn't have the guts to buy one, although he always asked Frank if he could plink cans with his. No one knew what Bryce carried, but it didn't matter anymore anyway because it was taken away along with everything else when he crashed in the Yukon River one summer day in 1999.

A lot of things disappeared forever when Bryce died.

If you knew someone who had been stuck on the ground in the boonies, then you knew the gun was necessary equipment. Tony grew up in Fairbanks and had a friend hit the side of a mountain and lay out there, stuck for hours with her passenger, waiting for a rescue with two broken legs and a cargo of chips and canned goods. The thought of being circled by hungry bears was enough to make anyone put a pistol in their flight bag. Sam just looked at it as another tool—he had a ratchet set, tie wire, and a pistol. And Frank? Frank took his with him to bed at night.

But that was Frank.

They packed bag lunches and thermoses full of hot coffee. They remembered to bring knives, forks, and spoons. If they were going to Galena or Barrow or Deadhorse, where they knew there would be a microwave and a place to eat, they carried TV dinners. If it was fire season, they angled for flights into Bettles or McGrath, where they could scam a box lunch from the fire service. In the winter they ate early, before their sandwiches froze on the floor beside them.

Tony dumped a packet of Instant Breakfast into his thermos of coffee to keep him awake on the early morning cargo run, while Casey just mainlined Mountain Dew no matter when he was flying. Frank brought lunch from home; Scott did too, until his wife left him, taking his kid, his dog, his money, and every single piece of Tupperware. He started eating out of the vending machines then, and raiding the company fridge.

Because he was addicted, Bob Stevens packed cigarettes. For a little while he wore a nicotine patch, but it didn't do any good. The patch couldn't defeat all the reasons Bob needed cigarettes, couldn't bring his father back from the dead or make him a decent man once he returned. It couldn't make his mother understand that just because her childhood was crap didn't mean that everyone else's had to be too, and it couldn't make that girl, that last girl he saw in Seattle, not tell him he was lousy in bed.

The patch couldn't stop Bob's palms from sweating, his heart from racing, or his mouth from going dry when he was faced with another day of flying an overloaded airplane into questionable weather just to prove to the Bosses who didn't give a shit about him, to the other pilots who barely noticed him, or to himself, who was too crippled to care, that he, Bob Stevens, was indeed man enough. He felt like the cigarettes gave him an edge, an image; they made it all seem possible, even enjoyable. He was the Marlboro Man out there, flying at five hundred feet looking for something to see. He almost felt good with the pack resting in his pocket, and the minute he landed he reached inside for more. After Bryce died, he started sneaking them in the air.

After Bryce, no one ever saw Bob without a fresh pack.

If they were based in the Bush, flying out of a place like St. Mary's or Aniak or Bethel or Kotzebue, then they flew with a specific set of habits. Out there it was about the snow and the ice and the wind. It was also about illusions, about pretending you could see when you couldn't and accepting that no one else could see either. They learned to trust one another in those places, or at least to trust every sane guy and avoid the ones who were nuts. Mostly though, they just learned to hate it.

Tony flew in the Bush years before anyone else. Scott served occasional weeks in the Y-K Delta, and Frank spent months convinced his bosses in Bethel were determined to kill him; they nearly succeeded. Bob did time in Bethel also, stationed there temporarily for the Company, as did Sam, who was stuck there longer than anyone else. He hated village life. Sam was so bored in Bethel that he nearly lost his mind.

Bethel was a "damp" village then, which meant you could import liquor or brew it yourself, but you couldn't buy or sell any within the city limits. No bars, no clubs, no comfortable tried-and-true chances to meet girls. Sam spent way too much time at way too many pilot house parties trying to persuade a girl, any girl, to go out on a date. These evenings usually ended up with someone's brother, cousin, friend, or former boyfriend taking a swing at him. And everyone was drunk. For a village that didn't allow the sale of alcohol, Bethel overflowed with it, and Sam was always getting into trouble. He begged the Company to move him into Town, but instead the Bosses offered him Barrow. He was so desperate to get out that he actually went. As it turned out, Barrow was just the standard sequel to your basic village nightmare—everything the same, only colder and darker.

Later, when he talked about his time living in the Bush, Sam always tried to end his stories with a laugh. But everyone noticed that it was a hollow sound, an empty sound. It was like he still couldn't figure out a way to make it all seem funny.

THEY LEARNED A NEW LANGUAGE. The earliest words were for the new hires; they called them newbies, cherries, or FNGs. These were familiar terms to everyone, echoing every war movie they had ever seen. They embraced the titles although they pretended not to, all of them recognizing the thought that they were now in some kind of combat—against the weather, the Bosses, or even one another. None of them thought the names were strange or wrong. They loved this kind of excitement in their lives; some of them were desperate for it.

Quickly other words seeped into their daily conversations. They began to scud-run, or fly low beneath the weather, and the weather itself was referred to as dogshit or worse. The planes were sleds or hos or bitches, depending on the make and model. Waiting for Anchorage Center to provide radar clearance for landing presented an entire string of words that no Outsider could hope to decipher. As Sam put it one day in Bethel, "I was in my sled at the end of the train in the racetrack waiting for the zone to pop up to a mile so Center would clear us to land. It took forever." Every pilot who heard this nodded in sympathy and agreement.

Along with the words, they also had to play the game—fly when it was legal but maybe not safe, and lie when it was illegal but definitely much safer. There was physical survival, job survival, and career survival to consider. Rarely did the three converge on any flight. They had to pick and choose which was most important and fake it when they made a mistake. Some guys figured this all out in the first day with the Company, but others never got it at all.

If they were the kind to worry, there were a lot of things to be concerned about. The planes they flew were old and tired. The exteriors were patched, the interiors stained, and in a hundred different ways each of them was suffering from some sort of neglect. They were used for hauling sled dogs and snow machines as well as any other freight that fit, and they looked it. There were a lot of things that went wrong, and flying a broken airplane quickly became part of the job, just another test of loyalty to a place too cheap to do things right.

Cylinders blew, a magneto came loose, a turbo quit, a diaphragm fuel pump froze-up, connecting rod bolts failed, a waste gate stuck open, cylinders broke completely loose from the engine block, the trim tabs froze up, hydraulic pumps failed, and then the classic: One day Scott was flying out of Bethel and a cowling came off and disappeared into the tundra. The passengers loved that one; nothing like having the hood come off your car while you're driving down the interstate.

The worst though were instrument failures, because the pilots usually didn't realize the instruments were broken until they needed them. There was the time Sam was flying back from Anaktuvuk, VFR in a single-engine, when the ceiling dropped down on him and he couldn't see a thing. He punched up blind through the clouds, aiming for an altitude that was five hundred feet above the highest mountain, and that was where he stayed until he was talking to Fairbanks Approach. As he was landing though, he realized there was something wrong with the altimeter. It was off by one thousand feet. Sam actually flew home five hundred feet below the highest mountain along his route. Lesson learned: Never trust your altimeter; although in this case he had no idea what else he would have done.

"WHAT THE HELL WERE MY CHOICES UP THERE?" he asked us later. "You can't see a damn thing, and mountains in all directions. What could I do?"

"Don't fly to Anaktuvuk if there's clouds," said Tony, trying to look serious.

"Yeah, right, I'll just go out on all those perfect CAVU days this winter, like waiting for those miracles won't get me fired." Sam thought for a minute and then said, "This job is going to kill me, you know; it is totally going to kill me." "You're a lucky son of a bitch," said Scott. "You know that?"

Sam shook his head, "I gotta start praying; I need to get religion."

"Get God or get drunk, either way you're still flying tomorrow."

And that was the bitch of it. Whatever happened today was over and tomorrow was still coming, no way to duck or hide. Tomorrow was always coming.

THERE WERE PITOT TUBES THAT CLOGGED WITH ICE, killing the airspeed indicator and forcing them to guess how fast they were going. Windshield heat failed, leaving them behind a sheet of ice. Prop heat failed, and the prop iced up or the deicing boots got so buried under ice that the leading edge of the wing looked like the rim of a margarita. Again and again and again, ice built up on the wings and the tail, and no matter how hard they tried to climb out of it, the ice dragged against them, stalling out the airplane over mountains and tundra and God knows what else.

Scott once flew one of the singles for thirty solid minutes with the stall indicator intermittently going off over the White Mountains. Lowering the nose increased the speed and stopped the stall, but as soon as he dropped it the slightest bit, he lost altitude and the plane wanted to keep going down. So he held it just right until he landed in Arctic Village and then pulled out a credit card and started chipping away at the inch and half of ice all over his airplane. When I asked him later how bad it got, he shook his head and said, "Peggy Fleming could have skated on my wings."

And everyone laughed about that for days because it really was funny, wasn't it?

Slowly, without realizing it, their comfort zones began to slide. They learned to navigate through the shifts, accept a new set of personal standards. At first it was about limits, like when Bob only wanted to take one flight a day and Casey wanted to verify the weight of his load before he would launch. They considered these necessary rules during training, standards they were unwilling to relinquish. Then they were put on the line, and immediately everything changed. You had to be fast and you had to be ready or you weren't going to get the flights. Before they knew it, each of them was taking off in conditions that seemed unacceptable just a few weeks before. And then, somehow, those conditions became comfortable, familiar. The zone shifted and scary became a fluid term, a dangerous gray area that was always getting grayer.

They flew in ceilings below eight hundred feet, then below five hundred, and then Tony dropped down so low over the Yukon River that water splashed on his wings. His wheels brushed the treetops on more than one occasion until, with awesome regularity, he found himself having to climb to clear islands or the houses at the end of the runway while on final approach into a village like Kaltag.

And he wasn't the only one.

Their visibility requirements dropped from three miles, to one mile, to maybe three thousand feet, and still they said it was flyable. Ice built up on their wings to a half-inch, and they kept flying. They flew with an inch and then collected two, all the while trying to boot it off but knowing the equipment was struggling and the deice boots were covered in ice as well. Scott hit a high point when he brought one of the Navajos in with three solid inches. If the planes could handle it, they discovered that they could as well. It was never easy, but they could do it; and after doing it for a while, they forgot all the reasons it had seemed wrong once, why it had ever seemed impossible.

They forgot everything but the last flight, the last hour on the job before they went home and got ready for the next one.

They flew fifty pounds overweight the first time and were angry about it. Then they took one hundred pounds more and then two hundred. In the single-engines they routinely went three hundred over and in the twins, five hundred. One summer day on a charter in a Navajo, Tony blew everyone's mind when he brought three thousand pounds of salmon roe back from Kaltag plus a single passenger who weighed in easily at three hundred pounds himself. The Company wasn't thrilled because if Tony had split the load and flown it legally as two flights, it would have earned the Owners twice as much. The customer gave him a hundred-dollar tip though, worth two hours of flight time. So if flying heavy got you done for the day sooner and the plane could handle it, then why not do it? Why not see just how heavy you could go? After a while, once everyone had done it over and over, there was no reason to ever stop.

It didn't take long for them to get jaded. They looked for telltale signs of pilot error in newspaper articles about crashes, began to see the unwritten things other pilots did wrong, all the things they should have done right. They could assess blame from a paragraph, a few sentences, or even less. A pilot trying to beat bad weather and losing—this was clear in a second. A pilot worrying more about giving tourists a good time than staying clear of glacier—this was evident right away. Overloaded, loaded wrong, not enough gas, not enough brains. Every crash was avoidable, every one preventable. And they knew that every dead pilot would be replaced in days by someone desperate for the same chance that had been squandered, for the golden opportunity to prove they were better. They stopped being surprised when it happened all over again. Some weren't even surprised that much by Bryce, only that it was Bryce and that it was into the river and that the weather was good and that he died.

Bryce was one of theirs; being surprised by his crash seemed like the right thing to do.

EVERYONE LIED TO THEM. The Company lied from the very beginning, promising higher paychecks, bigger airplanes, and a better schedule. Some of them actually volunteered to go to the Bush because the Bosses said it was the fastest way to career advancement. Once they were out there though, they were marooned, stuck hundreds of miles from civilization flying pieces of shit in and out of one godforsaken place after another. They called the Company constantly at first, asking for a timetable back to town, trying to get someone to commit to something concrete. But all they heard were the same pointless promises over and over again.

Sometimes Sam would tell everyone about the last flight into Barrow from Fairbanks, about the cold Dominos pizzas the Bosses put onboard for him as reward if he pulled off yet another miracle. Sometimes he left them outside for the ravens and watched while they tore the boxes apart, spreading cardboard all over the ramp. Lousy pizzas. And Tony and Frank and Scott nodded their heads, all of them thinking about cold burgers or greasy buckets of KFC that had been their rewards. Shit you bought teenagers who cleaned their rooms or got straight A's on their report card; that was what they were working for at the outstations, the approval of assholes who treated them like children.

But they ate it anyway, because at least it was something. The village agents lied about the weather. Some of them just didn't know what they were doing when asked how the conditions were, but a lot of them lied because they wanted the plane to come in no matter what. They were expecting freight or mail for themselves or had someone onboard who needed to be home, and so they told the Company that the weather was good. And so the pilot launched and then found out somewhere along the route that it was total shit and he couldn't see fifty feet in front of the airplane. Usually he kept going, because he was already more than halfway and it was easier just to go, dump the load, and leave than return to the base and wait for the weather to improve. But he was pissed. So the pilot yelled at the agent and the agent lied and said he told the Company it was lousy, and the pilot went back and yelled at Ops and Ops said the agent told them it was good, and the end result was that whatever the agent wanted he got and Ops was glad to have the stuff gone and the pilot got paid. If he pulled this off enough, the agents would start to brag about him. For a while Frank was called "Ninja Pilot" because he would fly virtually blind. He squashed that nickname as quick as he could though; it was the last thing he wanted the Feds to hear.

Ops almost always lied about the load, even when they didn't have to. Every pilot was given a load manifest for his flight prior to departure. It listed everybody and everything onboard the airplane along with their weights and destination. When they were newbies they ran the calculations, made sure all the numbers worked out to a legal load, and went on their way without checking the plane. But after a few weeks with the Company, they began to notice things. There would be a dozen boxes of mail onboard for Nulato, but no Nulato mail was listed on the manifest. They would arrive in Kaltag and the agent would ask for freight. They would look in the nose compartment and there it was, but it wasn't listed on the manifest either. Cases of beer for Last Chance Liquor in Koyukuk were supposed to weigh five hundred pounds, but when they unloaded them they realized there was more like eight hundred pounds onboard. One truck tire for the Company office in Galena would turn out to be two hidden behind the back seat. A dozen pumpkins for Ruby School weighing one hundred pounds were really thirty pumpkins weighing God knows what. It went on and on and on.

Sometimes pilots would complain and, to prove a point, might throw a few things off onto the ramp before they left. On one trip Tony had the Galena ramp crew remove every single thing from his plane and weigh it when he landed there, just so he could call Ops and bitch. The Bosses apologized at first, pretended to be shocked, but after a while there was no need even for that. You just knew the load was suspect, and it was up to you to refuse it or not. And refusing, well, that might lead to time in the penalty box. Ops would either schedule you exclusively in the worst piece of crap the Company flew (like 1MD, which was slow and had a notoriously shitty cabin heater), or you just weren't scheduled at all for a few days. Pretty quickly you realized it was the way the system worked; you might hate it, but no one had any choice. Pilots flew the load because it was their job, and Ops moved the freight and mail and passengers out the door because that was theirs. Lies were just the currency that kept everyone flying and, most importantly, kept the Company paying.

In spite of all the hazards, every company had a pilot like Casey who refused to worry. He would sail past Bob, standing on the ramp desperately sucking down a cigarette and checking out the clouds, and jump into the cockpit of his single-engine airplane and be long gone while Bob was still thinking about taking off in a twin. Casey rolled every airplane the Company had and excelled at flying through ice and snow and in temperatures that were just plain crazy. One time he was stuck in Galena with a broken heater, and the mechanic the Company sent down finally had to give up; no way to fix it without more parts. So Casey straps the guy in, climbs into the left seat and tells him not to talk and fog the windshield up. Then they fly for an hour and a half back to Fairbanks. It was fifty-two below zero, and that's straight temperature, no wind chill. The mechanic didn't stop shaking for a week. But that was Casey; cold wasn't going to stop him from his date that night. Nothing was ever going to stop him.

There was this picture-perfect summer day once, and Casey was flying the Owner's visiting cousin on a cakewalk tour flight up to Anaktuvuk along with the mail. He was going up the John River, just above treetop level looking for moose and talking up all the sights to this poor dumb woman from Connecticut who never hurt a fly and had no idea that her pilot was pretty much going to get them killed if he wasn't more careful.

The John runs through canyons—lots of deep, twisting canyons—and it is okay to follow it. Hell, everybody runs it in bad weather, but you have to know when to start climbing and what turns to follow. Casey didn't worry about those things though. He was too busy thinking about how much she was loving the flight and all the good things she was going to say about him and the size of the tip she just might be sliding in his direction if he gave her that sideways grin of his often enough. And she might have been near fifty but she was good looking, so he wasn't having any trouble flirting.

Then after a while he finally started climbing out of the canyon. It didn't take him long to realize though that he was in trouble. Any pilot can do basic math, especially the kind of distance versus altitude versus side of mountain impact crater formula. Casey never would have admitted any of this to anyone, but Scott was flying out there that day, and he could see Casey was in trouble and started talking to him over the radio. He told him to pour on the power and pull the nose back hard, and all Casey could say over and over again was "I'm not going to make it; I'm not going to make it."

"You just need to pull that sucker back, hold off the stall, and you'll be fine."

"I don't think so man, I don't think it's gonna make it."

"That plane has more power than you might think. It's a good plane; it'll do it."

"Oh shit," said Casey as the mountain got closer. "Does it look good from there? Does it look good?"

"You're fine, you're great. You'll clear it easy. Just keep the nose back, and don't let up on that power."

And then they held their breath, both of them, Scott watching out his window as the little Piper Saratoga struggled to get over the trees at the top of the ridgeline. He said later that Casey cleared the mountain by fifty feet, tops. By ten o'clock that night though, he was kicking back beers, laughing his ass off, and picking up the new waitress at Pike's. And that woman who was with him? She gave Casey $50 and her phone number. She never knew he almost killed her.

So this is how it happened with Bryce:

He was leaving Tanana in a Navajo, loaded with freight and mail but no passengers. It was a clear summer morning, and he probably took off thinking about nothing but his next stop. Maybe he was looking out the window admiring the view, enjoying the quiet. Then a couple of minutes after takeoff something quit, something failed; some system or some component ceased to operate, and then he was saying he was in trouble and turning back for the airport and not making it and crashing in the Yukon. And then Bryce was dead and no one will ever know how it happened.

Witnesses heard Bryce say on the radio that he had a problem; they heard the plane hit the trees; they heard it smash into the river. They said it was sudden and sharp; they said it was like an explosion. They said they had never heard anything like it in all of their lives, and they all agreed how loud it was and how strange the quiet was that came behind it. And then they said nothing and there was only blessed silence, no more words to distract from what was Bryce's death. There were just the Company pilots, all of them, one after another, standing on the banks of the Yukon or flying low over the shore and each of them wondering what had gone wrong. "It was beautiful out there that day," Frank said later, "if only you didn't know what the river was hiding."

If only Bryce weren't dead, and if only we weren't stuck with never knowing why.

IF YOU ASKED THEM, THEY WOULD ALL SAY that the last bush pilots died long ago and they were just guys doing a job. Most of them claimed they stayed with the Company to build flight time, to advance their careers, to get a shot with the majors. Some of them said it was all about the money. Not one of them would say he had something to prove. All of them were liars.

The truth is that their mothers abandoned them when they were children, their fathers were overbearing authority figures, their wives left them, girlfriends cheated on them, siblings overshadowed their accomplishments, and no one, absolutely no one, ever understood them. They came for a thousand different reasons, but they stayed for only one: Not one of them had anywhere else to go.

By the time he left Alaska, Sam held more than a dozen names in his memory, all of whom died while flying. Some of them were particularly dear; a few were irreplaceable. He wondered though about the ones he didn't have names for, the ones he didn't even know were gone. "How many guys did I talk to on the radio, did I see on the ramp in Barrow or Bethel or have lunch with in McGrath during fire season, that just aren't here anymore?" he asked one night. "How many of those guys I kind of knew but can't remember are gone now? I mean, do I really know fifteen dead pilots, or do I know thirty or forty?

"How many do any of us know?"

And for a minute, sitting over after-work beers at Pike's, we realized that together we might fill the room with our dead; we might fill the entire restaurant. There could be a hundred dead pilots we knew; there could be more. We found ourselves shocked at the thought, lost for words as we looked at the tables and chairs surrounding us and considered the faces that could have been there.

And then we all started talking at once. Because the honest answer is that we didn't know how many names there were, and on a good night we didn't care. On a good night we didn't even remember Bryce. But the truth was, there were never enough good nights, and everyone knew it.

We didn't tell anyone that though, not even each other.

STAN JONES

THE NATHAN ACTIVE MYSTERY SERIES FOLLOWS the twists and turns in the frequently intersecting professional and private lives of a police officer from the fictional Alaskan town of Chukchi. Active is Iñupiat born in the small coastal Arctic community, but adopted by white parents who raised him in Anchorage. As an adult he joins the State Troopers and is posted in his birth village–which he loathes–as his first assignment. Over the course of the books published thus far, he comes to terms with the community and, at the conclusion of the fourth installment, "Village of the Ghost Bears," resigns from the troopers in order to become head of borough public safety (regional governance in Alaska is divided into boroughs, not counties).

Stan Jones, author of the series, has modeled Chukchi on Kotzebue, a small community of 3200 people located on the windswept Baldwin Peninsula about forty miles north of the Arctic Circle, on Alaska's north-western coast.

An award winning former journalist, Jones has spent most of his life in Alaska. He lived in Kotzebue for five years over two different periods, and while he now makes his home in Anchorage, his connection to the village has never gone away. He told me, "I found the lovely, barren Arctic landscape absolutely mesmerizing, the extreme climate a joy, and the Native culture fascinating. I landed Bush planes on the sea ice, drove snowmachines—or 'snowgos,' as they're called in Kotzebue—over the tundra, hunted moose and caribou, and once helped paddle a sealskin *umiaq* in pursuit of a bowhead whale on the Chukchi Sea off Point Hope."

In *Tundra Kill*, the fifth book in the series, Jones offers a description of Chukchi that perfectly evokes the larger coastal communities along Alaska's northern and western shores.

At the south end of Beach Street was Chukchi Region Inc.'s newly renovated Arctic Inn, modern as anything in Anchorage, right down to an espresso stand, free wi-fi, and rooms with pay-per-view porn and professional sports on cable.

After that came a stretch of log cabins crumbling back to nature, some with caribou antlers lining the eaves as had been the custom until a few years ago. In front of the old cabins, cars, trucks, outboard motors, and snowgos rusted away—slowly in the dry, northern climate—in their effort to return to iron ore. A few were draped in abandoned mattresses, soggy and mildewed in summer, hard-frozen under the snow in winter.

The north end was marked by the towering cranes of the Chukchi docks, where everything that sustained the village arrived if it wasn't so urgent it had to come by air.

Beach Street was, in its way, a museum of Chukchi's past and present. Even its future, if you counted the near-complete seawall on along the shore.

While the series has generally tended toward Arctic noir, in *Tundra Kill* Jones poked fun at Alaska's most well known resident. In this story, the state's governor, Helen Mercer, comes to town to welcome her husband at the finish line as winner of an incoming dogsled race. Conniving, manipulative, ambitious, and drop-dead gorgeous, Mercer is reminiscent of a recent real-life Alaska governor, and Jones relishes the opportunity to offer up the complex feelings Alaskans have toward their celebrity former chief.

In the excerpt that follows, Active meets Mercer for the first time. It's an awkward and humorous scene where a pair of all-business cops have to contend with their governor, who is all about herself.

— From *Tundra Kill* —

"ME GUARD THAT WOMAN?" Active looked across his desk at Patrick Carnaby, commander of the Alaska State Trooper post in Chukchi. "Let me explain it this way: No. That's a Trooper job. It's not a job for borough public safety."

"Nathan, Nathan." Carnaby's face took on an expression of charitable piety. He tapped the green folder he had just dropped on the desk. "This is a marvelous opportunity, guaranteed to put you and your fledgling department on the map right out of the gate."

Carnaby waved his coffee cup at the move-in clutter around them in what, a few weeks earlier, had been the office of the chief of police for the city of Chukchi.

Now it was the office of Nathan Active, newly appointed chief of public safety for the newly created Chukchi Regional Borough. The borough had absorbed the police functions of the city of Chukchi and acquired jurisdiction over the surrounding eleven villages in the patch of Arctic coastline, tundra, mountains, rivers, and lakes known as the Chukchi region. The borough was bigger than fifteen of the United States, and now one-time Alaska State Trooper Nathan Active was responsible for the public's safety on every square foot of it.

"Not to mention on the evening news," Carnaby went on. "And cable news, talk radio, the New York Times, Flitter, and—what do they call those Internet things, globs?"

"The word is blogs. And it's Facebook or Twitter, not Flitter."

"That's it," Carnaby said with a twinkle in his eye. "Twitface. Anyway, you spend a couple of days bouncing around the countryside with our gorgeous governor in Cowboy's Cessna and you'll be an international celebrity. Your face will be on the cover of People Magazine right beside hers."

"Not so much," Active said. "The media don't follow her around like they used to. She only makes national news when she does something ridiculous and the papers here find out and it blows up. Remember when her limo hit the cat and the Juneau paper reported it and PETA got all over her?"

Carnaby chuckled. "Admittedly, her last try at national office was unfortunate. How many countries did she want to invade?"

Active shrugged. "I lost count."

"So did she, I suspect," Carnaby said. "The point is, she's determined to fight her way back into the headlines. Helen Mercer does not know the meaning of the word 'quit.'"

"Or 'mercy,' either, from what I hear," Active said.

Carnaby nodded. "When she played high-school ball here—well, that's when they started calling her Helen Wheels. Which takes us back to you, young man. You really want to stand in her way?"

"I just wanna dodge this bullet."

"Coming home to Chukchi to watch her husband win the Isignaq 400 is part of her master comeback strategy." Carnaby patted the green folder again. "You help the governor show herself heroically braving the Arctic skies in a tiny Bush plane while playing the loyal spouse and you get yourself not only her undying gratitude but, what, at least ninety seconds on Fox News? "

"Coming home? Ha. How long since she really lived here?"

Carnaby waved a hand in dismissal. "Granted, it's been some years since she graduated from mayor to the state legislature and then to the governor's mansion. But there's no place like home and now she's back and she wants you to watch her body."

"All right, let me explain it a different way," Active said. "No chance, no hope, and no thanks. It's a suicide mission and we both know it. My plan is to avoid her presence, cross my fingers, and hope she gets out of town safely. I've got all I can do right here in Chukchi trying to keep the lid on till the race is over, anyway. Plus, I need to go up to Katonak on the honeybucket murder—"

"Honeybucket murder? Do I know about this one?"

"No reason you should, I guess. Only happened last night and the guy turned himself in already. Apparently he and a buddy got into a fight over the ownership of an Igloo cooler full of homebrew, the honeybucket got kicked over in the fight and then there was another fight over that. And when the first guy woke up and saw his buddy dead, he staggered over to my village safety officer's house and turned himself in. Actually, he said he was sorry and begged my guy to shoot him, but all he got was arrested. And now I have to bring him down here."

Carnaby waved it off. "Let Alan go. Or have the safety officer bring him down. Sounds open-and-shut."

Active shook his head. "Thanks, but, I still gotta pass on this one. I want to check in with my safety officer up there and ask a few questions before I button it up."

"You may not exactly have a choice. She—" The door banged open and Carnaby jumped out of his chair. "Why, here she is now! Welcome home, Governor, this is Chief Active. Nathan, have you met our governor?"

Active masked his astonishment as she swept into the room, complete with the scarlet Helly-Hansen parka, the rectangle glasses, the weapons-grade cheekbones, and a cloud of the famous perfume, though he couldn't remember what it was called. And the calf-length high-heel boots—what was the brand? Something weird and a little suggestive, if he remembered.

She crossed the office, hand out. He rose without conscious effort and his hand met hers of its own accord.

"Chief Active." She shook his hand and held it a moment longer than necessary. "What a pleasure!"

Active stifled simultaneous impulses to ask why, and to punch Carnaby in the face. "The pleasure's all mine, Governor," he managed.

"Good to see you again, Governor." Carnaby put out his hand. Mercer turned her head away. The Trooper captain gave a slight eye roll. "Governor, I was just—"

Mercer shot him a frown and he shut up. Carnaby retreated to the only other chair in the office, which was against the back wall. She took his seat in front of Active's desk.

"Sit, Nathan, sit, we need to talk. We haven't met yet, right?"

Active dropped into his own chair behind the desk. "No, ma'am, you were already governor when I got here and—"

"I know, I know, I'm not home nearly as much as I'd like to be. It's so hard to do that, now, much as I love my Chukchi and I guess . . . well, our paths just haven't crossed."

"No, ma'am."

"Has Captain Carnaby told you how much I need you?"

"He was just starting to exp—"

"Yes, I want you for my bodyguard while I fly the Isignaq 400 and cheer my husband on for the next couple days."

Active gave Carnaby a fast look. The trooper threw up his hands in the international symbol for bureaucratic surrender.

"But, Governor, I think you'll be perfectly safe in Chukchi and the villages. And, anyway, don't the troopers usually—"

He froze at Mercer's look. Too late, he noticed Carnaby's grimace and warning head shake from behind the governor.

"I will not have a trooper anywhere near me." Mercer swung on Carnaby. His expression dissolved into bland impassivity. She turned back to Active. "The last one was guarding my body, all right. Especially my butt when I climbed the stairs to my office. I sent him back to Juneau this morning."

Behind her, Carnaby circled his ear with a fingertip.

"Of course my department will be happy to help in any way possible, Governor." Active snapped his fingers. "In fact, one of our officers, Alan Long, was born in a fish camp up the Isignaq and I'm sure he'd be only too happy—"

"No."

"I'm sorry?"

"I don't want Alan Long. I want you."

"Me?"

"Posilutely." She nodded and gave him the smile made famous on her campaign posters and book covers. "So we're all set!"

He shot another quick glance at Carnaby, who winked.

"May I ask how you chose me for this honor? I had no idea you were even aware—"

"Oh, I'm very aware of you, Nathan. I still have my sources here. You can take the girl out of the village, but you can't take the village out of the girl, am I right?"

"So they say."

"To be exact, I was very impressed by your interview with Roger Kennelly on Kay-Chuck the other night."

"You pick up Chukchi public radio in Juneau? I didn't know—"

"They stream it on the Internet, duh! Modern times, Nathan."

"Of course, what was I thinking?" He slapped his forehead, as she seemed to expect.

She shot him another grin. "I liked what I heard about your ideas for the new department you're creating here. I liked it very much. So much so that I've suggested to our commissioner of public safety that you might make a good director of state troopers in Anchorage the next time the job opens up. Which I anticipate will be soon."

Active rubbed his eyes. "Director of the Alaska State Troopers." He gave Carnaby a vengeful look. "Meaning I'd be Captain Carnaby's supervisor?"

Carnaby shuddered behind Mercer's back.

"Come to think of it, you would!" She shot Carnaby another blood-freezing glare, then turned back to Active with an expectant air.

"It's a great honor, Governor, but—"

"Suka."

"I'm sorry?"

"Please. Call me Suka. That was my nickname when I played basketball here. It comes from the Eskimo word for 'fast' and it's what my friends use." She leaned across the desk and touched his forearm. "I hope you'll be my friend now?"

"Of course, Gov—er, Suka. But there's so much I need to do here." He waved at the litter of file boxes and office equipment on his floor. "I just took over. We're still getting moved in."

Mercer glanced at the clutter and sighed. "The director's job can wait, I suppose. But when you're ready, you just let me know."

"Of course, Governor. Of course."

"And, meantime, you'll be my bodyguard for the race?" She widened her eyes and waited. "You have a reputation as a guy who won't back off, no matter what. That's exactly what I want if things go sideways out there, right?" She waited some more. "Look, Nathan, I, that is, the state, of course, we do fund over half your department's budget, right? And this seems like such a small thing to ask. You know, as one friend to another."

Active faked a delighted grin. "Of course, Suka. Absolutely. Your wish is my command."

She nodded with a gratified look. "Now, where was I? Oh, yes, your interview on Kay-Chuck. That network of women's centers you and

Grace Palmer want to set up around the region? I am totally in support of women's rights, other than contraception for girls, of course, and abortion. But if you need an additional appropriation, just let me— well, here." She scribbled something on a business card and handed it to him. "That's my personal cell number. You call me absolutely any time you need absolutely anything." She touched his arm again. "Anything at all, any time at all. You've got a friend in Juneau, Nathan. A true friend? Okay?"

Active nodded.

Mercer rose and swung on Carnaby, who let his game face slip a little under the pressure. "You have the information my staff emailed up?"

Carnaby pointed at the green folder on the desk. "I printed it all out."

"And you'll brief Chief Active on my schedule and make sure he has all the state resources he needs?"

Carnaby nodded again and started out of his chair.

"No! Don't get up!"

Carnaby sank back down.

Mercer turned back to Active. "Nathan, great to finally meetcha, I can't wait to fly the race with you and watch Brad win his third Isignaq 400! My staff arrives on the noon jet tomorrow. We'll meet them and get organized, and then we'll be off up the river with the legendary Cowboy Decker. Brad should hit Isignaq tomorrow afternoon to give his dogs their last mandatory rest stop, and cross the finish line here in Chukchi the day after, so we should be out for just the one night and two days. All good, Chief Active?" She snapped him a mock salute.

To his shock, he found himself picturing her in a tight sailor suit, the blouse open except for a knot at her bellybutton. Christ, what was this mojo she had? "All good, Suka," he said.

She wheeled and swept out of the office in another cloud of perfume. Active and Carnaby listened as her footsteps clacked down the hall. After a few seconds, Carnaby rose and peered after her.

"She gone?"

"Gone." Carnaby dropped into the chair before Active's desk and let out an exhausted breath.

Active waved the business card at him. "And I have her personal cell number."

"Not my circus, not my monkeys," Carnaby said. "Not any more."

Active tucked the card into his shirt pocket. "But what the hell was it about?"

"You heard what I heard. She wants you to guard her body."

"Because one of your Troopers looked at her butt? Seriously, her butt?"

"She thinks every man looks at her butt," Carnaby said. "Which most of them do, probably. Also, don't forget, she told that TV reporter she doesn't like people judging her by her chest size. So, don't get in front of her or behind her, and you'll be fine."

"But—"

"And I definitely wouldn't use that word around her."

"Jesus," Active said. "She's even crazier than people say."

Carnaby's eyes twinkled. "I hear she can see the White House from her house. You'd think we would have learned our lesson from the last woman governor we elected. But, no, we had to do it again."

"I mean, I heard the Juneau guys talk about her when I worked for you, but—"

"That's our governor," Carnaby said. "A woman of iron whim. Not for nothing is she known as Helen Wheels even to this day."

"I'm doomed. I ride around for two days with her in Cowboy's Cessna, she's gonna think I'm looking at her butt or her boo—er, ah, chest, for sure."

"Actually," Carnaby said, "you want my theory? It may not be the butt-checking at all. Maybe what it is, she does get any news coverage while she's out here in the Bush, she wants to make sure there's a Native face in the picture, so as to broaden her appeal in this multicultural society of ours. Mad she may be, but there's usually some method in it."

"Her husband's half Inupiaq," Active said. "Why does she need me?"

"The lady demographic maybe? You do wear a uniform and a Glock, and I don't have to tell you what that does to some women." Carnaby grinned. "But seriously. I didn't know this guy she just fired very well, but I'm told he was in all fairness somewhat lacking in emotional intelligence—an area where you excel, I might point out."

Active studied the trooper captain in the spring sun flooding through the third-floor windows. The Super Trooper, as he had been known when Active was at the public safety academy in Sitka, was six-two, square-jawed, and still looked fit at age sixty or so. But there was a hint of jowl under the jaw these days, a little gravel in the voice, a little more salt than pepper in the hair and mustache. The bifocals that had appeared a year earlier were pushed up on his forehead.

When Carnaby had first arrived in Chukchi, as Active understood it, he had a family in Anchorage and plans to return to it in a couple of years. But here he still was, with a live-in girlfriend, a boat, and a plane, and no word lately of the Anchorage family. And now he was retiring, what with the Chukchi Borough taking on the police powers once wielded by the Troopers. So far, he showed every sign of staying on in Chukchi. Maybe he had missed too many planes, as the saying went, to go home again.

Carnaby cocked an ear. "We got company?"

There was a rustle outside, then a tap.

Active grimaced. "Come in, Lucy."

The door swung open to admit Lucy Brophy, one-time dispatcher and office manager for the Chukchi police department, now office manager for the new borough public safety department. A blue folder rested on her prominent belly. "I wasn't listening when the governor was here," she said.

"Of course not," Active said. "The thought never crossed our minds."

"Not for one moment," Carnaby said.

"*Arii*, I wasn't. She's sure pretty, ah?" Lucy said it with what struck Active as studied casualness. He didn't respond. "I read she's a size six. I wish I was a size six." She laid the folder on Active's blotter. "Maybe I'll go on Amazon and order some Naughty Monkeys, too. You have to sign the paychecks."

"I do?"

"Sure, it comes with your new job. Finance sent them over." She snuffled a little as she said it, and felt around in the pockets of her sweater.

"You got a cold?" Active said

"No, it's just my allergies."

He handed her his handkerchief. She looked at it, then at him.

"Don't worry, it's clean."

"*Arii*, I know." She took it and dabbed her eyes, then blew her nose.

Active opened the folder and looked at the top of the stack. "I sign my own paycheck? Isn't that a conflict of interest or something?"

"Not if it's under fifteen thousand. Then the mayor has to sign it."

Active signed checks. Lucy looked at Carnaby. "Is Nathan going to Anchorage?"

"I thought you weren't listening," Carnaby said.

"I heard on accident," Lucy said.

"He's not going anywhere any time soon," Carnaby said. "You heard wrong."

"I don't think so," Lucy said. "I have really sharp ears."

Active handed her the folder. She offered him the handkerchief, which he declined.

She left and closed the door behind her. Carnaby looked at Active, then at the door, and raised his eyebrows.

"Thank you, Lucy," Active said in his command voice. "That'll be all."

They heard a bustle outside, then footsteps receded down the hall.

Carnaby chuckled. "Interesting life you lead, Chief Active. Your ex-girlfriend is your office manager?"

"She came with the package," Active said. "It's fine. She's a blissfully happy married woman now."

"And pregnant again," Carnaby said. "How far along? And how many is this?"

Active scratched his temple. "Six or seven months, and number two."

"And suffering from allergies, it seems. But in April? With everything still frozen solid? When did that start?"

"How would I know?"

"Maybe it started right outside the door when she heard you might go to Anchorage to run the Troopers."

"And maybe it's none of your business. Like I said, married, blissfully happy, number two on the way."

"And what are these Naughty Monkeys she wants?"

"That's it!" Active snapped his fingers. "The boots the governor was wearing."

"Mm-hmm. Well, you and Lucy have fun with your shiny new cop shop. Where were we, now? Oh, yes, your flight-seeing expedition with the governor."

"Oh, God."

"Assuming you can resist the temptation to induct her into the Mile-High Club in the back of Cowboy's Cessna, there may be a way out of this."

"What way?"

"If history is any guide, a few days in your company will be enough for our governor to get quite enough of you. She'll move on to something else. Or someone."

"How is it a way out if she ends up hating me? The state money for my department could go up in a puff of smoke. Like that bodyguard."

Carnaby tented his fingers and beamed over them at Active, who groaned. "It's all a matter of calibration, Nathan. Turn that emotional intelligence of yours up to 'stun' and make sure you're just cooperative enough while you're with her, but not more so. Gracious but reserved, if you will."

"What the hell does that mean?"

"You'll figure it out." Carnaby leaned forward, grinned, and touched his forearm just like the governor had done. "If not, you do have her cell number."

Active slapped away Carnaby's hand. "Maybe I could be sick tomorrow and send Alan Long."

Carnaby's eyebrows shot up. "That nitwit? After what she said about him?"

"He's not a nitwit," Active said. "You just—"

"You just have to watch him," Carnaby said. "I know. We've all had guys like that. In fact, I once supervised a young trooper who jumped out of Cowboy Decker's Super Cub in mid-air. Without a parachute."

"It was not mid-air and I did not jump," Active said. "Cowboy was hovering in a high wind and I stepped out onto a snow bank."

"And dislocated your shoulder."

"A gust caught us, is all."

Carnaby waved a hand in dismissal. "The point is, the governor likes you. Play it right and you'll be fine."

He flipped open the folder and ran his finger down the schedule for the week. "See, she got in yesterday to drop the starting flag for the race and she and her kids are staying at their place here in town tonight. Like she said, the race leaders will overnight in Isignaq tomorrow, Saturday, and finish here in Chukchi the next day. She'll park her daughters with her parents while you and Cowboy will fly her and the videographer, who happens to be her son, out to watch Brad mush into Isignaq. Then, while he looks to his dogs and sets up camp for the night, the governor stays with the family of the Episcopal minister there in Isignaq. The next day, Sunday, she barnstorms a couple of the upriver villages for *muk-tuk* eating and Eskimo dancing and such, then Cowboy does a 180 and whisks her back to Chukchi in time to cheer Brad on as he leads the pack down Beach Street, after which they spend the evening celebrating his victory in a manner not appropriate for minions like ourselves to speculate upon, however tempting the prospect might be. The evening of the next day, Monday, is the mushers' banquet, where she passes out the trophies, and the morning after that she jets off to Juneau, restoring peace and tranquility to our little hamlet on the tundra."

He passed over the folder. "Until next time."

NANCY LORD

"WHAT HAPPENS WHEN YOU INCREASE AIR TEMPERATURES by several degrees?" Nancy Lord asks in her essay "The Experiment," included in her 2009 collection *Rock Water Wild*. "I've used the word *you*," she continues, "because I mean *you*, *me*, the humans who, through our activities since the beginning of the Industrial Age, have added so much carbon dioxide and other greenhouse gases to the atmosphere that temperatures have warmed by one degree Fahrenheit globally and considerably more toward the Earth's poles."

In that essay Lord focused her attention on Homer, Alaska, where she has made her home since 1973 and where she was already seeing visible evidence of climate change. In her 2011 book *Early Warming: Crisis and Response in the Climate-Changed North*, Lord extended her attention to the the rest of Alaska and northern Canada.

In the excerpt that follows, Lord travels to Shishmaref, a small Inupiaq village on Sarichef Island in the Chukchi Sea, on Alaska's north-western coast. The decline of sea ice in recent decades, combined with rising temperatures, has resulted in severe shoreline erosion threatening the survival of the village and the culture that has developed there. Since the book was written, residents have voted (again) to relocate to the mainland, but how the endeavor will be paid for remains an unanswered question. It's entirely possible that that the people living in Shishmaref will become some of America's first climate refugees, forced to abandon their village and spread out to wherever they can find homes, their community lost forever. They're unlikely to be the last to experience this fate.

As shown by this selection, when Lord approaches a topic, the result is a carefully-worded argument written with clarity and concision. Drawn to facts rather than emotions, she bases her arguments on what can be demonstrated. In exploring how climate change is actively altering the north, she combines hard science with on-the-ground reporting, telling us what is happening, what is likely to occur next, what impacts this will have on communities caught in the way of changes beyond their capacity to control, and what we might all learn from those on the front lines about preparing for the future.

Two things Lord never does in her writing are panic or point angry fingers. Every sentence in her environmental writings is calm and measured. Her presentation of facts and her explanations of how these realities are affecting all forms of life—including human—are rendered all the more powerful by her complete lack of histrionics.

She also avoids the temptation to condemn people for their behaviors. This stems in part from her character, but also, I suspect, from her background. For many years she worked in commercial fisheries, a job that involves hard labor at the origin point of an extractive industry that feeds into the global economy that is the culprit for climate change. She doesn't hesitate to include herself as part of the problem, which is why she knows that any solution will require sacrifice on her part.

Regarding her approach, Lord told me, "I consider myself an 'environmental writer,' since most of my writing seems to be related to environmental issues—that is, the relationships that people have with the natural world. Writing is my way of learning about these connections, which involve cultural matters, science, and politics. Pulling all those aspects together into a story is the ultimate goal for me. Increasingly, I try not just to witness the world's tragedies but to look for positive stories that show how we might live in a more respectful and sustainable way."

— From *Early Warming* —
WHEN A VILLAGE HAS TO MOVE: SHISHMAREF

IF THERE IS ONE PLACE IN AMERICA most identified with global warming and climate change, that place has to be Shishmaref, Alaska. The Inupiaq community struggling for its very existence has been portrayed around the world as an early victim of climate change.

The story that has been told and shown, exhaustively now, is of the Inupiaq village on a small sand island on Alaska's northwest coast, eroding from storm waves no longer blocked by sea ice, and made more vulnerable yet as the permafrost that formerly held the land together thaws. As elsewhere along Alaska's northern coasts, waves have a longer "fetch" across open water and storm surges pick up more energy. In 1997 a fall storm took 125 feet from the northern side of Shishmaref's island, dropping buildings into the sea and necessitating the move of a dozen homes as well as the National Guard Armory. Storms since have continued to erode the shoreline, and emergency seawall protections have been but a temporary "fix." The entire island is four and a third miles long and only a quarter mile wide, with the high point twenty feet above sea level. In 2002 residents voted to relocate the community and in 2006, following a study of alternative sites, voted to move to the area known as Tin Creek, on the mainland.

Shishmaref is not alone in its exigency. A Government Accountability Office report from 2003 identified 184 of the 213 villages in Alaska as being affected by erosion and flooding, and the situation has only worsened since. Shishmaref is one of six villages on the "immediate action" list. It is also the one that has been most public about its situation and need.

Tony Weyiouanna, the principal architect of Shishmaref's public campaign, had brought me to Tin Creek to take a look at what he hoped—if the soil and other studies checked out—would be the new village location. He snugged the skiff up against the bank, and Fannie, his wife, jumped out with an anchor to secure us to shore. Weyiouanna, a kind man with a bushy mustache and the beginnings of gray in his dark hair, was born in Shishmaref and has lived there all his life, except for some time at college and in Nome. Since the late 1980s he's been a tireless advocate for relocating the village to higher ground—not because he or anyone wants to move, but because they know they must. From 2001 to 2007 much of his time as the village's transportation planner was devoted to an organization called the Shishmaref Erosion and Relocation Coalition, in which role he used his considerable computer, communication, and personal skills to bring Shishmaref to the world's attention.

But Weyiouanna was tired. It had been a long effort, and it seemed to him now that the local people were losing control. More state and federal agencies than he could count were involved in multiple layers of studies and planning, and it was not at all clear how or when a move would actually occur, whether the preferred site would even be approved, and how any of it would be paid for.

"We seem to be going backward," Weyiouanna had told me at his house earlier in the day, when I'd met him and Fannie for the first time. He'd been sitting at the kitchen table and sharpening ulus while Fannie set out a pile of sourdough pancakes and the younger members of the Weyiouanna household—they have four teenagers—drifted in and out. They'd all gotten home from their camp on the mainland just hours earlier, and the Ziploc bags of salmonberries they'd gathered—gallons of them—were piled in the entry, ready for the freezer. (Salmonberry is the local name for *Rubus chamaemorus*, otherwise known as cloudberry and, in Inupiaq, *aqpik*. It's the second-most important traditional subsistence resource in Shishmaref, after the bearded seal.) Weyiouanna is also an artist, and some of his whalebone carvings looked down at us from a high shelf.

Weyiouanna searched the kitchen for the right stone for his ulu sharpening, then told me that, although he'd given up the transportation planning job and his lead role with the coalition for a part-time position as the village's grant writer, he couldn't turn his back on the dire situation, the future of his family and community. It was just very frustrating to have so many entities involved in such a confusing and uncoordinated way and so little progress, and now the media had lost interest and was on to other, fresher stories. Senator Ted Stevens, so successful at delivering federal funds to Alaska's villages, had lost his seat, and who knew how that was going to play out?

Now, at Tin Creek, we disembarked onto tundra lit with the feathery heads of cotton grass, and Fannie and her niece Brenda set out with berry buckets. Weyiouanna and I started uphill so I could get a better view and sense of the country that might be Shishmaref's new home. The tundra growth was wound tight to the ground and into hilly tussocks, inter-twined with grasses, willows, Labrador tea, lichens, gemlike blueberries we paused to pick and eat, and an occasional single gold *aqpik* berry. Despite the advancing season, the landscape was still green, with leaves just beginning to suggest the yellows and reds of autumn. We staggered over the dry, prickly tussocks as they twisted and toppled under our feet, and I thought of what a biologist in Nome had told me—that the tundra surface was drier than usual, not for a lack of rain but because, as the "active layer" of ground deepened over thawing permafrost, there was more soil for the moisture to soak into.

"What's that dark thing?" Weyiouanna pointed toward the creek and a patch of willows, upstream from the boat and from where Fannie and Brenda were leaning over their yellow berry buckets.

I raised my binoculars. A caribou with smallish antlers was staring back at us.

Weyiouanna took his own look. "This is a closed area," he said, as though he wished it were not and he could go get the rifle from the boat. Caribou are a major subsistence food for his family and most others in Shishmaref. While bearded seals, the village's main source of protein, are threatened by the loss of sea ice, caribou, too, are having a time of it as snow conditions and vegetation change with the climate. Here on the Seward Peninsula, the now treeless expanse of tundra is expected to transition into spruce and deciduous forest within the next hundred years. A forested landscape would no longer support certain species, like caribou. Winter icing, elsewhere in the north, has already collapsed some caribou populations by blocking their access to nutritious lichens, and warming is also increasing the numbers of biting insects that drive caribou to exhaustion.

As we continued to wind our way uphill, we began to see over the land beyond the creek, to the water that was the lagoon and then across the twelve miles that separated us from the chain of barrier islands and Shishmaref. The islands out there are true barrier islands, long and nar-row and almost continuous, with a few breaks that open to the Chukchi Sea. They're made out of sand and, like all barrier islands, are hugely dynamic. That is, they're constantly being reworked by wind and waves.

Although the mechanics of barrier island origins are still debated, their development is linked to the end of the last ice age; when the glaciers stopped melting and the rapid rise in sea level slowed, the islands formed. Scientists note that rising sea level causes existing islands to move shoreward, typically by a process called "rolling over," when waves top an island and carry sand to the lagoon side.

The mirage effect over the water caused the islands to lift in the distance, and the village of Shishmaref looked like a shimmering line of tiny, boxy shapes, minimalist in such a massive landscape. What a crazy place to build a community, was all I could think. Who in his right mind would ever put six hundred people and all their modern infrastructure on a sandbar?

No one, of course, had made any such intentional choice. One thing led to another, until we have today's situation. Although Shishmaref's people claim four thousand years of habitation on the island (known as Kigiktaq—"island"—before explorer Otto von Kotzebue, working for the Russians, came along in 1816 and began renaming places), that habitation was nomadic and seasonal. Seals and other marine resources were, then as now, a mainstay of the Inupiaq food supply and culture. Eventually, because of the natural harbor in the shelter of the island, Shishmaref became a supply center for gold mining activities. A post office was established in 1901. Then came the school, the Lutheran church (on the highest ground in the center of town), the electrical system and fuel to run it, the government housing, and on, and on. Like so many other coastal places in Alaska, the location made it easily accessed by barges for unloading all the construction materials and fuel and now packaged foods and TV sets that barges bring.

And always, there was erosion—"natural," if you will, and increasingly related to the reduction in sea ice and the thaw of permafrost. For more than three decades now, as more and more infrastructure was piled onto the sand, there's been talk of moving. In 1974, the estimated cost of relocating the community to the mainland was $1 million. In 2006, an Army Corps of Engineers study set the estimated cost of moving at $179 million. Anyone can do the math; for 142 households, that's more than $1 million each. Who's going to pay?

The alternatives are scarcely less costly. The Corps estimated that the village could be "colocated" to either Nome or Kotzebue for about $93 million. To stay in place on the island but shield it with seawalls, at least for a while—$109 million.

Weyiouanna and I sat on the hummocky tundra while he pointed in one direction and another. We were somewhere on the grounds of the potential relocation site, the one selected by the community after a reconnaissance study had evaluated such things as space requirements, room for growth, and access to the sea. Over the hill lay Goose Creek, an important area for waterfowl hunting and the collection of greens, and beyond that rose the Serpentine Mountains, above the river where the Weyiouannas and other Shishmaref families have their hunting and berrypicking camps.

Since spring, a road study had been underway, drilling into the tundra to test the underlying materials and ice depth to determine the best route as well as likely development costs. The road—to cover about twenty miles—would go from the edge of Shishmaref Inlet across village corporation land and part of the Bering Land Bridge National Preserve (perhaps the least visited unit of our national park system) to the granitic Ear Mountain, from which rock and gravel needed for construction would be mined. The village site would lie partway along the route, approximately where we sat. Just the exploratory work on the road was costing some millions in federal highway funds, and the road itself was expected to be in excess of $30 million. Other studies were clocking wind speeds and directions at a potential airport location, to determine where a runway might be built and whether a cross-runway would also be necessary.

The tundra, the sky, the skipping-by small birds and the flocks of ducks over the river, the deep quiet, the sweet smell of the crushed plants beneath us—it was hard for me to sit in such a place and to anticipate a construction zone or a village. My mind stuck on the current village, with its poorly built government houses, four-wheelers parked by the post office, children playing, meat and fish hanging, smell of sewage, and steady drone of the power plant. But the new village would be built with a plan, and that plan would include new technologies and concepts of sustainability.

Weyiouanna talked, and it was clear he held a particular, perhaps even utopian, vision in his own mind. In the new village, houses would not be crowded on top of one another, and they would be built for energy efficiency. They would have plumbing and pump-out sewage tanks instead of water barrels and "honey buckets." There would still be a need for fuel tanks and fuel, but at least some of the electricity would come from wind or other renewable sources. There would be a new clinic and new school building. The village, in a safe and permanent place, might become a service hub for the rest of the region, might build an economy from that. Most of all, in Weyiouanna's vision, Shishmaref's people would be together and would still have access to their traditional lands and resources. Without the constant worry of living on a disappearing island, and with room to grow, young people and their families would stay in the community, would embrace and carry on the culture. Those who had left would want to return.

"I want us to use as little fossil fuel as we can," Weyiouanna said. He had told me earlier that both gasoline and fuel oil were presently priced, in Shishmaref, at $7.50 per gallon. "Subsistence is an important part of our lives—we don't have an economic base. It's important that, in our planning, we ask, 'How can we be more efficient in using resources?'" The ongoing studies were moving the project forward, however slowly. They would help identify the best, cheapest, most sustainable way to do the job. As the village grant writer, Weyiouanna was doing what he could, including applying for funds for small-scale projects, some wind and solar.

Below us, Fannie and Brenda were still picking, just feet apart, and I imagined they were talking together, too, the way that women do, everywhere, when working with their hands. Beyond them, sunlight glinted from the boat's windshield.

Shishmaref can show the way, Weyiouanna stressed. Shishmaref's relocation should be seen as a demonstration project to show how communities and government agencies can work together to both respect the cultures and needs of the relocating communities and be cost-effective. He didn't say it, but Weyiouanna's implication was clear: Shishmaref's climate-induced need to move was only among the first of the flood to come.

I LOOKED OUT AT THE OCEAN AND THOUGHT ABOUT ELEVATION. The country all around us was tundra plain, none of it along the coast very high. Ear Mountain, where the rock and gravel would come from, rose to twenty-three hundred feet, but the Tin Creek site where we sat was not at all high—perhaps something more than a hundred feet. I remembered maps I'd seen of different sea level rise scenarios; with more global warming and more glacial and ice cap melt, those graphic depictions showed the coast of western Alaska being inundated for miles inland. Most villages, built for good reasons by the sea and along rivers, would be flooded out.

The sun was losing some of its heat as Weyiouanna and I stumbled our way back over the tussocks to the creek, stopping for handfuls of blueberries along the way. This had not been a great berrying spot, but Fannie and Brenda had collected enough blueberries that Brenda was happily looking forward to adding hers to pancakes.

We motored back out the creek, racing with ducks, past a pair of sandhill cranes posing on the tundra like something from a Japanese print. We had another stop to make, at the next creek over, where sour docks grew in plenty.

Goose Creek, when we arrived, appeared to be well named. The banks of the creek and the adjacent lowlands were littered with goose poop and feathers, and flocks flew over us in scrawling lines. After anchoring the boat, we took pillowcases and walked away from the creek, across dried mud imprinted with caribou hoof prints, past scatters of Arctic daisies and Jacob's ladder, around thick stands of marsh fleabane and their dense yellow flowers turning to woolly cotton balls. I lingered behind, taking photos, while the other three beelined for the nearest reddish field.

Sour dock (*Rumex arcticus*), a member of the buckwheat family, grows on a tall red stalk with red bracts surrounding the small, dense flowers. The stalks, higher than anything else in the meadow, were easy to spot, but it was the arrow-shaped leaves at their bases we had come to pick. Cooked like spinach, they're very high in vitamins. The Inupiat traditionally fermented them with seal oil, often adding berries, and relied on them as a vegetable all winter long. Today, still an important food source, they're chopped and cooked, then frozen in Ziplocs.

This was the first Weyiouanna sour dock gathering of the year, and Fannie was unhappy to find the leaves already splotching into red. I joined in the picking, searching out the younger and greener leaves, pausing to sample a leaf. It tasted okay—maybe a little tough, a little sour. I wouldn't want to eat a salad bowl of raw greens, but I imagined that, cooked up and seasoned, they'd be as tasty as any spinach or kale. Fannie told me she usually added some sugar to them just before serving.

Each of us lost in thought, we worked from patch to patch, along a bank, past a slough spilling with ducks. We picked for more than an hour, through the sea of red, while the sun lowered into the kind of Arctic sidelight that brings everything green into fresh brilliance. Our pillowcases fattened. I've always liked gathering food (as opposed to either growing or purchasing it), with the sense of the earth (or the sea) freely providing, the so-clear connections among soil, sunlight, water, life, and health. I like, even love, the repetitions of motion and Zen-like state that softens the mind. Most of us don't live that way anymore, but surely there's something to learn from those who do, and value in maintaining their ability to do that, in the places they know and care for. In Alaska, we call it subsistence, a word wrought now with political meaning and conflicts over rights to resources, a word that reduces a way of life to something that sounds deprived.

All the rest of the summer and fall, back home and everywhere else I traveled, reddish dock plants I'd never noticed before would spring to my sight from meadows and roadsides. They reminded me of Shishmaref, Tin and Goose Creeks, the faces of people who welcomed me into their homes and homeplaces, cultural values we should hope to maintain.

When the pillowcases were full enough, we lugged them back to the boat and sat on the boat's benches to share the snack foods we'd brought along. My foods were a three-ounce bag of beef jerky from the Shishmaref store ($10.99), a green apple I'd carried from home (that is, from the Homer Safeway), and a liter bottle of water from the Shishmaref store ($3.81). My hosts pulled from their ice chest a dish of chopped bearded seal—some dark meat, some bits of intestine—soaked in seal oil, a spread of silver salmon to put on Pilot crackers, chopped sour dock also packed in seal oil, *agutak* or "Eskimo ice cream" of whipped caribou fat and seal oil, Spam, and store-bought cookies. I sampled the seal meat, sour dock, and *agutak*; the distinctive taste of seal oil is something few Westerners (myself included) take to, though it's easy to understand why it's been such a critical preservative and energy-packed food in northern cultures.

I was sorry that none of the Weyiouanna teenagers had come along with us. They were, Weyiouanna told me, having pizza that night at home. And salmonberries. Fannie said she had no sooner put the berries into the freezer than they were taking some out again.

WHEN I'D FIRST ARRIVED IN SHISHMAREF, I'd walked through the town to orient myself: from the Emergency Services building where visitors stay ($125 per night, no running water, a sign in the kitchen that reads *the sink is out of order—use the window*) to the Lutheran church and its cemetery, past homes surrounded by the snow machines and four-wheelers that are the tools of modern travel and subsistence, around the occasional chained dog and the odiferous bins into which "honey buckets" were emptied. The "streets" were more like dirt trails, and more sand than dirt—a fine sand at that, as fine as pastry flour. On the lagoon side of the island, viewed across open tundra, dozens of skiffs rode at anchor. It was early morning, and there weren't many people about, but everyone I met was genuinely friendly, recognizing me as a visitor and asking who I was.

I turned next to face north, to confront the Chukchi Sea, wild with frothing whitecaps even on a windless day. From the abrupt end of a sand street, I looked across part of the new seawall—giant rock boulders I'd heard had been barged from a quarry near Sand Point in the Shumagin Islands, about eight hundred miles away—at the huge yellow bucket top of a heavy-equipment excavator working on a section farther along the beach. This was phase two of the federally funded work—750 feet of new revetment being added to the 600 feet completed the previous year behind the school and teacher housing, close to the community's huge diesel tanks and electric generators. Buildings, including one of the village's two stores and its fuel tanks, lay just feet away from the back of the new seawall. I walked to the gap between the two seawalls and over some rocks to the beach. There, the remains of some earlier, less successful armoring looked pathetically unsubstantial: bunches of rocks sunk into the beach and scattered, hunks of twisted metal, shreds of fabric that had once held rocks and sand. None of that earlier effort, clearly, had withstood for long the force of storm-driven waves.

I walked past the big blue school—by far the largest building in town, and a stone's throw from the sea—to where the phase one seawall ended; the shoreline there was badly eroded, with the remains of buildings and trash scattered over the beach. The main town infrastructure ended, and

the bluff farther west was lined with simple tent and driftwood structures and drying racks—the places where people landed and processed
their seals and fish, all right at the edge.

The next two seawall phases, under design, would, in part, help protect the washeteria and its sewage lagoon farther to the east. But there
was no funding, as yet, for that substantial investment, some $20 million.

Besides cost, the problem with seawalls is that they don't really prevent erosion; they relocate it. I know enough about coastal erosion processes and seawalls to know that wave energy will erode downward in
front of a seawall, leaving no beach for sand on which to subsequently
rebuild, and will deflect to the sides of a seawall—into the gaps I was
looking at there in Shishmaref. I had personal experience. At my fish-
camp on Cook Inlet, for years every summer my partner, Ken, and I,
by hand, reinforced and added to barriers in front of the cabin that in
1972 had been built well back from the beach; the beach got steeper,
the erosion increased on either side, and at last, one fall after we'd left,
waves breached our barriers and tore them—concrete and rebar, bolted
timbers and the side of an old boat, heavy rocks and sandbags—apart.
We lost the cabin. And in Homer, a professionally engineered seawall
built to protect a city road and neighborhood failed immediately, was
repaired and reinforced, and still requires constant maintenance.

THE DAY FOLLOWING OUR BOAT TRIP, in the basement of the Lutheran
church, I sat in on a meeting of the Shishmaref Erosion and Relocation
Coalition. Thirteen members—drawn from the village (tribal) council,
the separate city council, and the Native corporation—sat around a couple of long tables to conduct their regular business—approving minutes,
reviewing a profit and loss statement, and planning for visits from government agencies. Since Weyiouanna had resigned as the transportation
planner, Brice Eningowuk had taken over that post and, along with it,
served as staff to the relocation committee.

Eningowuk is a handsome young man with army-short hair, rectangular glasses, and a ready smile. He did in fact do a stint in the army,
between enrollments in the University of Alaska, and he was still working on a college degree in rural development. He'd told me earlier that
relocation planning was a big part of his job, but he had other duties
and wasn't giving it the same emphasis that Weyiouanna had. He was,

however, overseeing a new study that was, again—even as all that work was being done over at the Tin Creek site—considering alternatives. The new study would come up with three locations, including the option of keeping Shishmaref right where it was, only with more protection. There were three criteria for the site selection: economic sustainability, cultural sustainability, and cost-effectiveness.

When I'd seen Eningowuk in his office, he'd pulled from his shelf the June 2009 Government Accountability Office report "Alaska Native Villages: Limited Progress Has Been Made on Relocating Villages Threatened by Flooding and Erosion." The GAO report noted that "federal disaster programs have provided limited assistance and no comprehensive relocation program exists" and that "without a lead federal entity to prioritize and coordinate assistance, individual agency efforts may not adequately address the growing threat." It went on to note a number of structural problems that prevent the federal government from being more responsive. For example, cost-effectiveness criteria are a problem when the value of infrastructure in need of protection is less than the cost of proposed erosion and flood control projects. And, while there's funding to respond to disasters, there's no program to help villages avoid disaster. This report identified thirty-one "imminently threatened" Alaska villages and twelve that were at least exploring relocation options. Shishmaref was one of four villages "likely to move all at once, as soon as possible" both because of its immediate peril and because its options for a gradual move were limited. Then there was this: Some "officials" feared that building new seawalls could slow the momentum toward relocating by creating a false sense of safety.

Eningowuk was clear himself about the need for Shishmaref to relocate. He showed me an aerial photograph of the island. "It looks like there's still a lot of room, but all this space"—he pointed to the green tundra on the south side of the island—"can't be developed because it's in the airport's clearance zone." And besides, when there were storm surges, the water came up on that side and flooded the area. Shishmaref was slated to get twenty-one new homes, but there was nowhere to put them. The newer houses in town—the ones on the old airstrip, which was abandoned when the island got too narrow—were set up to be plumbed, if they ever got water and sewer connections or were moved to a place that had them. Those houses had external septic tanks right now, so that "honey buckets" weren't necessary, but the tanks needed to be heated in winter, and people couldn't afford the cost.

Another major problem on the island was the lack of freshwater. Eningowuk had pointed to the map again—a rectangular "pond" on the east side of the island. It was just a hole in the ground with a visible white liner, and it collected rain and snowmelt. Aside from the rainwater that people collected from their roofs, that was the only source of freshwater on the island. In winter, the only water came from a tank filled before freeze-up, or from snow and ice melted by individuals. Running water and flush toilets weren't an option for the island, even if they were afford-able, because there simply wasn't the water.

And then there were drainage issues. The snowmelt used to drain, but now the seawalls were higher than the land and dammed it.

My head had begun to hurt from this litany of what seemed insur-mountable problems. I asked Eningowuk what he wanted to happen.

"Personally, I hope we relocate to the mainland, someplace close enough to the ocean, and within the next ten years. I'm supposed to be planning this all out, but I'm not the decision maker." He flashed his smile. "I hope we move a lot sooner than ten years."

And what would he want people outside of Shishmaref to know?

"People have the misconception we should do this on our own. We need help, just like the people of Louisiana."

I wasn't sure that, after Katrina, the people of Louisiana felt that they'd gotten very much, or the right kind, or cost-effective help. But I didn't say that.

At the school, which would open its doors to students in another week, I avoided touching anything near the *wet paint* signs. Science teacher Ken Stenek, wearing shorts, met me in his classroom and showed me on his computer the plant and animal encyclopedia he and his stu-dents had begun. The encyclopedia contains photos and science infor-mation along with community information that includes the Inupiaq name, local observations, and the role (often as food) in the culture. Stenek, who is married to a local woman and has small children, is one of the few non-Inupiat to live full-time in the village. For ten years, he'd watched the community grapple with change; he'd watched four seawalls be constructed and the first, made of sandbags, deconstruct. He'd seen permafrost thaw and sand crumble, and storms blow in over the open ocean. He'd seen ice thin and weaken. "This year was a good ice year," he told me, "but the two before that were very poor." Three years ago a young man fell through the ice and died, in a place that had never been a problem before.

There had not been a major storm since 2005, but Stenek was keeping an eye on a typhoon that had just killed dozens of people in Southeast Asia and required the evacuation of millions; its waves had been twenty-six feet high. The Chukchi Sea, he said, is known as "the graveyard of the typhoons," and the remnants of that storm could hit Shishmaref in another month.

Stenek taught his students, to the degree he could, about global warming and climate change. He was hampered by the school district standards, which were prescriptive about what students needed to learn. He worked it in, though. He taught about energy transfer and the albedo effect of ice, and he'd had the kids calculate the carbon footprint for the village. (The electric generators burn one hundred thousand gallons of diesel per year, adding six hundred thousand pounds of carbon to the atmosphere.) In 2007 he'd contributed an article to the magazine *Connect*, for teachers of science and math, called "Global Climate Change: What to Teach and When." In that, he wrote about the media people who descended on Shishmaref as the "poster child" of global warming and who asked young people about climate change as though they were experts on it. He'd given a lot of thought about how to teach what was not required but relevant to student lives, appropriate for each age group, and how to do that without either imposing a political agenda or creating panic. He believed in empowering our future citizens, wherever they may live, to help solve a global problem.

I asked, what did his students, now, think about the problem? Did they engage with it? Were they troubled?

"It's just something they live with," Stenek said. "If you ask a kid here, 'what's global warming?' he'll probably say, 'erosion.' I'm just trying to help them get the facts straight. A lot of it is correcting information they hear."

In Shishmaref, as elsewhere, most people had heard from the media about global warming causing higher tides. But that's not Shishmaref's immediate problem. The Arctic has small tidal ranges, and if there's a little more water—or water volume—out there to rise and fall, that doesn't make a huge difference. Stenek's effort goes into helping his students understand how storm surges not blocked by ice erode a coastline and how thawing permafrost loosens the sand.

ONE ALTERNATIVE THE PEOPLE OF SHISHMAREF had turned down unambiguously was "colocation"—that is, moving the community to another, established one. The likely places analyzed by the Corps of Engineers were Nome and Kotzebue, both regional centers near Shishmaref, both with much larger and mixed populations. "That's not something we want to do," Brice Eningowuk had told me, emphatically. "Everyone here is family."

Shishmaref residents are certainly aware of the example of the King Islanders. King Island, a steep volcanic island in the Bering Sea, about eighty-five miles northwest of Nome, was inhabited by Inupiaq Eskimos for at least a thousand years. As a winter home built along cliffs, it was surrounded by the biological richness of the Bering Sea—seals, walrus, fish, crabs, seabirds. In summer, the people typically migrated by boat to the mainland for different hunting, fishing, and gathering opportunities, and to trade. In 1959 the Bureau of Indian Affairs closed down the school, and the people were forced to move to Nome full-time. There, they lived on the south end of town in substandard housing and suffered economic and social ills along with outright discrimination. Some reversed the old migration pattern—for years, when school was out, spending some of the summer on the island.

Non-Native friends in Nome have told me that when they were growing up there the worst thing a person could be called was "a K-I-er" and that young people today still used the expression in derogatory name-calling. The community, described by outsiders as "clannish," struggles to maintain an identity that lives, in its heritage and heart, elsewhere.

We would not, in America in this day and age, either mandate moves or leave migrants and refugees entirely to their own devices, but the King Island experience lingers in people's memories and adds to their fears.

WHAT DO I THINK WILL HAPPEN TO SHISHMAREF? Many people I spoke with, including some in Shishmaref, told me that, despite all the best intentions and all the desire and effort, they don't expect that the community will actually move. The cost is too great, the impediments too many. The most likely scenario, I believe, is that planning and studies will continue, but that the residents of Shishmaref will get tired of waiting, the anxiety that comes with every storm, and doing without water and sewer and an adequate clinic—infrastructure they would have if they knew they were staying, or if they were building in a new place. I expect that they'll gradually move away—the young people who might make a start elsewhere, and family by family—scattering to other villages, to Nome and Kotzebue, to Anchorage, as they already have begun to do, until only the most determined remain. Some—the most committed to a traditional life—might well move to the mainland and "live out," as some people always have, and others might still return seasonally, as the King Islanders did to their island for years after their move to Nome. But the village itself will eventually be gone, dropped into the sea, and the community bonds and culture that flourished in its unique fashion for so very long will be gone with it.

When I was first beginning to think about the consequences of global warming and climate change for Alaska's villages, a friend said to me, "For these communities that are already stressed, climate change will either be the glue that will help hold them together, or it will be the straw that finally breaks them."

The same thing could be said for the rest of us, all of us who will, individually and collectively, either find new ways of living that sustain ourselves and the earth as we know it, or who will not.

Shishmaref is just the beginning.

In Shishmaref, so many people I'd met had looked me directly in the eyes and asked, "How do you like it here?" or "What do you think of Shishmaref?" or "What do you think of us?" I had thought at the time it was a way of trying to assess me, but also an expression of pride in who they were, and also, perhaps, a small show of insecurity. Do we matter? Are we important enough to save? Is anyone going to help?

PAUL GRECI

B REATHING NEW LIFE INTO A WELL-WORN LITERARY GENRE isn't an easy job, but it's one that Paul Greci accomplished with his debut novel, *Surviving Bear Island*. In this case it's the castaway story, a plot device dating back to oral mythology and popularized in modern times by Daniel DaFoe's *Robinson Crusoe*.

Despite being a novelistic cliché, it makes perfect sense to set such a story in Alaska, with its thousands of mostly uninhabited islands and tens of thousands of miles of largely remote coastline. It's an easy place to get marooned, as many people have learned, and not always with happy results.

In this young adult novel, which was a 2015 Junior Library Selection, Greci introduces readers to Tom Parker, a young teenager kayaking with his father near the mouth of Prince William Sound. Both are swamped by a large wave, and Tom finds himself washed ashore on Bear Island, far from any human settlements.

Unable to locate his father, Tom decides to find his own way to a spot on the island where the two had previously camped in hopes of rendezvousing with him there. Along the way he encounters bears and other wildlife, is exposed to rapidly deteriorating late fall weather conditions, and has to feed himself. Meanwhile he ponders his relationship with his widowed father, and recalls the teachings of both his dad and his late mother, a songwriter who conveyed lessons through lyrics.

Greci brings considerable personal experience to the story, helping to make it believable. He said, "I have spent twenty plus years sea kayaking in Prince William Sound, doing trips ranging from one to nine weeks, both solo and with friends. A few of the main character's experiences are taken directly from things that happened to me, and the rest are from me applying my imagination to my experiences and asking a lot of 'what if' questions."

He also knows kids well, having worked as a teacher for more than two decades, and the first person narrative provided by Tom in this story reflects his lengthy interactions with children's thought processes. Physically stuck on an island, and left with no one but himself to converse with, Tom struggles with his insecurities, his failure to emotionally connect fully with either of his parents, and the limits of his own abilities at meeting his needs to survive.

Greci uses the storytelling itself to present the landscape Tom finds himself in. Rather than offering extended descriptive passages that might lose young readers, Greci works the visual imagery into the narrative as Tom contends with it, making the island itself the only other major character in the book.

Originally from Indiana, Greci was employed seasonally in Alaska for several summers during the 1980s, working first on the Kenai Peninsula where, he told me, "I fell in love with the landscape, wide-open-spaces, and wilderness of Alaska." Later jobs took him to the Togiak and the Arctic National Wildlife Refuges. He moved to Fairbanks permanently in 1990.

As an educator, Greci was hoping with this book to reach children at a time when they are at risk of abandoning reading, a common affliction among junior high kids. By placing Tom in that age group, subjecting him to physical and emotional challenges beyond what most kids encounter, and exploring Tom's reactions and efforts as he slowly takes control of his destiny, Greci gives young readers someone they can identify with. He meets his intended audience on their level and then lifts them above it, the mark of any skilled teacher.

In this excerpt, Tom starts learning to read the weather on Bear Island, encounters wildlife, and attempts to catch fish with a hand-fashioned gaff.

— From *Surviving Bear Island* —

THE NEXT DAY GRAY PUFFY CLOUDS scudded across a blue sky. No rain, but the northerly breeze crawled up my sleeves and down my neck. Cold. Just plain cold.

But I'd noticed something. Rain clouds came from the south and stayed until a wind from the north blew them away.

Patterns. Weather patterns. Back in Fairbanks, who cared if it was forty below in the winter when you had a warm house to hang out in or all the right clothes to go outside if you wanted to? You didn't really need to deal with the weather unless you lived in it.

You only needed to pay attention to the things that were threatening you. I mean sure, you paid attention to other things, but you didn't have to.

Out here, I needed to pay attention to everything. Like where I put my feet so I didn't fall. Was the hook secure on my gaff? Was a bear following me? Did I have enough firewood to at least last the night? Little mistakes could turn into big mistakes. Like my dad said, when you're alone in the wilderness, everything is magnified.

I headed for the creek, ready to try my new gaff. At my kitchen, the coals from my cook fire had been scooped out and scattered. A pile of bear scat dotted with blueberries crowded the tree I'd slept under that first night.

We are all potentially food for something else.

Okay, okay, I thought. All part of the cycle. Everything is made of recycled nutrients. Berries, bears, people. And once you're dead, you're just a pile of nutrients.

Like, if I died out here, what happened to my body wouldn't matter. Bears would chew on me. Gulls would peck my eyes out. Bugs would gnaw on me. Flies would lay their eggs. They'd hatch, and the maggots would feed.

I kicked the bear scat out from under the tree. This was still my kitchen. I wouldn't turn into bear food—not without a fight.

I stopped to look and listen, then stepped out of the forest, squatted by the stream channel and drank.

I forded the first two channels, then walked across the gravel bar to the main channel, anxious to pull a struggling salmon from the stream. I scanned the water for signs of movement. For swaying dorsal fins.

But all I saw was empty water. I squinted at the channel, like if I looked hard enough, they'd magically appear.

"Where are they?" I said.

I glanced upstream. I wanted to fish out in the open. Where I could see. I didn't want to go up the creek, and be closed in by trees and brush. But there had to be some fish up there. That's where they spawn. But there had to be bears, too.

A cramp ran through my abdomen. I took a step upstream. My chest felt raw. Like I was breathing in tiny fragments of glass. The next couple lines of my mom's song about leaving the yard ran through my head.

It might be scary, especially at the start.
You've gotta take that step. You've gotta have some heart.

Where the gravel bar ended and the channels came together, the water ran deep. I backtracked a ways, crossed the side channel and followed it up to the same spot on the stream bank. In the beach grass I saw the rotting remains of bear-killed salmon.

Make noise to let the bears know you are there, especially if you can't see very far. The last thing you want to do is surprise a bear in a tight spot.

"Hey bear! Hey bear!" I called as I continued upstream, using the same phrase my dad used.

The beach grass ended and I entered the forest. The rush of the water seemed louder, echoing off the trees. My mom's lyrics about having heart kept popping into my head.

I'd taken like ten steps up the creek and was ducking under a fallen tree, when I heard a big splash. I jumped backwards, the back of my head slammed into the tree and I fell on my face. My teeth dug into the wounds in my mouth, and I tasted blood.

I rose to my knees.

"Hey bear! Hey bear!"

I stood up and rubbed the back of my head and spit bloody saliva. If a dead tree could take me out, I really didn't stand a chance against a bear.

There were no bears to be seen, but I made out the shape of a fish at the bottom of a deep pool. I raised the gaff and slammed it into the water but missed the fish, which moved but stayed in the pool. I nosed the gaff into the water and tried to ease the hook under the fish and pull, but the fish kept evading me.

A steady ache settled into the back of my head. I spit more bloody saliva, rinsed my mouth with creek water, and kept crawling over and under downed trees, bashing through brush, and shouting "hey bear," hoping to find a better spot.

I rounded a bend, and a flurry of movement burst upwards. My heart jumped to my throat as a bald eagle took flight from the bank.

I just assumed every surprise movement was a bear. I mean, how could I not? I wanted to be ready. But why did I have to jump backwards? And why did my heart have to beat so hard? Could I teach myself to relax?

To be alert but calm?

Well, I had the alert part down. I was like one of those smoke detectors that beeped when you boiled water. We had one of those. The fire department gave it to us. It was supposed to be really good. After a couple of days my dad took the battery out of it because we couldn't boil water without it beeping.

I rounded another bend. In water about four feet deep, half a dozen salmon, all facing upstream, sat in the bottom of the pool. The water ran shallow over small rocks where it flowed into the pool from upstream.

One fish sprang forward and powered over the rocky area, then disappeared upstream.

Perfect, I thought. Fish runs over shallows and I snag it like a bear.

So I waited, crouched by the shallow spot, ready to gaff the next fish to attempt the run.

I don't know how long I waited, maybe five minutes, and none of those fish moved. My fingers were going numb, so I rubbed my hands together. I didn't want to put my gloves on and get them all slimy if I gaffed a fish and had to grab it.

So, I just kept waiting, rubbing my hands, wiggling my toes because they were getting cold too.

"Come on, fish," I said softly. "You know you want to try it."

Still, no fish.

How long would a bear wait for a fish? A bear might not wait. A bear might just go into the water and try. Stick its head under and go for a fish.

Think like a bear, I thought. I knew I wasn't gonna dive in, but maybe I could get one in the deep water. This water wasn't quite as deep as the pool downstream where I'd bashed my head.

So I moved to the side of the pool. I focused on the closest fish, raised the gaff parallel to the water and swung it down. The fish scrambled, four of the five disappearing downstream, the fifth jetting up through the rocky area.

"I just can't win! I gotta catch a fish!"

Patience. Remember what you do and don't have control over.

"Shut up," I shouted. "Just shut up!"

I have control over how I act, not over how the fish act. They're trying to survive, too. But I needed one. At least one. If I didn't eat something besides berries soon, my belly button would be touching my backbone.

Okay. So the gaff only works when the fish are close to the surface. Yeah, I'd learned that, twice now. But to not try was worse than trying and failing. But I couldn't just try the same stupid thing over and over.

You can't learn nothin' if you don't leave the yard.

I glanced upstream. There had to be another shallow spot up there. A spot to snag a salmon.

I climbed over the rocks and continued upstream. The brush was thicker. In a couple of spots I had to part it with my hands like I was swimming the breast-stroke. And everything was damp, and the water started working its way up my sleeves. I tried cinching my cuffs down on my raincoat, but the Velcro kept loosening up on its own.

And the creek was a narrow, deep channel. I just hoped it'd spread out again.

I heard a branch snap, and this time I didn't jump out of my boots or slam my head against any hard objects but just stopped and looked.

A wall of black fur disappeared into the brush in front of me. I stared at the spot. I wanted to keep going upstream. I had to eat, but didn't want to be eaten.

I kicked at the moss covering a log until it came free, then stomped on it. Then I saw movement on the other side of the creek, branches waving in the wind, but there was no breeze. More black fur, then a bear was at the edge of the creek. A small bear, a cub.

I took a step back.

The cub lapped some water from the creek, its nose resting on the surface. It was cute, made you want to sit down and play with it, but I knew it was a death trap. Mothers protected their cubs.

I turned around and picked my way downstream, glancing over my shoulder every couple of steps. Alert but calm, I thought. I didn't freak out and do something stupid. I was starting to really get this. If you didn't threaten something, or act like you were super nervous, then whatever else was around mellowed out too.

I broke out of the forest and walked along the stream bank through the beach grass, relieved to be out in the open. I'd rather starve than get attacked by a bear.

If I had to eat berries, I'd eat berries. I had to eat something. The more energy I spent looking for food, the hungrier I'd get. I'd just spent a few hours crawling up that creek and had nothing to show for it, except I'd learned that my gaff only worked if the fish were close to the surface and that being calm is a good thing. And yeah, I'd left the yard and learned I had to keep leaving the yard.

I didn't have time to learn things the slow way, the way Mom said she'd become a better guitar player and writer. Slow and steady. That was fine if you weren't trying to survive. Sure, I'd concentrate on gaffing a fish if I found some, but I couldn't spend weeks figuring out where they were.

The creek flared to the right and the beach grass grew taller—neck high. I took a breath and reminded myself to be alert but calm. I took another step and a faint rustling invaded my ears. Then I saw white, and more white, and some gray. And I relaxed and just stood there. And that was my first mistake. Not looking where I was going as I backed up was my second.

A hiss like no other hiss I'd ever heard invaded my ears. Then this prehistoric beast was stretching its neck toward me, and flapping the biggest wings I'd ever seen. When I saw its bill was open and it wasn't stopping I took a couple big steps backward to avoid being pierced or bitten or whatever this thing was planning on doing. Behind it I glimpsed three or four more just like it, only more gray than white, before I went down.

Yeah, I caught my heel on something and landed flat on my back with my head in the creek. Two thumps on my chest and the monster swan was on top of me with its hissing bill descending toward my face. I turned and felt the water invade my mouth as my head went under, the swan's bill slicing my neck just below the ear. I came up choking, swinging my arms.

The swan danced back, still hissing. I spied the end of my gaff, scooped it up and kept advancing. All five of them turned and started flapping their wings through beach grass, eventually lifting off like jets with extremely heavy cargo.

I let out a breath, felt my heart pounding. My hand moved to my neck just below my ear and came back bloody. It stung like it had been blasted by a blowtorch. I'd just had my butt kicked by a bird. Yeah, it was a big bird. But still, it was a bird.

Okay, alert but calm doesn't work every time. And swans, they're tough. I'm just glad it hadn't connected with one of my eyes.

Mr. Haskins was always telling us weird animal stories but he didn't have any swan stories that I knew of.

I kept walking and broke out of the beach grass, I wiped more blood from my neck, forded the two side channels, the water pulling at my shins, then crossed the gravel bar. If I would've been thinking more clearly when that swan was on top of me I could've grabbed its neck and twisted. If I wanted to survive I needed to be ready to take advantage of any opportunity. If I'd been ready maybe I'd be cooking a big fat swan instead of wiping blood off my neck.

I approached the main channel of the creek and saw a splash. Like magic, a large school of fish filled the channel. I felt the power again; the whole place was humming. Only it wasn't a noise, it was more of a feeling. Like the fish were in charge. When they were here everyone noticed—the eagles, the gulls, the bears. Seals and sea lions ate salmon. And Killer Whales. Everything depended on them. Well, everything except for, maybe, killer-swans.

No fish earlier and now there were fish. I needed to figure this out.

Mom's lyrics rushed into my brain.

If you pay attention, you will know what the river knows.

I raised my gaff, brought it down hard, pulled a struggling fish from the school, then clubbed it with a rock.

I examined the gaff. The line had stretched, but just barely.

I waited. The fish returned, and I killed another. The gaff survived the second killing, but the lure was now half out of the barked-out area. I wanted more fish, but knew if I kept at it I'd lose my lure.

I cleaned the bigger of the two fish first. I took my knife, punched the tip into the opening just in front of the anal fin, and ran it up the belly, stopping just below the gills. I pulled the guts out and tossed them into the creek and let the gulls fight over them. Then I slit the bloodline, and, using my thumb while holding the fish in the water, I worked the blue-purple vein out of the fish, like my dad had taught me.

I cleaned the other fish, and paused for a moment when two bright pink egg sacs plopped out of the cavity. I knew people ate the eggs, but they looked pretty gross to me.

I tossed the eggs, along with the rest of the guts, into the creek, and rinsed my hands.

ROB MCCUE

A FRIEND ONCE TOLD ME THAT FAIRBANKS doesn't grow on you, it simply renders you unfit to live elsewhere. It's a sentiment that Rob McCue could relate to. Originally from Kansas, he came to Alaska in 1988, and after a stint at commercial fishing, wandered into the state's Interior and took up cab driving to pay the bills.

In *One Water*, his debut essay collection, McCue captures the bipolar nature of Fairbanks. It's an unattractive town where building codes and urban planning have never been priorities. Residents curse the government while their economy is shackled to military spending and a university. The climate alternates between hot summers with twenty-four hour daylight when the air can be clogged by dust and wildfire smoke, and frigid winters when the sun creeps just above the horizon for less than four hours and, on the coldest days, vehicle exhaust and wood stove smoke freeze on contact with the air, creating toxic clouds at ground level that are euphemistically referred to as "ice fog."

Yet it's where many choose to live because open country lies just beyond the pallid clutter of box stores and strip malls lining the city's streets. And the aversion to rules allows its residents freedoms not easily found elsewhere, something McCue describes in his book.

There's a wildness to this town that goes beyond the tens of thousands of square miles of wilderness that surrounds it. It's a town of misfits. People who weren't making it other places somehow find a home here. Nobody tells you how to build your house. Men are bushy and long haired. Women shoot moose and operate heavy equipment. People do what they want.

There's also an egalitarianism that's rare in America. As McCue explains elsewhere,

Class distinctions get blurred here. That is to say nobody comes here to be a member of the Fairbanks elite. The wealthiest guy in any room may be wearing the filthiest clothes.

One Water is unlike any other Alaska book. Essays alternate between daily urban life and adventures in the great open. When he's not driving residents, visitors, and the occasional unruly drunk around Fairbanks, listening to their stories, McCue is building his own home in a semi-rural subdivision north of town, paddling down creeks, hunting and fishing, or traversing the Alaska Range on skis and foot in winter. In all of these places he finds Alaska.

Explaining why he took the unusual step of exploring both the urban and wilderness aspects of Interior Alaska within a single volume, McCue told me, "The percentage of AK that's paved is minuscule. But most of us live in these few specks of urbanity, often dreaming of our next foray into the wildness just beyond the edge of town. So there's tension between the two poles. I liked using my experience driving cab and taking trips into the backcountry to explore this tension. Cab driving provides a unique perspective on the great folks who call this place home as well as those who travel here. Moving between the cab and the backcountry lends a human texture to the flow of the narration while imitating this elusive rhythm so many Alaskans share."

In the selection that follows, McCue describes a night of cab driving in Fairbanks in January during a brutal cold snap. It captures the desperation that sets in when the town sinks into an existential murkiness fueled by long hours of darkness and life-threatening temperatures. His passengers are a pastiche of Native Alaskans visiting from villages, elderly pioneers, drunks, soldiers, miners, and students, all making their way through the frigid night. Life keeps churning along. Because in Fairbanks, no one is allowed to cite cold and darkness as reasons for staying home.

— From *One Water* —

A Night on the Town, 2012

Interior Alaska in winter is a dark ocean, and we live miles beneath the surface. The cold resents our presence, our warmth an impediment to its equilibrium. It's nothing personal, just a fact of our planet's orientation to its host star: the axis around which the Earth rotates is tilted slightly relative to the orbit it traces around the sun, probably knocked out of whack by a meteor impact way back, before history. Due to this perfect imperfection the north is angled away from the warmth and light for months each year.

Don't get me wrong, I'm thankful for these circumstances. If it were otherwise the hordes from the Lower 48 would've swarmed here long ago and obliterated this place with the same urban sprawl that's chewed through the natural world to the south. The cold here in January freezes your flesh in seconds, and during the few summer weeks mosquitoes rise from the swamps by the trillions and our streets are littered with the sucked dry bodies of their victims. All in all, these inconveniences are boons.

Another good thing about winter is that it generates its own economy, sustaining us when we begin to second-guess our memories of summer. Mechanics, septic steamers, snowplow operators, tow truck drivers, furnace repairmen, woodcutters, drug dealers, cab drivers—we're in it together up here, consuming food, booze, sex, money, diesel, sharing our mutual desperation until the sun returns.

I've driven a cab here in Fairbanks for twenty years. When the cold comes, people's cars quit working. They lose their will to walk. They need to leave the house before they hurt someone, or get hurt. They call me.

It's 4:30 when I show up. The sun's been down more than an hour, early January, forty-five degrees below zero. The yard is layered in ice fog churned from the rumbling V-8 motors of the cabs waiting for night drivers. The warm water vapor from a car's exhaust is cooled nearly three hundred degrees within ten seconds of leaving the tail-pipe. The super cold air is too dense to absorb any of the vapor, so it turns into tiny hovering ice crystals. Add in the warm water discharged from the power plant; the emissions of all the woodstoves, furnaces, and boilers; and the exhalations of every living thing and our town is swaddled in a toxic gauze.

From negative forty on down, the taxis are left running to avoid the risk of freeze-up and lost revenue. Can't see fifty feet.

I walk into the smoke-filmed walls of the dispatch office that smells of stale cigarettes, fresh cigarettes, coffee, old dog, and microwave. Smurf is dispatching, talking on the phone. All lines are lit up. There are thirty-eight buttons on the board.

I throw five dollars on the trip log in front of him. Part gratuity, part protection money.

He turns to me. He has a big drinker's nose, a thinning mane of golden hair, and a wolfish Irish grin. I've watched him battle his personal demons for close to twenty years now. A trail of broken bottles, used hypodermics, meth memories stretching behind him, out of sight. Now, all that's left are the medications, the battered liver, the clogged arteries. The doctors told him he can have a new liver if he stays clean for a year. I hope he makes it. The man's got the love in his heart, and that's all that matters to me.

"What d'you want?" he asks.

"I don't know. I thought I'd try drivin' a little taxi cab."

"I don't know. You think you can handle it?"

"I'm not sure. I heard it requires great mental agility."

"Fuckin' A right."

"But they let you do it?"

"'Cause I'm fun to watch. What are you drivin'?"

"I'll take twenty-nine."

"Go get the Fred Meyer liquor for Regina."

"Thanks."

"You still here?"

I close the door as another wave of static breaks from the radio.

I feel like a pinball that Smurf has shot into the night. Like some intricacies of spin, velocity, and position have cast me to the inevitable.

TOWN SNEAKS UP ON YOU IN THE ICE FOG. Stoplights and other cars appear out of nothing, and then they're gone. It takes five minutes to get to Fred Meyer. When I enter the parking lot, I catch a glimpse of an old Athabaskan man in a Carhartt suit with the hood up. He holds a sign with big military surplus mittens. The sign says, "homeles veitnam vet plese help." No sooner than I see him he's gone in the fog and steaming train of headlights.

At the liquor door Regina comes striding out pushing a loaded cart with three kids under ten behind her, respectful. I pop the trunk of the Ford Crown Victoria and help load her bags.

As we leave the lot she sees the man with the sign. "Jesus Christ, is that Uncle Melvin, kids? Could you stop for a second?"

"Sure."

"Uncle, is that you? Jesus Christ, what you doin'? It's too cold to be stannin' around like that."

A big beauty of a broken-tooth smile breaks across the old man's weathered face like sunrise. He steps toward the cab and raises his hand.

"Uncle, get in the car with us, huh, we got moose stew at home. You can stay there."

The old man seems hesitant.

"We got beer there too, c'mon and get in with us." The smile gets bigger, and he climbs in. Cars behind us start to honk.

I take them to a house in the Hamilton Acres subdivision, a middle-class neighborhood north of the river. They give me $8 for a $6.20 meter. I thank the lady and help get the groceries to the door.

I CALL IN AND SMURF SAYS, "YOU'RE ONE CITY. I'm holdin' one South, you want it?"

I say, "Check."

"Get F.M.H. in the lobby for Richard."

Richard doesn't look well. He shuffles to the cab pulling an oxygen tank on wheels. He seems prematurely old. He's tall, and you can tell that he had once been a strong man but now he is shriveled and bloodlessly pale, his hair and lips the color of dried bone.

He tells me he's going to Yak Estates but wants to stop at a pharmacy on the way. I say no problem.

He's out of breath after the walk to the car and doesn't say anything for a couple minutes. Then, "Sorry, man. I move slow. I'm all fucked up."

"That's all right. You didn't take too long."

"No, but I will though, at the pharmacy. You're probably gonna charge me for that, huh?"

"Yeah, sorry."

"That's all right. You've gotta make a living. How old are you?"

"Forty-six."

He laughs fatalistically. "I'm only three years older than you. Found out a couple years ago I had hepatitis C. Now I'm dying. I got sclerosis of the liver and my knees are shot. I was hopin' they could fix my knees so I could take one more walk before my liver gives out, but it doesn't look good."

"Damn, man. Sorry about that."

"Yeah, they're just figuring out this stuff can live outside the body for years. I could've snorted a line of coke with a contaminated twenty back in the day, and it could've hung out in my nostril until I got a cut in my nose and that was that."

I swing into Fred Meyer west and up to the pharmacy door. He gets out and pulls his oxygen tank inside the mechanized whir of sliding glass and sits in an electric shopping cart and hums in to the din of the store. I turn the meter from mileage to time and let it tick, fifty cents a minute, thirty dollars an hour.

Ten minutes, the meter a bit over fifteen dollars. A guy on a mountain bike swoops out of the ice fog, hops onto the sidewalk, and coasts to a stop at the bike rack. His head, chest, and shoulders are covered with frost, and ice fog pours from his clothes and mouth. He has an empty backpack on over a down coat, snow pants, balaclava, mittens the size of beavers. There's a plastic five-gallon water jug strapped on a reinforced rear rack. A freakish strobe flashes from the back of the seat, and he forgets to turn it off when he goes inside.

Twenty-one minutes, the meter almost to twenty bucks, I see Richard roll back into the entryway with a couple bags of groceries. I hop out and carry them to the car while he wheels his oxygen. We're off. It takes him a few minutes to catch his breath.

"Man, it's like I'm invisible to people. Like I'm a ghost. I have to bump into people with the cart before they acknowledge my existence. I just want to shout, 'I'm still here,' sometimes."

I think about when I first saw him and felt a moment of dread knowing that he was my passenger. Like that made him real when I didn't want him to be. Didn't want this specter of death fucking with my perspective.

"Well, you seem real to me, man. A lot of people have it, right? I mean a friend of mine has it. He's doin' okay, gets tired easy. But you don't hear much about it."

"Yeah, more people have hep than AIDS in this country. They're calling it the silent epidemic 'cause, you know, who gives a shit about a bunch of old junkies and hippies with blood poisoning? I guess it's the price I gotta pay for all those years stayin' up all night dancin', drinkin', whateverin'. Man I used to love to dance. Loved the ladies. And you know what? If I had it to do all over again, I wouldn't change anything."

"There're some new meds coming out too. I'll just try and hang on till they get here."

We get to his condo, and I carry in his groceries. I wish him good luck and shake his hand. He manages a weak smile and something sparks in his eye. For just a second I can see him dancin' and makin' moves on the ladies in some bar with a band, and I kinda believe him.

Smurf sends me to the Holiday House Apartments, and I pick up three young engineering students from India and take them to Safeway. They speak in Hindi. I listen to the cadence and bubbling tones, and they soothe me. I like hearing languages I can't understand, all that yearning stripped of meaning and removed from me, an instrumental, a symphony.

I can't get through on the radio. Smurf's in a rage because a cab ran the stoplight at Geist and Johanssen. "It's busy as hell in here, Cab 16, and now I've got to tie up the phone lines takin' complaints, and not for the first time either, about your crappy driving."

Sibilant static leaps from the radio and explodes in my inner ear. From it emerges a panicked beep. I clamp my hands over my ears and stifle a whimper. It's Morse code. A few years back the Federal Communications Commission decided that in the interest of national security and personal freedom, all registered radio frequencies need to beep out their call letters and frequency at a tympanic tissue-piercing pitch every fifteen minutes. We're all thankful.

Eventually I get through. Get sent to 15 Farewell. There's an elderly lady in the entryway. She steps into the night and asks if this is for Opal. I tell her it is, and she asks if I could help with her things, pointing to a brown paper sack filled with hot food in aluminum foil. I put this in the backseat, and she gets in the front. "Where to?" I ask.

"I'm going to the Elks. Do you know where the Elks is?"

"Yes, ma'am."

"You just go down this road. I guess it's Farewell or something and go past the first few stoplights and then turn left and then right and go in that way."

"Okay. How are you doin' today?"

"Oh, all right I guess. I'm just going to meet my friend. We always get together on our birthday and have some drinks and talk about the good old days."

"Well, happy birthday."

"Thank you, young man. It is my birthday. I'm eighty-four."

"Congratulations."

"I don't know that congratulations are in order, but if you help me get my stuff inside that'd be appreciated. Eighty-four's a bitch, young man."

"I'll carry the stuff."

"I came up here with my World War II hero in 1947. After the war he was having a hard time, and he asked me if I wouldn't mind giving it a try up here. So that's what we did. I met the lady I'm going to meet now not too long after we got here, and we found out we had the same birthday. We've been friends ever since."

"Wow, you've seen some change, huh."

"Oh, yes. This town's about ten times bigger now than it was then. All that Bentley land, my husband used to look for moose there. Now, I won't even go."

"I liked it better when it was woods, myself," I say, referring to the several square miles on the northeast end of town that in the span of the last decade has been leveled, buried in gravel, paved, and developed into Walmart, Home Depot, Sportsman's Warehouse, Sports Authority, Barnes and Noble, a new Fred Meyer, Old Navy, Chili's, Carl's Jr., Boston's, the Holiday Inn, the Hampton Inn, and a host of other chains.

"It's like aliens came and dropped the Walmart from space. I'll just stay with Safeway."

"I go to the old Fred Meyer," I say as we pull up to the Elks.

"All right, I like that one. How much do I owe?"

"Five's fine." She gives me six and gets out. I carry her bag in, let her hold my arm on the ice. Smurf puts me four North. I gun it past the Big International Bar, the oldest joint in town, dating to the forties. There was recently an effort to have the building removed to make room for a new bridge over the Chena River. The outcry was loud enough that the city decided to remove every building but the Big I and build the bridge around it—proving that you can rip down any historic Fairbanks building you want, as long as it's not one that serves alcohol.

I OPEN MY EYES WHEN I HEAR A RAPPING ON THE WINDOW. There's an older Athabaskan man smiling at me. He's wearing a royal blue cap with a white bow in front. Dark eager eyes shimmer behind tinted glasses. He's just a spruce needle taller than the cab. I smile and release the power locks. "Jeremiah!" I say as he ducks into the car. "How are you, my friend?"

"I'm good, good. Good to see you, my friend."

"Good to see you too." His lips are a shade gray from the cold. I am, as always, impressed by the size of his hands relative to the rest of him. Big meaty mitts always open and ready to begin some undiscovered chore his eyes are constantly seeking. "You have that baby, yet?"

"Yeah, man. But he's not much of a baby anymore."

"Same one I meet that time, huh, Michele?"

"That's her."

"Oh, that's good. Good for you. You guys bring that baby up Venetie, huh? We go around that country. I got new boat this year."

"Jeremiah, we'd be honored. That sounds great."

"Hey, can you give us a ride? I got some lynx skins I want take to the buyer. You know where, huh?"

"Alaska Fur?"

"Yeah, that place. Can you take us?"

"Yeah, sure."

He hops out of the cab and waves to a younger man standing by the door of the hotel with a large black trash bag. The man jogs over, and they both get in. We take Tenth to the expressway and head north to Farewell.

"How many lynx you got?"

"Only six right now. I only go out for couple weeks, though. I got sick really bad this winter. Had to go to Anchorage for operation. No good. No good."

"Geez, that's too bad. How're you feeling now? You look great."

"Oh, I feel good now. Ready to go back trapping. The price is good. He say maybe thousand dollar for six skins."

"That is good."

"He was really sick, though," the man with the bag says.

"Oh, yeah?" I look at him.

"Yeah, he make us all nervous, didn't you?" He slaps Jeremiah's shoulder with his leather gloves.

"Oh, I guess. I make myself nervous. No good at all. But I'm better now."

"How're you, man?" I say to the friend.

"I'm good. I've been in town waiting for job out of Carpenters Union but nothing yet. Maybe I go back to the village soon if nothing come up. Try again later."

"Not much happenin' this winter, though, huh?"

"Economy's no good I guess. I been okay, though." He smiles. We're pulling into the driveway of a small house on a residential street. Nothing marks the house as a business other than a small, neon OPEN sign in the window of the garage door. Jeremiah and I agree to have coffee tomorrow. I wish them well.

A car clears North as I'm grabbing my mike. Smurf puts him six. I don't bother calling until I'm in the city.

Smurf says, "United 29 get the Comet Club for Leroy."

I go in the squat block building on the airport access and shout, "CAB! UNITED TAXICAB!"

A row of regulars looks over their shoulders from the horse-shoe bar and then turns back to their drinks and smokes. "That'd be me, partner," a short, wiry guy in a cowboy hat and bolo tie says, his blond hair and beard half gray.

In the cab I say, "Where to, my friend?"

He says, "Man, why don't you take me to the Mecca. See if I can't find me an Indian gal to keep me warm tonight. What'd'ya think about that?"

"Sounds like a winner, man. You'll never know if you don't put your boat in the water."

"Ain't that the truth. Hey, where you takin' me? The Mecca's over that way. You got to go right here."

"All right, but it's over this way, too. Remember 'cause it's a one-way street I have to go up to . . ."

"Hell no, man. I've been up in this town thirty years. I know how to get to the Mecca. Don't go runnin' me around, jackin' up the meter."

"I wasn't runnin' you around. I told you I have to go to Cushman before I can get there."

"Bullshit, I know which way the Mecca is. Don't be tryin' to fuck with me, 'cause I know better."

"You don't know shit, and I don't like people accusing me of cheating them."

"You know, I think I'll just get out here. I don't need this crap."

"Fuckin' A right you will." I said pulling the cab to the curb.

"How much I owe you?" he says pulling some bills from his chest pocket.

"Nothin'. I don't want your money. If you leave any in here I'll throw it out. Just get out."

When he's standing outside with the door open he says, "What's your name, man. I call this company all the time."

"Fuck you, man." And I gun the car and the door shuts itself and the guy disappears in the ice fog. Remain calm, I keep saying, restarting my breathing. I call in a minute later and get sent to Chena Courts. I say check, but there's no one in number nine so I return to the car, fight through the radio, tell Smurf it's a dud. He says, "You're back one City."

Then he asks if I want one on Post, and I say check and drive to the visitor's center at the main gate of Fort Wainwright and park and go in to get a pass. This is a U.S. Army installation. The MP examines my paperwork and licenses behind bulletproof glass. Scrutinizes my face even though he's issued me at least fifty passes since he's been stationed here.

I put the yellow pass on the dash and roll through the gate where the private security contractor examines my licenses and pass again. Then I call in on the radio and say, "United Cab number 29, advise."

And Smurf says, "29 take it to 3206 room 231 bravo for Menendez."

And I say, "Check," and drive to the barracks. It's a sprawling three-story concrete cavity that houses close to a thousand soldiers. Most of them returned home from Iraq a couple months ago. Since then they've consumed enough alcohol to make up for the year they were gone.

The Stryker Brigade has only been here a few years. Before that the fort was a sleepy base where guys who liked the woods ended up. I remember the euphoria that swept the town those first couple years as a few hundred million dollars were spent building new housing and infrastructure. All the businesses in town were rocking and people couldn't cut down trees fast enough to build more big stores.

Now, a couple deployments later, the economic lift the brigade gives is no longer a bonus but a necessary slice of the pie if the town is to sustain the enlarged commercial base. A bunch of local stores have closed. Crime is up. And there's gonna be a spike in the number of single mothers in a few months.

The war economy. It's changed the town.

But this is nothing new. The paranoid Cold War climate that followed World War II military spending here and at Eielson Air Force Base, southeast of town, quadrupled Fairbanks's population in less than ten years. It's continued to be one of the primary economic engines driving us ever since.

I roll in front of the barracks and three shadowy forms holding the collars of jackets over faces dart from the glass entry to the cab.

"Holy shit, man, it's cold out there. You mind if I smoke?" the guy who grabbed the front says.

"Go for it. Where you headed?"

"How about San Diego?" the Hispanic guy in back says. The other two laugh.

"Sounds good to me, man. But I'm gonna need some money up front."

"Yeah, no shit, huh. No seriously, dog, take us to Kodiak Jack's."

"All right, man."

"So how long you been up here?" the Hispanic guy asks me.

"Twenty-five years, now."

"No shit?" There are exclamations of amazement from around the car. "How can you stand it? What do you do here?"

"Well, I like the country, like the woods, you know. This is as good as it gets."

"Shit, man, I like that country down in Texas. I can go outside and barbecue in it anytime I want. Plus there's like a hundred times more women down there."

"Yeah and there's way more hot chicks, too," the skinny, sharp-faced kid sitting behind me says. "Up here it's all fat chicks. And the ones who aren't fat are like the queens of the fuckin' universe, you know. Even the fat ones act like porn stars. Hell, I wouldn't even be lookin' at 'em back in Chicago. Here you gotta fight through like ten guys just to talk to 'em. I hate this fuckin' place." Everyone nods in agreement.

"It is beautiful in the summertime, though. I've seen some truly beautiful shit here in the summertime," the Hispanic guy says.

"Yeah, whenever it's not all fuckin' smoky from forest fires or raining, it's fabulous," the guy from Chicago says.

"Where you from?" I ask the guy in front.

"West Virginia."

"You like it there?"

"Yeah, I'm from the western part, in the Smoky Mountains. It's nice country, kinda like the mountains north of town. Not many jobs, though."

"You got deer there, huh?"

"Yeah dude, tons. Whitetails. My family eats a lot of venison. Wild turkey too."

"How's that?"

"Like anything, it's good if you do it right. If somebody knows what they're doing."

We're pulling into the lumpy parking lot of the bar. "I'd eat some whitetail tonight," the Hispanic guy says.

"Fuck, I'll eat any kinda tail I can get my hands on," the Chicago guy says.

"Fifteen dollars," I say. They give me seventeen and shout fuck when they open the doors and run to the building.

On the radio Smurf is telling Cab 93 that he has a personal call, or PC, at the Bentley Mall.

"Well, I'm on another trip right now. Why don't you send another cab and let her know I'm sorry."

"She's your personal, 93; she already knows you're sorry. Next."

I get through after a couple others and let him know I'm red City. He sends me to 653 Eighth Avenue. I double-park beside a row of buried-in-snow cars in front of a gray split-level across from the state office building. I honk the horn, hop out, knock on the door, get back in, hit the meter. The woman comes out four minutes later. She's in her late twenties with thin brown hair and baby fat in her cheeks. She's wearing gray sweats a shade lighter than her eyes. "Take me to the Golden Nugget, please." She's crying.

"Okay."

"I'm sorry."

"It's okay, don't worry about it." I hand her a McDonald's napkin my relief driver left in the door well.

"Thank you. I'm just, I was supposed to go out with my boyfriend tonight, but he turned off his phone, and he's probably out having sex with another girl right now and . . ." She dabs at her eyes. "And I'm just gonna get a room for the night. Figure out what I'm gonna do."

I pull up to the door. "You seem like a good person. It'll be okay."

"Thanks. What do I owe you?"

"Two bucks."

"I'm sorry I can't afford to give you a tip. I know it's a short trip."

"Don't worry about it. Have a good night."

"Yeah. Good night."

I PULL INTO A PARKING SPACE BEHIND a red-and-gray bus in a slot on the Lacey Street side of the garage. There are people getting off the bus with duffel bags and backpacks. One of them walks to my cab. "Hey there, you here to pick up Stick?" the man drawls.

"Yep, I am. You need the trunk?"

"Nah, I can just throw it in back here. I'm goin' out to the airport?"

"All right, no problem." A terrible noise blurts from the radio followed by the shrieking beep. We slap our hands over our ears.

"Goddamn, what the hell was that?" Stick asks.

I explain to him about the FCC.

"That sounds like our government, all right. I'm a gold miner and you should see the hoops they make us jump through. You can't even fire up a piece of equipment without gettin' an environmental 'impasse' statement. I'm from Montana, and that's completely shut down. I have to come up here to work."

"Is that where you're headin' now?"

"Yeah, back to the family for a couple weeks and then back to the mine for a month."

"That's a hell of a commute."

"Yeah. Well, at least I'm workin'. Price of gold stays where it is, this job'll last awhile too. Got a family to support."

I drop him at the departures door, and he tells me to keep the twenty, and Smurf tells me to pick up at Pike's, a bar-restaurant-hotel on the way back to town.

THERE ARE PEOPLE WAVING IN THE STREET in front of the bingo hall. I recognize them. They're the local bingo babes, and none of them are going farther than five dollars, but Mary goes to Sandvik Road, twelve dollars away. She's the queen of the bingo babes. Plus she's cool.

She's between the two sets of doors, an eighty-year-old five-foot-tall Athabaskan woman with stylishly coifed silver hair. She walks to the cab making efficient use of a cane with a spiked fitting over the end for sticking in the ice. I get out and open the door for her.

"So how'd the bingo go?" I ask.

"Oh, I make enough for my cab ride that's all. But I won twice this month, already. Maybe I'll try again tomorrow. I just like to go and see people, really."

"See anybody interesting?"

"Some people from Fort Yukon. That's where I'm from. But I haven't been there in twenty years. Everybody from Fort Yukon comes to bingo sooner or later, though. Really, though, I was from Chalkytsik."

"On the Black River?"

"Yes, but we were nomadic too. We moved around all over that country.

"I remember when I was a girl. My mother marry her third husband, and he was not a good man. He try to abuse us, me and my sister, you know. He try to touch me and one time he raped my sister, and he held a knife up against her face and tell her that he cut her all up if she ever tell anybody.

"One time I was with him in camp, and he came and got into my bed. I jumped up real fast and said 'Oh I have to go to the bathroom.' And I got the gun and put it on him, and we sat like that all night.

"He tell me I don't need the gun anymore, that I can put it away 'cause he's better now. But I said, 'No, I don't believe you.' And I tell him to get the dogs ready. We were traveling by dog sled then. I held that gun at him all the way back home.

"When we got there my grandmother ask me what was the matter. So I tell her and she told me, 'You go to bed now 'cause you gonna wake up early.' And she get me up real early the next day and tell me get dressed. And she put her hands on my shoulders and said 'You remember those three long lakes you pass yesterday?' I said yeah.

"'You going to go past those and go this way.' She was doing with her arm like this 'cause she was speaking our native language, and we don't have word for right. She said, 'You're going to follow that trail to Black River where your auntie stay.' The whole time she talking to me I feel power coming into me from her hands. She was a shaman, you know. Then she tell me get going.

"I walked all day, but you know I don't remember any of that walking. I only remember seeing my auntie and she ask me 'How was your trip?'

"I say 'I don't know. I don't remember any of it.' We looked at my boots. I was wearing those canvas mukluks and they were completely dry and this was in April when everything was wet. My auntie say that my grandma had made me a wolf for that trip, and I believe her 'cause I walk all that way and I don't remember any of it and my boots were dry when I got there."

We were coasting into the handicapped space in front of the door to her building. "That's a great story."

"I been thinking I'd like to tell that one to somebody. That one and I got some others, too. Maybe somebody could write them down while I still remember. Is twelve dollars okay?"

"Yeah, that's good, thanks." And soon, Mary too is gone in the fog.

JONATHAN WATERMAN

"I AM HAUNTED BY DENALI," Jonathan Waterman tells readers in the introduction to his modern Alaska mountaineering classic, *In the Shadow of Denali*. America's tallest peak has rested at the center of Waterman's life as a climber, professional guide, and adventurer, as well as his career as an author. He's reached the summit multiple times, and the mountain is the focus of four of his fourteen books. And while his excursions have taken him to many other places as well—particularly the North American Arctic—it's to Denali that he keeps returning, both physically and on the page.

Few people are as knowledgeable as Waterman about Denali and its climbing history, and no living author has written as well about both. He conveys a lyrical sense of wonder about being so high atop the world, personal insights into the downsides of the climbing industry that he's helped fuel as both guide and writer, and perhaps most importantly, an informed understanding of what it takes to get to the top, and how and why things can go wrong and people can fail and sometimes die.

In his latest book, *Chasing Denali*, Waterman applies all of this knowledge, along with historical sleuthing skills, to an examination of one of Alaska's most popular legends: the claim that Denali's northern summit, the lower of its two peaks, was successfully scaled for the first time in 1910 by miners from Fairbanks who had no previous climbing experience. It's an audacious story, beloved by Alaskans as an example of working man know-how eclipsing the expertise of wealthy Outsiders in the race to be the first to reach the mountain's top.

Over the course of many decades of exploring and thinking about Denali, Waterman grew increasingly skeptical about the Sourdough story, and the bulk of this book is given over to his dissection of the historical claims about the climb, which he scrutinizes through the lens of his own intimate familiarity with the mountain. He also sifts through written documents from the time, compares the conflicting accounts of the participants, and employs digital tools unavailable to previous historians, before ultimately passing judgment on whether or not the miners made it. His conclusion won't be revealed here, but it is convincing. And in the process of explaining how he came to it, he offers readers a rollicking tale of pioneer Alaska and the formative days of northern mountaineering.

In the introduction and epilogue of the book, Waterman recounts his own return to Denali in 2016, a trip that coincided with his sixtieth birthday and which he indicates will likely be his final visit to the mountain that has defined so much of his life. The following excerpt is drawn from these passages. On his way up he contemplates the toll that age and activity has taken on his body, ponders the inherent dangers of climbing, considers turning back, and confronts the many changes in mountaineering on Denali that he's seen in his four decades of climbing there, all while once again basking in the wonder of it all.

Asked about what he seeks to accomplish through his writing about Denali and the North, Waterman, who makes his home in Colorado, said, "There's no question that, compared to the Lower 48, Alaska really is the Last Frontier. As the largest state, more than half of its acreage is designated wilderness (California, with 14 percent wilderness, is not even a close second). More than anything else, we have the chance to do things right with Alaska: to prevent the oil derricks from festooning the Arctic; to save the wild salmon runs in Bristol Bay; and to prevent dams from being built on its free flowing glacial rivers. By sharing the wonders and beauty of the Alaskan outback, there's a chance that we can keep its pristine spaces eternally."

Although he's not an Alaska resident, through his writings Waterman has told many stories about Alaska, and through his excursions up the state's mountains and down its rivers, he has himself become part of Alaska's story.

— From *Chasing Denali* —
Prologue: June 2016

I pulled the balaclava down over my frosted chin, shivering, as the bottom half of Denali fell into shadow. A raven flew past holding wind in its wings and all of the mountain in its eyes. I sat fifty yards from our 14,300-foot medical camp and right next to the dead body of Pavel Michut.

Several days earlier, this Czech ski mountaineer stepped into his ski bindings halfway up an hourglass-shaped snow chute called the Messner Couloir, sixty degrees steep and rising a vertical mile to the 19,500-foot summit plateau. He made three jump turns, caught an edge, fell head over heels, and continued plummeting toward camp—knowing, in his horrified last thoughts, that dozens of climbers in the basin below were helplessly watching him fall—over rocks and cement-hard ice, until he stopped 1,500 feet later, bent and irreversibly broken. Hot sunlight reflected off the snow and burned his skin, slowly dispersing the atoms that made up his forty-five-year-old body into the mysterious universe of our beginnings.

When the clouds cleared below camp the park service helicopter would fly in from sea level and carry his remains out. I stood up and gave a respectful bow to him there on the landing pad that we had stomped out in the snow.

Death on a mountain foils all the best-laid plans. If you repeatedly spend time on Denali, it's inevitable—lacking a near miss or even losing a friend—that you'll witness a fatality or help with a body extraction. This can feel like the height of folly, taking on these great tests only to earn such wretched consequences. To continue amid such adversity, and to counter the perception that climbing is solely a game of risk addiction, committed climbers also depend upon camaraderie, challenge, the beauty of mountains, and inspirational legends to sustain them through both storm and sunshine.

The addiction to risk—with its brain chemistry rewards—never goes away but can be balanced and put in its corner through mastery and judiciousness. Camaraderie often vanishes outside the intensity of expedition life. Beauty can be as elusive as stormy weather in the high ranges. And even the physical challenge fades as oldsters become incapable of their once youthful feats.

EXACTLY FOUR DECADES HAD ELAPSED SINCE the first time I stumbled up here on the west buttress route with my scout troop from Massachusetts. In that peculiar way in which only young people can commit themselves wholesoulfully, I had found a path that gave my life meaning.

I wanted to climb mountains and run rivers and spend my days on long journeys through remote landscapes because the physical challenge of adventuring appealed to me through the blood, on a cellular level. If I wasn't out in the mountains or planning the next trip, I succumbed to depression—like most climbers do. Life simply seemed meaningless when I was sleeping on a mattress indoors without wind in my face or untracked horizons to explore.

WHILE I DIDN'T PLAN ON RISK-TAKING IN 2016, as I climbed higher I was preoccupied about turning older. These are the thoughts, I remembered, that you have to process after a mountaineering fatality. Bury these experiences and they'll come back to haunt you. The only alternative, for me, is to learn from them.

So while seeing lifeless bodies on a mountain is provocative and unforgettable, the experience can serve as a safety net for climbing. Because each step you or your friends takes comes with consequences. Forty years ago, we made the right decision, as weather deteriorated in the face of my high-altitude headache and nausea, to turn around before the summit. That expedition spurred me into figuring out how to reduce risk on big mountains, let alone launch a career—based on sharing lessons about safety and history—that kept me in the wilds.

Now, nearing sixty, I refused to accept the idea of retirement. Besides, I made my living from these trips, writing about the adventure along with history, culture, and conservation. Rather than rusting, I planned to go out dancing, despite the broken bones and surgeries and arthritic setbacks that come with letting the animal of your body love what it loves. It didn't matter that I had lost some lung capacity and flexibility and strength. By training hard, if I couldn't set the pace or break trail, I could at least keep younger partners in sight. Experience, technique, and knowing how to conserve energy also gave me an edge—or so I hoped on this final Denali trip.

While I planned to stay fit for another quarter century, the thought of celebrating my June 12 birthday on top, on the day that I would become a sexagenarian, seemed like a karmic invitation into disaster. So I kept this fantasy to myself. As in a new relationship, I repeatedly gazed toward the distant summit and declaimed: No expectations.

Until recently, I had abandoned mountaineering as if it were part of a past that didn't belong to me anymore. Aging, of course, has a way of directing you onto different paths. But I wanted to change that.

In the years that had passed since my last visit, the culture of climbing had evolved on North America's highest mountain. My teammates were watching movies downloaded onto their cellphones, climbing traffic had nearly doubled, and in good weather, tourist-engorged, scenic-flight planes swarmed the mountain.

Climbers now pay a $365 fee, submit their registrations two months in advance, and carry park service–issued, plastic-bag lined "clean mountain cans" (CMCs) so that their feces can be disposed of in pre-marked crevasses. Only the bravest climbers carry their full CMCs all the way back down the mountain.

On my 2016 Denali climb as a park service volunteer, two of my six companions—all half my age—had been here before. We spent a full week acclimating at 14,300 feet, frequently hiking or skiing a thousand feet higher to accustom our bodies to the altitude. We treated, then evacuated, two frost-bite victims from our medical tent. We posted daily weather forecasts, advised climbers, played Yahtzee, and read books.

On the day that we left for the 17,200- foot, west buttress high camp, it appeared that no one in the group had anything to prove. Worried about being the pensioner slowing down young teammates, I had trained up to twenty hours a week through uphill running or cross-country skiing in Colorado. Rather than ordinary workouts, I went alone up a cold mountain and repeatedly pushed myself to exhaustion and beyond. Then, week after week—listening to my body—I extended these limits with a tolerance for suffering that I'd learned through decades of conditioning outside the gym. I had to keep up with companions a lot younger than me.

As the saying goes in Alaskan mountaineering, there are old climbers and there are bold climbers, but there are no old, bold climbers. So those partners (particularly youthful ones) who claim that they don't consider the possibility of dying or getting hurt on a mountain like Denali are climbers whom you should never rope up with. Fear—of falling, being avalanched, hit by a sudden storm, dropping into a crevasse, or contracting altitude sickness—tends to sharpen your focus and make you pay more attention. Still, since vigilance, luck, or all the experience in the world can't stop a falling rock or any number of other random hazards, I had prepared and left a will with my family in Colorado.

I could accept not making the top again. I'd turned back repeatedly because I preferred a hollow sense of incompletion to more frostbitten digits or the prospect of others risking their lives to rescue me. Or worse. Also, this time, as a soon-to-be sixty- year-old, I had good excuses in case I failed.

Complicating matters, on past trips to these uninviting elevations I had been clobbered with headaches, vomiting, forgetting partners' names, battling insomnia, and nearly drowning in my own fluids—regardless of acclimatization. My family ancestry didn't include high-altitude genes.

Fortunately, compared to the Sourdough route, the west buttress is a relative walk- up, given several days of good weather (uncommonly found up high) on Denali. But below the fixed ropes, parboiling in a snow basin that resembles a fry pan, I developed urgent misgivings.

Being towed up at the end of a rope, breathing hard and sweating profusely felt miserable. Plus, we were queueing up for a mountain that I'd never see lines on. At least a hundred other climbers were heading up this day.

What am I doing here? I thought. I had two young sons who had tried to convince me that I was too old for Denali. While my role modeling might show them how to deal with their own aging, they would never talk to me again if I didn't come home. This was prompted, of course, by imagining how wrecked the ski mountaineer Pavel Michut's family would be.

Shaken up by these thoughts and sweat soaked at the base of the fixed ropes, I shouted to our unflappable lead Ranger Bob Tomato: "I'm going down." The rest of the team avoided meeting my gaze, as if I had suddenly become the party crasher. Tomato, lithe and thick-lipped, bowlegged like a bull rider from his many extreme ski descents, strode over and looked me in the eye. No one else said a word.

"You feeling okay?" he asked, sotto voce.

"Yeah," I replied, "physically anyway."

In the first week out, tacitly acknowledging that he would lead without sharing leadership, and that I would write about Denali, we agreed to change his name in print to Bob Tomato—which gave him great pleasure. During the two strenuous weeks that I had observed him in action, to my knowledge Tomato had never breathed hard or broken a sweat. Ten days earlier, when our teammate Bobby Cosker had an erected tent snatched out of his hands and blown out of sight down the glacier by the wind, Tomato scooted after it on his skis and somehow caught it a mile away on the lip of a crevasse. To a mountaineer, particularly a guide or a park service ranger, losing a tent to the wind is the Nascar driver's equivalent of falling asleep at the wheel and totaling a car—a stigma Tomato would never live down. But as a thoughtful leader, he took the whole event in stride, without issuing any reprimand, acting pleased that Cosker's blunder allowed such a brisk and heroic ski rescue. The rest of the team, however, couldn't resist a rejoinder, and thinking of our hapless partner Bobby flying away under a tent held like an umbrella, my hard-hearted teammates began calling him "Bobby Poppins."

Before Tomato switched jobs to what the guiding community referred to as "the dark side," working for the feds as a park service mountaineering ranger, he had completed his guide certification and successfully escorted many clients up the mountain. Under his skilled protocols, we all understood our role as secondary volunteers. To keep the peace, I acquiesced because real leadership is defined by an ability to follow.

While repeatedly trying to make this dead-serious bergführer smile, I observed that Tomato was incapable of laughing unless it was at his own joke. As far as he let on, history concerned old dead guys and the sourdoughs were loaves of bread.

Physically speaking, since the altitude didn't slow him down, you couldn't help but wonder whether Tomato had Sherpa DNA. But before I could verify his lineage, a week ago an unfortunate, dawn meeting of a full, yet topless, pee bottle and two sleeping bags had forever banned me from his tent.

There at 15,200 feet, awhirl with clouds, I caught my breath. And Tomato's shrewd leadership skills would prevail yet again. "You can't go down alone," he said. That settled it—as he knew it would. Since I didn't want to prevent someone else from summiting while they accompanied me down, I had to continue up. This whole climb wouldn't be such a big deal, I thought, if my teammates were all thirty years older.

I clipped on my crampons to the bottom of the plastic double boots as a set of dangerous-looking claws. More than any other piece of gear, the crampons are vital to high-altitude mountaineering. The evolution of this tool over the last century—from four-point, iron strap-on creepers to fourteen-point, stainless steel clip-on spikes—explains how climbers have tackled and succeeded on increasingly difficult climbs on Denali. By stomping each spiked foot into the icy steps leading to the crest of the west buttress, our feet stuck as secure as astronauts' Velcro boots to the space shuttle walls.

In my left, over-mitted hand, I clutched a twenty-inch-long ice ax, jabbing its end spike like a trash-picker stick into the snow. Compared to the eight-pound, four-foot-long, hickory-shafted, step-chopping alpenstocks used by pioneers, the fifteen-ounce carbon fiber shaft lanyarded to my wrist was as space age as the crampons. In my other hand, I pushed a jumar—from its Swiss inventors (Ju)gen and (Mar) ti, which locks when you lean back on it and slides as a one-way clamp—up a rope that had been tied down into pickets and permanently "fixed" on the mountain a month earlier by mountain guides. We also tied into one another with our climbing ropes.

Having all of this modern, lightweight equipment might make a high-altitude climb seem more straightforward, but proper use of the gear is not a journeyman's trick. Two of my very fit teammates, Sergeants

Jeff Hamilton and Cory Inman, had never climbed Denali. I could only imagine their trepidation. Still, as armed air force pararescue medics, they had frequently deployed to Middle East combat zones more hazardous than a subarctic mountain. But up on the fixed-rope headwall, they neglected to flex their ankles and climb the forty-five-degree slope flat-footed in order to engage most of their crampon spikes, instead of just their frontpoints. Shouting instructions or trying to teach hard-to-learn and less-comfortable techniques mid-climb wouldn't have worked. So they repeatedly frontpointed and kicked their feet straight in, perpendicular to the slope, straining calf muscles while expending extra time and energy—showing how long-in-the-tooth mountaineers can catch their breath amid muscular, young war heroes.

Our packs were made of the same lightweight spectra-nylon used in bulletproof vests. We wore Gore-Tex bibs and jackets that would keep us dry in storms but allow our sweat to pass through ingenious nylon pores. We kept two-ounce packets of easily digested, vanilla or fruit flavored, mucous-consistency "Goo" gel in outside pockets in case of diminishing blood sugar. Fleece gloves under nylon-shelled pile mitts kept our fingers warm.

Seen from the historical context, we were highly evolved climbing machines. In body and mind, we exploited decades worth of technology and knowledge about the mountain, essentially standing upon the shoulders of those canvas-jacketed, hatchet-handed, creeper-footed Sourdoughs who may or may not have preceded us.

After stomping a monotonous, over-ballasted upward jig all afternoon, we finally crested the top of the ridge, crampons singing like rusty hinges in tight snow, and walked down onto the broad, sloping 17,200-foot basin. With the mercury hugging the balmier single digits, we felt thankful that it was windless—but this could change instantaneously. So without hesitation, as if expecting an artillery barrage, we began digging in.

For several hours, we quarried out large, rectangular snow blocks with aluminum snow saws, then carried and stacked them around our three tents in a towering barricade. These snow walls would buy us just enough time to dig a more bombproof snow cave in case the all- too common, Denali tent-shredding blizzard should hit.

To my surprise, I had an appetite for the disagreeable freeze-dried food. I slept soundly. When I woke up bound tight as Rameses II in my

mummy bag with frost fallen from the tent walls melting on my face—
feeling as if resuscitated from major surgery—I had no headache. Still,
acutely aware of my age because of the stiffness in my joints, or the relentless call of the bladder, I decided to forgo the summit and call 17,200 feet
my high point. For the next two days, just strolling a hundred yards on
the flats at this altitude left me gasping and contemplating a raid on the
emergency oxygen bottles stashed in the nearby rescue cache.

When June 12 dawned, our next-door neighbors—young snowboarders sponsored by The North Face—began singing "Happy Birthday"
across the snow-wall fences. Somehow word had gotten out. Although
not pleased to be so publicly reminded of my age, I looked forward to
one more day of repose in the tent before descending to thicker air.

Unexpectedly, Ranger Tomato then announced—in his dropped
"r"s drawl—that I would continue to the summit, escorting our teammates while he and Justin Fraser stayed behind and supervised a helicopter lifting out trash from the basin. Everyone heeds the rangers of
Denali, or at least they did during my own park service patrols back
in the day before Tomato's Sherpa parents sowed and raised Tomato.
While relieved to be romping up with my teammates instead of following our leader's brutal pace, taxpayers everywhere would have been
impressed that Tomato, a clocked-in government servant, elected trash
removal over a summit attempt.

The summit morning felt a blur, wondering how I would be able to
keep up with the stallions I had roped into, skeptical that I would make
the top. We repeatedly passed slower climbers who warbled out oxygen-
deprived versions of "Happy Birthday" to me, the frosted graybeard.
Apparently, the whole roof of the continent had been let in on my secret.

We finished slugging from our water bottles, peeing, and squeez-
ing Goo into our mouths. I suggested that Inman take a Diamox tablet
for his headache, caused by a traumatic brain injury earned in combat
and aggravated by high altitude. I thought of both Jeff Hamilton and
Cory Inman as selfless models for service to our country, and while I
would do most anything to see them make the summit, they probably
wouldn't need my help. Then we pulled on our packs and headed slowly,
ever so slowly, up into clouds. No way we're going to make the top, I
thought. And if this weather turns, we're screwed.

MOLLY RETTIG

DESPITE THE OUTSIZED ROLE IT PLAYS in the state's history, Alaska's Gold Rush was a brief event. The lure of easy riches that brought tens of thousands of people from the United States and beyond pouring into the North is the foundational myth of Alaska. But it didn't last long. Most stampeders returned home empty-handed within a couple of years, while corporations with the capital required to extract gold from Alaska's lands displaced them.

The few remaining independent prospectors, whose image would become the de facto symbol of what became known as the Last Frontier, were lucky if they broke even. Today some can still be found in remote areas, clinging to the dream, and as a friend of mine who dabbled in such work once put it to me, "spending a lot of money making a little money."

Clutch Lounsbury is a third generation Alaskan gold miner living in Ester, a quirky community a few miles west of Fairbanks. His neighbor is Molly Rettig, a former reporter for the Fairbanks Daily News-Miner who came to Alaska in 2010 expecting an adventure for a year or two before moving on. Like so many of us, though, she found that moving on was impossible. She had fallen in love with the land and its people, and stayed.

Rettig befriended Lounsbury, and in doing so was faced with a quandary. He loves the land as much as she does, but while she approaches it from a preservationist perspective, he tunnels into it, seeking to continue making a life on his own terms, maintaining a family tradition begun by his grandparents.

Rather than pass judgment on another person's livelihood, Rettig listened to Lounsbury. His family's story is one of four that she shares in her book *Finding True North*, a collection of oral histories that document the ways that land, resources, and people interact in Alaska, and exploring the relationships those making their living through resource extraction develop with the land.

Rettig had quickly learned during her tenure as a journalist that resource extraction is Alaska's economic driver. Nightly news reports keep Alaskans updated on the current prices of a barrel of oil and an ounce of gold, financial indicators that rarely draw media attention elsewhere, but that Alaskans live by.

Lounsbury undoubtedly keeps a close watch on gold prices. But he keeps closer watch on the land he lives and works upon. Rettig found herself enthralled by his deep knowledge of that land, and of the history of those who walked it before he did. He's living a piece of Alaska's mosaic that most of us only read about as part of a bygone era.

That Alaska still exists, but barely. By documenting the lives and family histories of Lounsbury and others, Rettig went looking for the ways that Alaska developed over the twentieth century, and how these ways of being persist today. She didn't simply interview her subjects. She spent long stretches of time with them, often joining them as they worked the land.

In the following excerpt, she tells of a summer afternoon on Lounsbury's claim near Wiseman, a tiny community nestled in the Brooks Range, about sixty miles north of the Arctic Circle, where she tries her hand at finding an elusive nugget.

I asked Rettig what she learned about herself and Alaska as she engaged in an activity she wouldn't have dreamed of doing a decade earlier, when her thoughts on land and resources largely sprang from an urbanized outlook

"I hate to think that I saw the world in black and white, but I definitely grew up thinking resource developers were a little evil. That's where this reporting project changed me so much. To meet someone like Clutch at the local saloon, to learn his family history and visit his mine, showed me where he was coming from and why he was here. And it wasn't greed, it was love for this place and this remote wilderness lifestyle. It really wasn't that different than what brought me to Alaska. Now, when I meet someone I disagree with, I try to rewind a few generations to imagine why they might hold these views."

Spending time with Lounsbury and others connected Rettig to Alaska in ways that her background couldn't match, and forced her to broaden her views. She didn't abandon her principles, but she did come to appreciate and admire viewpoints that, on the surface, seem vastly different from hers, but that originate in a common love for the beauty and possibilities of Alaska. In an age when Alaskans, much like other Americans, are increasingly cocooning themselves among like-minded people while regarding others as mortal enemies, Lounsbury and Rettig listened to each other and found that their commonalities greatly outweigh their differences. There's a lesson for all Americans in this.

— From *Finding True North* —
HOT ROCKS

EITHER THE BUGS OR THE HEAT WAS GOING TO KILL ME, I was sure, before I found any gold. The sun pounded down on us and radiated up from the rocks under our feet. It had been shining twenty-four hours a day for two weeks straight, heating up the trees, rocks, and air to a temperature I never would have thought possible at seventy-five miles north of the Arctic Circle.

Clutch squatted in the creek and set a 45-inch sluice box in the current. It looked like a water trough for a pig pen, a skinny aluminum tray with high walls on the sides, except it was open on both ends so water could shoot right through.

"Let's dam up the mouth and get some more flow going through the box. You want about two inches runnin through there," Clutch said.

I ripped some moss from the tundra—soft and squishy, like a big organic sponge. As I stuffed it around the opening, I could already feel my toes going numb in the water. Above us glaciers clung to the walls of the canyon, shelves of dirty ice protected by caverns of shade. Even in the middle of June, winter never fully went away here at the top of the world.

From our little spot on the creek, the Brooks Range unfolded in every direction, a great wall across northern Alaska separating the Arctic coastal plain from the Yukon River valley. The mountains were wrapped in green vegetation, except at the top, where fins of schist jutted into the sky. Wildflowers lit up the meadow—purple lupines and fiery-red Indian paint brushes. In this collage of color, it was hard to believe that for most of the year the ground was frozen solid, the animals were sleeping, and this whole valley was blanketed in white. That the air was so cold it turned snow into dust and made ground squirrels freeze solid. It wasn't an easy place to live, and there were only a handful of villages scattered across an area larger than Colorado.

Ahh, Colorado. I hadn't taken the job at *High Country News*. It was hard to turn down, probably the hardest move I'd made in my relatively short career. In the end, it wasn't some lofty decision about saving the earth or falling in love or any one thing at all. I just couldn't bring myself to leave Alaska. It would have been like putting a book down before the ending, or leaving a soccer match when it was just getting good. I wasn't the first one to find myself in this predicament. I'd met plenty of people up here who concocted elaborate escape plans over the winter, vowing to head south at the first sign of spring. Then, when the sun came back and the world turned green, their resolve seemed to evaporate with the snow. They called it "seasonal amnesia," but it seemed more like an addiction to me. Either way, there was no known cure.

So here I was, standing with Clutch in a bone-chilling creek three hundred miles north of Fairbanks, learning how to sluice for gold. We were just outside of Wiseman, a tiny gold rush village where Clutch had been prospecting since before I was born. He laid a piece of black bristly turf in the bottom of the sluice box, then attached the riffle tray. The horizontal steel bars created eddies in the water, allowing gold to settle out onto the turf.

"Go ahead and start shovelin," he told me.

The sun bored down on my shoulders where I had rolled up the sleeves of my T-shirt. Had I known it would be this hot in the Arctic, I would have brought a tank top. I scooped some gravel from the creek and dumped it into the top of the box. It was wet and heavy, more work than I expected. But I was forty years younger than my companion, and I couldn't really complain. Clutch had brought me here to show me what prospecting was all about. I had learned a lot about the history of mining: how a single nugget had sparked a global stampede; how prospectors had filtered into every major river valley in Alaska, bouncing around the creeks like pinballs every time a new one was discovered; how the large dredges and drift mines had taken over, in typical capitalistic fashion; and how, ultimately, World War II had reshaped the entire economy, putting an end to the small-time miner.

I had hiked in the footsteps of GL and Nellie and explored the dark recesses of Lloyd's tunnel. I had accompanied Clutch to local miners' meetings and listened to them rant about environmentalists, Obama, and the EPA, silently biting my tongue among a roomful of hard-core miners. But I had never actually squatted in a creek, with my feet soaking in the icy water, and searched the gravel for gold. And really, that's what mining was all about—sifting through millions of ordinary pebbles in the hopes of finding a few precious flakes.

I brushed hair out of my face and squinted at Clutch.

"So how do you know where to look?" I said.

Surely there was a method to the madness. I couldn't possibly comb through every foot of gravel in this canyon.

"Oh, there's some tricks," Clutch said, with that hint of mystery I had come to expect. Clearly he wasn't going to share them with me. I'd have to figure it out for myself.

I watched a white rope of water gushing over some boulders, and I tried to imagine where I would be if I were a little particle of gold.

"I've been fooled," he continued. "I've seen places that looked like they had gold and didn't, and places that didn't look like they had gold and did. I'm just as miffed as the average guy."

At least I knew we were in the right neighborhood. Less than two miles away, in the same drainage, a palm-sized nugget was plucked from the water in 1901, creating the boom that gave birth to Wiseman. It weighed 34 ounces and 5 pennyweight, yielding $696.50 (or $42,000 today).

Clutch rattled off more local history as he cleared out the tray, working as deftly as a surgeon in an operating room or a bartender making drinks. It was easy to see he had spent a lifetime handling gravel.

"The next year they found a nugget twice that size, just three miles up the road from my place. They found a 60-ouncer and eventually a 150-ouncer. There was just huge nuggets lyin' all over this area."

"Do you think there's any—Oww!"

I dropped the shovel as something stabbed into the tender flesh above my elbow. The moose flies had found us. Super-sized horse flies with two pairs of scissors in their mouths, they could draw a pint of blood from a moose in a single day, making mosquitoes seem as friendly as butterflies. I dropped the shovel to put on a rain jacket and a head net, choosing sweat in a beekeeper outfit over bleeding in the breeze.

Clutch was still sluicing away, wearing only a T-shirt under his tan overalls. Apparently one could get used to the flies over time. Clutch watched me flail around, arms waving spastically over my head.

"So whaddaya think?" he said, sounding amused. "You wanna be a miner yet?"

I slapped another fly that was drilling into my back.

"Ha," I said. "We'll see how it goes."

Actually, I was surprised. So far, prospecting wasn't much different than how I usually spent my weekends, hiking up mountains or paddling down rivers. It was never glamorous, per se. Compared to the sunny skies and well-marked trails of Colorado, Alaska was a total wild card, a place where any outing was likely to include bushwhacking or mosquitoes or possibly even snow, registering somewhere on a sliding scale between suffering and fun. Like earlier this summer, when Josh and I were on the Chatanika River—one second we were paddling through some innocent-looking riffles and the next he was bobbing down the river trying to retrieve our capsized canoe. The X factor is big up here, but if you can handle it, the rewards are even bigger.

As we settled into a rhythm, Clutch told me how he got these gold claims in the first place. He began coming up to Wiseman back in the seventies with his older brother, George, who used to make deliveries in his Beechcraft Bonanza. One of his customers was an old miner named Harry Leonard. Like many of the sourdoughs who lived in the Bush, Harry wasn't known for his social graces. He had a crude metal shack on the north side of town, across the footbridge from everyone else (there were sixteen residents living in Wiseman at the time, about six more than today).

Though Harry didn't have many friends, he took a shine to the two young Lounsbury brothers. Clutch and George started visiting often to help with chores and hear his stories. Harry had been a cowboy in Texas before moving to Alaska in 1928. He got a job at the machine shop in Fairbanks. But his southern-belle wife didn't fall in love with the north like he did, and after a messy divorce, Harry needed a change of scenery. Hearing reports of giant nuggets in the Koyukuk region, he tracked down some mining supplies and a plane ride north. He staked some claims on Gold Creek and burrowed into the side of the mountain. For fourteen years, he lived there alone, miles away from the next human being. He worked the creek with a pick and a shovel, without a single piece of mechanical equipment. Over the years, he picked up more and more claims as other prospectors left, living on wild food and finding just enough gold to scrape by.

By the time the Lounsbury brothers came along, Harry was pushing eighty, and it was getting harder to work alone. So he asked Clutch if he wanted to join his venture. The younger miner didn't hesitate.

Though Clutch had spent his life working with coal, gravel, and oil, his first love had always been gold. In 1980, they started mining a small tributary of Hammond Creek. They set up camp on a grassy bench above the creek, just up from where we were sluicing. I could still see Clutch's old trailer parked there, plywood skirting around the edges and a piece of sheet metal slapped on the roof. The outhouse behind it was made entirely of Blazo boxes, crates used to deliver fuel in the old days. The squares of wood had been nailed to the frame like oversized shingles. To me it looked like a festering mosquito trap, but to Clutch it was something special.

"It's actually a historical monument," he said. "It was built in 1934 by, I believe it was Verne Watts."

For Harry and Clutch, this had been home away from home for the mining season: not much in terms of creature comforts, but surrounded by the quiet beauty of the Brooks Range. During the summer, they dug gravel from the streambed with a Caterpillar and a backhoe, and piled it on the banks. There it grew, day after day, like a squirrel's grand cache of acorns. In the fall, as the tundra burst into color, they shifted gears as well. Pumping water through a pipeline they'd built from the stream, they blasted paydirt into the sluice box to see what came out the other end.

Though they mined this site for three years, Harry and Clutch never got rich on Hammond Creek, nor any of their other creeks. In fact, that was the biggest thing I had learned from my jaunt through gold rush history. For many of the miners, it wasn't about money.

"My dad told me, 'Don't get gold fever,'" Clutch said.

"Meaning what, exactly?"

Clutch paused for a moment, something he rarely did, and I leaned in a little closer.

"Everybody thinks they're gonna get rich right away, but it's not gonna happen," he said. "Trust me."

Of course, all miners were obsessed with gold. They talked about it constantly, could quote the exact size, shape, and weight of a nugget, to the hundredth of an ounce. And in private, they all fantasized about stumbling upon a chunk of gold the size of a baseball, no doubt. But what were the odds of that happening? The main reason they were out here, shoveling gravel at sixty below zero, was because it beat working at a factory or living in a high rise, following the strict set of rules society required. The goal wasn't to have an easy life, but one where they lived on their own terms, at their own pace and by their own rules. They may have come to Alaska with the hopes of getting rich, but they stayed for some other reason, maybe the same thing that gripped us all, yet no one could fully define.

Now that I was up here, in Clutch's favorite place on earth, I felt like I finally understood my quirky neighbor. Certain things were obvious from the first day I met him, strumming the tub bass at the Golden Eagle; he was clearly proud of his family's history and eager to carry the torch. But standing in the creek, which he had probably invested more into over the years than he'd taken out of, I realized something else. Clutch was trying to hold onto something, to the joy of exploring a wild canyon, to a way of life that was disappearing. That's why he loved sharing his family's history, and why he cherished the old sourdough stories. That's why he still spent the summers in Wiseman, even though he hadn't actively mined here in years. He loved everything about it—the excitement, the grit, the raw outdoors.

"I never really cared about gettin' rich, ya know." He threw a fistful of gravel back in the water. "It was more of an adventure, like going over the Chilkoot Trail, lookin' at the next drainage."

Yet Clutch was born just as small-time mining was dying out: it was getting harder to compete with the big corporations, more expensive to comply with the rules. In a way he was born too late, and he was still living in the past. It made me sad to think of him grasping at something that was slowly slipping away. Perhaps this was the dark side of my environmentalism. I had always focused on protecting the land, on humans being good stewards of fish and animals, of putting trails and habitat before roads. But, like everything else, conservation had a cost. Not just jobs, but the identity wrapped up in those jobs. As a third-generation miner, gold was in Clutch's blood. Just like the coal miners in Pennsylvania, whose livelihoods had been lost to automation and the rise of cheaper forms of energy, prospectors seemed to be losing not just their jobs but something bigger. The world was moving on without them.

Clutch leaned down to examine the tray, almost dunking his hat in the creek.

"Well, that's probably good for one day," he determined.

I peeked into the five-gallon bucket, where we had been emptying the contents of the sluice box for the past hour. It was half full. Meanwhile, my shoulders were aching and I was getting hungry.

"Looks good to me," I agreed.

Clutch removed the turf from the sluice box and folded it neatly into the bucket. I grabbed the handle and carried it up the side of the creek, careful not to tip it as I picked my way through the willows. There was no way of knowing what was in there—a life-changing nugget or just a bunch of worthless muck.

NICK JANS

RESOURCE CONFLICTS HAVE LONG BEEN ENDEMIC to Alaska. Disputes over fisheries played heavily into arguments first over establishing territorial status, and later during the push for statehood. The battles over developing the Prudhoe Bay oil field and building the Trans-Alaska Pipeline transformed not only Alaska's landscape, but its political culture as well.

Large scale resource extraction projects continue to be proposed in Alaska, undertakings that would excavate and permanently alter large swaths of essentially untouched wilderness. Environmental groups unsurprisingly oppose these plans, but often the fiercest resistance comes from nearby residents who are dependent on fish, wildlife, and plants, the survival of which they consider threatened by industrial activity. They fear losing their livelihoods and lifestyles.

In the Utukok-Kokolik uplands area in the far northwestern corner of Alaska that Nick Jans visits in the following essay, one of the largest coal deposits on Earth has been explored and staked out for development. The few local residents living near the region, meanwhile, are almost all Inupiat engaged in a largely subsistence-based economy, dependent, among other things, upon caribou that calve on land that could be stripped away and hauled out to power industrial economies on the other side of the globe.

Jans is one of Alaska's most well known and widely published authors. In 1979 he arrived in the interior Arctic Inupiat village of Ambler. He lived in the Arctic full time for the next twenty years, working as a teacher, writer, and photographer. His essays about his life in the north, which explored the nuances of living among the Inupiat, have been a regular feature in Alaska Magazine for many years. He has written 13 Alaska books and contributed to more than a dozen anthologies.

In 1999, Jans married and relocated to Southeast Alaska, but he has kept the house he built in Ambler and returns there every fall, using it as a base for his continuing travels. He describes Ambler as "the only place where where when I step off the mail plane, people take off their gloves to shake hands and say welcome home."

An advocate for keeping things wild, Jans told me, "For most people, supporting the idea of preserving wild Alaska is a no-brainer. The Great Land is one of the last reservoirs of large-scale wilderness on this rapidly shrinking rock we all call home. But as an Alaskan who's lived in, traveled, and studied Arctic wilderness for four decades, I feel a special responsibility to advocate; and the fact that I'm a writer and photographer, with the ability to reach out to others and provide accurate, first-hand information, strengthens that obligation to report from the front lines. One might argue that I'm simply engaging in NIMBY (Not In My Back Yard); however, wild Alaska—what the Inupiat call Nuna, The Land—is a legacy to the world, an invaluable treasure that we all must conserve and guard for future generations."

He added, "it's been a rare year when I was not in the Arctic at least part of the time; and I write about the Arctic and study and read all the time. I will be returning to travel the country until I am no longer able, and hope my ashes will end up somewhere in the Brooks Range."

"The Big Empty" appeared in Jans' 2016 collection *The Giant's Hand*. Since being published, Alaska has elected a different governor from the one mentioned here, perhaps its most pro-development one yet. And while coal mining in the Utukok-Kokolik thus far remains uneconomic, if some company decides it wants to make a go of it, it will will be greeted with a welcome mat in the state capital of Juneau, a city as far from north-western Alaska as Florida is from Minnesota.

— From *The Giant's Hand* —
THE BIG EMPTY

TWO HUNDRED FEET BELOW MY PERCH ON A ROCKY BLUFF, the Kokolik River carved a meandering arc toward the Chukchi Sea. Around that silvery thread, rolling tundra stretched over the horizon and off the edge of the earth in a vertigo-inducing sprawl. I'd long since learned not to trust my eyes in such country. A knoll I'd guessed a mile distant was, instead, only a few hundred yards; a blink transformed a standing grizzly into a ground squirrel. Without perspective, even gravity itself seemed suspect. All that kept me anchored was the skyline, and the sight of camp a half-mile upstream.

It was August 2006, and I'd tagged along on a Sierra Club sponsored float trip. We'd come to glimpse a vast, seldom-visited area: the uplands on the far northwestern edge of the Brooks Range. Overshadowed by other spectacular arctic wilderness tracts, this country, much of it lying within the NPRA (National Petroleum Reserve Alaska) and most of the rest owned by the state or the Arctic Slope Regional Corporation (ASRC), remains a forgotten corner of Alaska. In this oblong expanse stretching inland from the villages of Point Hope and Point Lay, along the northern foothills of the Brooks Range, you might travel a hundred miles without seeing anyone. It's hungry, treeless, wind-blasted country, where life clings in crevices. Patches of tundra rise into mesa-crowned badlands and low, elongated ridges—some rounded, others marked by limestone outcroppings resembling the vertebrae of great, long-vanished beasts. My home country of the upper Kobuk and Noatak valleys seemed almost tropical by comparison.

That austerity, though, is paradoxical: the Kokolik River drainage and the abutting Utukok Uplands are in fact a rich and critical chunk of wilderness. The Western Arctic Caribou Herd, Alaska's largest at more than 200,000 strong, migrates to the area each spring, one constant in a lifetime of movement. The barren ridges and tussock flats of the upper Utukok and Kokolik are the herd's ancestral calving grounds. Predator numbers in the area are generally lower than elsewhere, and the near-constant wind, coupled with well-drained ground, help keep hordes of mosquitoes and parasitic flies somewhat at bay—though local infestations can be intense on the few windless summer days. As the snow melts, emerging cotton grass shoots and other new growth provide vital, high-quality nutrition for nursing cows. Making this long, hard journey, through melting snow and across ice-flowing rivers, translates into survival for the collective being of the herd. Rather than a wasteland, this harsh terrain is a necessary haven; and the caribou themselves are the lifeblood of an enormous ecosystem extending as far south as the Seward Peninsula.

The Western Arctic Herd's steep decline in the past decade from a historic high of more than a half million highlights the importance of these barren sweeps. For reasons open to debate (climate change, elevated numbers of predators, possible human overharvest, and natural cycles) the herd is surely under stress. Things need to go well on the calving grounds over the next few years, or the herd, diminished by half and still one of the world's great masses of hoofed mammals, may wither to a skeletal presence. Pregnant cows shy away from disturbances, and may calve instead in spots far less favorable for their young's survival. While thousands of calves in the best of years are destined to die in their first year of life, there's little wiggle room for excess mortality if the herd is to maintain itself, let alone recover to its former might.

THANKS TO RECENT RAINS, OUR PARTY OF SEVEN, traveling in two rafts, was able to put in relatively high up the Kokolik. Riding the clear, shallow current down riffling pools, we journeyed away from the mountains and out through an autumn-tinged tundra sea. Over the next three days, the land would blaze into surreal reds and golds that peaked and just as quickly began to fade. Though signs of caribou lay everywhere—tracks, deep-grooved trails, bones, and droppings—we would see just one lone bull and a cow-calf pair on the entire trip. But many thousands had passed, and would again. As we sipped morning coffee at our first camp, a lone gray wolf stood on a hillside a quarter-mile upstream, announcing our strange-scented presence with a series of agitated howls. The next day, a red fox trotted through camp as if we were invisible. In our entire four-day float of 80-some miles, that was it for bigger-than-a-breadbox mammals. Still, every gravel bar was marked by tracks, some of them hours old: grizzly; wolf; musk ox; moose. Sparse as it seemed, the land coursed with life.

Meanwhile, we'd hit a banner year for lemmings and voles, and the tundra swarmed with them, as well as their pocket-sized predators. Short-tailed and least weasels bounded along the banks; one of the former scurried to within arm's length, black nose twitching, as if sizing me up for a possible buffet. Birds of prey, too, had gathered to feast. Groups of juvenile short-eared owls swooped low over our heads, peering wide-eyed down at us; peregrine falcons and rough-legged hawks keened from their cliff-side nests; shrikes, jaegers, and northern harriers by the dozen hunted the tundra, fattening up for their long journey south.

The true story of this place, however, lay in the rocks themselves. Much of this part of the Brooks Range was formed from uplifted and folded sedimentary rock. Strata of soft sandstone, limestone, and shale had weathered over countless seasons, rounding the land into elongated, east-west trending ridges and exposing lower, ancient layers. Time had scraped the country down to its bones; now fossils lay scattered at the surface as if dropped by a great, careless hand—everything from tableaux of ripples on a long-vanished shore to imprints of ferns, and casts of tree-like algae and minute, shelled creatures. Up one creek bed I hiked, chest-thick chunks of petrified redwood lay, annual rings and beetle holes in the bark as clear as if the trees had fallen not a hundred million years ago, but the day before. Some gravel bars seemed composed almost entirely of fossil-rich stone; others were littered with strange, glistening, green and red-marbled metamorphic stones that seemed to have fallen from space. Among these ancient remnants lay more recent leavings: shards of mammoth tusk from the last glacial epoch; a fragment of caribou horn sled runner lost by an Inupiaq traveler, perhaps centuries before; bleached remnants of a wolf-killed caribou from the previous winter.

Halfway through the second day, we spotted dark strata woven into a riverside bluff. Later that day, a geologists' helicopter racketed overhead, a link to the survey markers we'd seen driven into the tundra here and there. Part of the fossil record we'd marveled at translated into a primordial swamp that had flourished several hundred million years earlier. Layers of rotting plants had been deposited, buried, and compressed over the eons, creating the fuels on which we've come to depend: oil, natural gas, coal. Most proven, large-scale reserves of the first two lie farther north and to the east, on the edge of the arctic coastal plain and offshore. Before us, vast seams of coal lay just below the hooves of the caribou and the nests of falcons, over hundreds of millions of acres, almost as far east as the pipeline. Entire bluffs we passed were black with the stuff.

These contiguous coal fields north of the Brooks Range cover 30,000 square miles—a bit larger than the entire state of West Virginia, where companies have happily removed entire mountain tops to reach a single rich seam. In arctic Alaska, we're talking not billions, but as many as 4 trillion tons, much of it just sub-surface or even fully exposed—up to 9 percent of all the coal on the planet, in one of its wildest corners.

It's not just any coal, either. Much of the Utukok-Kokolik uplands area, as well as tracts further east is lignite—low-sulfur, clean-burning sub-bituminous and bituminous coal, among the best of its kind anywhere. Also, it's relatively close to coal-fueled Asian markets. In China alone, new coal-fired power plants go online steadily, and India as well is sprinting toward a vastly expanded, coal-reliant power grid. As the Arctic continues to thaw at an accelerated pace, the ice-free season for the Arctic Ocean continues to lengthen, and with it, the window for direct, more economical shipping routes. A barge port, built for the massive Red Dog lead-zinc mine, already exists near Kivalina, on the Chukchi Sea coast. All that's needed to make it go is a transport link connecting the coal to that port, or to a yet-to-be-created and closer new port.

The incredible size of these deposits was enough to entice BHP Billiton, the world's largest mining company, in partnership with the Native-owned ASRC, to spend 2006-2008 probing an especially rich feature near the coast around Point Lay known as the Deadfall Syncline, as well as drilling exploratory boreholes into promising areas across 175 million acres of ASRC land. Meanwhile, 300 miles to the east, just north of the central arctic Inupiaq village of Anaktuvuk Pass, another mining company, Millrock Resources, actively explored another huge lode on state land.

The potential scale of operations for arctic Alaska coal extraction is mind-boggling. Imagine a network of enormous mine pits and clusters of prefabricated steel buildings stretching over the horizon, linked by a network of gravel roads swarming with house-sized Terex ore trucks and giant excavators—all this dwarfed by a landscape that today remains as primordial and boundless as any on Earth.

Of course, development on such a scale, in such an extreme and remote location, poses a number of intertwined challenges. The most obvious involves access; either a heavy-duty road or rail bed that can bear the weight of massive equipment and material going in, and hundreds of millions of tons of coal going out. The cost of building such infrastructure spanning delicate permafrost soils, wetlands, and hundreds of stream crossings is breathtaking—millions of dollars per mile, a cost that is bound to rise over time. Then there are environmental issues, including the tricky business of safeguarding groundwater and reclamation once the mining is done.

Developers of course hoped the state would dig into its coffers to provide a transportation corridor, as it did with Red Dog, the world's largest zinc mine, in the late 1980s. In his 2011 state of the state address, then-governor Governor Sean Parnell affirmed that the state would provide $8 million to the Department of Transportation for preliminary work on a road reaching to Millrock's prospect and westward to the outpost of Umiat, deep in the heart of the central arctic coal fields. The move was part of an ambitious and aggressive statewide pro-development program titled Roads to Resources. Though the sum represented drops in a huge bucket, the state had pushed an ante onto the table, and the game was on. With ASRC, the mining companies, and the state shoulder to shoulder, the prospect of some sort of major development seemed inevitable as an approaching (albeit slow-motion) tsunami.

Directly in that wave's path lay the small Inupiaq community of Anaktuvuk Pass; and skirting the coal fields to the west, the remote coastal villages Point Hope and Point Lay—altogether, fewer than 1500 souls, the only people close enough to be directly affected. Despite enthusiastic promotion by their own regional Native corporation, and the fact that many villagers were dividend-reaping shareholders of ASRC, and stood to benefit as well from a much-boosted economy, the majority in each of these three communities remained adamantly opposed to coal development. They had their reasons.

Though the 21st century pours onward, bringing change at a dizzying pace—sod huts and dog teams to Internet and cell phones in three generations—residents still depend on the land and its gifts, for both material and spiritual sustenance, as they have for centuries. There are few, if any, Native households in the region where caribou meat, berries, seal oil, and more aren't regarded as prized and necessary resources. The general fear is that mining on such a scale, while providing good-paying jobs relatively near home villages, will disrupt centuries-old patterns of subsistence. Residents of Point Hope and Point Lay have complained that exploration helicopters have already altered caribou movements; and in the case of Anaktuvuk Pass, Millrock's proposed mining area lies square across a main migration path for the Central Arctic Herd. Considering that the Anaktuvuk people are descended from nomads who relied on the pass to funnel caribou to their waiting bows and lances ("Anaktuvuk" roughly translates to "Place of Caribou Droppings,") no surprise that the village tribal council stands united in its opposition to potential coal development in their area.

However, the seemingly inevitable mines weren't so inevitable after all—at least, in the short run. BHP in 2009 suspended their active prospecting in the area after concluding that high development costs and current economics would make mining unprofitable. Nonetheless, in 2010 they filed the necessary paperwork to keep their fingers firmly in the pie. Millrock, like Billiton, also shelved development plans. But a sizable boulder had been trundled a few yards uphill; and gearing up production if things changed would be that much faster—even if development shifted hands to other corporations.

On top of that blow to pro-development forces, Parnell was defeated in the 2014 gubernatorial election by fiscal conservative Bill Walker. The latter's reining in of state spending was more a matter of necessity than philosophy, as Alaska's operating budget dwindled and worldwide oil prices continued in a downward spiral. The Roads to Resources initiative ground to a halt.

Today, Alaska's oil revenues continue to waver and fade. The state economy is strapped; even basic school and road maintenance budgets have been decimated. No doubt The Great Land is searching for its next big fix. Royal Dutch Shell's much-ballyhooed offshore oil exploration in the Chukchi Sea, off the state's northwest coast, proved disastrous, and the multinational giant called off the effort in September 2015. Governor Walker has focused on promoting a long-touted plan to build a natural gas pipeline from the North Slope, to the east of the major coal fields.

However, such a mega-project is considered by many industry watchers to be every bit as much of a pipe dream as arctic coal, given current costs and realities; while permitting and other paperwork is moving forward, the project is still floating, but dead in the water.

OUR RAFTING PARTY—FOUR OF US ALASKANS, three visitors from Outside—sat up the Kokolik valley, warming our hands before a campfire kindled with dry willow and stoked with chunks of coal we'd gathered from the gravel bar around us. The black stuff ignited with little coaxing, and, burning with an acrid, black smoke reminiscent of burning tires, rose and swirled downwind. Our fire represented a tiny model of the final, ironic effect of arctic coal development. Not only would this land be utterly transformed by its removal, but burning it en masse, even afar, would hasten the already astonishing rate at which the western Arctic has warmed—five to eight degrees Fahrenheit average daily temperature in the past 40 years—and become a receptacle for atmospheric pollution. Already, the prevailing upper-level winds bring weather and contaminants straight from Asia to northwest Alaska and Canada. Once-crystalline air is now often tainted with a visible haze laden with sulfur dioxide, mercury, and greenhouse gases traced directly via chemical signatures to coal combustion. Heavy metals precipitate over water and land, and become increasingly concentrated as they move up the food chain, which ends with bears, seals, whales, walrus, and humans.

A similar slow-motion tsunami looms a couple hundred miles to the southeast, on the rim of the upper Kobuk valley. Plans and permitting for a half-billion dollar-plus, 200-mile road into my home country are well underway, aimed at a concentration of rich but fragmented mineral deposits sprawled along the geologically up-folded southern flank of the western Brooks Range—gold, copper, zinc, silver, and more. These lodes have been known and staked for decades, labeled by the state as The Ambler Mining District. Along with the North Slope coal and natural gas deposits, all these are referred to by promoters as "stranded" resources—a term that implies an urgent need for rescue. Just build that one gravel highway, they say, and a local network of more roads, to make development and extraction viable, and open a floodgate of riches.

With an eerily similar enthusiastic blessing of the region's Native corporation, NANA (The Northwest Arctic Native Association), preliminary studies have already been completed, and $26 million been spent by the state alone. Representatives for NANA and Canadian mining corporation Nova Copper have conducted community meetings across the region and beyond, assuring villagers that the mines will provide high-paying jobs and keep the NANA dividends flowing, and that the road will be closed to all but industrial use, thereby preventing a flood of pressure by outsiders on local resources. Some Inupiat and neighboring Koyukuk Athabaskans are buying into the dream, while many others oppose what they see as a looming nightmare of trailered-in boats, snowmobiles, and ATVs swarming over the land, driven by outsiders from Fairbanks, Anchorage, and beyond, all competing for local resources and stressing a fragile landscape.

Then there's the very real issue of acidic leaching from millions of tons of exposed waste rock finding its way down Kobuk tributaries and into the main river—not just for the decades of a given mine's life, but essentially forever. The especially toxic waste given off by these particular sulfide ores neither degrades nor goes away; and even trace amounts of heavy metal contaminants have been found to affect the ability of salmon to find their natal streams. Larger amounts threaten the entire food chain. The record of large-scale, long-term contamination from similar mines, elsewhere in Alaska, the U.S., and the world, is dismal.

Supporters of the mines and road avoid those points; they insist that the highest environmental standards will be adhered to. They also blur past the fact that once upon a time, the state of Alaska made a similar promise about the oil pipeline haul road being forever private—and practically overnight, it was opened to the general public. How could the approximately 800 people of the upper Kobuk avoid being overwhelmed by the world beyond?

As I stood by that coal-fueled campfire on the Kokolik, I couldn't avoid the hollow realization: even if every one of these projects were delayed for two or three decades or longer, even if I might not live to witness their completion, the numbers would eventually match up, and the roads and mines and gas pipelines would come. Tropical swamps to arctic wilderness to a rural industrial park of giant strip mines, and whistle-stop villages connected by alternately icy and dusty ribbons of gravel—just a function of pressure and time. We've heard the argument that the Arctic's people can have it all: caribou, wild country, and decades of prosperity. But as I stared up at those tall, dark bluffs along the Kokolik, all I felt was empty.

ALEXIS BUNTEN

WHEN ALEXIS BUNTEN WENT TO WORK for Sitka-based Tribal Tours, a nonprofit subsidiary of Sitka Tribe of Alaska, her objective was to embed herself in a Native-run tourism business as part of her PhD work in cultural anthropology. Along with that degree, which she obtained from UCLA, her experiences also resulted in a lively book that explores the complexities of maintaining Native identity in a rapidly changing world, and presenting that identity to the broader public through cultural tourism without whitewashing it in the process. The book also examines the impacts of tourism on local communities that come to depend on it for economic opportunities, and the daily experiences of being a seasonal worker. She accomplished all this and more while maintaining a persistent sense of humor in what remains one of my favorite works of contemporary Alaskan nonfiction.

"So, How Long Have You Been Native?" condenses Bunten's two summers of work into a single season, capturing the broader arc of temporary employment in the tourist industry while focusing on how it plays out for a small company trying to sell day tours to cruise ship passengers.

Tribal Tours is engaged in a difficult balancing act. Part of the Tlingit history being taught to tourists involves the severe mistreatment Southeast Alaska Natives suffered at the hands of Russian and American settlers in Alaska. Conveying this to people on vacation in a manner that is informative without being offensive is one of the struggles Bunten and her coworkers deal with as part of their jobs.

Another challenge springs from how the tour guides are tasked with selling the culture, yet somehow need to avoid commodifying themselves. Tourists, meanwhile, arriving with set notions of what Native "authenticity" is, sometimes struggle to grasp that the Tlingit and other Alaska Native groups are as much a part of the modern world as urban Americans of European extraction. That disconnect extends all the way to the book's title; one of her coworkers actually was asked by a tourist, "So, how long have you been Native?"

Bunten proves to be the perfect go-between. She is is of Unangan Alutiiq (Aleut) and Yup'ik, as well as Swedish descent. She grew up enjoying summers in Alaska, but spent most of her life elsewhere. With a mixed identity that tilts strongly to her Native Alaskan roots, but with experiences largely had in the broader world, she's able to see both sides of a divide she views as bridgeable. She considers tourism a legitimate means of making needed connections.

Explaining her objectives with this work, Bunten told me, "In writing this book, I wanted to share the complexities and tensions of maintaining Indigenous identity in the complex world we live in. Our lives are messy. Many of us Alaska Natives struggle to maintain our cultural identities, and I think that tourism is a beautiful way to make a good living that also makes the world a better place by building intercultural bridges. Ultimately, I love learning the back story of events, places and people, and I hope that Alaskans, and people traveling to Alaska, also enjoy reading what happens when you pull the curtain back on cultural tourism."

Bunten lives in California, where she leads the Bioneers Indigeneity Program, engages in a range of academic pursuits, continues her studies to engage in Indigenous tourism, and publishes widely about Indigenous and environmental issues in academic and mainstream media outlets.

— From *So, How Long Have You Been Native?* —
JULY: MEETING THE TOURIST GAZE

CHRISTINA WARNED US THAT IF WE DIDN'T FIND OUR OWN WAY of giving tours, we would have a hard time making it to the end of the season. In order to become really good at our jobs, we needed to create "tour guide personas," facsimiles of our real personalities tailored to the tourism experience. Olga's brother Matthew called us "Stepford Natives" for our ever-pleasant demeanors. "Stepford Natives" only tell one side of a story. They don't get caught up in painful details. The past is an idealized place, where our ancestors lived off the land, in peace and harmony. Shamans don't exist. Nor does alcoholism, neglect, jealousy and violence in the world of the Stepford Natives.

The veteran guides carved out larger than life personas. The more they personalized and stylized their tours, the more they seemed to enjoy their jobs. Their personas helped them to cope with the challenges of tour guiding year after year. It protected them from having to deal with the painful truth that many of our guests came to us with imaginary ideas about what it means to be Native that we could never live up to.

IN AN ATTEMPT TO HELP THE NEW GUIDES, Heather, Pam and I, to personalize our tours, Christina encouraged us to shadow the veteran guides on their tours. I decided to ride along with Jackson. I was attracted to Jackson's sense of humor; he reminded me of a beloved Vegas performer, who repeats the same corny material night after night to the hair curler set. In other words, the cruise ship visitors loved him.

Jackson's wife Vickie picked me up for work to meet Jackson at the bus barn, where he was getting the motor coach ready to pick up a pre-arranged tour with the Carnival Spirit. "Everything OK?" I asked Vickie. "You look tired." "Yeah, just had a late night last night," Vicky admitted. "Jackson and I are sharing a car right now, and I've got to work a double shift for the next couple days, so it's going to be rough." We picked up mochas at the drive through coffee shop, and headed over.

"I've got to run! No time to hang around this morning" Vickie dropped me off. "See you later Vickie." She was already out of the parking lot before I finished my sentence. If they had a late night, Jackson didn't show it,

"Hi!" he greeted me brightly as I handed him his mocha. "Ready to go on tour?" "Yes, I am. Thanks for letting me tag along, Jackson. I really want to learn from the way you give tours. I want to make them laugh."

We picked up the tour group, "Welcome everyone . . . For how many of you folks is this your first trip to Sitka?" As we drove the regular tour route, Jackson told such dry puns that only someone with his show-boat demeanor could possibly deliver them without eliciting a chorus of groans. As he drove past Sheldon Jackson museum, Jackson delivered rapid-fire commentary:

SHELDON JACKSON BUILT THIS SCHOOL ORIGINALLY to educate Alaska Natives, to give them the skills to compete in the new American culture. In 1897, he built that octagonal building you see there. That building was the first concrete building in Alaska. Do you know why he made it concrete? He made it so that the building would not burn down in case of a fire, because it is the first museum in Alaska. At the same time that Sheldon Jackson was assimilating all the Sitka Natives to white ways, he traveled all aroundAlaska to collect and preserve artifacts that showed our ways of life that he believed were quickly disappearing.

[Jackson's speech slowed down]

Now it's a world-class museum, folks, that showcases art and artifacts from every major Alaska Native culture. There are eight major Alaska Native cultures: Inupiaq, Yup'ik, Siberian Eskimo, Alutiq, Athabascan, Tlingit, Haida and Simpshian, but I am going to pause and take a minute to talk a little more about the Simpshian people who are originally from an island just south of here called Metlakatla. And the reason I want to talk about this is because some time ago there was a double murder so brutal . . . A man murdered his ex-wife and her new lover with a carving knife. All the evidence pointed to the ex-husband as the murderer, but after a drawn-out trial, he was acquitted. And do you know what that man's name was?

[Pause]

O.J. Simpshian!

The audience laughed heartily; only a few of them groaned.

I SPENT THE NEXT WEEK DEVELOPING MATERIAL to improve my own tours, trying out lines that I saw work for the other guides and testing new ones. One schtick that worked particularly well for me played off an auto insurance commercial popular that summer. As I pulled up to the Sitka National Historical Park, I began, "Do you see all those totem poles at the edge of the forest?" "Yes," the group responded.

"When we get off the bus, I'm going to tell you all about the meanings of the images carved on those totem poles, but first I want to give you some background information. Those totem poles you see there were not originally carved here. In fact, some of them are not even Tlingit poles. Some of them are Haida and Simshian poles brought here to the park by the territorial governor from the Northwest Coast Exhibit at the 1904 St Louis World's Fair. Why, you may ask, do we have Haida and Simshian poles here? It's a long story, but you're going to hear it.

"Down the end of the trail here is the site where the Tlingits fought the Russians in the 1804 battle for Sitka; as a result of the battle, the Tlingits retreated to the other side of the island and deeded Castle Hill— the hill you may have seen from the dock where you landed this morning, where we started this tour—to the Russians. As soon as the Tlingits retreated, do you wanna know what the Russians did? They proceeded to burn down the Tlingit village in what is now downtown Sitka, and that inevitably included some of the totem poles, to make way for the new Russian town, Novoarkangelsk. [Here, tourists would gasp.]

"But overall, the Russians didn't try to end the Tlingit way of life. No, that job was for the Americans. After Russia sold the territory of Alaska to the US in 1867, the transfer took place in town here at Castle Hill where Baranoff's castle, and the headquarters for the Russian American company were located. Because at the time Novoarkangelsk was capital of Russian America. When the American missionaries got here, they immediately and mistakenly identified the remaining Tlingit carvings as idols to false gods. By this time there wasn't as much to destroy as there was before the Russians came. So the American Missionaries finished the job. So they burnt down any remaining totem poles and put a ban on the carving of heathenistic idols. [Tourists would gasp louder this time, some commenting "Oh no!" and "How horrible!"]. But it's really not that bad, you guys. ["What do you mean?" a voice from the back always shouts out.] Well, despite the fact that first the Russians burned the original village, and then the American missionaries finished off the job, there is a positive side to all of this.

[Pause]

"I just saved a lot of money switching to Geico!"

This non-sequitur punch line, much like Jackson's "OJ Simpshian" never failed to elicit peals of laughter from my groups of tourists.

The kind of jokes that Jackson and I favored fit a category of humor called, "shaggy dog stories." This comedic genre got it's name from a classic joke about a man who went through considerable trouble to return a shaggy dog to a family in England for reward money only to get a door slammed in his face with the remark, "he wasn't that shaggy." These kinds of jokes are defined by their long-winded, detailed introductions that end in an absurd or ironic twist that undermines the very telling of the story. These jokes play upon and audience's preconceptions of how story should work. Listeners pay attention to a story with certain expectations, which simply do not happen not, or are otherwise met in some entirely unexpected manner.

The "Geico" punch line made the story safe; it lightened a tense mood. It allowed me to bring up important aspects of history that are uncomfortable. Having no conscious familiarity with the Shaggy Dog joke genre when I made it up, my Geico joke was masterful in this regard. The set-up for the joke was a long-winded account of the decimation of Native culture in Sitka at the hands of colonizing Russians and Americans. As I explained how Sitka lost its totem poles not once, but twice, the audience became more and more uncomfortable. Most people don't expect to face dark periods in history when they plan a vacation to Alaska. They want to experience nature on a grand scale and meet friendly locals. By the time I reached the punch line, my tour groups were rapt with sadness over the sequence of events I presented as they gazed at the magnificent totem poles at the Sitka National Historical Park. So when I abruptly changed the subject, just as my audience was deeply drawn into a story of cultural genocide, I let them off the hook. I distorted their emotional reactions to my story with a flip comment about saving money. I shifted the tone of the tour from the dangerous territory of being a Native tour guide who bears the painful legacy of manifest destiny to a fun visit with a regular person who knows what's funny on TV right now.

My coworkers and I were painfully aware that our clients wanted an Indigenous experience, but that some tourists viewed an Indigenous encounter as potentially "hostile." By making jokes, we relieved our tour groups of any fear of Native "backlash" against them by helping visitors to discover that we are just like them. This desire to identify with a superficially dangerous experience, within an overall structure of safety that many of our visitors shared is not limited to the tourism setting. It takes place anywhere members of a dominant group are drawn to a historically oppressed group within a context that allows interaction between the two under the security of rules and expectations set forth by those in power. It happens when professors are banned from saying anything that might be construed as unfair to powerful political interests, like teaching about Israel as an apartheid state. It happens when suburban, white teenage boys listen to gangsta' rap, but are afraid to set foot in the "ghetto" neighborhoods that inspire the music. It happens when middle class baby boomers change out of their suits and into just bought stiff leathers to attend the annual motorcycle rally in Sturgis, South Dakota.

We knew that Alaska tops the list in the American imagination as the most rugged, wild and dangerous place to visit. We understood that in order to do our jobs well, we needed to titillate tourists a little bit with our Native perspectives. Hell yes, we hunt and fish for our dinner! We perform 'spirit dances' at ceremonies hidden behind carved masks and elaborate robes. We told fantastical stories about how raven created the world by opening the box of daylight, the woman who married a bear, or how mosquitoes came to be . . . Over time, we developed a heightened "double consciousness," or what African American scholar W.E.B. Dubois, described over a century ago as the idea that one is always looking at one's self through the eyes of others.

I slowly became more adept at "reading" groups of visitors, molding my presentation of self to match what I thought they wanted of me. If the group seemed energetic, I might take them for an extra long walk in the park and include more information about local plants. Or if the group laughed at my first joke, I would continue to tell more jokes. If the group became very excited when I pointed out a few bald eagles or Hershel, the Sea Lion who hung around the lightering facility, I detoured from my regular route to places where I knew we would be likely to see more wildlife. Far from mechanically reciting the same tour to each group, I allowed different aspects of my knowledge and personality to surface in response to the dynamics of each group.

All successful Tribal Tours guides had the ability to tailor their situational identities. For education-focused groups such as those organized by Elderhostel, guides gave informative, historically rich tours, adapting their presentation to that of a more formal, slightly detached instructor. On exclusive, family-group tours, guides became a closer facsimile to their informal personalities outside of the workplace, sharing more of their personal experiences than they would on a larger tour. But most of our clients were retirees from the Midwest who enjoyed humorous, lightweight tours. This typical kind of visitor had probably shaped Jackson and Sandy's guiding styles over the years.

Some Tribal Tours workers were never quite able to tailor their personalities to match different tour groups, much less deliver a tour that went beyond the tour script. A few weeks into driving tours, Heather still struggled to present any kind of tour. "I just can't talk like that! I'm shy," Heather complained, after Malia tried to give her a pep talk. "Don't worry about forgetting the tour script. Just tell visitors about what its like living in Sitka. That's what they would really like to know." Malia was not aware that Heather grew up with her Tlingit grandmother who instilled in her the cultural restriction from talking about oneself in an autobiographical manner. Asking Heather to simply "get over" her difficulty delivering tour content was tantamount to telling someone who is afraid of heights to "just try" bungee jumping. But Heather needed to make some money before the baby would come, and she would have to quit working for several weeks. So she kept trying her best.

Malia didn't know that the way Tribal Tours requires workers to talk about themselves can be considered quite rude in some local contexts. While the ability to speak confidently about ones' personal experiences might be valued in mainstream American culture, there is a time and a place for it in traditional Tlingit culture. People who are truly respected in traditional Tlingit society allow others to speak for them, to talk about their accomplishments in the right context. In pre-contact Tlingit culture, the depth of interpersonal communication depended on specific relationships between people, as well as inter-clan relations. Too much grandstanding was a sign that the individual is too self-centered to put their clan first, or just plain socially retarded.

Tourism workers operate within a complex cross-cultural world that is not immune to contradiction. Some of my coworkers, like Heather, had a very traditional upbringing, and others, like Erik, had no prior exposure to the culture. The degree to which Tribal Tours' workers gave preference to Tlingit cultural rules was up to each individual. What might be taboo for one guide to talk about with tourists was perfectly fine for another.

AMONG THE MANY CONVERSATIONS ABOUT what is appropriate to share on tours, Shamanism was one of several topics we tended to avoid. Talking about cultural genocide was a tough call. That's why I approached the subject in the form of a joke about car insurance, to lighten the mood and open up a safe space to discuss these issues. "Remember when you had Heather, Pam and I join your tour last month?" I asked Natty. "I liked the way that you talked about the Russian and then American colonization in a way that was straightforward, but didn't in any way, blame the tour goers, or induce any kind of 'white guilt'. I know a lot of people still have a hard time with that period because it continues to impact our lives now. What's your philosophy for talking about bad things that happened in the past?"

"I went through a lot of painful years when I was younger. I spent nearly a decade drunk or high on peoples' couches. But I never drove, thanks the creator, and I never hurt anybody. I only hurt myself. And I was angry. Really angry. But I have learned not to let anger rule me. All I can control is what happens from now on. I had to learn to forgive those who caused myself and our people harm otherwise I never would have healed. Making the tourists feel bad for something that happened before their time is counterproductive. It doesn't lead to any kind of healing."

"But isn't it important that our visitors understand what really happened in the past? I don't believe in sanitizing the past. If we are teaching people about Sitka from a Native point of view, I'd say understanding the impacts of Russian and American takeovers are a pretty important part of our perspectives today. I don't celebrate Columbus Day, you know what I mean, Natty?"

Natty didn't want us to relive traumatic events as part of the job description. And we newbie's had learned by now that we would come across as 'hostile' towards our tour groups and make them feel uneasy if we expressed too much charged emotion against European and American colonization. We also understood that if we discussed tragic events in history, we would be in danger of calling forth our own internalized pain over the past. We knew that once these feelings rise to the surface, emotional labor cannot always suffice to bring us back to our tour guide personas.

I DROPPED OFF MY LAST TOUR GROUP in front of the Naa Kahidi Community House around 2 p.m. I was beaming from delivering what I thought was my best tour to date. After parking the bus, I went inside to punch out my timecard to see who was around and to find out what was happening after work. I wanted to spend my tips! As I started to chat with Malia and Kylie about plans to cook some crab down at the beach, Melanie walked in, visibly shaken.

"Is everything OK?" I asked, putting my arms around Melanie to give her a big hug. Melanie, who was usually very even-tempered sniffed, "No. I had a really hard time with someone on my last tour. I really wanted to boot her off."

"Do you feel comfortable telling me what happened? Maybe we need to report that person to someone?" I said, thinking of a story I heard about a visitor the year before who had harassed the other tourists on board the motorcoach, and had to be escorted back to the cruise ship by the local police.

"No, that's OK." Melanie's voice went from sad to angry to sad again, as she recounted her story: "I was giving my tour, and it became apparent right away that I had a know-it-all on board. Every time I said something about Sitka, this lady in the back of the bus corrected me, 'No, it did not happen this way, blah, blah, blah, I read it in a book,'" Melanie sing-songed the offender's comments in a whiney, nasally voice.

"How does she know that her book is not more accurate than my clan's stories? I always get so nervous around tourists who read up on Sitka, and think they know it better than me, even though I have lived here my whole life!"

"As if writing it down makes it more legit than oral history!" Malia backed her friend up.

"So we get to the park, and I am walking the group down the path to the river explaining the battle of 1804, and the Tlingit survival march after they were forced to surrender Castle Hill at the end of the battle. I explained that because the Kiks.ádis were in such a hurry to keep the Russians off their tail, and because they had to pack up and leave in such a hurry without many of the necessary supplies, many of the weak members of the group, elders, children and infants, perished along the hard trek across the island. I explained that this was a very sad time for our people, to lose our loved ones. Then this know-it-all lady pipes up and tells me that, no, I am wrong. She announced loudly, talking over me, that my ancestors were 'bloodthirsty cannibals' who slaughtered their own elders and infants to prevent the Russians from locating the clan's location along the march. I told her that she was wrong, while there were instances of ritualized cannibalism among the Natives, that was a false rumor. We did not savagely murder our grandparents and children!"

"Hey, that was very professional of you!" I offered weakly. "I'da maybe told her where to shove it." Of course, my freedom to tell people to "shove it" hinged upon the reality that this was my summer job, and not my livelihood. I didn't have a family to feed.

Melanie continued, "The know-it-all began to shout that I was wrong, and I didn't know what I was talking about. At that point, I just stopped telling the story, and started talking about the berries along the path. Her ignorance really hurt me!"

Melanie finished, tears streaking down her face now. "I don't know how I am supposed to handle somebody telling me that my people are less than human, animals that would kill their own babies!"

"You shouldn't have to deal with that! Why don't you come and eat some crab with us tonight? We're going to get a bottle of chardonnay," Malia enticed Melanie. "No. I think I'm going to go home, hang out with my kids and work on some beading tonight." Melanie left the office for the day, and didn't come to work the next day, too upset by the buildup of emotions that resulted from hearing the insistent claims made by the callous, know-it-all tourist. Melanie wasn't just drained from that one short exchange, but a number of little encounters that added up over the course of the season, and now began to take its emotional toll. She needed a few days off.

We processed our work experiences in the back office of the community house. These conversations involved a high level of awareness among us about the master narratives lurking just under the surface of the tourism encounter. Yes, we could talk about the survival march, one of the keystone events in recent Kiks.ádi history. But if we chose to do so, we'd better be prepared to come up against the idea that Natives are not so human, that they will kill their own children if they have to.

Christina often reminded us that we needed to fit the way the tourism industry works, not the other way around. "We are not on Indian time here, people!" Christina proclaimed at a staff meeting:

"People think that being on "Indian time" means that you will show up whenever it suits you, but the concept of "Indian time" has been distorted. Being on time is part of our culture. Do you think our ancestors showed up late when it was time to pick berries, to gather herring eggs, or to fish for salmon? Back then, running on 'Indian time' meant you got there on time to get the work done because if our ancestors were late, do you know what would have happened? They would have starved. died. But they didn't. They thrived off of what the land provided and they built great wealth because they were ON TIME. So when you get a schedule for the week that asks you to be at the docks at 6:30 a.m., it is for a reason."

"I'm going to be real on-time tomorrow then," Melanie whispered, "because I'm going fishing with my brothers tomorrow morning. Wanna come?" "Hell yes, let me see if I can get the day off." After the meeting, I pleaded my case to Natty. He let me go, only if I promised to help process fish that weekend.

The next morning, I met Melanie and her two brothers at Crescent Harbor. I jumped in the skiff wearing my waterproof gear from head to toe. As we took off I smiled as I watched the two cruise ships docked in Silver Bay became smaller and smaller, and then non-existent as we rounded the corner. The mountains reached all the way down to the ocean and little islands dotted the blue and green landscape. I scanned the shore hoping to spot a bear. Everyone kept quiet throughout the forty-five minute ride. The motor was loud and no one wanted to distract Melanie's brother, Mark, from steering the boat. There were too many unseen rocks and other hazards we could easily run into into. We steered through a narrow passageway carved out by glaciers thousands of years ago to Redoubt Lake and up to the base of a waterfall. Red-bellied sockeye salmon fought their way up the falls, their hooked lips gaping in the open air.

"Look!" Melanie pointed up the other side of the waterfall. A black bear and her two cubs were fishing at the top of the falls. "Good thing we are in a boat!" she added. Mark steered the boat closer to shore, while Luke, her other brother reached out for a log and tied the boat to it. "Here," Mark motioned for me to take the wheel, "make sure we don't get turned around while we are fishing." Mark and Luke pulled out large nets on the ends of metal poles and began dipping for sockeye. It was hard work, scoop after scoop, and the brothers did not pull any fish in for the first twenty minutes. "Let us girls try!" Melanie insisted and we traded places with the boys. I almost hit Melanie on the head with my first dip. "I'm sorry," I knew better than that. I needed to keep an eye on where I was swinging that net around. "Keep it low, just like fishing" Luke advised. A few minutes later, I dipped into a group of sockeye visible at the surface. Most of them scattered. The steady water tension became a forceful set of jerks yanking the net in multiple directions. I pulled up and almost dropped the heavy net, just as Luke gave me support by grabbing the pole from behind. Four sockeye lopped onto the floor of the skiff. I descended on them quickly with the butt end of a hunting knife, stunning them to death with a quick blow to the fishes' heads. "Nice job!" Melanie congratulated me. "Check her out!" Mark teased. My arms were wobbly from exertion. "I think I'll go back to steering the boat." "No you don't girl," Melanie wasn't about to let me off the hook. "We each get 25 today." "It's bullshit," Mark muttered, "we should be able to take what we need for subsistence."

We stayed for two more hours, taking turns with the dip nets until we reached our maximum limit. The bottom of the boat was covered in slick, red-bellied carcasses. Melanie, Luke and I cut fish the entire ride back to town, throwing guts into the ocean as we worked. My fingers froze solid handling the damp fish as we steered back to town facing the cold wind. Natty met us at the dock. We loaded the fish into his truck while Melanie's brothers cleaned up the boat. We dropped off about half the fish at Melanie's house, where she would freeze most of them for all of us and took the rest to Natty's house. Natty lived in a modular home with his mother, Olinda, and father, George. We went to the shed out back to prepare the fish for the smokehouse. Natty's father had been cutting alder all day in preparation to smoke fish. We spread out buckets of salmon at opposite ends of a large work table and started cleaning and cutting some more, filleting the gutted fish into strips for hanging on the racks in the smokehouse. We finished by nightfall. Melanie, Mark and Luke joined us at Natty's house. Kendra and Betty came with them. I was suddenly starving when I smelled the fresh sockeye Olinda had baked for us. I realized I hadn't eaten all day. Betty brought a large bowl of fish dip, made with last year's smoked salmon mixed with cream cheese, mayonnaise, fresh garlic and onions. Olinda put out a box of pilot bread on the table to eat with the dip.

"This is delicious!" I smacked my lips. "We'll eat some of this fish, but most of what we caught today is going to go to Olga's pay off party," Melanie explained. "Do you want to come help us jar it after we're done smoking the fish? You can take a few jars home." "YES!" I rarely got my hands on home smoked and jarred fish down south in California. And I was so spoiled by eating home-smoked fish my whole life, I couldn't stand lox and other forms of commercially smoked fish sold in supermarkets.

"Hey," I realized this was the first time I had seen Kendra socially since the beginning of the summer. I spent down time with Melanie and Olga every other week or so, but Kendra rarely joined us. "Where's your ball and chain?" Kendra's lips began to quiver. "She and Kyle broke up last night," Melanie spilled. "He wanted me to go all the way," Kendra explained. "I can't have sex until I am married. That's my commitment to God." "Good for you, Kendra!" I gave her a little hug. "He can wait or he can go fishing somewhere else," Melanie said. "I bet he's already with someone else RIGHT NOW," Kendra wailed. Olinda shot her a nasty look from across the table. "He's a teenager. He's got crazy-hormones. I doubt he's waiting around. But he won't find anyone as pretty and sweet as you," I tried to comfort Kendra from the perspective of someone with ten more years life experience under my belt, "Just wait. You'll do better." "She'll be fine," Melanie assured herself more than her daughter. "Yeah, you'll be fine."

As we feasted, Natty reminded Melanie and I, "ready for work tomorrow at 6 a.m.?" "Oh, you are evil," I teased Natty. "It's a good thing we were raised to work this hard." "Someone should tell my college students that," I recalled working as a teaching assistant at UCLA. "I don't think they can put in more than a few minutes at a time hard work, unless they are cramming for a test." "We're cramming for a test in a way," Kendra offered, brightly in contrast to her mood five minutes before. "It's called life. If we don't get our subsistence foods, we will not make it to the next level." "I just wish I could have gone with you guys today," Natty remarked sadly.

That weekend, I worked alongside Melanie, Natty, Kendra, Olinda and George prepare fish for winter, just as some of our ancestors had summer after summer for thousands of years. I remembered the stairs to the basement of my grandparents' house, flanked by wooden shelves stacked heavy with jars and jars of fish, jam, and other home-pickled foods. Even as a small child, I noticed that many of them were very dusty. I thought about those dusty old jars as I helped my grandmother to stir berries in a big pot with sugar and pectin for next year's batch. I think my grandparents just had too much canned food to eat. Or maybe they forgot to eat it in their old age, but they couldn't stop the habit of preserving food for later.

After a long weekend smoking and jarring fish, it was almost a shock to go back to work on Monday morning. I began my first tour of the day finally ready to abandon the script, and just talk about what it means to be Native Alaskan.

"Over on the other side of where your ships are docked," I gestured, "is a place where the locals go fishing for subsistence. I was just there catching sockeye salmon and helping to smoke and jar it for next winter.

In the distant past, all summer would be devoted to getting ready for winter. People would leave their permanent clan houses and head to fish camps to gather beach greens, seaweed, pick berries, fish and hunt. The elders described it as hard work, but always very fun. Of course, they were very young children when that lifestyle made way for cash jobs that did not permit their parents to spend months away gathering foods. Their parents needed cash to survive now, and so fathers became commercial fishermen, and mothers worked in the canneries cutting up fish or in logging camps cooking for white settlers instead of their families.

Some people say that the subsistence lifestyle, living off the land, is what defines Alaska Natives. Maybe what defines us is the value of working hard for something that matters. "I'm going show you some of the things you could eat right now." I pulled over. Everyone filed out of the motor coach and lined up along the bridge over looking the Stargavin Estuary seven miles out the road from downtown. It was an unusually sunny day. Do you see the salmon swimming up river?" Everyone's cameras went click click click. "See those bushes over there? In about a month here, they will be just covered with berries. That weed over by your feet is what we call, 'Indian celery.' It's a little strong, but I like the flavor." "Is that 'cow parsnip'?" someone else asked. "I think so. I'm not sure. Over there on the beach if the tide were low, we could gather gumboots. They are a kind of chewey mollusk you can eat. And there's several different kinds of seaweed you can choose from for your salad. If you were brave enough to dive in the cold water just off the rocky point over there, you could gather abalone. I heard it's going for like 100 dollars market price in San Francisco. Yeah, no one ever had a problem living in Southeast Alaska so long as they were willing to work hard."

"Do all Natives live this way?" someone from the back of the bus shouted out. "Nope. No. Some do. Many do in Alaska. But you've got to know what to eat. That's not hard if you grew up doing it, but imagine if you got dropped off on one of these little islands here. Do you think you could survive off the land?" "I have been watching those shows on cable about mountain men, so I think so," he replied. "Maybe," I laughed.

"It depends on if you have the time to gather subsistence foods, if you know how to do it right. You have to know how to give thanks to your creator for these animals so they will continue to provide for us. If you screw that up, you're going to be in trouble. And, you have to know what time of year to gather what. You can't just get everything you need all at once. Right now, it is the end of July and there's a lot to eat. You can fish for king salmon, silver salmon, sockeye salmon. You can also gather lots of berries and wild rice from now right up through September. Traditionally, the Tlingit would be working hard right this time of year to gather up many of the foods that would feed them all winter. But it takes all year to have a well-rounded diet. Fall time is deer season and a good time for dunginess crab. In winter, you've pretty much got seal meat, geoducks, clams and more crab. Everyone gets excited for March. That's when the herring come in and spawn. I love herring eggs. Late spring, its time to gather different kinds of seaweed. As it gets closer to May and June, the fresh spruce tips come out. They are tangy and lemony. You can also pick the fiddleheads, or baby ferns, goose tongue, which is a type of green, and the early berries. All the while, you'd be eating and preserving for later. Oh man, if I could have everything all at once, I'd have some slow roasted deer with wild rice, a fiddlehead salad on the side, oh yeah and something totally sacrilegious like a casserole with layers of halibut, crab and king salmon, dried fish dipped in seal oil . . ." I was beginning to distract myself. "You should have an Alaskan foods only cooking show!" the man who watched a lot of cable TV shouted out again. "Yeah, I'm hungry now," someone else interjected. "Where's a good place to eat." "Unfortunately, most of the restaurants in this town are terrible," I admitted. "But there is one place. Listen, you are all my last tour for the day. I'll walk you over to where you need to go after the tour, and maybe I'll sit down and have some food with you. I think I just made myself hungry!" I admitted. I finished the tour and kept my promise. It was fun to hang out with a handful of my guests without my tour guide persona on. We laughed and traded stories. We didn't see each other through "tour guide" and "tourist" filters. No more double consciousness. No more masks. No hard feelings as stereotypes and expectations were temporarily suspended over a nice meal. I enjoyed their company, even if it was temporary. As Sandy always said, "tourists only travel in one direction."

TANYO RAVICZ

Tanyo Ravicz could not have picked a more perfect title for his 2007 short story collection than the one he used, *Alaskans*. The stories Ravicz tells are of everyday Alaskans, most of them working class, who aren't so much awed by the the state as they are resigned to it. They live through its hardships and reap its bounty and get up the next day to do it again.

Born in Mexico City, Ravicz spent his childhood in Los Angeles. He graduated from Harvard with a degree in English and American literature and language. After living on the East Coast and in Europe, he came to Alaska in 1986.

Ravicz told me, "I didn't come to Alaska to write about Alaskans, but I came with a writer's outlook, an openness to experience and an open-eyed acceptance of people as I find them."

During his time in Alaska, Ravicz lived in Fairbanks, Anchorage, and Kodiak, and worked the sort of hard labor jobs that can provide substantial volumes of material for someone paying attention.

"My parents were anthropologists and had this relentless curiosity about people and places."

Ravicz's ear for conversation is what is most distinctive about *Alaskans*. He said, "How people express their humanity in this great, diverse land, their distinctive preoccupations, the ways they talk about the things they talk about—this fascinates me." This shows in his characters, who *sound* like Alaskans. In a scene from the story "One Less Black Bear," a wildfire crew whose food supplies are being ransacked by a bear copes with the situation on the ground and the bureaucracy in Fairbanks that prevents them from resolving it themselves:

> *"Any word about the fire?"*
> *"They're talking about a backfire."* His eyes closed over the smoke from his cigarette. *"You heard about the blackie?"*
> *"They're gonna shoot it,"* John Ritchie said.
> *"I figured."*
> *"These jokers in overhead."* Ritchie laughed his gimpy weak-chested laugh. *"Can't kill a bear without going up the chain of command."*

Brief exchanges like this are found throughout Ravicz's book and lend it its sense of realism. It's the same with the characters in the story presented here. A trio of cannery workers in Bristol Bay make a liquor run to the nearest town. Their conversation is rambling, profane, and very male. The beauty of the locale barely captures their notice. They've come to Alaska with the longterm objective of saving up a bit of money, and the short term goal of getting drunk. The three are not the sort of people most would choose to befriend, but in remote parts of Alaska, and especially when working seasonal jobs, they're the sort of people one finds for company.

Ravicz left Alaska in 2000 and returned to California, but he maintains a homestead on Kodiak Island, about which he is presently writing a natural history. The state remains central to much of his writing and thinking. "Homesteading was for me such a fulfillment that in a way I've never left Alaska," he explained.

— From *Alaskans Fishes and Wine* —

Jimmy Biggs had journeyed to Alaska all the way from Tucson hoping to make enough money to pay for college one day. Whenever an older hand like Ratface, tramping the beach beside him, asked Jimmy how he liked cannery work, Jimmy answered that he didn't mind it for now but he wanted to do something better with his life. He was nineteen.

Ahead of them, Lucky Tyler marched over the wet sand with a strut, swinging his arms as if to keep time with some inner passion. When he stopped to wait for them, he hooked his thumbs in his belt-loops and hiked up his jeans and shouted "Let's go, turkeys!" Tyler was a squat man with a large head and a thick nose that doglegged from an old break. A Pancho Villa mustache swooped down the sides of his mouth.

"What's his hurry?" Ratface grumbled.

"You didn't hear about the bet?" Jimmy said.

A party had started up in the bunkhouse shortly after dinner, and as soon as it was obvious that there wouldn't be enough booze to keep everybody happy, these three had agreed to make the run into Naknek, the only town in walking distance on this remote shore of Bristol Bay. The cannery's two forklift drivers—Lucky Tyler was one of them—always vied for popularity among the lesser line workers, and when the second forklift driver heard that Lucky Tyler was going to town, he laughed scornfully and gave odds that Tyler wouldn't make it back to the cannery before midnight.

"Hell if I care about his bet," Ratface said. "I'm on my own time."

"That goes double for me," Jimmy said, glad to have nobody to answer to for a change. It was late in May, the herring run had ended, and for the first time in weeks he had an evening off.

The end of a bandage dangled from under Jimmy's blue flannel cuff, and as he walked he tried stuffing the bandage back around his wrist. His wrist ached from tendonitis contracted from handling too many herring too diligently—scooping the fish off conveyor belts, packing them into waxed boxes for export—and whenever his wrist ached especially much he told himself, This is all part of doing something with your life, Jimmy boy, eight-hour days'll be a cinch after this.

The three men walked abreast, picking their way among the slick dark rocks. Muddy bluffs rose to their left, buttressing the tundra, and to their right a shining mudflat sloped a hundred or more yards to the water. The tide was out, and far out there you could see the fish tenders lying at anchor. A few lights glimmered on the boats but it was early yet, not half past eight, barely twilight in this part of Alaska.

"What's your hurry," Ratface demanded.

Lucky Tyler had gotten ahead again. "I'm thirsty, that's what."

"No, it's that other forklift driver," Ratface said.

"That old motherfucker said I can't hike three miles twice and bring back a rack of beer without falling on my ass."

Jimmy drew closer. "He only said that to get you to go out and buy the beer."

"Damn right," Tyler said.

Ratface was doubled over in one of his coughing fits, scarlet-faced, his mouth wide open.

"Quit coughing on us," Tyler said.

"Can't you cover your mouth?" Jimmy said.

"Goddammit I told you it ain't contagious," Ratface cried, and lashed his empty duffel bag, the one they had brought to carry the booze in, against a rock.

Ratface was a slight and beady-eyed man who had been drifting on the seafood circuit for years. He always ate his meals alone and as soon as he was done eating he would get up and leave the mess hall. Many years ago Ratface had gone to Cuba to pick sugar cane for Fidel Castro and nobody knew what to make of him when he told them this. He was often seen talking to himself.

"You should've seen it when that old motherfucker dropped his pallet," Lucky Tyler was still stewing about his nemesis back at the bunkhouse. "Drove his forklift smack into the freezer door and dropped two thousand pounds of fish. Cary Sue saw it."

"Cary Sue," Ratface muttered balefully.

"Crashed his forklift and he's got the nerve to tell me he's a better driver."

"He said he's better than you?" Jimmy said.

"Calls me a forklift driver," Tyler said. "He's a forklift operator but I'm a forklift driver."

"That's just words," Jimmy said.

"You like Cary Sue?" Ratface asked.

"Sure, I like her," Jimmy said.

"You don't care if she's a dyke?"

"No, I don't care," Jimmy said.

"Well," Ratface said after a moment, "neither do I. But I wish she was more up front with us about it."

"Maybe she didn't think we'd follow her orders if she told us on the first day she's a dyke," Jimmy said.

"It spoils everything when the foreman's not up front with you," Ratface said.

"Hell, I like her," Tyler said. "It's a shame, though."

"What about?" Ratface said.

"It's a shame when a woman's getting more pussy than I do, but she's a damn good foreman," Lucky Tyler explained.

The others laughed. Lucky Tyler lit a cigarette. He was called Lucky Tyler because a bomb burst his foxhole in Vietnam twenty years ago and he was the only man of three to come up out of it. He wore a brown corduroy jacket over his t-shirt, the dirty white t-shirt bulging over his belly.

A cold wind was whisking around them and Jimmy buttoned the top buttons of his flannel. They still had a half mile to go up the beach and another mile inland into town. They walked briskly, sometimes tossing stones along the shore or pivoting and hurling them at the black face of the bluff. Up there on the bluff a line of old cabins straggled, abandoned until June when the setnetters would return to fish for salmon.

"That old motherfucker only gave me six bucks for drinks," Tyler said.

"Quit thinking about him," Jimmy said.

"I can't help it. How much cash'd you guys draw from your checks?"

"I took fifteen," Jimmy said.

"Twenty," Ratface said.

"Now why do you suppose that old bastard motherfucker only gave me six bucks?"

"Maybe that's all the money he had," Jimmy said.

Lucky Tyler threw down his cigarette and hitched up his jeans the way he always did before mounting his forklift. "Let me see my paycheck, Jimmy."

"I don't have it."

"You don't have it?"

"I left it under the bunk."

"You did not."

"The idea was you weren't gonna cash your check," Jimmy said. "What's it matter if I don't have it if you're not gonna cash it?"

"I'm not gonna cash it, I just wanna see it." Lucky Tyler stopped walking and frowned at him, and Jimmy pulled uneasily at the bandage trailing from his wrist. He withdrew some checks from his back pocket and handed one to Tyler.

"Hah, you see!"

"The kid was doing you a favor," Ratface said.

"Then why's he tell me he hasn't got my check when he's got it right there in his back pocket?"

"I don't care," Jimmy walked ahead, "I really don't care about your check."

"Hey, I'm sorry," Tyler called after him.

When they caught up to Jimmy, Lucky Tyler asked him again to guard his paycheck.

"No way. It's your check, you do what you want with it. Just don't ask me to cash mine."

"I won't."

"I'm not touching mine till I put it in the bank."

"Fine."

"All right then." Jimmy plucked the check from Tyler's hand and slipped it in his back pocket. Then they turned and watched Ratface, who had gone over by a driftwood log and was bent over hawking, shooting phlegm from his mouth.

"That sounds bad," Tyler said.

"You all right?" Jimmy said.

Ratface nodded and they walked on.

"How can you be sure it's not contagious?" Tyler said.

"Because it's cured," Ratface said wiping his mouth.

"I didn't know they could cure tb."

"Well now you know," Ratface said. "Almost had my lung cut out."

Lucky Tyler threw his hands up and said to Jimmy, "You see why a guy wants a drink now and then?"

"I know why a guy wants a drink," Jimmy said, "but I don't know why anyone would work for three weeks and blow his paycheck in three hours."

"No one's blowing any check," Tyler said. "I just hope a hundred cash'll cover what we need."

"It should be plenty," Jimmy said.

"That old motherfucker only gave me six bucks," Tyler said. "I know what things cost. It's seven bucks for a sixpack of Rainier."

"That's the cheapest they got?" Jimmy said.

"Cheapest brand. Twenty-two dollars a case. Hell, I don't wanna drink with that old fart anyway."

"I'd like to pour some Calvert down Cary Sue's throat and see what happens to her," Ratface said.

"Like what might happen to her?" Jimmy said.

"I don't know. But it ruins everything when the foreman's not up front with you."

To their left some water was flowing down a gully that slanted down the face of the bluff to the beach. They danced their way up this gully to the top and then jogged across the tundra looking for the dirt road that Tyler and Ratface said was nearby, jumping from tussock to tussock to avoid the water in the low places. It was still early in the year, May, and the grass was not very green yet, just a flat expanse of dull grasses and mosses and low berry plants stretching for miles.

Once they had found the dirt road, they slowed again to a walk. In the distance Jimmy saw a radio tower poking up from the flatness.

"I was working in a pea cannery down in Walla Walla," Lucky Tyler reflected. "There's a little college down there with a heated duck pond, can you believe it? I used to ride by on my bicycle."

Jimmy had rolled his sleeve back from his wrist and was trying to reattach the clip on his loose bandage. "How do you know it was heated?"

"I'm telling you, it was heated," Lucky Tyler said. "To keep the ice off it. So the college kids could have ducks to watch."

"College kids," Ratface said. "That explains it."

"Man, was I sick of peas," Tyler said. "We'd go out behind the cannery and pee in the pea field just to do it. Someone's peas might have my pee in it, ha!"

"I worked on a surimi ship where we did the same thing," Ratface said. "Just peed right there in the fish."

"I'll never eat another green pea as long as I live," Tyler said. "I couldn't even eat dinner tonight."

"You don't like stew?" Jimmy said.

"I love beef stew but not if there's peas in it."

"Get yourself something in town," Ratface said.

"Yeah, maybe I'll get a cheeseburger," Tyler said.

"Should be enough time for it and still make it back before midnight," Jimmy said.

It was late twilight, nine o'clock or so. Pink and violet undershimmers swam in the evening sky and reminded Jimmy, not happily, of a school of herring. The road to town was rutted from whatever few trucks had driven here and back; there really was nowhere to drive but on the dirt roads that petered out across the tundra. To their right the treeless sweep was interrupted by a silvery little pond.

"How much'd you bet him you'd be back before midnight?" Ratface asked.

"Thirty-five bucks," Tyler said.

"That's why he only gave you six," Jimmy said. "He knew he'd lose the bet."

Tyler nodded sourly. "Maybe I'll spend his six on my cheeseburger and not give him any beer."

"Oh, I don't know," Jimmy said.

"Don't know what?" Tyler said.

"If that'd be fair."

Tyler ignored that and lit a cigarette. "Maybe I'm a little out of shape," he said, "but he's dead wrong if he thinks I'm a soft gut." He blew his cigarette smoke at Ratface.

"Cut it out," Ratface said.

Lucky Tyler elbowed Jimmy. "I didn't think people even got tuberculosis anymore, did you, Jimmy?"

"I don't have tuberculosis," Ratface said. "That was ten years ago."

"When I got out of jump school I had a twenty-eight waist," Tyler said. "Asshole tells me I got a soft gut."

Jimmy unwound the flapping bandage from his wrist and stuffed it in his pocket.

"I'm short one toe and got rebar in my leg and my hearing's fucked up and some old queen tells me I got a soft gut?" Tyler had quickened his pace and Jimmy and Ratface hopped to keep up with him.

"It just don't matter what he told you," Ratface said.

Tyler grunted and glanced at Jimmy. "You hear me, Tucson?"

"I don't think you're fat," Jimmy said.

Tyler grabbed a roll of flesh at his side and with his fist began beating himself in the belly. While he walked he kept slugging himself as if he were beating a drum. "I'm Airborne," he yelled, "I'm an Airborne moth-erfucker and don't anybody forget it!"

"Why don't we get a drink before starting back," Ratface said. "We'll stop in at Fisher's."

"Maybe so," Tyler said hotly.

"Fisher's a bar?" Jimmy asked.

"That's right," Tyler said. And to Ratface, "Help me figure this out. If we get four cases of beer, that's eighty-eight bucks. Plus a bottle of tequila would throw us over a hundred. You remember how much Nat gave me?"

"No."

"There probably won't be time to stop in any bar," Jimmy said.

"But I know Bandy gave you his whole draw," Ratface said.

"Then he gets his fair share," Tyler said. "Fair is fair. But if a guy gives me six bucks—I'll tell you one thing, the only bottle I spring for that old lard-ass forklift operator is the one he splits his lip on."

"There might not be time to get a cheeseburger if we start going in the bars," Jimmy said.

Lucky Tyler looked at him. "Listen, Tucson, the only way we can fill this duffel bag is if we go in a bar. The liquor store is part of the bar. They sell from stock in the back room. That's how it is in this town."

"He's right," Ratface said.

"You don't have to drink a drop," Tyler said. "Course they won't cash your check for you unless you buy a drink with it."

"Nobody's cashing any checks," Jimmy said.

"I'm just telling you how it works," Tyler said.

"That's how it works, is it?" Jimmy slowed his pace but the others pulled him along. "The whole economy's just fishes and wine. You make your money and give it right back to them. Of course they're happy to cash your check as long as they get a piece of it."

"No," Tyler said, "the only reason we'll need to cash a check is if that bottle of tequila throws us over a hundred."

"It's one bar or another," Ratface said.

Jimmy gazed ahead at the dusky faceless buildings of the town. He saw nobody on the outskirts. "What's the choice?"

"Well, there's one bar not even worthy mentioning," Lucky Tyler said. "And the Red Dog has some chairs and tables in it. That's a nice place for a college kid to sit. And then there's Fisher's."

"Fisher's," Jimmy said. "We'll go there."

Ratface let out a strange yip when he heard they were going to Fisher's.

Lucky Tyler said, "Now listen, Jimmy, don't tick anyone off in there, all right?"

Naknek is built on the bank of a river, and coming into town they saw the water edging silently by, broad and smooth and faintly aglow. Warehouses and canneries fronted the river and yardlights shone down from the high roof corners. Seagulls stood below in the circles of light.

They passed a grocery store and a hardware store, both shut for the night. Ratface and Lucky Tyler crossed the road to a sunken wooden building with a light burning on the porch. Jimmy heard men's voices inside. A white mutt got up on the porch and wagged its tail at them. Ratface and Lucky Tyler tramped noisily up the porch steps and Jimmy followed more grimly. The saloon doors swung inward when they entered and swung shut behind them.

Heads turned and Jimmy swiped the cap off his head. The bar ran around three sides of the room and men stood along the length of it. Pool balls clacked in the heart of the room where men shot pool under low-hanging lamps. It was crowded inside with just enough elbow room but no empty stools to be had. The place was smoky and full of talk. Jimmy kept his eyes moving or he met with unfriendly stares. They were wiry men, their faces creased and bearded and stained.

Lucky Tyler and Ratface gravitated toward the white-aproned bartender, and Jimmy went after them. "We buy the stuff and go," he whispered.

Tyler nodded, but distractedly, bargazing at all the colored bottles and pretty glasses. With his thumb and forefinger he kept smoothing down the sides of his mustache. He raised his hand to catch the bartender's attention.

The only woman in the joint was high up in the corner on a video screen, a young blonde wriggling around on a tropical beach. Jimmy watched her doing what she was doing for a minute until he realized nobody else was watching. When the bartender approached, Jimmy turned his back and tried to concentrate on the game of pool. "You know how to play snooker?" Ratface asked him.

"No." Jimmy felt warm and undid a shirt button.

Lucky Tyler finally rejoined them and said he had placed the order.

"Good. Ten o'clock," Jimmy said. "We'll make it."

"Where's the booze?" Ratface asked.

"Bartender's packing the duffel bag," Tyler said. He watched the game with them a minute, then cautiously cleared his throat and hiked up his jeans. "Can I see my check, Jimmy?"

Jimmy stared at the green of the pool table. "What for?"

"I just wanna see it."

"We brought enough cash to cover things."

Lucky Tyler wiped his hands on his hips. "Well maybe I want something for myself."

Jimmy looked at him and looked away again.

"Tucson, man, I already ordered us a round. Ten bucks is all."

Jimmy turned and saw the bartender setting down three Budweisers: brown bottles, bright red and blue on the labels. Some stools had come available and the bartender murmured Sit down, boys and Tyler went ahead and sat down. Jimmy turned to Ratface but Ratface only shook his head and said, "Hey, I'm a drinking man too, but if a guy is dumb enough to blow his paycheck on booze, I'm not gonna stop him."

Jimmy took the third stool. A thin, unshaven man slouched next to him, head propped on his hand and grinning bleary-eyed at Jimmy. The man's lips were shut and moving in a circle as if he were chewing tobacco. Goddamn, he stank. Like the bottom of a herring hold he stank. Jimmy turned away but the stranger clamped a hand on his shoulder and hissed words in his ear. Jimmy shoved the hand away and sat rigid, his heart bucking. He didn't know what the man had said and he didn't ask.

Lucky Tyler demanded his paycheck again and this time Jimmy gave it to him. Tyler unfolded it, and there was just that piece of paper he had sweated for, pale and fragile in his palm.

A hush had come over the room. The men around the bar had stopped talking and they all seemed to look at Lucky Tyler as if they all had a stake in his paycheck, as if they had seen this little drama many times before. Their keen, sad faces made Jimmy shiver.

Jimmy glanced up again at the girl on the video screen, but nobody in the bar gave a damn about her and neither at the moment did Jimmy. In his friend Lucky Tyler he was looking down through the insides of a man to a region where duties and scruples blow along like dry leaves before a fire. There is no answer for that, or none that Jimmy could give from the height of his barstool.

Lucky Tyler handed his paycheck to the bartender and received cash in return, and Jimmy heard what sounded like a long sigh go up through the room, followed by a riffle of long swallows and a soft knocking of glasses one by one upon the bar.

VICKY HO

T HERE'S A LONG RUNNING JOKE, even among residents of Alaska's largest city, that wherever you are in Anchorage you're never more than a half hour away from Alaska.

It's not really a fair thing to say. Despite being a midsized urban metropolis, there are many things about Anchorage that are distinctively Alaskan. Chief among them is the city's location. Anchorage is bounded on one side by the Chugach Mountains, which are thick with bears that sometimes wander into the city proper, and where countless backcountry opportunities await. On the other side lies Cook Inlet, where whales can be found swimming. And the city can be quickly escaped with only a few minutes of driving. So perhaps a better way of expressing the notion about Anchorage is that wherever you are in the city, you're never more than a half hour away from Alaska at its finest.

Vicky Ho discovered this upon her arrival in the state. Born and raised in the Houston area of Texas, she migrated to Alaska in 2015 when she was hired as a copy editor by what was then the Alaska Dispatch News. She also took a part-time job with REI. Though never much of a hiker previously, she was surrounded in both jobs by people who encouraged her to hit the trails. She wasted little time following their advice, and before she knew it she was an outdoors maniac.

By 2017 the Alaska Dispatch News had reverted to its original name, the Anchorage Daily News, and Ho had launched a recurring column called "Cautionary Tales." As someone who was in the midst of graduating from novice hiker to pro, she wanted to share both her accomplishments and mistakes so that those just starting to explore Alaska would be encouraged to get out and do it, while hopefully absorbing valuable lessons on what to avoid.

The early installments in the series found Ho in the greater Anchorage region, but more recent columns have taken her as far afield as the Brooks Range. She's gone ice climbing, fat biking, skiing, and more. As she's gained skills and knowledge, her articles have become less about mistakes and more about possibilities. She's also used the space to tell stories of some of the state's most intrepid and under-recognized adventurers. What ties all of her work together is a constant enthusiasm for whatever she's doing, wonderful descriptive abilities (in the essay here she describes the snow she traversed as having "the consistency of cake batter"), and an unstoppable sense of humor (one article is titled, "My knee itched, and then there was all this blood").

Asked what she looks to convey with her writing, Ho said, "We live in a place that can be unforgiving and intimidating when it comes to the outdoors. My hope is that readers laugh at my mistakes and learn from them. Lessons learned the hard way aren't easily forgotten. I'm just trying to spare others some growing pains."

As one of Alaska's emerging writers, Ho has yet to publish a book. Hopefully at some point she will. Her writing is a lot of fun, and she continually encourages readers to get out there for themselves. She knows some of the best places in Alaska are just a short drive from her doorstep, and once out of her car, all she needs to access them are her own two feet.

The selection that follows has not been previously published. It's adapted from a tale she shared at a storytelling event in 2017 describing her early experiences as a hiker in Alaska. On a solo winter overnight in the Chugach Mountains, things start going wrong. But in the end they go unexpectedly right. That's the theme of many of her Cautionary Tales. If you stick it out despite the troubles, it usually turns out just fine.

— From *Alone in the Chugach* —

I'm used to doing a lot of things alone.

That wasn't always the case. Before I moved to Alaska from a ski town in Colorado, I would have never camped alone, or hiked alone.

In 2015, I moved to Anchorage, the state's biggest city, by myself. My boyfriend planned to follow later on. Before my move, I was fielding questions from our friends about the northern lights and the Palins and winter darkness and grizzly bears. I had few good answers.

Then a few months after I got to Anchorage, my boyfriend dumped me. Which prompted me to ask the question: What the hell was I doing in Alaska?

I had a tough time figuring out my place and meeting new people in Anchorage. The mental and physical distance from what felt familiar only enhanced my sense of isolation. Instead of having a social life, I threw myself into work, opting to fill my days with time spent around co-workers instead of shrinking into the quiet of a dark, empty house. I'd work 70 hours a week, not out of necessity, but out of loneliness.

Alaska, to me, was a sorry place to be alone.

After the breakup, I shuffled around in a haze of lost time. Finally one day, sick of wallowing, I forced myself into a decision: I could squander my life away feeling sorry for myself, or I could try to make the most of where I was.

So, on a co-worker's suggestion, I started hiking. On those first outings, when I was still upset about the breakup, I'd start at an angry pace, taking out my frustration on the trail with a stomping gait. I'd grow saddened and pissed off thinking about how things fell apart.

As I would hike, though, those feelings gradually dissipated, replaced by awe as dramatic, jagged ridge lines came into focus. I delighted in the delicate flowers that clung to steep tundra slopes, and in the alien vegetation that looked like it belonged on the ocean floor, not on a mountainside in Chugach State Park. Sunlight would play off the waters of Cook Inlet and Turnagain Arm, shimmering like fish scales in the distance. This sensory overload stole my breath away each time, and it compelled me to think about here and now instead of there and then.

I followed my feet to indulge my curiosity. In the process, the mountains grew to be a more familiar place. I returned again and again, and my irritation and insecurities would drift away.

Solo hiking is like free therapy. At the end of these trails, immersed in a sea of mountains, I would marvel at the world and I'd wonder: What was I so upset about, anyway?

My solo day hikes gave way to solo backpacking trips. It wasn't long before I took up solo winter backpacking.

When I took the plunge going it alone in the winter, though, I questioned—at least for a moment—the wisdom of my solo approach.

Late one April night I pulled up to the Rabbit Creek trailhead, one of the entry points into the peaks of the Chugach front range, which tower like sentries guarding over the eastern side of Anchorage. I'd just gotten off work and thought I could squeeze in an overnight trip to Rabbit Lake, about 4.5 miles back on easy terrain, and climb South Suicide Peak nearby before returning to work the following afternoon.

I strapped on my snowshoes and headed out. I was gleeful with anticipation. This'll be great—or so I thought.

The first warning sign: The snow at that point in the season had the consistency of cake batter. Having snowshoes on felt like overkill. Taking them off, though, I'd be postholing in shin-deep sludge.

I kept pushing forward.

And then the wind picked up. It wasn't too bad at first, but even my rookie experience had taught me that the farther I headed back into the Rabbit Creek Valley, the worse it would be.

Once I spotted a flat spot off the trail, I set up my tent, staking it into the gloppy snow as well as I could. With a quiet prayer to the mountain gods, I climbed inside.

In the movies, when engineers are testing equipment for space or flight, they flip a switch and a wind tunnel blasts to life. That's what it sounded like as soon as I entered the tent.

Wind thrashed violently against the tent's bright orange fabric walls, which bowed inward, pummeled by an invisible force. When I got too close, the walls of the tent slapped me in the face. The lights of Anchorage were visible through the tent's tiny window, a smattering of twinkling pinpoints seen through clear plastic that shuddered in the cacophony.

Amid the thunderous roar, the city lights gave me comfort. I started to sink into slumber.

Then, a half-hour later, I was jolted awake by the strangest sensation. My tangerine fabric world was bowing and flexing around me, and my whole body was moving. Not just me; everything was in motion. My sleeping pad, my backpack, the entire tent. Disoriented, I realized what was happening: My tent was sliding downhill in the snow.

From inside my traffic-cone-orange prison, I couldn't grasp how bad the situation was. As everything kept moving around me, I screamed words too colorful to publish. My mind raced for some way to stop my tent from sliding farther.

I tried digging an elbow into the snow in a half-hearted attempt at arresting my fall, with the floor of the tent separating me from wet misery. But then the wind howled again, and I continued slipping farther downhill.

A tangle of brush halted my descent. But still, each gust threatened to send my tent tumbling end over end—a scenario I dearly hoped to prevent.

I dug my elbow into one corner of the tent and the heel of my foot in the opposite corner. With my back bracing against the wall, slammed by blasts of wind, I was playing the world's worst game of Twister.

If only someone else were here, I thought, this wouldn't have happened. Maybe the tent wouldn't have blown downhill with the weight of two people. Maybe my imaginary camping partner would have talked me out of sleeping out here on such a windy night. Maybe, at least, they could've helped me out of this body-contorting position.

I thought about heading home. I thought about sleeping in a soft, warm bed surrounded by solid walls and a sturdy roof. But in my solitude, I'd grown stubborn. So I held that position in the tent, my body stretched and twisted. I dozed off with my head propped up by my elbow, and I woke up every time the wind rushed through the valley—which was often.

Two hours passed before I abandoned my plan to camp and started packing up.

When I stepped outside for the first time, keeping a firm grip on my tent for fear it would sail away into nothingness like a runaway kite, I mentally prepared myself for a survey of the damage. Earlier I felt like I was sliding downhill for such a long time. Where had the wind pushed me? How far away was the trail? Had I slid down all the way down to the creek?

Then I saw: My tent had moved all of 15 feet. In my mind, though, it might as well have been 1,500 feet.

I slogged back to the trailhead, dodging piles of scat from a bear who'd woken up early from hibernation and vowing to check the weather conditions more diligently before my next solo winter trip. By the time I reached my car, gray clouds had given way to a brilliant sunrise. It was a beautiful morning, and even though I was exhausted, I thought: It'd be a shame to waste such a nice day.

Driving, I wound my squeaky station wagon around the curves of Canyon Road. A stop sign gave me pause. Drive straight, and I'd be on the route home. I peered up through the windshield at the glowing pink-and-orange sky, now receding into a clear, bright blue.

On impulse, a woman possessed, I felt my hands turn the steering wheel right and I ended up at the trailhead to nearby Wolverine Peak, a local favorite.

And up I went.

Few things make me appreciate where I am the way hikes do. It happens every time: I'll reach a summit, absorbing the views, and tell myself anyone who isn't right there at that moment is crazy for missing out on such an experience.

That morning at Wolverine Peak, even after a hellish night at Rabbit Creek, was no different.

I stood on a rocky perch above Anchorage, my gaze flitting over the same neighborhoods I drove through when I first arrived in town. My body ached and my mind was almost delirious with weariness.

I took a deep breath and drank in the freedom of solitude, the freedom to make my own decisions and my own mistakes. The bone-deep understanding that when it's just me in the mountains, I have to answer for everything I do, and that accountability is the tradeoff for the liberation of being beholden to no one but myself.

And then I thought: Alaska is a terrific place to be alone.

JULIA O'MALLEY

No aspect of Alaskan culture is as deeply misunderstood beyond the state's borders as whaling. For Iñupiat and Yup'ik peoples of Alaska's northern and western coasts, whales have been harvested for food for centuries. Annual whale hunts are also a means of preserving ancient cultures and passing them on to each generation. Taking a whale and sharing it with other residents of a village—particularly the elders—is crucial to holding communities together and maintaining Native identity.

A whale can feed an entire village, helping residents afford to remain in places where grocery costs are exorbitant, job opportunities scare, and incomes often limited. Unfortunately however, even in the information age, the historical, cultural, and nutritional aspects of Arctic and subarctic whaling are largely unknown outside Alaska. So when a young man of 16 from the village of Gambell on St. Lawrence Island took his first whale and reports of his success were shared on Facebook, the news quickly went viral and he began receiving hate messages and death threats from all over the world.

The story of the cultural collision that ensued is told here by Julia O'Malley, who explains how a teenager following an ancient custom became the target of vicious abuse from people who have no understanding of Native cultures or subsistence, but are well versed in venting their rage on social media.

O'Malley, a third-generation Alaskan, is a longtime writer for the Anchorage Daily News, where she has distinguished herself with her ability to write sensitive and thoughtful pieces about controversial and sometimes traumatic issues. From 2009 to 2014 she penned a metro column where she sometimes wrote on topics she felt strongly about, and respectfully sought to understand those on the opposing side rather than simply using the space to expound on her own viewpoint, a rarity in an age of hyper-partisan journalism.

Discussing her approach, she told me, "I look for stories that I suspect might take me somewhere I've never been, surprise me, change my mind or let me walk in some else's shoes, especially when they are someone I might not like or agree with." She added, "I think journalism is the story of a place in thousands of messy episodes."

O'Malley has also been published by the New York Times and the Guardian among other prestigious outlets. And she and has held the Atwood Chair of Journalism at the University of Alaska Anchorage.

The following piece, which won a James Beard Foundation Journalism Award for food writing in 2018, first appeared in High Country News and was subsequently included in The Best American Food Writing 2018 anthology. It's an example of O'Malley's skills at storytelling, and an examination of what happens when two ways of living and thinking, completely isolated from one another, collide off the shores of one of the most remote places on Earth.

— From *The Teenage Whaler's Tale* —

BEFORE HIS STORY MADE THE ANCHORAGE PAPER, before the first death threat arrived from across the world, before his elders began to worry and his mother cried over the things she read on Facebook, Chris Apassingok, age 16, caught a whale.

It happened at the end of April, which for generations has been whaling season in the Siberian Yupik village of Gambell on St. Lawrence Island on the northwest edge of Alaska. More than 30 crews from the community of 700 were trawling the sea for bowhead whales, cetaceans that can grow over 50 feet long, weigh over 50 tons and live more than 100 years. A few animals taken each year bring thousands of pounds of meat to the village, offsetting the impossibly high cost of imported store-bought food.

A hundred years ago—even 20 years ago, when Gambell was an isolated point on the map, protected part of the year by a wall of sea ice—catching the whale would have been a dream accomplishment for a teenage hunter, a sign of Chris' passage into adulthood and a story that people would tell until he was old. But today, in a world shrunk by social media, where fragments of stories travel like light and there is no protection from anonymous outrage, his achievement has been eclipsed by an endless wave of online harassment. Six weeks after his epic hunt, his mood was dark. He'd quit going to school. His parents, his siblings, everybody worried about him.

IN MID-JUNE, AS HIS FAMILY CROWDED into their small kitchen at din-nertime, Chris stood by the stove, eyes on the plate in his hands. Behind him, childhood photographs collaged the wall, basketball games and hunting trip selfies, certificates from school. Lots of village boys are quiet, but Chris is one of the quietest. He usually speaks to elders and other hunters in Yupik. His English sentences come out short and delib-erate. His siblings are used to speaking for him.

"I can't get anything out of him," his mother said.

His sister, Danielle, 17, heads to University of Alaska Fairbanks in the fall, where she hopes to play basketball. She pulled a square of meat from a pot and set it on a cutting board on the table, slicing it thin with a moon-shaped ulu. Chris drug a piece through a pile of Lawry's Seasoned Salt and dunked it in soy sauce. Mangtak. Whale. Soul food of the Arctic.

SOON CONVERSATION TURNED, ONCE AGAIN, to what happened. It's hard to escape the story in Chris' village, or in any village in the region that relies on whaling. People are disturbed by it. It stirs old pain and anxiet-ies about the pressures on rural Alaska. Always, the name Paul Watson is at the center of it.

"We struggle to buy gas, food, they risk their lives out there to feed us, while this Paul Watson will never have to suffer a day in his life," Susan Apassingok, Chris' mother, said, voice full of tears. "Why is he going after a child such as my son?"

ON THE DAY THEY TOOK THE WHALE, Chris and his father, Daniel Apassingok, were cleaning a bearded seal on the gravel beach when they heard a cousin shouting. A black back cut the waves a few miles offshore. The three of them scrambled to their skiff.

Every whale is different, Daniel had told his son many times. An experienced crew captain knows to watch how each one moves and to calculate where it will surface. If they get it right, the boat will be 5 to 10 feet from the animal when it comes up. Then everything rests on the acuity of the striker in the bow, who holds a darting gun loaded with an exploding harpoon.

Daniel works as the maintenance man at the village school, supporting Susan, Chris, Danielle and Chase, 13. Daniel is a decent hunter, but Chris is something else. The boy was born with a sense for the direction of the wind, an eye for birds flashing out of the grass and animals bobbing in the surf, Daniel said. He could aim and shoot a rifle at the age of 5. By 11, he'd trained himself to strike whales, standing steady in the front of the skiff with the gun, riding Bering Sea swells like a snowboarder.

"He started out very young," Daniel said. "Chris kind of advanced a little bit faster than most people, even for me. He's got a gift."

From the boat, Chris and Daniel's village appeared in miniature, rows of weather-bleached houses staked in the gravel, four-wheelers parked out front, meat racks full of walrus and seal, cut in strips and hung to dry. Across the water the other direction, mountains on the Russian coast shaped the horizon. Chris removed his hat to pray and scanned the glittering chop, his compact frame taut, his expression slack as always. Daniel nudged the tiller.

When Daniel was a child, the village hunted in skin sailboats, chasing the whale in silence. Then as now, a boy started young, mastering one job, then another, until, if he was talented, he could try to make a strike. Daniel started as a striker at 19. He'd taken two whales so far.

The weather seemed to have changed permanently since he was a boy. He believed it was climate change. The ice didn't stay as long and wasn't the same quality. Whales passed at a different time. There were fewer calm days and more ferocious storms. The village was still recovering from one in 2016 that damaged 60 structures on the island, including their house.

Along with whale, the village relies on bearded seal and walrus for food. In 2013, hunting conditions were so bad, the village required emergency food aid to get through the winter. Subsequent harvests have been below expectations.

"It's always hard," Daniel said. "But it's getting harder."

They were a few miles offshore when the dark oblong of the whale passed their boat. Adrenaline lit up Chris. Just a few feet off the bow, the bowhead's back split the sea. Chris raised the darting gun, a heavy combination of shotgun and spear. He aimed.

"Please let us get it," he asked God.

He squeezed the trigger. The harpoon sailed, trailing rope.

Alaska Natives have been hunting bowhead in the Western Arctic for at least 2,000 years. The animals were hunted commercially by Yankee whalers from the mid-19th century until the beginning of the 20th century, decimating the population. Since then, whale numbers have recovered, and their population is growing. In 2015, the National Oceanic and Atmospheric Administration estimated there were 16,000 animals, three times the population in 1985.

Alaska Native communities in the region each take a few whales a year, following a quota system managed by the Alaska Eskimo Whaling Commission (AEWC). The total annual take is roughly 50 animals, yielding between 600 and 1,000 tons of food, according to the commission.

Subsistence hunting of marine mammals is essential for villages where cash economies are weak. The average household income in Gambell, for example, is $5,000 to $10,000 below the federal poverty level. Kids rely on free breakfast and lunch at school. Families sell walrus ivory carvings and suffer when there isn't enough walrus.

Store-bought food can be two to three times as expensive as it is in Anchorage, depending on weight. In the village grocery, where shelves are often empty, a bag of Doritos is $11, a large laundry detergent is more than $20, water is more expensive per ounce than soda. No one puts a price on whale, but without it, without walrus, without bearded seal, no one could afford to live here.

The harpoon struck, but the wounded whale swam on. A second boat took another shot. The great animal lost power. It heaved over, belly to sky.

Soon Chris had congratulations in his ears and fresh belly meat in his mouth, a sacrament shared by successful hunters on the water as they prayed in thanks to the whale for giving itself. He had been the first to strike the whale, so the hunters decided it belonged to his father's crew. They would take the head back to the village and let the great cradle of the jawbone cure in the wind outside their house.

They towed the whale in and hauled it ashore using a block and tackle. Women and elders came to the beach to get their share. Every crew got meat. Whale is densely caloric, full of protein, omega-3s and vitamins. People eat it boiled, baked, raw and frozen. Its flavor is mild, marine and herbal like seaweed.

People packed it away in their freezers for special occasions. They carried it with them when they flew out of the village, to Nome and Anchorage and places down south to share with relatives. Everyone told and retold the story of the teenage striker. Then the radio station in Nome picked it up: "Gambell Teenager Leads Successful Whale Hunt, Brings Home 57-Foot Bowhead." The Alaska Dispatch News, the state's largest paper, republished that story.

IT USED TO BE THAT RURAL ALASKA communicated mainly by VHF and by listening to messages passed over daily FM radio broadcasts, but now Facebook has become a central platform for communication, plugging many remote communities into the world of comment flame wars, cat memes and reality television celebrity pages.

That is how Paul Watson, an activist and founder of Sea Shepherd, an environmental organization based in Washington, encountered Chris' story. Watson, an early member of Greenpeace, is famous for taking a hard line against whaling. On the reality television show, Whale Wars on Animal Planet, he confronted Japanese whalers at sea. His social media connections span the globe.

Watson posted the story about Chris on his personal Facebook page, accompanied by a long rant. Chris' mother may have been the first in the family to see it, she said.

"WTF, You 16-Year Old Murdering Little Bastard!," Watson's post read. "... some 16-year old kid is a frigging 'hero' for snuffing out the life of this unique self aware, intelligent, social, sentient being, but hey, it's okay because murdering whales is a part of his culture, part of his tradition. . . . I don't give a damn for the bullshit politically correct attitude that certain groups of people have a 'right' to murder a whale."

Until then, Facebook had been a place Chris went occasionally to post pictures of sneakers and chat with his aunties. He heard about the post at school. By evening, messages arrived in his Facebook inbox.

"He said, 'Mom, come,' and he showed me his messages in his phone, calling him names like, 'You little cunt,' and 'I hope you choke on blubber,' you deserve to die and 'You need to harpoon your mom,'" Susan said.

A deluge of venomous messages followed, many wishing him dead.

Cleaning up after dinner, Danielle said she tried to keep count. She got to 400 and they kept coming, from across the country and from Europe. Chris has only been out of Alaska once, to a church conference in Indianapolis, she said.

"There was this one message saying that, I read on his phone, that they hope that our whole community dies," Danielle said.

"It was pretty cruel," said his brother, Chase.

Chris said he tried to ignore the messages, to laugh them off. When he heard his parents and siblings talking about them, his eyes grew wet and he clenched his jaw.

"It never stops," he said.

Across the Arctic, people responded to Watson's post with comments, petitions and private messages in opposition. The Alaska Eskimo Whaling Commission reported it to Facebook. Eventually, it was removed. Across the region, whaling captains reminded hunters not to put pictures on social media.

Watson wrote another post, refusing to apologize.

"This has been my position of 50 years and it will always be my position until the day I die," he wrote.

Watson and Sea Shepherd declined to be interviewed for this story but sent a statement.

"Paul Watson did not encourage nor request anyone to threaten anyone. Paul Watson also received numerous death threats and hate messages," it read. "It is our position that the killing of any intelligent, self-aware, sentient cetacean is the equivalent of murder."

Villagers have been familiar with Watson's opinions for many years. They have seen him on cable, and many remember 2005, when Sea Shepherd sent out a press release blaming villagers for the deaths of two children in a boating accident during whaling season.

Many environmentalists who object to subsistence whaling have a worldview that sees hunting as optional and recreational, said Jessica Lefevre, an attorney for the whaling commission based in Washington, D.C.

"The NGOs we deal with are ideologically driven; this is what they do, they save stuff. The collateral damage to communities doesn't factor into their thinking," she said. "To get them to understand there are people on this planet who remain embedded in the natural world, culturally and by physical and economic necessity, is extremely difficult."

The organizations are interested in conservation, but fail to take into account that Alaska Natives have a large stake in the whale population being healthy and have never overharvested it, she said. Some NGOs also benefit financially from sensation and outrage, she said, especially in the age of social media.

IN THE SUMMERTIME, VILLAGE TEENAGERS LIVE in a different time zone in the forever light of the Arctic. At 1 a.m. in June, their four-wheelers buzz down to a large wooden platform basketball court in the gravel by the school, where Drake pulses out of cellphone speakers. The girls wear polar fleece jackets, sparkle jeans and aviator frames. All the boys have Jordan sneakers. A half-dozen fidget spinners blur.

On a recent night, Chris stood on the sidelines of a pick-up game. There was a girl with him. They didn't talk, but they stood close. Occasionally, someone threw him a ball and he made a basket.

It is hard to be alone in a village. Even if the adults are inside, someone is always keeping track. Between blood relations, adoptions and marriages, Chris' family is huge, with relatives in many houses. Many are paying extra attention to him now.

Chris' grandfather, Mike Apatiki, lives just down from the basketball court. He has a freezer full of meat his grandson brought. He worries less about Chris leaving school—hunting seasons have put him behind for years—than he does about him feeling shamed.

"These people do not understand and know our need for food over here," he said. "Like the rest of Americans need to have a chicken and a cow to eat out there from a farm, we need our whale and seal and walrus. Makes us healthy and live long."

"Neqeniighta," the Siberian Yupik word for "hunter," doesn't have a perfect equivalent in English, said Merle Apassingok, Chris' uncle, who lives across the road from his grandfather. It means something broader even than the word "provider," and is tied to a role men have played for generations that ensures survival and adaptation. When a boy is a good hunter, he is poised to be a leader, Merle said.

"Hunting is more than getting a permit and fulfilling that permit with a grizzly bear or a Dall sheep or whatever," he said. "There is happiness when a boy gets his first seal, there is joy. There is sadness when we have a tragedy. How can we isolate the word?"

He wishes that Chris' story never left the island. He worries his nephew has not lived long enough to process all that's happened.

"As far as day-to-day dinner on the table, hunters are everything in the village," he said.

After basketball, when most of the village is asleep, Chris sometimes packs his backpack with ammunition, slips on his dirty camouflage jacket and pumps up the leaky four-wheeler tire. Hunting, he told his mother once, is like a story: Suspense, conflict, resolution. He always prays the ending will be the animals showing themselves so he can take them back home, she said. As twilight edges into sunrise, he heads out alone down the coast, his rifle slung on his back. After a long ride, he crawls into a seal blind tucked behind driftwood on the beach, where he can stay for hours with only the birds and the smell of grass and the racket of the sea.

ZACH FALCON

"**W**HERE ARE YOU SUPPOSED TO GO *when the last fucking frontier is ruined for you,*" a drunken young man asks a friend as they stagger through Alaska's capital city of Juneau in one of Zach Falcon's pieces of short fiction. "*Where else? What am I supposed to do, Silas?*"

Some variation of this question underlies the dilemmas of many of the characters found in Falcon's story collection *Cabin, Clearing, Forest*, which explores the lives of people who have either come north seeking redemption from their failures, or have spent the entirety of their lives failing in Alaska and find themselves incapable of escape.

Falcon's tales are grim but enthralling. Set primarily in Juneau, where he grew up, as well as Kodiak, where he was born, they examine the dark side of a state renowned for its beauty and wilderness, yet one where economic opportunities can be hard to come by. It's an Alaska where hoped-for new beginnings can quickly be lost through hard luck and personal shortcomings, and where small towns that appear unpretentious and down-to-earth on their surfaces can be brimming with social complexities. It's a lesson learned the hard way by a physician's assistant fleeing from New York City who finds himself working on Kodiak in the story "Every Island Longs for the Continent."

"Alaska was not what he anticipated," Falcon writes. *"It was not the simple frontier he imagined from the Saturday westerns. Instead of wilderness and moral clarity, he found himself in a shabby plywood-built fishing town as complicated in its workings as anywhere else."*

In the following selection, two homeless men, each adrift for his own reasons, are brought together on the streets of the state's capital. When I asked him where his plot originated, Falcon explained, "I wrote this story during a time I was thinking about community. My hometown of Juneau is like other communities in that it includes some and excludes others. As a settler colony, it also has a shameful history, and lingering present, of dispossession. My hometown of Juneau is unlike other communities in its isolation. It is difficult for some of those marginalized to leave; it is painful for some of those dispossessed to stay. In that circumstance, in that extremity, what new communities arise? Anyway, that's what I was thinking about at the time."

Homelessness is a huge problem in Alaska's urban enclaves. Statistics are hard to pin down, but the past decade has seen an enormous surge in the number of people panhandling and showing up at emergency shelters. Obtaining accurate numbers is complicated by the ease with which the homeless can slip into squatters' camps in the woods that are immediately adjacent to Anchorage, Fairbanks, and Juneau. As in other American cities, Alaska's homeless population encounters violence on the street and police who won't take their side when they are preyed upon. They carry the added burden of exposure to Alaska's extreme weather, which claims the lives of homeless Alaskans every year.

Falcon attended Columbia University, the University of Michigan Law School, and the Iowa Writers' Workshop. He practiced law in Juneau from 1999 to 2006, the final two years as an assistant attorney general for the State of Alaska. He's now a professor of conservation law at Unity College in Maine, as well as the fiction editor for *Hawk & Handsaw Journal of Creative Sustainability.*

— From *Cabin, Clearing, Forest* —
BLUE TICKET

IT WAS EARLY OCTOBER AND RAINING and near dark when Amos arrived at the squatter's camp. Russell watched him come up the trail and stop, uncertain. Amos looked boyish, eighteen at most. Scrawny and hollow faced. It appeared that he'd cut his own hair, hacked his own thin beard, with a knife. The only thing he carried was a scrap of visqueen that he rolled about himself to keep the rain off while he slept, tucked into the one-walled crease of a roofless mining bunker.

The squatter's camp was a mile south of Juneau, hidden in the woods two hundred feet back above Thane Road. Fifteen or so sagging tents and various lean-tos made from blue tarps and warping plywood. The forest was littered with the remnants of the Alaska-Juneau Mine: concrete ruins and rusting hulks of inexplicable machinery. The squatters lived among the ruins and between the spruce trees, adding their wreckage to the decaying past: soggy mattresses and drifts of beer cans. Some people stayed for a week, others longer. Russell had been there since June and was scared he would die there alone and unacknowledged.

The next morning, Russell pushed out of his sleeping bag and unzipped the door of his tent. Amos sat on a log next to a dead fire, wet and shivering, hands between his legs as though in hidden prayer. Russell regarded him for a moment before speaking. The boy's clothes were ragged. A pair of duck-cloth pants, a homemade plaid shirt with carefully matched seams, a thin parka. All soaked through. He looked worse off than Russell did when Fat George took him under his wing. With Fat George gone, Russell felt the obligation to help the boy.

"Hey," Russell said. "Get any sleep?"

Amos dipped his head in a nodding shrug, seeming to fold further into his frame. Russell waited for him to raise his head and meet his eyes, but he didn't. Russell coughed wetly and leaned out of the tent to spit. He set his stiff leather boots outside the tent and stepped into them as he emerged. "Give me a second," he said. He shuffled to a patch of devil's club and pissed and then walked back to where Amos sat by the dead fire, pausing to turn his torso sharply, cracking his spine.

"What's your name?" asked Russell.

"Amos."

"I'm Russell. I bet you didn't sleep at all."

"I've slept worse," said Amos. His voice was a strange mumble. It sounded somehow antique.

"I'll make a fire," said Russell. He'd never built a fire before getting stuck in Juneau, but now he prided himself on his skill at nursing wood into combustion. When the fire held, he squatted across the fire pit from Amos and fed larger, wetter branches that popped and hissed in the dawn. The heavy smoke stung his eyes, but the fire was warm. He watched Amos unfold and ease in the heat, straightening his back and letting his legs splay open. Steam rose from the cuffs of his pants. Russell fed another branch into the fire and sat back on a log. It satisfied him to see the boy warming. He felt an impulse to make coffee or hot chocolate or oatmeal. Something to offer. For the last week he had been finishing a tub of peanut butter, scooping it out with his fingers in a way that would be depressing to an observer. The grooves of his fingers against the greased plastic jar were depressing even to him. It could not be shared. But in the hierarchy of human need, when it's raining, food comes second. So Russell considered that.

"That tent over there is empty," said Russell, pointing. "You can sleep in it until you figure something else out."

Amos stared at the tent, a lime-green A-frame style with a single ridgepole across the top, sides sagging. "Whose is it?"

Russell could hear the camp stirring. The usual coughs and groans.

"It belongs to a guy named George. Fat George."

"Where's he at?"

"Lemon Creek." Amos's face remained blank, leaving the question in the air. "Jail," Russell added.

Amos stared at the tent again, seeming to weigh the option. "For what?" he asked.

Russell shrugged. "A cop tapped him on the shoulder while he was pissing in the doorway of a restaurant downtown. George was so drunk he turned around and splashed the cop's shoes. He'll be out in a week or so." Russell added another branch to the fire. "George won't mind. He likes to help people out. You warm now?"

Amos nodded.

"Then get some sleep." Russell checked his watch. "It's not even eight yet."

After Amos disappeared into the tent, Russell stared at the fire a while longer. He felt the pinch of his stomach but the idea of the peanut butter made him ill. He had $40 left. As he listened to the camp waken, as puffy-eyed men straggled to the fire and sat heavily, he decided to walk to town and spend some of it. Make a meal he could share.

Russell's remaining $40 represented a heroic act of financial management. He had $500 when he came to Juneau in the spring. He'd gone to Alaska to escape Seattle. To get away from Second and Pike. He hitch-hiked to Bellingham and took the ferry north to start over and make money and get clean. At thirty-two, a fresh start still felt possible. He rented a week-rate room at the Alaskan Hotel and looked for a job. Everyone said he'd come at the wrong time. Summer jobs were booked. Maybe try back later, after the seasonal turnover. Maybe in the fall. After that first week Russell had $232 and a tent and a sleeping bag. Another week's rent would clear him out, so he turned back his key. He camped the first night in Cope Park where a mustached cop moved him along before dawn. He shivered in the bus shelter downtown for hours until he met Fat George, who wandered south toward Thane in the evening and told Russell to follow. After four months, Russell felt much older.

Here's how Russell aged: Early on, in June, he visited the library every morning and perused the paper. He scanned the sparse want ads in the *Juneau Empire* and followed the news. Occasionally he would leaf through a GED study guide and jot answers on a piece of scrap paper with a stubby pencil from the tray by the card catalog. In the afternoon he would spring four dollars for a bagel and a cup of brewed coffee from Heritage and stroll along the cruise ship docks, feeling faintly superior to the tourists. He was young and local and regenerating and clean. The squawking rain-ponchoed hoards were just visiting. In the evening he ambled back toward camp. He had a rod and reel and angled off the beach below Thane Road, catching Dolly Varden or humpy for dinner. It was not bad. Almost civilized. He could conserve cash and wait until fall. But the want ads stayed sparse, and the dirt took its toll. By August the tourists looked away from him with studiously blank expressions. Homeless is homeless no matter where. He skipped the library and ate the free bum lunch at the Treadwell Kitchen on South Franklin. Some nights he loitered at the Imperial Bar, drinking water or cheap burnt coffee. Waiting for a happy drunk to win big on rippies and ring the bell. A round for everyone. Then he'd walk home. By September, Russell's cheeks had sunk and his beard had grown and he left the camp only if he had to.

The camp changed through the summer, too. For a month of good weather it was like a drunken carnival swap meet. There were late nights and bonfires. The northern lights curtained the sky above the mountains. People came and went and shared suitcases of Rainier and convenience-store cold cuts. Their laughter echoed off the mining ruins and their humping shadows splayed on tent walls. Then came September and the raucous parties died in the rain. Some kids, semi-pro hippies, would show up for a day or two and change their minds. A panicked phone call and a Western Union later they'd tack back to the land of plenty, leaving nothing behind them but the scent of patchouli. Their odor was replaced by old men who stank of mouthwash and aftershave and perfume. Fat George, with a traveler of whiskey, roaring and shaking his hairless belly in the firelight. Russell had a phone number and had called it twice in his adult life. Once it paid for rehab and the second time it said no. He didn't want to call it again.

It was an hour walk to Foodland from the camp. Down the muddy trail gnarled with spruce roots and hedged by devil's club. North on Thane Road until it turned into South Franklin Street at the edge of town. A dispiriting strip of shuttered tourist shops intermixed with bars. The Great Alaskan Tee Shirt Shop, The Rendezvous, Columbian Emeralds, The Lucky Lady, Northland Fur Company, The Arctic Bar. At the corner of Franklin and Front, Russell passed the enclosed city bus shelter where he'd met Fat George. Some people called it the Crystal Palace. Later in the day and through the night it would be full of people from the squatter's camp and other like-minded hobbyists. Drinking from paper bags and marking time by the arrival and departure of busses none of them rode.

Russell crossed Franklin and walked down Main Street, past the Triangle Club and the Imperial Bar. Already a short line of old men fidgeted outside the door of the Triangle, waiting for it to open. Russell walked the rest of the way watching his feet.

When he reached the Foodland parking lot Russell saw two police cars with their disco-lights rolling near the entry. A man he knew from the camp slumped unsteadily on a concrete parking bumper with his legs outstretched and his hands cuffed behind his back. Jerry's pants and the lower half of his white T-shirt were dark with what appeared to be blood. Russell stopped short. Two cops stood nearby with a woman dressed to the store's code, a maroon vest and a name badge. A stack of plastic-wrapped meat and two disposable cameras tottered on the hood of one of the cop cars.

"Hey Russell," Jerry drawled, grinning, as though his situation was a fine joke. "Thought they shot me but it was just the steaks in my pants broke open." One of the cops turned and stared hard at Russell. Jerry kept talking. "Keep an eye on my shit will you?"

"Move on," said the cop. Russell nodded and went into the store. He spent nineteen dollars on coffee, three cans of condensed soup, two boxes of tuna helper, oatmeal, and a box of powdered milk. He decided against the hot chocolate and the new toothbrush. A young Filipino girl took his money without looking at him.

It was drizzling when Russell made it back to camp. The fire smoldered but there was no one about. Russell stowed the groceries and then stood next to the lime-green tent, listening for Amos's breathing. He heard the boy stir. "You awake?"

"Sort of," said Amos.

"Sleep more if you need to," said Russell. "I'm going fishing. Catch something for lunch. Come if you want." Russell gathered his gear and was heading toward the trail when Amos unzipped his tent. Russell waited for him to catch up and then proceeded. Thane Road runs along the shore of Gastineau Channel, a cold, deep finger of the Pacific that cuts between the mainland and Douglas Island. Russell and Amos crossed the road and stepped down the steep embankment onto the rocky beach, grabbing at branches of scrub willow and alder to steady their descent.

The tideline of the beach was littered with scoured logs and driftwood and marine trash: chunks of cork from seine floats, sun-bleached and deflated buoys, milk jugs, useless lengths of fraying rope. Russell led the way down the beach toward the stubby point where he liked to fish. Amos followed, walking carefully on the slick barnacled rocks, his arms outstretched for balance.

At the point, Russell geared up his rod. It was a short button caster, the kind generally used by children just learning to fish. Russell found it at Sally Ann's for three dollars—a package deal with four pixie spoons.

He set his feet and cast awkwardly. The drizzle continued from the low mat of gray cloud, but there was no wind to stir the slack ocean. The spoon arced out in the air silently, like a raised eyebrow, hitting the water with a fleeting gulp. Russell reeled back quickly and cast again.

"This has been an okay spot for me," he said. "I caught a lot of humpies in the summer. Dolly Varden too." He cast easily now. Another fleeting gulp. "We'll catch something. Even if we don't, I got some other groceries."

Amos stood a few paces behind and to the left of Russell to be out of the way of the hook on the backswing. He held a mussel shell in his hand, rubbing his thumb in its smooth pearled chamber. "Thank you," he said. Russell shrugged his shoulders slightly.

"I mean it," said Amos. "I thank you for your kindness. I didn't know what I was going to do."

Russell looked back at him over his shoulder. "It's nothing," he said, casting again. Gulp. "Where are you from?"

"Skagway. North of Skagway."

"Take the ferry down?"

"No. I walked."

Russell turned back and looked at him. "You walked?" Amos nodded. "Jesus," said Russell loudly. Amos's face flinched, a momentary squint and twist of his cheeks, as though something had been thrown at him. Russell took a moment to reel in the line.

"You walked with no tent? Nothing?"

Amos looked down, focusing on the nacreous shine of the mussel shell. "I had things," he answered simply. "I just lost them is all. I had to swim once and I lost them in the water."

Russell shook his head, marveling. "Well that is something else, my friend. You're lucky to be alive."

Amos gave a fleeting half smile, an abbreviated twisting grin. "I was scared," he said. "I shouldn't say so, but I'd be lying if I said I wasn't."

"Everybody's scared of something," said Russell. "It's okay to say so."

They fished a while longer, following the lapping edge of the water as the tide ebbed slowly down the beach, uncovering rust-orange rockweed and wet pockets of squirming blennies. Things trapped and left behind by the sea. Russell caught two small Dollies in quick succession. He gutted them out on a flat rock, leaving the ropy entrails for the ravens eyeing him from the branches of a nearby cottonwood. Amos gathered an armload of driftwood for the fire and they headed back to camp, struggling up the muddy trail, breathing hard.

Amos built a fire on the coals left from the morning while Russell wrapped the fish in a creased scrap of tinfoil and read the instructions on a box of tuna helper. With the fire going, Amos sat back and began to whittle on a long thin piece of flat driftwood with a pocketknife. Russell put a rack on the edge of the fire and set the fish upon it, together with a pan of water for boiling.

"So what are you scared of?" asked Amos.

Russell snorted. "Bears. Everything."

"Bears come around much?"

"Once or twice this summer. People get sloppy with their food. I do too sometimes. But we make enough noise, I guess." Russell pushed the fish around on the rack with a stick. His voice grew serious. "I'm scared of being stuck here forever. I've got to start looking for a job again. Can't even afford to leave Juneau right now. Stupid to come to a town with no roads." Then he snorted again. "And I'm not crazy enough to try to walk out of here."

Amos grinned sheepishly. "I wouldn't recommend it to you."

Russell gave Amos his plate and heaped it high when the food was done. He ate his own portion directly from the pan after it cooled. They stared into the fire as they ate. Midway through their meal one of the squatters returned up the trail. A taciturn man named Hugo who never said much but sometimes shouted out in his sleep. Russell offered him a bite, but Hugo shook his head and disappeared behind the flap of his lean-to. Amos scraped his plate clean and belched softly. "It's not so bad when your belly's full, being stuck here. There's worse places."

Russell nodded. He thought of Second and Pike, of waking up sick after lost time, not knowing where he was. "Sure," he said. "I suppose there is."

They remained in camp all day, staring into the fire, talking off and on until nightfall. Russell yawned and dozed and awoke with a start. Amos kept shaping his piece of driftwood until he seemed pleased with it. It was oblong, with notched edges and a dull point, shaped like a spearhead. He carved a hole in one end and asked Russell if he had any twine. Russell nodded and yawned and stood. He shuffled to his tent, feeling the air bite cold away from the fire. He found a tangle of bristling brown twine, the same twine that held up his too-large jeans. He stood over Amos as he watched him fix a length of it to the wood and then begin to twist it.

"What've you got there?" asked Russell.

"It's a wolf roarer," he said. "To keep the bears at bay."

"What, you hit 'em with it?"

Amos looked up with his half smile. "No. It makes a noise. We used to have sheep and goats at our place, and my brothers and I would make these to keep the wolves off. Listen." Amos stood and swung the piece of wood around his head like a lasso, letting out twine so it swung in a widening circle. The wooden piece spun on its axis as the twist in the twine released. The sound it made, doppling as Amos swung faster and wider, was like a slow chain saw, growling and screaming in the dark. There were some half-hearted protests from the men in their grim tents, but Amos kept swinging the wolf roarer, his face lit with firelight. For Russell, the noise was comforting. It gave fear a sound and made it a warning to the surrounding darkness. It echoed in his head as he slept.

In the days that followed, Russell and Amos fell into an easy pattern together: fire and coffee in the morning, fish if they were lucky, or lunch at the Treadwell. Part of each day was dedicated to getting out of the rain. Damp amplified the cold, and they were always damp. Their clothes stank of mildew and wood smoke. Sometimes they spent time in the atrium of the State Office Building. With its skylights and potted trees, the SOB was like a vacation. In the center of the atrium stood a totem pole that Fat George claimed came from his family, but the plaque made no mention of it.

One cold night they went to the Imperial Bar and sipped water while it was still empty enough for the bartender not to care. Russell kept an ear open for someone ringing the bell, but no one had any luck with the rippies. Amos sat uncomfortably, eyes down. He didn't say much, or talk about his past. Russell had gathered that he came from a large religious family that homesteaded land and kept to themselves. His father was dead, and Amos had left for reasons he didn't say. Russell didn't press.

At the other end of the bar, playing pool and feeding the jukebox, clustered a group of loud young men with close-cropped hair and braided belts and gym arms. They laughed and pushed each other and called each other faggots. Russell recognized them as a type and avoided looking their way. When he went to the bathroom though, one of the men was standing at the sink, a small black kit bag open on the counter, a syringe in his hand. Russell froze. He felt his heart lurch and a small sigh escaped him. The man, tall and bulging, with tiny cauli-flower ears on either side of a head that itself seemed well-muscled, glowered at him. "What?"

Russell stammered. "Nothing, man. It's just that you shouldn't, you know. I used to—"

"I'm a diabetic, asshole," spat the man. "You homeless hippie faggots make me sick. Get the fuck out of here." Russell's face burned as he left. Amos followed and didn't ask what happened. Russell appreciated that. Sometimes you just left a place quickly for reasons you didn't have to say.

Another week passed before Fat George returned, and when he did it was a big to-do. He embraced everyone, hooting as he pressed them to his stomach. He embraced Amos and thanked him for watch-ing his tent. They made a bonfire and someone supplied hotdogs that they ate right off the sticks with Tabasco sauce. Fat George, fully rested and enjoying a fifth of Country Club, stood on a log and performed his story of pissing on Officer Vandiver's shoes with great animation. "He said to me: 'In the olden days, we'd blue ticket your ass for what you did to my shoes, kick you out of town.' And I said to him: 'You can't blue ticket me, motherfucker, I am Wooshkeetaan, Wolf Eagle, I blue ticket *you*, motherfucker!'" The assembled cheered and Fat George took off his shirt and danced slow and Tlingit in the firelight, singing a song to himself, eyes closed.

It was late when everyone crawled off to sleep, and Russell saw Amos looking uncomfortable, sitting by the dying fire. "Sleep in my tent," said Russell. "There's room. We'll find something else tomorrow." Amos nod-ded, relief on his face.

When they finished arranging themselves in Russell's small tent, tucked in their sleeping bags and blankets, they were comfortable as could be expected. The camp went quiet but for the creak of the sur-rounding spruce trees and the occasional ember popping in the fire. Russell felt his breath lengthening, becoming even and heavy as he eased into sleep. It was his favorite time, feeling his body go slack and the heaviness come and his chattering mind go silent.

"Russell?" Amos whispered. "You awake?"

"Huh."

"You awake?"

"Yeah."

The boy was silent for a moment. Then he whispered again. "I was thinking, maybe tomorrow you could cut my hair right. Or we could find someone to cut my hair right. Those people in the bar were looking at me like I was crazy."

"Your hair's a bit uneven," said Russell. "You could wear a hat."

"It used to be long. My beard, too. But it was wispy. My papa said my beard would go full after I had seventeen years but it didn't. He was wrong about that. I cut my hair off with my knife after I left home. I was eager to be rid of it, but I wasn't thinking what it would look like."

Amos's voice came low and ragged. He was on his back, face directed up to the roof of the tent. "I used to think God lived in Papa's beard. When I was a boy. His beard was so long and white and sometimes when the light hit it right it looked like it was on fire. His beard moved and danced when he spoke, and all he spoke was God's word." Amos took a deep breath. "Or he said it was. I suspect he was wrong about some of that, too."

There was a long silence. Russell felt he should say something. "He passed on, didn't he? Your dad?" Russell heard Amos's nodding head scrape against the sleeping bag.

"He's dead enough," said Amos. There was another long silence but Russell did not break it. In a moment, Amos spoke again, as though he was picking up from where he left off. "Before I left I took a map that Papa had on the wall in the room where he kept books and other forbidden things. It was a big map, some three foot square. It had never been folded before I folded it. It showed the coast between here and Skagway. I thought I needed it but I didn't. All you do is follow the coast. I didn't need a map for that. Nobody does."

"What do you mean forbidden? You couldn't read books?"

"No," said Amos. "We weren't to read or write. Just to listen when Papa spoke out of his beard."

Russell turned and propped himself up on his elbow, looking at the shape of Amos's face in the darkness. "So you can't read?"

"I can read some. Mother taught us some, on the side."

"So you've never been to a library?" Amos didn't answer.

"Well," said Russell, "that's just crazy. Tomorrow we'll go to the library. It's a good one. We'll go in the afternoon." Russell dropped back flat onto his sleeping bag. "No books allowed," he said, mulling it over. "I can't imagine it. It sounds like leaving was the right thing. Jesus."

"Came here to be punished and ought to be punished," he whispered.

"What?"

"It wasn't just the books that made me leave." Amos's voice was choked, thickening. "I've done bad things, Russell." He heaved a sigh that broke into a jagged sob, the crying of a child, face wet with snot. He rolled on his side and brought his knees to his chest, curling into a tight ball.

Russell let him cry for a time and then reached his hand over and rubbed his back, soothing him. "It's okay, Amos. We've all done bad things."

The next day Russell found some scissors and evened out Amos's hair as best he could and found a hat for him to wear. In the afternoon they walked together into town and went to the library. Russell sat with the want ads while Amos wandered the aisles for an hour, picking up book after book and setting them back as gently as if they were eggs. The library had a cart with tattered paperbacks for twenty-five cents apiece. Russell counted out five dimes, and Amos spent another hour looking through the paperbacks for the two he wanted most. He finally chose them based largely on their lurid covers. Russell scanned each one and handed them back to Amos with a shrug. "Have to start somewhere," he said.

It was already growing dark when they left the library and strolled along the empty cruise ship docks. The hulking mountains that fenced the town were silhouetted against the dim gray sky. They left the docks and cut through town before heading back south down Thane. Amos chatted about the library, asked if they could go back tomorrow, what it took to get a check-out card. Russell considered the job situation. The want ads were a bust, but he figured it was time to stop treading water. He would catch the bus out to the job center. He would at least make an effort.

"How long does it take you to read a whole book?" Amos asked. They were on Main Street, heading toward the Crystal Palace. Russell could make out the usual small crowd of people in and around the bus shelter.

"Depends on the book," said Russell. "Depends on what else I'm doing."

"I'm going to read books all the time."

There was a clutch of smokers around the door of the Imperial. Russell and Amos stepped off the sidewalk to move around them. "Well, you've got two. You're off to a good start," said Russell. He looked up absently as they passed the smokers and locked eyes with the man with the cauliflower ears from the bathroom.

"What are you looking at?"

Russell looked down and away but the man advanced out of the group. "What are you looking at, you piece of shit?"

Russell raised his hands, moving away into the street. The man advanced toward him quickly, flicking his cigarette at him and grabbing at his jacket, shaking him. "What are you doing here? Didn't I tell you to get out?" Russell leaned back, trying to pull away. He felt himself going limp. Then Amos was between them, shoving at the man, trying to break his grip on Russell. The man spun, knocking Amos in his face with an elbow, hurling him to the ground. Amos seemed to crumple and the man kicked him, making awkward contact against Amos's shins. Amos curled into a ball. Russell stood trembling, his hands yet raised in the air. The man cleared his throat loudly and spat, a wet smack landing in Amos's hair. For a moment everything was still. Then a voice came booming from the Crystal Palace.

"Hey, you."

Down the street came Fat George. Not running but coming fast— he seemed to almost float. His arms were outstretched in the pose of a mounted grizzly—his shirt was open, exposing his hairless belly. "Hey, you fuckers. I'm gonna eat your face."

The crowd of smokers tightened and pulled back. The cauliflower-eared man stood his ground. "Stay out of it, you drunk muck," he said.

"Haaa," roared Fat George, coming faster.

The cops were on Fat George before he could take a swing. They came at a flat run, utility belts jangling, and combined their momentum with Fat George's to spin him hard into the rough wall of the building. They cuffed him as a cruiser pulled to the curb. The crowd of smokers relaxed, observers again. Russell reached for Amos and pulled him to his feet. Blood from his nose smeared the boy's cheeks. Russell pulled him away from the crowd now watching the routine and unremarkable arrest of Fat George for drunk and disorderly conduct.

"My eyes are watering. I can't see," said Amos.

"Hang on to me," replied Russell. "I can see fine."

Two cops, each taking an arm, led Fat George off the sidewalk and leaned him against the cruiser. He looked back at the crowd. "I blue ticket *you*, motherfuckers. I am Wooshkeetaan, Wolf Eagle. Aak'w Kwáan Tlingit. And I blue ticket all you."

Russell looked back at Fat George as he led Amos away. Fat George nodded at him and called out to Amos. "You watch my tent okay. You keep it good." Then he grinned to himself and raised his eyebrows at the cop standing next to him. "Hey, Officer Vandiver, you got real nice shoes on today."

By the time they reached camp, Amos's nose had stopped bleeding. They paused at a creek that cut through Thane Road in a culvert, and Russell wet a handkerchief and washed away the blood. Amos's face was swollen, and he did not speak. In the fight he had lost both the books.

Russell helped Amos into the tent. The boy curled into a ball and went silent. Russell made a fire and warmed a pan of powdered milk and brought it to Amos in a mug. "Drink this," he said. "You will feel better."

"Came here to be punished and ought to be punished," Amos whispered.

"No," said Russell. "Drink this and you will feel better."

Russell left the mug and backed out of the tent. He noticed the carved piece of wood wrapped in twine. He took it and stood, unwrapping the wolf roarer and letting it dangle. He went through the steps as Amos had done and began to swing it slowly over his head. He stood next to the tent in the light of the fire. He swung it until it sounded a pitch, a scream, a warning to the darkness. To keep the bears at bay.

SETH KANTNER

I N HER 1996 BOOK *DISAPPEARANCE: A MAP*, former Alaska Poet
Laureate Sheila Nickerson described the north as a place where,
when people go missing, it's the land itself that takes them. In much
of the world the assumption when someone vanishes is that some sort of
foul play involving another person has transpired. But in Alaska, where
the wilderness is vast and the humans found in it few, to disappear
implies a fatal misstep. Someone is traveling the land alone, and then
someone else starts wondering why they haven't returned or reached
their destination. A search commences, and oftentimes the missing person is never found. No one knows what befell them or where their body
might be, or even if they're actually dead.

It's an idea that Seth Kantner picks up in the title piece from his
2015 essay collection *Swallowed by the Great Land*. A lone adventurer
traveling the south side of the Brooks Range during the transition
from fall to winter failed to emerge from his travels, and Kantner,
who knows the country well, is as curious as anyone to learn what
happened.

Kantner and Alaska's Western Arctic are inseparable forces. Born in a sod igloo in Alaska's northwest, he grew up a part of the land. It was where he played, a place where there were no roads or traffic, where animals roamed freely, where his food came from and where it first had to be caught. It was a place, he wrote noted in his memoir *Shopping for Porcupine*, where "*people* were the exotic creatures."

Kantner's parents had come to the Arctic voluntarily, but he was born into it. In the 1970s, when most of his fellow white kids were watching television sitcoms and attending rock concerts, he was running dog teams and trapping and hunting wildlife to help feed his family.

"The land provided everything when I was a kid," he told me. "The weather decided what we did each day, and we spent our time gathering food and furs, hauling water and wood, eating most meals from the land, even insulating and building our home from trees, moss and dirt. Back then, people were the most uncommon part of life, and the most confusing. Books about Alaska were even more confounding. Why did they never tell it the way it was? A bear on the roof was normal; telephones and TV were alien devices."

Kantner now lives in the coastal arctic village of Kotzebue. Since the 2004 publication of his bestselling autobiographical novel, *Ordinary Wolves*, he's been Alaska's most prominent writer. And in a place where the work of so many authors is drawn from their connection to the land, Kantner's writing feels the most deeply rooted. Perhaps this owes to his having always known this land rather than having discovered it as an adult. Alaska didn't change him, as has been the case with so many others. Alaska created him.

Or as he explained, "It wasn't until later that I began to realize how different my perspective of the wilds is compared to most people. Out here these creatures and this land, the fireweed and cranberries, caribou and ravens and the rest have always been hard-working fellow citizens, the closest I've come to being part of a community. And I can't help worrying about them now. And me too, in this tenuous position of being best friends with the natural world."

— From *Swallowed by the Great Land* —
Swallowed by the Great Land

RECENTLY MY FRIEND DON REARDEN SENT ME A NEWS STORY of a search in the Brooks Range for a missing "survivalist." His only comment: "White boy lost by Ambler."

I was teaching a class, and busy. I glanced at it only because Don sent it. We both grew up in and out of villages—separately—and have navigated miles and years acutely aware that locals get a big kick out of a white guy screwing up in the country. I guess making fun of ourselves is all part of traveling prepared.

As I read the article, the word "survivalist" made me picture a cult member cramming underground bunkers full of canned Spam and ammo. The story said the man was from Wisconsin, an instructor from some Teaching Drum Outdoor School.

Instantly, I knew Alaskans were going to come down hard on this guy. People would recall Timothy Treadwell, eaten by bears, and Christopher McCandless, the skinny boy from Into the Wild who starved to death in an abandoned bus.

Many of us are lifelong Alaskans, and plenty are from the Lower 48, too, and the majority spend our days in heated buildings and much of our time in the country riding machines. All the same, we seem to reserve a special place in our hearts for despising Outsiders who walk into the wild and find trouble. Maybe we feel they haven't paid their dues or done the tedious time to gain experience. Or we think they lack respect for our hardearned, unquantifiable knowledge.

Regardless of our reasoning, as I read along, I felt a twinge of that contempt myself. Immediately I didn't feel too kind, and suppressed those feelings. I've certainly enjoyed my thousand risks out on the land and ice, and had my hundred lucky breaks.

I thought of my dad. When I was a kid he'd welcome any newcomer as having exactly as much right to be there as he did. He never had an ounce of that I-got-here-first attitude. He learned from sourdoughs and Natives alike. He would tell any stranger his favorite spot to pick cranberries, and graciously help them out when they foolishly shot a moose in the river, or had poor footwear, or no snowshoes, or no clue about the terrain they were headed into.

Reading, it dawned on me: I'd met the missing man, Thomas Seibold, in Ambler this past September. He was heading upriver with our friend Gitte Stryhn and her son. He seemed like a nice guy. He had big hands, and I wondered how he'd been received in the village with his ponytail. Later, I had asked Mary Williams in Ambler about him. Her face brightened. "Yeah! Real nice guy, Gitte's friend."

Don Rearden sent a second story. I skimmed it. The reporter seemed to be gluing together misinformation. The search area was out of reach to all of us without airplanes, and I wasn't interested in speculation. I had plenty of that in my own mind. I did recall Kobuk acquaintances mentioning that the flooding river had frozen high and the shelf ice was dangerous. I felt bad for the guy. This was a tough year to try to learn ice, and I figured he was under it.

Another friend, Nick Jans, called from Juneau. Statewide commentary was harsh, he reported. We compared stories of inexperienced white guys who had dropped into the region over the decades and somehow survived. We agreed that walking up the Ambler River valley during freezeup in a flood year, whether armed or unarmed, with matches or without, with the right footwear or without—this fella had to be tough.

From calls to Ambler, I got the feeling that people there were sympathetic. It's one thing to harvest enjoyment when an Outsider messes up, but nobody wants another drowning, another person frozen to death. Too many people here have had friends and relatives go that way. We wanted him found.

I tried to forget about it and headed out on my snowgo, looking for caribou. There was little snow, long stretches of clear ice. My hands kept getting cold. My thoughts kept circling back to falling through the ice, and how easily I could go from happy hunting to freezing in minutes. Actually, I've lived those minutes. Many local hunters and travelers have. I couldn't despise someone who has died in those minutes.

I remember walking from my camp to Ambler during breakup, hypothermic, jumping ice pans coming down creeks, for rafts, barely grasping willows to cling to cutbanks. Or at freezeup, kayaking across a river full of moving ice to get a wounded Canada goose, and getting swept partway under, certain I was gone but somehow clinging to a wedge of ice.

No one would have known where I'd gone. I don't leave detailed notes saying, "Energetic, bored, lonely, and restless today—crossing big river on retarded errand—back in two hours." No one would have found me. I can only hope folks wouldn't have written unsigned commentary about how I deserved it.

That stuff was in my mind about the time state troopers suspended the search. I looked forward to getting on with winter, getting back to feeling normal again when crossing ice.

But just then our longtime friend Gitte called with concrete details: where she and Thomas had gotten a moose, what kind of clothing he was wearing, and so on. Yes, he was carrying matches, she said, and yes, he was very capable.

A man named Tamarack called from the States—Thomas's friend and employer.

Equally out of the blue, on the morning jet, Gitte and two women, Lety and Makwa—Seibold's extended family—arrived from Healy and from Wisconsin. Stacey offered them breakfast and invited them to stay as long as they needed—these three women, kind people all, generous and saddened and missing a loved one. In those minutes the news story that Don had forwarded came alive at our kitchen table. I put down my coffee and everything I was doing, everything I intended to do. Their search became my search.

I can't pretend to know the country well, but I've traveled it. I don't know the local pilots well, but I've flown with them. I found phone numbers, grabbed maps, and stuffed parkas and socks and binoculars and cameras in packs. The sun cleared the horizon as we headed east with pilot Jim Kincaid in a Northwestern Aviation Cessna 206.

Peering down at the endless empty miles, all I could think about was how I would make it forty days over freezeup in the Brooks Range with no gun and poor winter gear. My thoughts jumped to humor—the warmest thing around would be a bear turd, still in the bear.

The second day we landed briefly in Ambler to pick up Alvin Williams. He knows the country and has always had better eyes than me. We continued up the Ambler valley in the short daylight.

The hours became surreal as we hunched at the small windows in the sky, pawing at maps, pointing out valleys, peering down at rocks and ice and tracks and trees—some of the most rugged and remote wilderness around. We were intense and focused, determined to spot a person, dead or alive.

We saw only one thing—a circle drawn in a sandbar, previously discovered by searchers. I refused to accept it as a sign of exultation or some sort of circle of life. I wouldn't make such a thing out in the wild, with wet feet and bears around, so I stuck with the belief that this guy wouldn't either. But what could it mean?

Nights, back in Kotzebue, we pored over maps and the photos I'd taken, and traded ideas. That wolverine relentlessness of mine wouldn't give up. I'd believed Thomas was dead, but I was starting to harbor faint spells of hope. Humans, I know, can be impossibly tough.

Toward morning I had a dream: I could see his legs—one twisted and broken—in yellow-soled boots and orange snowpants across big black rocks, and nearby an upright steel pole topped with a perfect stop sign. Why is that here? I wondered. I tried to examine his legs, but awoke with a start.

I got up and made coffee. By the stove, I asked Gitte what Thomas had been wearing on his feet. Steger mukluks, she said, and Sorel boots with light-colored bottoms. He had two sleeping bags with him, too, she added. One was orange.

The phone rang. It was Nick. "I had strange dreams last night," he said. "Nothing clear. Just that circle in the sandbar, really sharp, then I woke up."

"I'll let you know what we find," I said. I didn't say anything about my dream; I was still thinking about it.

That day Thomas's childhood friend, Makwa, brought home his belongings from the Kotzebue branch of the state troopers. Early on in the search they had found his diary and some of his possessions at Gitte's remote cabin on the Ambler River, where Thomas had spent the fall. When I laid out the tattered pieces of his USGS map here on the floor, a big piece was obviously missing—the entire upper Ambler River valley, and both passes north to the Noatak.

That evening Lety, Makwa, and Gitte got back on the jet, heading home. I couldn't stop studying Nakmaktuak Pass and the other fork of the Ambler. I envisioned myself alone for two months at Gitte's cabin on the river—I would try to walk that loop. And I certainly could get myself lost, hurt, chased around by bears, or under ice.

Just before midnight, Greg Dudgeon, an old friend and the superintendent of the Gates of the Arctic National Park, returned my call. I told him the route I would have tried to follow on foot. By morning he had made arrangements with local National Park Service officials, and Eric Sieh, a Kotzebue pilot who knows that country as well as anyone, had a small plane gassed and ready.

The weather was perfect, calm and clear. We skimmed the mountains on a direct line to the Cutler, upper Amakomanak, Imelyak, and Kavachurak.

We saw the blood of wolf kills, countless caribou trails, wolverine signs. With his years of experience tracking from the sky, Eric spotted caribou, a wolf pack, and tiny ptarmigan tracks. For hours he banked the plane in tight timbered valleys, flying low over the ice and level with vertical rock headwalls.

We saw nothing.

In the fading light, we turned west. It was a lowering kind of feeling, coming down over the sea ice, coming off the crazy intensity of this search: giving up. That mixed with the strangeness of staring down from the sky at so many square miles it has taken me a lifetime to cover on the ground.

It was hard to give up. I'm not family, not related. All I did was say hi to this man once. I liked his friends. And I figured the same thing could happen to me. I think he's under the ice, or he fell down rocks, or a grizzly bear stuffed him somewhere, but I don't know.

DAVE ATCHESON

DAVE ATCHESON CAN BE COUNTED AMONG the thousands of Alaskans who came for a summer and got hooked. In 1984, while still in college, he headed north from New York State, seeking adventure and some quick cash. He found both by getting hired onto a fishing boat out of Seward.

A year later, Atcheson was back to stay. For many subsequent years he found employment in Alaska's fishing industry, lured by what he calls Seasonal Work Syndrome, a common affliction among Alaskans who will work insane hours for a few months each summer in exchange for winters off and the chance to hunker down in a cabin or head for the tropics.

Dead Reckoning, Atcheson's memoir of his years working on Alaska's waters, introduces us to the vagaries of life on a fishing boat, where days of tedium suddenly give way to hours of frantic work during brief openings when crews attempt to haul in their allotted take before the state shuts things back down. He also explores the delicate social balance found on the vessels, where small crews are confined together for long periods of time. Everything good and bad about each member rises to the surface and impacts everyone's degree of success.

There's no guarantee of a good outcome when a fishing boat sets sail, Atcheson shows. Weather conditions, tides, problems with fellow crewmen, incompetent skippers, and just plain bad luck can cause any number of problems. And then there's the completely unexpected.

In the excerpt that follows, we join Atcheson on board the fishing vessel *Iliamna Bay* in 1997. Short of money that year, and waiting for the season to come into full swing, he signed on for a quick trip out to Bristol Bay, where the herring run promised a big paycheck. Things went well until they didn't. Immediately after filling the ship's hold, a riptide set in, causing calamity for the numerous boats whose crews were celebrating a successful haul.

Reflecting on his life and winding career path, Atcheson told me, "I've never been an adrenaline junky, and despite a popular misconception about fishermen most of those I've encountered while working at sea were hardly thrill seekers. What we did share was a sense of wanderlust, often a respect or innate love of nature, of the outdoors, and especially of the sea. We also shared a longing for adventure, the need to seek out something different, that might challenge you personally, but not to the point it puts you on edge or endangers your crew. It's a similar perspective I often attempt to render in my writing as well.

These days, Atcheson lives in Sterling, on the Kenai Peninsula, where he writes for numerous periodicals, teaches college courses, and advocates for resource conservation, especially in Bristol Bay, where a proposed mining development threatens salmon runs. Much of his adult life has been spent both harvesting those salmon and admiring their role in Alaska's ecological balance. Working to protect them from harm and preserve them for the future has provided a focus for his writing and his work.

— From *Dead Reckoning* —

MAYBE THINGS HAD BEEN GOING TOO WELL. We'd seemingly had such good luck, a considerate crew that worked together so well, a big payday in Cook Inlet, and splendid weather for our crossing of the Bering Sea.

But with our late arrival, had our luck finally taken its inevitable turn for the worse?

Tim had been running the engine nearly full bore for almost twenty-four hours. As we entered Togiak Bay, news broke over the airwaves that the fleet had been put on "twenty-minute notice," signaling an opening was imminent. It came with the usual scuttlebutt, the excited calls, and the last-minute planning that always accompanies the desperate plunge into a herring roundup. We fielded calls from our pilot and the other boats, requesting our location as we called out frantically, attempting to locate the tender that carried our seine. We were hoping, probably beyond hope, that we might somehow load it aboard and be ready to fish, but the closer we came, the more the realization crept in: nearly six days of travel, and if we'd arrived an hour earlier, if we'd only hurried our refueling on the Aleutians or not paused somewhere to check the engine and give our ears a break, we'd be out there now with our partners circling a school of herring. It could almost be read in Tim's eyes, seen in the way he held himself at the wheel, his stance settling from tenseness into a posture not really relaxed but simply loose, urgency briefly succumbing to anger before finally falling into stubborn acceptance. Oh, he'd still try, but we all knew there was just no way we were going to make it.

Still, there always remains that slight ray of hope. The tender that carried our net was not far away—in Kulukak Bay taking herring from gillnetters. The gillnetters, many of whom were locals fishing from small skiffs, had been open all day. Because this tender was assigned to them rather than a seiner, they were stationary, and this bought us a little bit of time. We'd already unchained our skiff and prepared the boom to lower it into the water as we pulled alongside the other boat. Seiners would not be fishing immediately adjacent to us, but the sea was alive with vessels and the sky suddenly became a tapestry crisscrossed with weaving aircraft. As we placed buoys between us and fastened the two boats side by side, we heard it, first broadcast in unison from outside speakers on each of our decks and then echoed across the water from various vessels—a ripple effect of bad news reaching us in increments. It was the announcement that fishing was open and the final acknowledgement that there was no way we'd have our seine unpackaged, loaded, and ready to fish by the time the twenty-minute seine opener was over.

We all slowed down and for a minute just watched the madness commencing around us—without us.

"Damn," muttered Karl, expressing a feeling of utter helplessness in a single syllable. We all felt it. There was the chance—however unlikely— that the boats could fill the entire season's quota during those twenty minutes, and we'd have come all this way for nothing; we'd have to turn back around and start the long voyage home. We continued without urgency to unload the seine from the hold of the tender onto its deck; then we dragged it across the rails of both boats and onto the deck of the *Iliamna Bay* in the anticipation that we would need it.

When we were finished, we found a resting place on the east side of the bay inside Anchor Point. Finally we were free from the constant drubbing of the engine; there was complete quiet broken only by the modest hum of the generator. At last, after nearly a week, we pulled the small foam plugs from our ears and took our first long walks on the rocky beaches of Bristol Bay.

Awaiting the official report, Tim was likely more anxious than the rest of us. Apparently our partners had not fared well. This was perhaps a sign that no one had and that there might be another opener or maybe two. I was relieved, especially because Tim had insisted, not being here in time, that we wouldn't be part of the co-op for this opener. Thankfully Tim's argument that we not share in the catch, an argument made against his crew's wishes and the other skippers' insistence, was rendered moot by the poor catch and the report broadcast that evening by the Department. Like our partners' catches, most of the herring had been "green" and unsalable and so were released back to the sea. Apparently our luck was still with us and we still believed in it and the inevitability that we'd hit it big this next opening.

So, here we were again reciting the fisherman's refrain of "hurry up and wait". We whiled away a good part of a precipitation-and-fog-filled week raingear-clad walking the beaches or squirreled away in our bunks reading. Occasionally we'd raft up with our partners the *Rafferty* and the *Sea Mist* so the skippers could talk.

Butch Schollenberg, skipper of the *Sea Mist*, had been fishing practically his whole life. As a kid he'd gillnetted with his father on Cook Inlet, and bought his first boat in 1976—just two years after graduating from high school. Greg Gabriel had done just about the same, starting on a beach site with relatives when he was thirteen, running a setnet skiff during breaks from school; he had graduated only a few years following Butch and bought his first boat soon after. The two now ran their own salmon seiners in Prince William Sound: this was the second year Greg had joined Butch's crew for herring. Though they were only in their early forties, they had a lifetime of fishing experience between them, which included innumerable Oh Shit Moments.

Like the other skippers, Grant Henderson of the *Rafferty* was experienced and had fished his entire life, but to me he seemed a bit different than the others. He was slightly more high-strung and seemed a tad younger than the skippers in our group, though on second glance probably wasn't. He just carried himself that way. Like Tim he kept clean-shaven, but he seemed more professorial than the others, reminding me of someone I could have taken a class from in college rather than an Alaskan boat captain. Like Tim he was rather meticulous, but he was also a bit of a contradiction. He suffered from motion sickness but loved boats and had his pilot's license. He claimed to be cautious and unlikely to take chances—and he appeared that way—but had also seen more Oh Shit Moments than just about anyone out there.

The skippers' chats usually took place aboard the *Sea Mist*, the largest of the three vessels, but could easily spring up just about anywhere. That was probably around the first time I heard Tim say that he had made a pact with himself never again to set past Usik Spit—which meant out past Bristol Bay proper and close to the invisible demarcation that signals the edge of the often turbulent Bering Sea. I asked him why and he was a little vague at first, saying it was just a nasty place to fish. "It's unpredictable," he said later. "Scares a lot of guys off. It's definitely not a place for beginners. The pilots though, they like it—there's not a lot of competition and it's a good place to pick up a lot of fish . . . a good place to lose them too." Come to find out Tim had done more than lost fish out there, he'd twice ripped his gear, once completely in half, and he'd witnessed more than a few boats roll in the erratic currents. "No," he said. "There's no way we're going out there."

With the constant wet weather, the deckhands tended to keep to their own vessels. Each night we'd listen to the reports from test fishing. The herring reached ripeness and maturity in a matter of days—though it seemed slow to us—and as the week wore on the fleet went from twenty-four hour notice to six, and then finally to one. At last we were going to have a shot at these fish. But as it turned out, the fog was as thick as chowder and the ceiling low—we likely wouldn't have the help of our spotter plane.

Earlier that morning, however, I had entered the cabin to hear Tim urging our pilot, Brad Heil, over the radio to please play it safe and stay grounded like most of the other planes. But Brad thought he could get airborne and since there weren't many planes in the sky, he easily ducked in and out, above and below the clouds, and after a couple hours in the air—with Tim shaking his head in both dismay and appreciation—he reported a possible spotting of several small schools of herring. They were spread out over the area and there was only one extremely large school. Unfortunately, it was just inside Usik Spit, on the edge of what Tim referred to as the danger zone.

The herring were congregated in a fairly tight ball, and it was determined by the skippers that just one boat should risk itself on what could very likely turn out to be—as it always was in this area—a dicey but very profitable operation. I don't know how it was decided that Tim would make the set, but I suspected—even after what he'd said and the pact he'd made with himself—he'd volunteered. My guess was that he just couldn't stand to be the one *not* fishing, the one standing by, because, after all, he was a fisherman. And fishing was what he did and that's what he had to do.

"I don't think there's any skipper that wants to go there," Tim said as we set a course toward Cape Pearce and the edge of the Bering Sea. It was still early afternoon and we had about an hour run out to where we would fish in a strait formed by a large island and a distinct point of land, ranging from eight to twelve miles across. Here, a series of narrow bays dotted the northwest shore, one of which held our quarry. "We might not even make it out there by the time they call the opener," said Tim, almost sounding like he was hoping that would be the case. He knew what he was doing, though; by now I had complete confidence in him and this boat and its crew. And despite the fog and low ceiling, the waters remained calm.

As is usual at the outset of an opening, a bit of hysteria ensued. Before setting out, we'd frantically tried to locate our pilot in order to refuel him. When we found him, Tim once again attempted unsuccessfully to persuade him to stay put. But both men knew there was little hope of us re-locating the large ball of herring without his eyes in the sky. He'd at least take off and attempt to pick his way through the clouds as we set course and once again pushed the engines of the *Iliamna Bay* in a race to reach the fish before an opening was called.

When we arrived on scene, it was already mid-afternoon and what we found was odd. With only two other boats in sight—and then a long way off—it was a far cry from the war scene that usually raged on the herring grounds. We figured the other boats' pilots had likely risked an earlier flight, but there was no sign of them now. Only one plane—ours—passed low between the falling cover and the eerily calm seas.

In the flat light and haze it was difficult to find the fish. At the pilot's suggestion, Tim climbed into the crow's nest and steered the boat from there. He circled the boat, following the pilot's instructions until he finally spotted the school. When he did, he marveled at its dimensions; the school, maybe millions of fish, turning the water black along a sandy beach at the far head of one of the small bays. "All in all, a pretty good place to set," he shouted down to us. That was, of course, if they stayed put.

We all wondered what Fish and Game was waiting for—maybe they were deciding at the last minute whether to even have an opening at all. Maybe the roe wasn't quite ripe or perhaps the weather was too bad and they wanted more planes in the air. On the other hand, maybe they were glad there weren't more planes flying, so the catch would be limited.

In the meantime, the two other boats, knowing our pilot was the one in the air, had changed course and were beginning to head our way. That's when Tim took immediate, evasive action, turning off the fish in the hopes of luring the other vessels away. His deception worked—the other boats began to veer off. But the fish also began to move. They were now streaming down the beach and out of range. Then, as it does with herring, everything happened at once. The Department announced the opening was on and soon thereafter, the countdown began: 5-4-3-2-1. We had just twenty minutes, but the fish were no longer anywhere nearby. Where in the hell had they gone? We could also no longer hear our plane; the pilot likely thought we were on the herring and had headed to safer skies. Five minutes had passed by and we still hadn't spotted our herring. Perhaps they were moving faster down that beach than we thought—maybe even out into the open. That's when the sound of a lone engine, lost in the soup somewhere above, pierced the breathless air. Tim had obviously relayed our situation to the pilot, that we had lost the fish, yet at the same time assuring him that we would find them and that he should leave us to it. But now ten minutes had gone by and we still hadn't spotted them. Then we all watched in wonder as our plane—in what Tim would later refer to as the most courageous and talented move he'd ever witnessed—angled down out of the clouds through a sudden hole. With barely a wingspan of sky and wisps of sunshine behind him, he appeared as if through a small door, allowing him just enough leeway to sweep in before it closed. Down the beach he sailed in search of our lost fish, finally dropping a wing and pointing out exactly where they had gone.

Moving much faster than we'd ever anticipated, the herring were still fleeing en masse, veering along the mainland, and at each interval hiding themselves in a continually worse spot. Tim made a quick calculation and throttled ahead, taking a bead on the fish like a linebacker heading off an escaping ball carrier, deciding in this case where to lay our gear. Unfortunately, in this game there was no referee to blow the whistle, to call them out of bounds, and we went ahead and made our set, now just outside the slight protection the little bay afforded and within view of the outstretched finger of land separating us from the open sea.

UNLIKE SALMON SEINING, WHERE TIME IS USUALLY in large supply and the crews often work by rote, no two herring sets are ever the same, nor has an opener ever gone off like clockwork. Each one borders on the slightly insane, even when there are no other vessels to fend off. Due to the lack of time, an unfamiliar location, or the position of the boat, lashed off quickly to the tender and the net in a myriad of odd ways—it is extremely dangerous, even under the best of conditions. Then, if you are lucky and have a good catch, there's enough fish tied off between you and the tender to potentially sink your vessels. All of it compounds the strain both on the equipment and on your psyche, on the gear and rigging and your nerves. And as we adroitly closed this set off, we knew it was big. Tim estimated it was at least two hundred tons, maybe as many as three hundred or four hundred, and at three hundred dollars a ton it was a major payday; this made the whole process that much more tense and intense.

The lone tender that had followed us pulled along the outside of our gear, between us and the mainland, as we hurriedly pursed the seine, pulling the lead line up under the fish and sealing them in a bag of net beneath us. The tender crew quickly tied the cork line to their boat any way they could, in the usual slap-dash fashion, using the slight sway of the ocean to lay the line—burdened by the weight of thousands upon thousands of these small fish—onto a series of hooks attached to a thick steel cable festooned for just this purpose along the side of their vessel. Once it was fastened, a company representative tested the fish for ripeness; the higher the percentage of ripe roe, the higher the price we would be paid. It looked good, very good, and as they began to suction the herring aboard, filling their hold, we began to relax and to feel the throes of celebration set in. We were all going to be rich—at least several thousands of dollars richer!

Over the next several hours the fish were tested and pumped, and evening began to settle in. By the time the eighty-five-ton capacity of our tender was reached, it was turning toward dusk. Another tender, which would tie up along the outside of this one and "pump across," was at least three or four hours away, and a third, which we'd surely need for such a large haul would certainly be sent by the company, and hopefully just behind it. With our tender anchored and holding us in place, we'd wait. It was calm. The sky actually looked like it was beginning to clear a little.

Butch, the skipper of the *Sea Mist*, likely had far more experience herring fishing than just about anyone in our group, and from the beginning he had expressed qualms about even heading out to where the set had been made. He knew, however, that he had a duty to his partners to be there now to help out and to make sure all went well with us. He and his crewmen, including Greg, had watched as the net was sealed, the set finished, and the tender began to pump fish aboard.

"In my mind it was in the bag," Greg said later, but Butch hadn't been so sure.

"We're not going to go far," Butch insisted, even after our first 85 tons were pumped and his crew, after enduring what seemed an interminable period of standing by, had long grown bored. "I've been in these deals before. Sometimes catching the fish, that's the easy part. They're not ours until they're on the tender. Actually," he said, amending his initial statement, "they're not ours until we've been paid for them."

It was something Greg would always remember. He'd been fishing long enough to know Butch was right. Still, waiting is never easy even though fishermen are used to it, and Butch could see his crew was antsy. He was too. After all the build-up, all the running around, they hadn't even made a set themselves and some of that energy remained. After several restless hours, he sent Greg and his skiff man over to see if there was something for them to do, any-thing to get them off the boat for a while. "Might as well go over there and help babysit the set," he said. "You never know."

On the *Iliamna Bay*, we were in celebration mode. After all, our work was done. The other tenders would arrive, finish pumping our fish out, we'd do a little clean-up and go to bed, and tomorrow we'd wake up much wealthier than when we started the day. But we waited and kept waiting. We ate dinner, we had a beer, and Karl even suggested it might be time to break out the whiskey. I initially thought why not? If nothing else it would be a good way to pass the time. I was a little surprised when Brad declined. "Let's wait until we're really done," he said and I agreed. Karl too. It was getting late and we all wanted it to be over with, to be unloaded and on our way. So instead we played a game of cards. I even laid down for an hour, but I couldn't sleep. It had grown dark as we marked our time, continually wondering where in the hell those tenders were.

"Still on their way," said Tim each time we'd ask. He'd been on the radio with them at least a dozen times. The company obviously hadn't thought we'd set so far out or hadn't planned on us catching so many fish. Besides, these big boats are slow, some only traveling seven or eight knots an hour, which might mean as many as four or five hours of travel time to where we were. And I'd worked for these companies before—who knew how long it had taken them to decide which boat to send. They may even have had the boats run an errand first.

I went to the deck and scanned the horizon. It was pitch black by now, and I could only see a couple small twinkles, boat lights like stars lost in the distance, so far off they might as well have been in another galaxy. That's when I heard the skiff. It seemed to almost pop out of nowhere and into the bright glow of our halogen lights, which swept in a semi-circle just out beyond our deck. These giant lights lit up the *Iliamna Bay* like a stadium, but also left you wondering what was happening just beyond them, on the periphery, where everything just dissolved into the darkness. The skiff entered from behind a black curtain, appearing as if by magic at the side of our boat.

"Butch sent us over to see if there's anything we can do," announced Greg as he climbed over the rail. We welcomed him aboard but told him there really wasn't much.

Still we were glad to see a couple new faces, hear a new story, anything to break up the monotony. Brad was on his way across to the tender to take a shower. "Might as well not let that boat and all their water go to waste," he said before climbing to our bow. We were tied off, our bow to the tender's stern, by a line that had grown exceedingly tight. Brad had to take a step or two across it like a tightrope walker to get to the other boat. I watched him suspended a few feet above the ocean, then noticed that the water below us was no longer placid and had begun to stir. It was running like a river between the two vessels now, signifying a tide change. We'd been through at least one since we'd set, so I didn't think too much of it at the moment. But the tide had just started shifting and I really hadn't paid too much attention to the clock either, other than logging off the hours waiting for an additional tender, so I didn't know it was just beginning to roar. If I had only made the connection, that the tide had just started and was already running so hard, I might have known what was brewing and relayed it to the others.

Back on deck we still hadn't noticed much of a change in the ocean. Karl offered our guests something to drink as we hashed over the usual topics—the price of fish and how ready we were to head home. But before long, we couldn't help but notice it. It came first on the *Iliamna Bay*. The two boats tied together were facing opposite directions, the back of ours aligned with the bow of the tender, which was anchored into the short, oncoming waves. With our stern into the waves we took the brunt of them as they abruptly built into a froth, at first just rocking the *Iliamna Bay*. And then, seemingly without warning—though in reality these churning seas may have been intensifying for as much as an hour—they erupted, now rocking even the larger boat, the one facing into them. Our initial thought, after having sat stationary, with nary a breath of wind for so long, was "what the fuck is going on?" I saw the tender's skipper peer out of the door on his bridge a story above us, his face creased with a look of bewilderment and concern. The way he hurried back and forth didn't rest well with me. We all thought the weather had taken an immediate and drastic turn. Oddly, there was still none of the wind that would accompany a squall, but no one seemed to notice in the increasing frenzy. We were trapped in our little sphere of light, like one of those globes that hold a winter scene, only we were held tightly to the now roiling whitecaps, building in force, beginning to wash over our stern. Our situation, having all at once gone from one of celebration to one of dread, had taken a precipitous about-face.

MONTE FRANCIS

A WIDELY PUBLICIZED 2018 REPORT from the Seattle-based Urban Indian Health Institute found that murder is the third most common form of death for Native American and Alaska Native women. That same year, the Anchorage Press noted that thirty-one Alaska Native women and girls were either missing, or their murders remained unsolved, while nine cases were absent from law enforcement records.

Monte Francis, a television and print reporter from San Francisco, suspects that at least three of those women whose cases remain unresolved, as well a murdered African American woman, were slain by Joshua Wade, a serial killer who operated in Anchorage around the turn of the millennium who has confessed to five other killings.

Francis traveled to Alaska after reading of the unsolved murders, which took place in 1999 and 2000. Noting the similarities the cases bore to the 2000 murder of Della Brown, an Alaska Native woman whose killing Wade eventually confessed to, he went digging.

The resultant true crime book, *Ice and Bone: Tracking an Alaskan Serial Killer*, is among other things an examination of the dangers Alaska

Native women face in the state's largest city, and an exploration of the impact Brown's murder had on her family and community.

Della Brown's life was tragic from conception. Her father raped her Inupiaq mother, who gave her away at birth. The white man who raised her, Brown would later claim, sexually abused her from the age of seven. As an adult she sank into a cycle of alcoholism, substance abuse and violent relationships.

On the night of September 1, 2000, Brown was discovered passed out on a road in Anchorage's Spenard district by Wade and three companions. Several hours later her sexually violated corpse would be discovered in a nearby shed.

Prior to the discovery, Wade had taken friends to see Brown's body, and bragged about having killed her. He was arrested, and in 2004 tried. However, owing to poor police and prosecutorial work, an absence of physical evidence, easily discredited witnesses, and a crack defense team, the jury returned a not guilty verdict on all charges except evidence tampering. The public was enraged, but Wade walked away.

In 2007 a psychiatric nurse practitioner named Mindy Schloss vanished and was soon found dead. After using Schloss' ATM card to withdraw money from her account, Wade was tied to the murder. The fraudulent use of the card elevated the crime to federal status, leaving Wade exposed to a possible death sentence, a penalty Alaska state law disallows. Rather than risk execution, Wade made a plea deal, admitting to the killings of Brown and Schloss in exchange for life without parole. He subsequently confessed to killing three men as well.

In *Ice and Bone*, Francis carefully documents the sequence of events for each killing and the prosecutions that followed. He also makes strong cases tying Wade to the unsolved murders that occurred around the time of Brown's death.

In his book, Francis recounts his conversation with Brown's mother, Daisy Piggott. Brown had finally reconnected with her as an adult and the two were struggling to build a relationship when Brown was murdered. Piggott, who has endured multiple tragedies herself, was left to come to grips with the fate of a daughter she barely knew.

Additionally, Francis spent considerable time with the since deceased Alaska Native activist Desa Jacobsson, a charismatic, tireless, and highly media savvy advocate for Native rights who was well known in

Anchorage. It was Jacobsson who helped Francis understand the failures of the justice system to address crimes against Alaska Natives. Francis' conversations with Piggott and Jacobsson are excerpted here.

Reflecting on writing the book, Francis told me,

"I first became aware of the epidemic of rape and sexual violence in the Native Alaskan culture when I read a 2014 article in the Atlantic entitled "Rape Culture in the Alaskan Wilderness." I was shocked to learn the scope of the problem and the lack of public awareness about it.

"As I researched unsolved crimes, I learned about the efforts of Desa Jacobsson to bring attention to the murders of Della Brown and other Native Alaskan women. I decided to give her a call. I never imagined that initial call would evolve into a friendship with Jacobsson nor could I have imagined that she would become such a support and constant cheerleader for me."

He added,

"I also wanted to pay proper tribute to the families and friends of the victims, who are so often forgotten in the telling of these tragedies. "

If Francis' suspicions are correct, Wade killed at least five women, but was only convicted when he chose a white victim. At a time when increased attention is being paid to the disappearances and deaths of Native American and Alaska Native women, *Ice and Bone* has taken on additional significance. Although he's never lived in Alaska–or perhaps because of this–Monte Francis has been able to tell us a story about the dark side of life in the Last Frontier that, for the rest of the state as well as the country, is criminal to ignore.

— From *Ice and Bone* —

DURING THE FALL OF 2014, WHILE RESEARCHING UNSOLVED CRIMES, I came across a story in the Anchorage Daily News that piqued my interest. The article, dated September 28, 2000, had the headline: "'THERE'S NOTHING WE'RE NOT DOING'—POLICE GIVE PRIORITY TO SOLVING SIX SLAYINGS." The story recounted the killings of five Native Alaskan women and an African American woman who had been murdered within the span of sixteen months. There was no clear indication the slayings were linked, but fear was spreading among the residents of Anchorage that a serial killer was on the loose. The cases shared a number of similarities: most of the women were intoxicated at the time of their deaths and all of them were last seen alone and outside during early morning hours. However, the women had met their ends in different ways: three had been stabbed, one strangled, one drowned, and the sixth had her throat slit and her skull crushed by a rock.

Quoted in the article was a Native Alaskan activist named Desa Jacobsson, who had gone on a twenty-eight-day hunger strike to pressure federal authorities to investigate the cases, claiming that police were not taking the deaths seriously enough. Jacobsson, sixty-seven, intrigued me because she spoke to a larger systemic problem, namely, the victimization of Native Alaskan women and society's failure to protect them.

"If this was Chelsea Clinton this was happening to, they'd be on it like white on rice," Jacobsson proclaimed to me over the phone, matter-of-factly. My call had taken her so off guard, she later told me, she initially couldn't speak.

"Are you still there?" I had asked, after several seconds of silence.

After a long pause, she said, "I didn't know it was going to affect me like this. Whoa."

Fourteen years had passed since the murders, and she said that my call, which came out of the blue, had caused all of her memories from that time to come rushing back.

"I thought everyone had forgotten," she told me. "Here I thought I was just going to retire, eat bonbons, and become a cougar," she told me during one of our many meetings that followed, making a joke about dating younger men, and letting out a hearty laugh. She then lowered her gaze, and a look of earnestness returned to her face. "But when you called, I realized, we have unfinished business."

In the months following the murders, Jacobsson had not only blamed the Anchorage police for failing to aggressively investigate the cases but also faulted the tribal leadership in Alaska for its apathy, saying as far as the six dead women were concerned, "The silence was deafening."

During our first conversation, Jacobsson was quick to point to crime statistics that showed Native women were far more likely to be sexually assaulted than white women in Alaska.

"We lead the nation in violence against women and children and sexual violence. And predators know the police here don't respond," she said.

According to figures compiled by the Justice Center at the University of Alaska Anchorage, just 18 percent of the rapes reported to the Anchorage police are prosecuted, a figure that is almost 20 percent below the national average. It is a statistic that is all the more troubling given that Alaska has the highest number of rapes per capita of any U.S. state, and Native Alaskan women are more at risk than any other group. The Justice Department estimated in 2012 that one in three Native Alaskan women have been raped, and the reality is undoubtedly much more unsettling. At least one hundred of the 226 Native villages in Alaska don't have any kind of law enforcement—many of those same villages don't have road access or dependable phone service—making the reporting of such crimes impractical if not impossible. The Alaska Federation of Natives has estimated the rate of sexual assault in many Alaskan villages to be twelve times the national average.

As for the larger cities such as Anchorage and Fairbanks, Jacobsson contended, a complacency on the part of public officials with regard to Native women leads to victim-blaming rather than pursuing the perpetrators. It's why, she conjectured, rapists and murderers have long been attracted to Alaska.

"I don't know what you know about predators, but these are the most practiced manipulators on earth. They know what they're doing, how they're doing it . . . their radar is always on."

THERE WERE FEW PEOPLE MORE OUTRAGED by the jury's verdict in the Della Brown case than Native activist Desa Jacobsson. The sixty-seven-year old–whose first name is pronounced *Deesa*—is a wonderfully eccentric woman, a descendent of the Gwich'in and Yup'ik tribes, who can dispense motherly advice and utter a string of four-letter epithets in the same breath. Often the sole protester at government events in Anchorage, she keeps her salt-and-pepper hair in a fashionable bob and is never without one of her signature pink scarves around her neck. Before following her political aspirations—which included a run for governor as the Green Party candidate in 1998—Jacobsson headed a citizen crime prevention brigade she dubbed the "Rat Patrol." The group was made up of five women, who in white T-shirts patrolled the main thoroughfare in downtown Anchorage late at night, trying to protect Native women from predators. One night, Jacobsson said, she watched as a group of more than a dozen men lined up outside a bar frequented by Native women, ostensibly ready to pounce when the bar closed its doors.

"One of them had a case of beer, and I thought, what are they waiting for?

At first I thought for a cab or something, but no, they were waiting for vulnerable Native women to come out . . . so they could do what they wanted with them. Nobody said a thing."

Shortly after Wade's acquittal, Jacobsson announced she was beginning a hunger strike to protest the verdict. She vowed to live on only coffee and water until the police chief resigned and until federal prosecutors indicted Wade for violating Della Brown's civil rights.

"It wasn't a strike, it was a fast," Jacobsson clarified. "The word 'strike' has violent connotations."

Jacobsson's feud with Anchorage Police Chief Walt Monegan stemmed from what she deemed a "sloppy police investigation" and from comments Monegan made on a radio program suggesting that Native women should not put themselves in the vulnerable position of being drunk and alone at night. Jacobsson considered this victim blaming.

"I don't care what kind of life you lead," Jacobsson quipped. "Nobody deserves to be slaughtered."

Monegan insisted that Jacobsson had misconstrued his comments, telling the Anchorage Daily News, "I think it's part of my duty. If there's a threat out there, I should be warning people about it. . . . No one deserves to be a victim."

Most important, Jacobsson saw that Della Brown's murder was already fading from the public's consciousness and she didn't want Della to be just one more Native woman the public would forget. Two weeks into her twenty-eight day fast, weak yet determined, Jacobsson led a ten-mile memorial walk in memory of Della Brown and the other five women who had been slain. Thirty-five women, mostly Native Alaskan, followed Jacobsson quietly in a solemn procession from the foothills east of Anchorage to downtown and then on to Spenard, where Della Brown's body had been found. There, the women held candles and some of them wept under a darkening sky.

"We were all screaming inside, 'Someone do something! Say something!' And no one did," Jacobsson recalled. "Even the Native leaders said we were being purely reactionary. And we said, 'No, we can do something, we can hold a candlelight vigil, and let everybody know that this is not okay.' You see, it's the silence that's dangerous."

MUCH HAD GONE WRONG IN THE PROSECUTION of Della Brown's murder, but it was unclear to me what role racism had played, if any, in the outcome of the trial. I could point to a number of missteps made by the state that appeared unintentional; at the same time, after almost a year of research into these cases, it was hard to ignore the fact that Wade wasn't convicted and put away until he murdered a middle-class professional white woman.

"Do you know what apartheid is?" Desa Jacobsson asked me, as we sat in a cafe one day, sipping coffee. "Well it's alive and well here in Alaska."

Jacobsson insisted that we drive to Bean's Cafe, a soup kitchen in Anchorage's Ship Creek neighborhood. The area surrounding the cafe and an adjacent shelter, where most of the city's homeless dwell, lacks the bustle and sophistication of downtown, just a few blocks to the west, and retains the industrial feel of the Port of Anchorage, a short distance northwest, which ranks among the most productive fishing ports in the world. On that November afternoon the temperature was just 18 degrees Fahrenheit, and I was shocked to see a few dozen people out on the streets, unfazed by the bitter cold. Unoccupied tents and sleeping bags lined the sidewalk, where many of them had apparently spent the night.

"Look at their faces," Jacobsson said. "These are the landowners!" She exclaimed, pointing excitedly. She repeated this phrase more than once, each time becoming more agitated. "The LANDOWNERS! The LANDOWNERS!" she said raising her voice, her outrage so palpable I thought she might jump out of my rental car. It took me a minute to realize what she meant: the faces of the men and women outside the soup kitchen appeared to belong mostly to Alaska Natives. These indigenous people of the state, whose tribes once thrived on this vast, fertile landscape, had been relegated to living on the streets, and the very thought enraged her.

Jacobsson later explained to me that the intensity of her reaction had come from a general sense of injustice, but it was also personal. She said that much like Della Brown, she had survived sexual abuse during her childhood, and as an adult had become addicted to alcohol. Thirty years ago, she quit drinking and decided to devote the rest of her life to victim advocacy. For eight years, she worked in shelters for abused women and children in rural Alaska, seeing firsthand the prevalence of alcohol dependency in Native communities and the devastating effects of fetal alcohol syndrome on a whole new generation of Alaska Natives.

The condition, which results when a mother drinks during pregnancy, besets a child with a range of physical and mental defects such as low body weight, learning disabilities, and poor coordination. Researchers have found that those affected with FAS are more likely to drop out of school, end up in jail, and to end up themselves, addicted to alcohol or drugs. The statistics demonstrate nothing short of an epidemic of FAS among Alaska Natives; state health records show between 1995-1998, a staggering 40 percent of children born to Native Alaskan mothers were at risk of having FAS, dramatically outpacing any other ethnic group. (Only 2.7 percent of white mothers were at risk of having children with the condition.) Health officials in Alaska have since made great progress lowering the numbers, but Jacobsson explained that for a generation of Natives, the damage had already been done.

Later, when our conversation returned to Della Brown and the other women who had been killed, Jacobsson told me that she feared all her efforts to draw attention to the unsolved cases over the years, had been ineffective.

"They have been forgotten," she said, referring to the murdered women. "And the only reason they were remembered again briefly, was because Wade killed again, and because Mindy was white."

Alaska has a history of discrimination against its Native people, mirrored in some ways by the prejudice faced by African Americans in the U.S. before the Civil Rights Movement. In the capital city of Juneau in the 1940s, it was not uncommon to see signs that read "No Dogs, No Natives" and "We serve to white trade only." There were "white only" sections at movie theaters, and Native children were forced into schools where their languages were neither taught nor understood. The state's earliest and perhaps most important civil rights figure, Elizabeth Peratrovich, herself an Alaska Native, founded a group called the Alaska Native Sisterhood and successfully lobbied the state government to ban the discriminatory signage in Juneau. Alaska Governor Ernest Gruening signed the Anti-Discrimination Act of 1945, which was the first law of its kind in U.S. history.

"Have you heard of the Paintball Attacks of 2001?" Jacobsson asked me. I shook my head.

"When you get home, Google it," she advised, assuring me that overt acts of racism in Alaska were not just from a bygone time.

A quick internet search revealed the story: On the night of January 14, 2001, three young white men in a car cruised the streets of downtown Anchorage with paintball guns in hand, videotaping their attack. The footage showed Alaska Natives flinching and shielding their faces as the young men opened fire, erupting in laughter each time they hit one of their targets. As The New York Times reported, the attacks appeared to be racially motivated:

- The youths, a 19-year-old and two younger teenagers, appeared to be looking for Eskimos. "Shoot him! Shoot him!" one voice on the tape said. "You need to shoot that guy." Another voice replied: "No. He's Chinese."

- Some of the victims called police, relaying the car's license plate number. Detectives traced the vehicle to a home in a suburb of Anchorage, but citing a lack of evidence, they did not arrest the three young men until two months later. The Alaska House of Representatives would condemn the attack as a hate crime. The oldest of the assailants, a nineteen-year-old, was sentenced to six months in jail.

ALTHOUGH JOSHUA WADE HAS SPENT ALMOST A DECADE behind bars, his evil acts continue to have repercussions in many people's lives. The FBI is confident Wade has killed at least five other people and we can speculate about at least a few other unsolved crimes, but the true number of his victims reaches into the dozens. That's because murder is never just a solitary act; the consequences for the victim's loved ones often play out in the most unfortunate and tragic of ways for years following the crime.

Most of these additional victims are people Wade never even knew. Della Brown's grandchildren, for example, are now growing up without their grandmother. Della's siblings, who were just getting to know her, will never have the chance to develop full and satisfying relationships with their sister. Gerri Yett now faces the prospect of retiring and growing old without her best friend and companion, Mindy Schloss. Robert Conway and Kathy Hodges continue on in life without the friendship and affection of a woman they both deeply loved. The families of John Michael Martin and Henry Ongtowasruk are left to make sense of their unresolved murders, destined to never fully understand how two such harmless men fell prey to a violent predator. The children of Michelle Foster-Butler—if she is, indeed, another of Wade's victims—are each, in their own way, continuing to cope with the loss of their mother, a wound inflicted on them at the most vulnerable of ages, and one they have carried into adulthood.

Wade's own family continues to suffer. His sister Mandy struggles to reconcile the love she feels for her brother with the unfathomable cruelty of his crimes. Wade's father, although far from a sympathetic character, lives with a torturous sense of guilt and regret.

For those closest to the victims, the void created by their sudden and unexpected absence is profound. No one truly overcomes such a loss. When a murder happens, those left behind are forced to find the courage to go on living, to find a source of strength somewhere from within. They struggle to trudge through the sorrow and to rise again. Sometimes, the darkness is too much to overcome.

Before my first meeting with Daisy Piggott, I had been warned by Desa Jacobsson and by three of Daisy's children that she was in a fragile state. The guilt Daisy felt for abandoning her daughter as a girl had proved debilitating and ultimately, insurmountable. She still felt responsible somehow for all of the turmoil in her daughter's life, and she continued to blame herself for Della's death. The feeling had so overwhelmed Daisy that during the summer of 2014, a few months prior to our meeting, she attempted suicide. Gloria Durham, one of Daisy's daughters, told me that Daisy had downed a bottle of antidepressants, an entire bottle of Tylenol, and two fifths of whiskey.

"When I got [to the hospital] she was hooked up to every machine

Much to her family's relief, Daisy recovered. About five months later, on a day in November, we spoke on the phone, and she told me that some days were better than others. At times, she felt like talking, and on other occasions, she felt like shutting out the world.

"Today is a good day," she said. "Why don't you come over now?"

I drove from the bed-and-breakfast in downtown Anchorage where I was staying to the trailer park where Daisy lived, on the eastern side of town. It was a bitterly cold and snowy day, and when I arrived, Daisy came to the door and quickly ushered me inside. She introduced her husband, Kenneth, who was in the living room reading the newspaper and who, she explained, had recently suffered a stroke. Daisy and I entered the den, where sunlight streamed through yellow and red curtains, creating a soft, golden glow in the room.

"I hope you don't mind if I smoke," Daisy said, sitting down and lighting the first of several cigarettes.

Daisy is a diminutive woman, and her voice has the pitch and timbre of a child's. She has thinning gray hair (she explained she suffered from alopecia) and wore moccasin-type boots lined with fur, black pants, and a blue sweatshirt with wolves embroidered on the front. During our conversation, she was at times animated and at other moments in despair. She readily admitted that she was battling depression, and a couple of times she wept openly.

For the first two or three years I couldn't say 'He killed Della.' Because at that point, I didn't want to accept that he did. So you go through a lot of stages. Now I can say he's a murderer. He killed my daughter. My firstborn."

Daisy admitted that on a day in June, she had experienced an emotional breakdown. She said the ordeal had given her insight into what Della must have felt just prior to her death.

"She was in an abusive relationship. I think it was her way of self-medicating. I can see it because I'm . . ." Daisy paused and then began to cry. "I almost killed myself. I almost succeeded. So I know how powerful depression is."

Depression, fueled by guilt, had driven Daisy to her lowest point. She couldn't seem to talk herself out of being responsible for all of Della's misfortunes.

"I know logically it isn't my fault," Daisy said, tears streaming down her face. "Even if I was here in Alaska, [Della's murder] could have happened. But you can't convince me. I know you can't go back. You can't make it all right, and I tried. I tried so hard."

At Della's funeral, Daisy had connected with Della's daughter Nora, who was adopted more than thirty years prior by a couple in the village of Shishmaref, Alaska. Nora's adoptive parents had made the 600-mile trip south so that Nora could attend her biological mother's funeral. Since then, Daisy had stayed in touch with Nora and even made a trip to Shishmaref to become acquainted with Nora's three boys. Daisy got up from her chair, disappeared into a back room, and returned with photos of her three great grandsons.

"We are a family now," she said proudly, showing me the snapshots of the boys. "So not everything was bad that came out of it. There were lots of struggles, sure, but those little bitty ones, that's what you live for."

I asked Daisy how Della's son was doing. She explained that Robert, who was eighteen when his mother was killed, had been battling drug and alcohol addictions.

"He's had his problems, but he's starting to mend," she said. A stern look came over Daisy's face.

"Unfortunately, the perp never has just one victim. He has a whole slew of victims," she said. "It's like a tidal wave. One little drop, there's the body," Daisy said, descending an index finger in the center of an imaginary circle. "But then you're affecting the friends, family members, in this case a whole community," she said, holding out both of her palms.

Daisy said that one of her sisters, who is a devout Christian, had been urging her to forgive Joshua Wade.

"At that time, I was seeing a psychologist. And I was breaking down, crying all the time, making all kinds of noise with my sobbing. And I asked my psychologist, 'Am I now crazy? Have I finally met crazy? Am I getting lost?' And that was scary. What I realized is that I don't have to forgive. All I have to do is remember to breathe. And if I want to, down the road, I will. But in my heart, no, I can't. Not now, and I may not ever. But that's my choice. It's something I have to live with."

Daisy's daughter Gloria had told me she and her siblings worried that Daisy might attempt suicide again. Daisy said she was getting a handle on her depression and grief, and she was in a better place. As for whether Wade should have been given the death penalty, Daisy said she was never ambivalent.

"Death was too easy. This way, he has to live, and he's quite young. He has to wake up to whatever size his cell is and remember why he's there." Raising her voice and speaking more deliberately, Daisy added, "I like where he is. Because he's paying for it every day of his life, until he dies. And he'll never get out of prison, ever."

As we finished our conversation, I asked Daisy why she agreed to talk to me. She said that talking about Della was cathartic.

"This is kind of a healing," she explained. "You don't realize that's what I'm doing right now, but it is. Also, my daughter doesn't have a voice. So I will always be her voice. And I didn't want Wade to have the last word."

"What do you want the last word to be?" I asked.

"That he didn't get away with it. And this is my way of saying she lives here," Daisy said, bringing her right hand to the center of her chest. She pinned her shoulders back and let out a long sigh.

"Now," Daisy said. "Can you drive me down the street to get some cigarettes?"

"Sure," I replied.

It was snowing as we left the trailer, and the afternoon sun was just slipping from view. Daisy shifted her face toward the day's last flight, as a flock of migrating birds crossed the sky in a V-formation, instinct guiding them toward a warmer horizon, their wings beating madly against the wind.

JILL HOMER

"**M**INUS TWENTY-FOUR ISN'T UNUSUAL OR EXTREME for this part of the world," Jill Homer explains in her book *Into the North Wind*. "Minus twenty-four would be fine, really, if I'd worn all the correct layers to begin with, and I wasn't soaked in my own sweat. But because I was wet, a chill clamped down the moment I stopped, and every second compounded the danger. If warmth becomes violent shivering in five minutes, one can only surmise the proximity of deadly hypothermia."

Homer was racing along the historic Iditarod Trail. But unlike mushers coming through at the same time, Homer wasn't being pulled a dog team. She was on her fat tire bike, racing in the Iditarod Trail Invitational, a human-powered scramble wherein entrants bike, ski, or walk those 938 miles across Alaska, but with considerably less fanfare and a bare minimum of support.

In 2016, Homer won the women's division with a time of seventeen days, three hours and forty-six minutes, a record still standing. *Into the North Wind* is the story of how she got there.

Homer came to Alaska in 2005 to work as a journalist in, appropriately enough, the small coastal city of Homer. She saw locals riding the winter trails near town on fat bikes and decided to give it a try. It looked like fun she said.

She had never been an endurance athlete, but in 2006 on a lark she entered the Susitna 100, a one hundred mile, human-powered winter race beginning and ending in Big Lake, north of Wasilla. She was hooked, and during the ensuing decade completed more than fifty endurance races on four continents.

In the year preceding the 2016 Invitational, Homer experienced physical setbacks and other difficulties in every race she entered and battled pneumonia to boot. The best she hoped for setting out was to finish, and she lacked confidence that even that was attainable.

Into the North Wind is Homer's tale of dragging herself over the starting line and trekking across Alaska, taking in the state's beauty while struggling with both the elements and her own mind and body. In addition to lending insight into what a race like the ITI demands of its entrants, the book also provides vivid descriptions of the trail itself. Readers will feel as if they're riding alongside Homer the entire distance. And owing to her engaging personality as a writer, they'll likely find themselves on the edge of tears when she crosses the finish line.

Explaining why she embarks on these ventures, Homer told me, "On the surface, adventure racing through Alaska during the winter might seem like the pinnacle of egotism and masochism. My experience has always been the opposite of this, an opportunity to feel the depths of humility as a human at the mercy of an unpredictable and inhospitable environment, and the heights of joy in communion with a vast wilderness. Fatigue, discomfort, and yes, what one might call suffering are an important part of the experience. It seems a paradox, but we find we feel most alive at the frayed edges of existence."

She added that, "I write about these experiences in an effort to try to make sense of them. I also hope to inspire others to take leaps outside their own comfort zones."

Although she left Alaska in 2010 and now lives in Boulder, Colorado with her partner Beat Jegerlehner (who walked the course in 2016), Homer makes frequent trips north, where she continues to get outdoors and recreate, and where she remains well known and well liked among the state's adventure sports community.

In the two excerpts that follow, Homer, having already traversed the Alaska Range, tells of the run from McGrath to Carlson Cabin, and then describes her arrival in the village of Ruby, where she reached the Yukon River.

— From *Into the North Wind* —

AT 10:30 FRIDAY MORNING, AFTER SPENDING TWENTY-FOUR HOURS in the lavish oasis of McGrath and finally not able to stand it one minute longer, I made my break for the unknown. Mike wasn't being facetious when he told me he didn't do early starts—he was still grazing from the breakfast table when I announced that my pent-up anxiety would explode if I didn't get out of there. Two other cyclists who had laid over in McGrath—Sam and Katie, a couple from Durango, Colorado, who were not part of the race but were planning to tour the entire Iditarod Trail—also were in no hurry to leave.

Remounting my bike after a full day felt like prying open rusty hinges in my joints. I pedaled through a maze of snow-covered streets, following Peter on his snowmobile. He hopped off at a crossing of the Kuskokwim River and pointed to a lone pyramid-shaped mountain to the west.

"Stay to the right of the mountain, and you'll be fine," he said gruffly. I reached out to give him a hug.

"Thanks for everything you do," I said. I figured his was the last friendly face I'd see for a while.

Pedaling away from town, I assessed my physical state. The injured arm and hand were tender and numb, but the rest of my body was surprisingly nimble. My butt wasn't sore, and my legs felt strong. During my two previous 350-mile finishes, I arrived in McGrath sufficiently broken. In 2008, I struggled to drag myself up the stairs after the six-day bike ride. In 2014, a week of dragging a sled for eighteen hours a day left me with painful shin splints and crushing fatigue. Those experiences made Nome seem physically impossible, and it took a big leap of faith just to challenge the notion that 350 miles of the Iditarod Trail was truly all I could handle. Even though I believed I could surmount pain with mental toughness, I continued to be astounded by how efficiently a focused mind can drive my body. Simply by deciding that I wasn't close to being done, my body wasn't close to being spent.

Despite feeling fresh and strong, the tears started to flow when I looked back toward McGrath's radio tower and remembered what I was actually doing. The village of Takotna was just fifteen miles away, and beyond that was a depth of remoteness I had not yet experienced. The two-hundred miles separating Takotna from the Yukon River were inhabited by no one. There were a few abandoned mining camps, but this swath of the Interior saw no winter travel beyond the Iditarod races and the occasional snowmobile-driving tourist. The land was so desolate that even hunting and trapping were infrequent, because there were few animals. It was, I reminded myself, the kind of place where one could wallow in deep snow and minus-fifty temperatures for ten days without encountering anyone.

This day was gray and mild, with temperatures around twenty degrees and intermittent snow showers. I fell into a quiet rhythm, climbing along the base of the pyramid mountain and descending into Takotna. The village was eerily quiet for the early afternoon. Chained dogs slept in front of shuttered homes, not even barking at me as I passed. Beyond Takotna, the trail veered back into the hills, rising more than a thousand feet on an old road bed, then traversing a ridge beside the fog-shrouded peaks of unnamed mountains.

Forty miles passed quickly, and I didn't even pause until I reached the ghost town of Ophir. This cluster of uninhabited log cabins left over from the Gold Rush was used as a checkpoint for the sled dog race, but sat empty the rest of the year. Ophir was the landmark where I intended to camp for the night and ponder whether I was ready to make the full commitment. The first Iditarod mushers wouldn't pass through for five more days, so I hadn't expected to see anybody, but smoke was billowing from one of the cabins. A woman emerged from a barn-like building next door and waved at me.

"Do you need anything?" the woman called out. "Do you want coffee?"

At the place where I was supposed to do my solitary gut check, this unexpected offer caught me off guard, but I nodded gratefully. She directed me toward the wood-heated cabin. The woman and her husband were Iditarod volunteers, preparing the checkpoint for mushers' arrivals. She heated up water for instant coffee and told me about the origins of the cabin, which was built in 1910. As I gulped down scalding coffee, she offered up a bag of cookies, then encouraged me to take two extra for the road.

"You need the calories more than the volunteers," she said.

"I don't know about that. I have a ton of food." In anticipation of potential storms and becoming stranded in three feet of snow like Beat had the previous year, I'd left McGrath with nearly twelve pounds of food—about five days' worth—which was everything I could fit on my bike. But I gratefully accepted the cookies and then surprised myself when I turned down an offer to sleep in another unheated cabin.

"I'm hoping to make it to Carlson Crossing," I said, referring to a public shelter cabin maintained by the Bureau of Land Management. "It's what, about twenty-eight miles from here?"

"We saw Phil on Wednesday. He told us it's sixteen from the airstrip, and that's only a mile from here."

"Oh wow, seventeen miles would be fantastic," I said, even though I didn't remotely believe her. I may have been a Nome rookie, but I knew not to invest too much trust in any information regarding weather or distance, no matter how well-intentioned it was.

Mike still hadn't caught up as I pedaled away from Ophir an hour later, and I was beginning to wonder whether he had decided to leave McGrath at all. He'd been hedging over his sore knee, and he did look particularly comfortable when he was sitting down to a big plate of man-cakes at ten in the morning. Sudden loneliness struck, because although Ophir's coffee and conversation had been unexpected, it was truly my last chance for outside interaction.

Twilight descended in darker shades of gray as I pedaled past collapsing cabins, skeletal frames of old front-end loaders, abandoned 1970s-era trucks, rusted barrels and piles of twisting metal—all remnants of the mining activity that proliferated in this region during the past century. Gold mining hadn't been all that lucrative for a few decades, advancing the state of decay. I peeked inside one of the cabins, which looked like a time capsule from 1978, with moldy upholstered furniture and labeled canned goods sitting on shelves. I questioned what was more unnerving—a pristine wilderness ruled by wolves, or a blighted one that had been abandoned by humans in a hurry. Either way, I was entirely at the mercy of the elements in a place so harsh even animals stayed away.

For twelve miles after Ophir, the route contoured hills above a narrow river valley. The trail followed the bed of an old road, complete with concrete bridges across what might otherwise be treacherous ice crossings. I was making great time and anticipated reaching the cabin for early bedtime, until the trail veered around a steep mountain and split at a junction. To the left was the Iditarod Trail's southern route—used during odd-numbered years by the Iditarod Sled Dog Race, this equally remote trail was put in place solely to guide mushers to villages at the southern end of the Yukon River. To the right was the northern route, used during even-numbered years by the sled dog race, every year by the Iron Dog snowmobile race, and the one we'd follow this year as well.

I walked a short distance out the southern route to appease my curiosity. It wouldn't be traveled by any racers this year, but there was a smooth and fairly hard-packed trail broken by unknown snowmobilers. The northern route, conversely, was an utter mess. As soon as the road bed ended, the smooth base and any use by sane snowmobile drivers disappeared. What remained was the result of two-hundred Iron Dog racers tearing up the trail at more than sixty miles an hour, after two feet of snow fell onto bare, partially thawed ground. Their hard accelerations and aggressive turns dug into the powder and tossed it in every direction. Now that two weeks of hard freezes and occasional thaws had passed, the trail had solidified into a bumpy disaster—ridges up to two feet high and sheer drops into exposed tussocks and frozen mud.

As a mountain biker, I'd compare this terrain to riding over the dry bed of a mountain river, with endless finessing over and around large boulders. For snow biking, it was exceedingly technical—fun when you're looking for a challenge, but less fun when you're tired and hungry and just want to be somewhere. The sun set, and temperatures quickly plunged below zero. I was working so hard to navigate the moguls that I felt no need to add layers.

Even though I was sitting in the saddle and pedaling the entire time, the first four miles of this frozen-boulder trail took nearly an hour to complete. By the end of that hour, my leg muscles were in knots and my emotions were nearing a full-tantrum meltdown. Much of this frustration stemmed from misdirected expectations. I anticipated being alone in a wasteland, facing forty-below temperatures, powering through steep climbs and descents, and managing complete self-sufficiency for the next two-hundred miles. I didn't anticipate a strenuous technical challenge that was going to demand more strength and patience than I had to spare.

Just as I stepped off the bike and held gloved, clenched fists against my ice-encrusted eyes, I noticed a headlamp beam approaching from behind. I turned as its source called out an enthusiastic "Wooooo!"

It was Mike, of course. The dude's body language was exuberant, with shoulders raised and a grin visible from a distance, even in the gray twi-light. He barreled over the snow boulders like a teenager in a terrain park.

"How are you doing? How's your knee?" I asked as he pulled up behind me.

"It's okay," he said. "A little stiff. Hey, you don't have any KT tape on you, do you?" hook my head. "I have some Leuko tape that I use for blis-ters. Might work. Do you want some?"

"I'll wait until we get to the cabin. We're almost there."

I shook my head. "It's twelve miles away. Could be three, four more hours if these bumps continue."

"No," Mike said with over-exaggerated indignation. "The lady said it was sixteen miles from Ophir. That's what Phil told her."

"You believed her? We've already gone sixteen miles since Ophir. It's twelve more. Trust me. I wish it were anything else."

Mike considered this. "I'm not even sure I can make it tonight," I continued. "I'm exhausted. I may need to camp before Carlson Crossing. You go. You're faster than me."

"We'll make it. We'll make it together!" Mike yelled, his exuberance returning.

Mike launched ahead and I shadowed closely behind, attempting to mimic his maneuvers because he seemed more technically skilled than me. His overstuffed seat post bag swayed in a humorous fashion, and I lost concentration and toppled over onto an exposed patch of tussocks. He didn't notice and pulled away. I thought he was gone, but five minutes later, I found him leaning against his bike next to a stream bank, waiting for me.

"How far do you think we've gone?" he asked.

I looked at my GPS. "Three quarters of a mile."

"No. Is that all?"

"Sadly."

When we rode together on the first day of the race, Mike and I discussed some of the races I've run. After I vehemently defended sled-dragging, he assumed I was primarily a runner who only occasionally rode bikes. As we resumed bopping along the bumpy trail, he asked, "How fast do you think you could run this stuff?"

"Probably same speed, four or five miles per hour," I said. "But not with a sled. With a sled, I'd be ridiculously slow. And even more grumpy."

"I bet we can do ten-minute miles," he said, turning the comparison back to running vernacular. "Two more hours."

The pedaling effort was already more strenuous than any ten-minute mile I had ever run. Enduring twelve miles at that pace would be like running a half marathon up a steep and rocky mountain, with a heavy pack. Mike surged ahead and I summoned all of my reserves to keep up.

"I might need to let you go ahead," I gasped. "I'm having trouble breathing." He slowed again. We resumed the fifteen-minute-miles as I concentrated on taking deep breaths through a face mask that was soaked with respiration. After a few more trundling miles, I wasn't entirely sure his slow speeds were for my benefit. His body language was decidedly more subdued. Conversation ceased. Mike stopped in the middle of the trail to shovel food in his mouth, so I did the same. He handed me a log-sized frozen sausage stick from which I gnawed little chunks, and I shared handfuls of M&Ms. Mike and I could make a good team, I thought, like the odd couple—Mike being the eternally optimistic, goofy young guy, and me being the pessimistic, realist old guy.

Nearly two hours later, after covering a blistering six miles, I announced we were halfway there. Mike was incredulous.

"I don't like that GPS," he said.

"I love GPS," I countered. "GPS tells me the truth, and it never lies. I'd probably go crazy if I let myself believe the cabin was sixteen miles from Ophir. By now it's been five hours, so it must be right around the next corner. How do you cope when it's not?"

Mike shrugged. "I'd get there eventually."

The truth can be its own burden, though, when the night stretches out indefinitely and fatigued concentration pulls thoughts into a place where time and space are fluid. After days had passed and GPS still displayed a three-mile gap, I was beginning to wonder if I was losing my mind.

"Maybe there is no end," I whispered into a cloud of my own breath. Mike was a hundred feet ahead, head lowered and shoulders hunched as his bike bucked and swayed through the yawning darkness. "Maybe this is all there is." This would be a proper purgatory for me—seeking respite that never comes, with a companion in sight but too far away to feel connected, riding a bicycle at my physical limit to achieve walking speeds, in the dark, in the cold, on terrain so technical that I could focus only on pedaling and steering, and couldn't retreat to deeper thoughts or happier memories.

Still, when Mike stopped and pulled out his sausage log and a bag of crushed potato chips, the angst momentarily faded. We'd fill our mouths with salted satisfaction and stare up at waves of green light making their way across an unobstructed sky.

"Maybe this is heaven." I always suspected that if there is an afterlife, the contents of it will reflect life experiences—a sort of ongoing consciousness rather than physical existence. Maybe heaven and hell are not only individual, but one and the same.

It wasn't our turn to slip into eternity yet, although it felt that way by the time the cabin finally appeared around the next corner. It was well beyond two in the morning. The cabin stood on a wind-swept bank at the edge of the Innoko River, flanked by birch trees and barren ground. Mike and I propped our bikes against the porch and robotically launched into a flurry of chores. I hauled a pot and empty dry sack out to the river to skim snow off the ice, then fired up my stove to make drinking water. Mike found a couple of big logs and dragged them to a clearing to split them apart while I stripped to my base layer and hung sweaty jackets and socks on the wall, anticipating the drying warmth of a fire.

With the fire started and our bagged meals rehydrating in hot water, Mike again went outside. He was still absent ten minutes later when I realized the snow sack was empty, and left the cabin to collect more. Out on the river, a hundred yards upstream from where I crouched without a headlamp, I saw Mike. He was standing on the ice wearing only boots and bike shorts, rubbing snow into the bare skin on his scalp and chest. As best as I could tell, he was bathing, which I thought was an impressively brazen act in a place far beyond the sensibilities of civilization . . .

a place where truly no one cared if we smelled like sweat and sausage log
... a place where taking a shower meant dousing one's naked body in
snow when temperatures were below zero. We'd just left McGrath that
morning, so I still felt relatively clean, but I could hardly imagine ever
feeling so wretched that I would endure the cold to that degree.

I didn't tell Mike I had caught him bathing when he returned to the
cabin, smiling and shivering. "There's some hot water," I said, pointing
to his Nalgene bottle.

"Oh great, I've been out of water for a while." I also found this statement
interesting—he was out of drinking water and no doubt was as hungry
and tired as I was, but his first priorities were fire and personal hygiene.

Mike took the water and produced a small bottle of Fireball—cinna-
mon whiskey. At this point I was incredulous. Did this guy take anything
seriously?

"It's great in hot chocolate," he said. "Try it.""Oh no, no, whiskey is the
last thing I need," I said. "I'm about to lose consciousness as it is."

"Just try some," he urged.

I reluctantly poured a few capfuls into my own mug of hot chocolate and took a sip. The cocktail was a taste sensation unlike any I had
experienced—a sharp injection of warmth and vitality infused with
sweet and spicy richness. "Wow ... that's just ... amazing," I stammered, genuinely floored.

"Told yah," he said. "It's extra weight but worth it."

We finished up our bagged meals and settled in to sleep in the lap
of luxury—the musty interior of a log cabin that smelled of pine wood
and gasoline, with dust clouds swirling near the windows, capturing the
silver moonlight.

MORNING WAS ROSE-TINTED AND COLD, SO COLD—which is always the
case when transitioning from a billowing down cocoon to the white,
frozen world. I did jumping jacks between frantic motions to pack up
my belongings, and took off in a sprint when I finally had everything
more or less strapped to the bike. I was grateful for the early climb, but
as soon as I generated enough heat to feel lucid, the weight of my fatigue
clamped down. Why was I still so tired?

Breakfast on the bike was a difficult affair—steering with a balled-up
mitten beneath my numb right hand while scooping trail mix out of a

"gas tank" top tube bag with my left hand. My body still wasn't warm enough to stop for long, but I suspected my low energy level was the result of a calorie deficit. Although I needed to consume more than five thousand calories a day, the technical terrain didn't allow me to eat on the bike, I didn't take many breaks, and my six-hundred calorie breakfasts and one-thousand-calorie dinners weren't quite filling in the gaps. The sheer bulk of food still weighing down my frame bag proved I'd been on an unintentional diet. No wonder I was tired and cold.

Three miles past my camp, I approached a cluster of dilapidated cabins. Mike's orange bike was propped against one of the buildings—he must have passed me while I was sleeping. I peeked inside the shack, which had no door. One corner held a few dirty plastic barrels, and the rest of the interior was piled with paper and garbage. A down sleeping bag was spread across the only bare spot on the floor. Mike's nose poked out from a small opening. I didn't intend to wake him, but he spoke without even stirring.

"What time is it?"

"About eight o'clock," I said. "What time did you get here? I never heard you pass, and I was up past midnight."

"Maybe two a.m.," Mike said. "I saw your camp spot. Almost stopped, but I thought I might find a cabin if I kept going."

His shelter wasn't much—particle-board walls and a sagging roof, missing both windows and the door. But it did block the wind.

"It was a nice night," I said. "Did you see the Northern Lights? I must have spent a half hour watching them."

"Mmm hmm," Mike hummed. He seemed to be drifting back to sleep, but then said, "Galena today?"

"I don't know. It's thirty more miles to Ruby, and I think it's going to be hilly the whole way. Then it's fifty more to Galena. That would be a really long day. Too long. I feel awful this morning."

"Mmm hmm," Mike hummed again.

I left Mike to let him snooze until what would almost certainly be an afternoon hour. He'd still probably catch me before Ruby. Mike was strong, but he was clearly on vacation. I envied his happy-go-lucky attitude, but if I slept as much as he did, spring would probably beat me to Nome.

The sun rose in sync with the long climb, pulling back a curtain of forest shadows to reveal a bright, warm day. Only it was still ten degrees, and my body fluctuated between shivering and sweating. I felt dizzy and flush. Something was clearly wrong with my system. Electrolyte imbalance? Potassium? I realize it's not healthy to subsist on nuts and candy, but a body doesn't become malnourished in three days. I tried to shake off this gnawing fatigue by focusing on my immediate surroundings.

Human debris became increasingly more frequent past Mike's cabin. A surprising number of abandoned vehicles sat rusted and half-buried in snow drifts. Although the lightly traveled trail revealed little evidence of a road bed, there were actual mile markers—numbered green signs sticking a few inches out of the snow—that clicked slowly backward. These sprinkles of civilization were oddly fascinating, and I rubber-necked every rusted rim and detached snowmobile windshield that I passed. Each one caused a pang of sadness, and I wondered why I felt so lonely. Only three days had passed since I left McGrath, which is not even close to the longest I've gone without outside human contact. When I was twenty-two years old, I spent nine days backpacking in the Utah desert with only two friends for company. We didn't even follow trails—we wound our way along a shallow river at the bottom of a sheer canyon, where there was no human debris. I recall jumping in surprise when a jet flew overhead on day seven.

Still, there was something about this no-man's-land that felt even more isolating than the desert. During that ninety-mile backpacking trip, I understood that we had sequestered ourselves in a narrow crack in the Earth. Above us on the plateau, cattle were grazing, ranchers were herding their stock, and cars were streaming along a smooth highway. The corridor along the Innoko and Poorman rivers was a hundred and fifty miles long, surrounded by thousands of square miles of nothing. The wind blew incessantly and ten degrees was a hot day. The fact that anyone ventured here at all remained fascinating.

Four miles from Ruby, the satellite phone finally patched through a call from Beat. He was just about to leave McGrath, he said, and was traveling with Peter Ripmaster—the man who fell through the Tatina River ice—and the physician from Utah, Eric Johnson. Beat had the usual foot and leg pain, but he was finally starting to feel strong. It was just like Beat to take three hundred and fifty miles to warm up.

"I'm so tired today," I admitted. "I've been getting a ton of sleep—you'd be ashamed—but it's still catching up to me. I don't know. Maybe it's the cold, or not enough food. Maybe it's just living out here, just keeping myself warm. It's hard."

"It is," Beat agreed. "Get some rest in Ruby. That's a long section you went through, and you still have lots of time."

As much as I anticipated conversations with Beat, I always hung up the phone feeling acutely lonely. These calls were so brief that they left many questions unanswered, which in turn emphasized our absence from each other. I missed Beat, but I didn't feel truly alone until I heard his voice crackling over a connection that was tenuously held together by a distant object hurtling through space. This yearning wasn't unlike the wistful sadness I felt while staring at a piece of trash alongside the trail. I realized the reason this wilderness felt so isolated was because it was littered with remnants of humanity. Relics, like too-short phone calls, are only reminders of companionship, displaced by time and distance. I longed to see Beat again, but Ruby would come first, so I anxiously anticipated that.

Mile-marker three brought a four-hundred foot climb. The effort bolstered my angst, as it took my ragged legs a half hour to make the mile-long ascent. At the crest of the hill I could see Ruby, nestled against a steep river bluff, with homes built most of the way up the hillside. The village wasn't what I imagined—I'd pictured something flat and sprawling, a settlement to match the expansiveness of the Yukon River. Beyond Ruby was a white strip of ice, at least a half-mile wide. On the far side were more domed hills, interrupted by sheer limestone cliffs.

"The mighty Yukon," I breathed out. The statement sent a chill down my back. I did this—I actually pedaled a bike to the Yukon River.

One last frigid descent brought me to the River's Edge Bed and Breakfast, where I'd sent my supply box. The proprietor was a Native woman with a number of children in the house—I counted at least four. She hastily showed me around then apologized when she had to go back to work. This also didn't match my preconception of Ruby, as I imagined a slower pace of life on the Yukon. I was impressed that a woman with multiple children and a day job also ran a B&B.

She asked if I was staying for the night, and looked surprised when I answered yes. I suspected she disapproved of my own relative laziness. It was an embarrassingly early hour to stop for the day in the middle of an adventure race—two in the afternoon—but I made the usual justifications. I'm tired. I'll put in a long day tomorrow. Beat agreed it was a good idea.

The hot shower was sublime, even on wind-burned, chafed skin. My appetite soared. I didn't want to go rifling through a stranger's kitchen, so I gnawed on an astronaut ice cream sandwich from my box, and a bag of beef jerky left over from one of the cyclists who had been through Ruby two days earlier. The jerky tasted particularly amazing, and I wondered if not eating enough protein was partially to blame for my fatigue.

The afternoon dragged on as I fiddled with my gear and grappled with the inevitable onset of town anxiety. Comfort was something I wistfully anticipated, but once removed from the trail, down time proved to be more nerve-wracking than relaxing. Eventually I'd have to return to cold solitude, and this knowledge kept me on edge. I sorted my food, then laundered my clothing and arranged it in piles. My gear looked simultaneously inadequate and burdensome. How would I coax myself back out into the cold, yet again?

Sam and Katie arrived at sunset, and stepping outside to greet them brought a shocking chill. Sam had stories to share about breaking creek ice to collect drinking water and finding their own perfect campsite, but I could only handle the cold for a few minutes. I mumbled an excuse, then rushed back into the heated house and climbed into bed.

Mike arrived about an hour later. Unable to sleep, I ventured back outside to fiddle with my bike bags one more time. The temperature had fallen to five below zero, which burned on my bare hands. It would take a few more minutes before convulsions started, so I worked quickly, reminding myself that an afternoon of acclimating to indoor temperatures—rather than weakness or fear—was to blame for how sinister subzero air suddenly felt. Sam and Katie were still sitting on the porch in their down coats, sipping on tea that they heated on their camp stove.

"Are you guys staying here tonight?" I asked. "Maybe," Katie said. "We haven't decided yet."

I turned to face their view of the river. There were still wisps of crimson light to the south, and a purple curtain of stars to the north. The river ice reflected moonlight that was still hidden behind towering river bluffs, and silhouettes of cliffs on the other side of the river created a spooky contrast.

"The Yukon River," I said. "Can you believe it?"

"It's beautiful," Katie nodded. "We were just talking about spending the night out on the ice, under the moon."

"Huh," I said. If it was five below on this hillside fifty feet above the river, it was probably fifteen or twenty below down on the ice. "That would be amazing," I agreed. "Tomorrow night, maybe."

The chill cut deep by the time I retreated indoors, and I was shivering profusely when Mike approached to ask when I was leaving in the morning.

"First light," I said. "I set an alarm for six."

"Six? Why not eight?"

"Ha! If you want to leave with me, great. Otherwise I'm sure you'll catch me somewhere on the river tomorrow."

This night, even more so than my nights in Anchorage and McGrath, I wondered where I'd find the courage to leave comfort and safety for the ever-widening jaws of the unknown.

DAVID A. JAMES

I'M A MOUNTAIN BIKER AS WELL, although not as adventurous as Jill Homer. But it's a sport that I took up shortly after moving to Fairbanks, and that has been my primary means of exploring my surroundings ever since. It's a also a subject I've returned to repeatedly in my own writing.

In the late summer of 2020 I was asked to contribute an essay to be one of several included in a forthcoming revised and reissued edition of the late Alaska historian Terrence Cole's *Wheels on Ice,* which explores the role bicycles played in Gold Rush Era Alaska.

Initially I felt I had nothing to add, but shortly before the snow flew that fall I embarked on a ride up Ester Dome in Fairbanks, accompanied by my dog Loki. During a year that had been marred by political turmoil and a pandemic, I realized that I had turned to my bike and the trails that span out from Fairbanks in all directions as an escape from the stresses of a world gone sideways. As I rode my thoughts turned to the roles cycling and Alaska have played in my life. The following essay, which initially was published by the Anchorage Press resulted.

In Fairbanks, we're blessed with the best combination one can find in Alaska. A medium sized city with all the conveniences of modern life completely surrounded by wild lands where anyone can go play. There are no admission fees. The trails are public. As I note in the essay, it's possible to go on an adventure on your way to the grocery store. One can go from a shopping center to deep woods where wild animals dwell in a matter of minutes. I know of no other city of this size where this option is available. It's a large part of why I continue to live here.

— From *Last Ride of the Season* —

BRILLIANT SUNSHINE burns through the stand of denuded birch trees, one of my favorite things to witness in Fairbanks. It's one of those perfect late fall days, when the reality of winter is closing in, but the lingering promise of summer has not yet given up hope. When the sunny places feel warm, but morning frost in shaded spots still loiters.

I pause to take a photograph and also to rest. I'm on my mountain bike and I've just begun ascending Ester Dome, my fifty-six-year-old legs nearly as much on fire as the sun. They're tired from climbing the same hill the evening before by a different but equally challenging route.

I hadn't intended to go riding this afternoon. But the weather forecast is calling for snow, and I've lived in Alaska far too long to let a day like this get away. Because rarely will the next day be its match. I figure I can make the top of the Dome. It's only a 1700 foot climb.

Coming down won't be a problem.

WHEN I WAS four, my dad took bought me a used spider bike that was my chariot. After a few spills I quickly mastered the art of propelling myself forward and never quit doing so. The spider bike gave way to a three speed, and later a ten speed. My grade school was close enough to my house that I began riding there in first grade. My junior high and high schools were further away, but I kept riding anyway. Even after obtaining a driver's license.

I grew up on Vashon Island in Washington State, and by my early teens had ridden nearly every one of its roads and frequently boarded the ferry boat to Seattle or Tacoma to ride through cities and rural areas alike. In the late seventies and early eighties, friends and I rode to campgrounds on the Kitsap and Olympic peninsulas for overnight stays, bike packing before we ever heard the term.

I rode all through college. And for three long years in Seattle after graduating, I continued riding everywhere. From my University District home, I could get downtown faster by bike than by bus, and often even by car given the city's notorious traffic. And I'd have more fun getting there, joyfully rushing past drivers who rarely looked happy.

A MAZE OF old mining roads crisscrosses Ester Dome. Finding gold in this hill has been the goal of everyone from lone prospectors to multinational corporations for over a century, but it's never paid. Meanwhile, private residences crept up its sides and a few sprouted on the very top. These days it's a nearby recreational destination for Fairbanks residents. From my house, at the Dome's foot, it feels like my backyard. I've spent thousands of hours running and biking it.

Right now I'm ascending one of those old road beds. The birch trees give way to aspen and spruce. My dog Loki springs back and forth, fruitlessly chasing squirrels and grouse, wondering why his companion is so slow. He's the third dog to join my Alaska travels, and after a lifetime of black lab mixes, my first sled dog. His energy is remarkable. These distinctively Alaskan dogs have no lineage papers. They've been bred for one thing: speed. They're gangly critters with skinny torsos atop ridiculously long legs and can bound through deep snow. And unlike people, they never seem to tire.

A good sled dog can just as easily come from the pound, as Loki did as a puppy, as from a champion musher. Loki was spared a life in a dog yard and will occupy the living room couch with as much self-entitlement as the most spoiled canine. But the trail is his natural habitat. Observing his athleticism never ceases to astound me. I've often said I need to get him his own GPS so I can compare his mileage to mine. I suspect he averages about 30 to 50% more distance than I do. And if I stop too long to rest, he barks demandingly at me to get going again. It's advisable that I do so, if only to avoid hearing damage from his protests.

I DIDN'T PLAN on becoming an Alaskan or a mountain biker. Both happened on their own, even if the roots extend back to my childhood. Growing up in Western Washington, Alaska was ever present. On any visit to Seattle's waterfront piers, signs of Alaska abounded. Cargo containers heading north, ferries returning south, and tacky Alaskan mementos cluttering busy souvenir shops. As a schoolchild, I read Jack London and Robert Service and felt the lure of the North. During college, when friends returned from summer jobs and told stories of their adventures, they kept the seed alive.

I talked about heading north countless times. Then, rather suddenly, it happened in the spring of 1990. College classmates who lived in Fairbanks came to visit. I met them for dinner. While catching up, I told them that I was working an enjoyable but futureless job, my apartment lease was about to expire, and my latest relationship already had. I wanted money to travel, I told them. I wanted to get as far south as I could go. They suggested I solve both dilemmas by coming north. I could earn money and hit the road come fall.

That night, like so many times in my life, I went for a long bike ride and did a lot of thinking. Truth be told, I'd already made up my mind. But riding helped clarify plans.

Three weeks later I was in Fairbanks, having left Seattle, right then the hippest city in the known universe. "What a dump," I thought upon seeing the Golden Heart City. "I'll bet I end up living here."

Eventually I did, but first I would spend five summers and a winter in Denali National Park, meeting my wife in the process.

CONTINUING UP the roadbed, I turn onto a narrow pathway worn in by mountain bikers over the years. It used to lead to a crumbling old miner's cabin. I once took a photo of my kid on its porch, holding his ski pole like a sourdough aiming his rifle. A few years ago, the Department of Natural Resources removed it and a few other old cabins that once stood scattered along trails on the Dome. Presumably it was to discourage squatters. But it felt like yet another uprooting of our history, something Alaskans are as skilled at doing as anyone else.

From there it's a steep climb to another fallow mining route, then onto a bandit trail that will put me near the top of the Dome. The ground is littered with leaves, but it's dry. On wet days I can blame the combination of wet slippery leaves and roots snaking along the surface of the ground for destroying my traction and forcing me to push up the steepest parts. Today I don't have that excuse. But the fatigue I felt earlier has faded, and instead of a quick ride to the top and back to my house, I'm making grander plans.

MY LIFE HAS centered on Alaska for over thirty years now, and my Alaska life has centered on mountain biking for most of them. I was still fairly young when I first ventured north, and expected my encounters with Alaska's outdoors would mostly happen on foot. Mostly they did early on and still often do. Hiking into alpine country is something I'll always treasure. What I didn't anticipate was that the time I would spend mountain biking would overwhelmingly outweigh time spent on all other outdoor activities combined.

I also didn't anticipate the trails around Fairbanks. My wife and I chose to live here for its proximity to Denali, and for its slower pace and smaller population than Anchorage. And for the dryer weather. It was only after arriving that we learned that hundreds of miles of trails litter the Tanana Valley, where the city of Fairbanks lies. Many cross through private property, but owing to easements, longstanding right-of-way laws, and a generally accepting attitude from many property owners, it's a dreamland for recreational travelers, be they cyclists, skiers, hikers, joggers, mushers, skijourers, and ATV or snowmachine riders.

I took to those trails like nothing else in my life. As GPS units rose in popularity, I started tracking my miles, and every year they run into the thousands. In summers I'll frequently head up Ester Dome after dinner. The endless daylight from May until early August means there's no real curfew. In the shoulder seasons between summer and winter, it stays light late enough to allow lengthy sojourns. And headlights make winter night rides a joy. As often as possible, I'm out the door and in the woods.

It's become my default way of life. The urban cycling I did when young now seems drab and pointless. "Pavement sucks" has become my mantra. Even when riding into town, I know a system of trails that can keep me almost entirely off roads most of the way. In Fairbanks, a quick trip to buy milk can turn into a mountain bike adventure. Where else is this possible?

I'VE OFTEN SAID that riding a mountain bike on Ester Dome is akin to those choose-your-adventure children's books. You can pursue any number of routes from bottom to top and back again. But it's good to know the seasonal variabilities. Head down the northwestern side in winter for one of the funnest descents in the Fairbanks vicinity. Try this trajectory in summer, however, and prepare to push though miles of muskeg and muck.

Most trails on the Dome lead to the top, and today the climb pays off both athletically and aesthetically. The workout has me energized. I follow a grassy four wheeler pathway looping the north summit of the Dome and head for an outcrop that marks the final high point before the steep rutty unmaintained gravel road dropping to Goldstream Creek.

A couple of weeks ago some friends and I headed this direction to connect with another old road bed that ascends to the southern summit. Like so many rides I've taken, it bottomed out in a swamp. If you're going to mountain bike in Interior Alaska, plan on wet feet, wet legs, and possibly a wet torso as you shove through fetid water. Or try riding through it, with half your wheels obscured by mud and goop. Aim for the far shore and pedal like crazy and don't be surprised when you lose momentum and splash sideways.

But on top of Ester Dome it's bone dry. I prop my bike in a rock cleft and start taking pictures. Murphy Dome dominates to the northwest, and the White Mountains spill across the northeastern horizon. To the southeast, the city of Fairbanks, such as it is, is dwarfed by the immensity of this land. And by the endless sky as well. This is the reward in climbing. You gain perspective.

WHEN I brought my bike to Denali I discovered riding on the Park Road. The long climb from to Mile 9 took me out of the forested creek drainages and up to the tundra, where caribou meander, bears lurk, and mountains span as far as can be seen in all directions. As you ride deeper into the park, you overlook valleys, cross rivers, climb and descend, climb and descend. And sometimes, when the wind is blowing hard, which it frequently does, riding downhill can require more effort than going up. Rarely have I pedaled as hard as I once did coming down the park road on the long downhill drop on Mount Margaret, hail stones peppering my face, driven by frigid gales hell-bent on preventing my progress.

This was in July. Summer in Alaska.

Once I found myself close to a grizzly lounging near a bend in the road. My riding companions and I pondered how quickly we could retreat down the hill and if we would be faster than a pursuing bear. We nervously made the requisite jokes about who the slowest would be. But the bear was more concerned with taking a nap on the tundra than feasting on a trio of seasonal workers. It barely acknowledged us. So we rode onward.

Decades after moving to Fairbanks, I rode beyond the Teklanika rest stop on a visit to Denali and noticed a large animal just ahead. Wondering who had let their dog off leash, I stopped. That's when I realized it was a lynx. The sizable feline noticed me and stopped as well. We stared inquisitively at each other for several magical minutes until the cat evaporated into the brush.

That remains my best lynx sighting, although a close second happened just two months later on a September midnight, after darkness had returned. Barreling down the Equinox Marathon Trail on the University of Alaska campus, my headlight caught movement. It was a lynx scrambling across the path. I came to halt and turned my headlights into the woods. There it sat, and again I found myself in a staring match with one of Alaska's more elusive animals. Eventually it got bored and wandered off. I rode home through the night with a warm chill, if there could be such a thing.

I've come close to colliding with moose on several occasions while zipping down trails. Grouse, which almost invariably fly in front of oncoming traffic, have many times come fluttering toward my face, nearly leaving me with a mouthful of feathers. A scampering fox vanquished one attempt at setting a personal best time for descending Ester Dome Road. It dashed in front of my bike so quickly that only my instinctual swerve to the right prevented what could have been a badly injurious collision for us both. My dog at the time, Sugi, pursued it into the woods. My attempt at a land speed record was cut short not by the wild canine, but by the domesticated one I had to retrieve.

Only once have I actually flushed a bear. While riding with friends on logging roads near the Tanana River southwest of Fairbanks, I surged ahead on the winding route. A black bear suddenly emerged a few yards ahead. It turned, stopped, stared, and snorted. I slammed the brakes and shouted. "No bear! Go away!" My friend Eric pulled up behind me, and the bear, perhaps realizing itself outnumbered, turned and charged into the trees. The rest of the group missed it entirely. We huddled in close together as we passed through those few yards of trail, hoping against —and laughing about— the bear's possible return. But we didn't see it again. Undoubtedly it was eyeing us though.

AFTER REACHING THE top and looping the cell and radio towers that are forever self-replicating on this hilltop, I opt to follow the Out & Back, a four wheeler trail shooting off to the southwest. It's part of the Equinox Marathon route, an annual race in September that sends runners up Ester Dome then partway down this side of it so they can turn around and top the hill a second time. On the best years, marathoners are treated to views of the Alaska Range, including Denali, dominating the southern horizon. It's entirely out today, and unlike runners racing the clock, I have the option of stopping and admiring this place I've called home for three decades, gazing at mountains of staggering beauty across the entire southern horizon.

I'm not running the marathon, so I go partway out, but not back. Part of the adventure I've chosen is to go down the Gravity Trail, a narrow and very steep descent that pops out on the Tricon Road, which leads to Ester. Most people don't know the Gravity Trail exists. It's an open secret among mountain bikers.

THE TRICON ROAD was the sight of my first ever mountain bike ride in Fairbanks. My first ever real trail ride. In the summer of 1998 I showed up for one of the Fairbanks Cycle Club's Tuesday night mountain bike rides, led by local cycling legend Doug Burnside. I'd read about them in the paper. It sounded like fun. I didn't realize it at the time, but this was when my road riding would succumb to trail fever. Before long I was avoiding roads. They're never so exciting as trails.

The ride began in Ester, west of Fairbanks. It was mid-May, so daylight wasn't a concern. We headed out the Ester Mine Road and onto the Fireplug Trail, the route of a since discontinued dogsled race. We hung a right at a steep ascent leading to the top of Ester Dome, some 1600 feet higher. The trail was boggy and brushy and generally terrible and our feet were soaked as we did a lot of pushing, eventually attaining the far end of the Out & Back. We rode that to the Tricon, which we bombed back down. Twice I was nearly taken out by other riders as I clung to my brakes on a very steep, deeply rutted descent. It was terrifying. It was gratuitously stupid. I was back for more the following week. And I've been back nearly every Tuesday night during every single summer since. I help lead those rides now.

IT'S NO LONGER summer, so today daylight is a concern. It's already 5:00. It will be dark by 7:00. I can head back to the top of the Dome and be home in under half an hour by road. But what's the fun in that? I brough a headlight and a fully charged battery. Loki is barking furiously because he knows going downhill is the only time he has to keep up with me instead of the reverse. And he knows this descent. He has a sled dog's memory for trails. I've always felt confident that if he were to become separated from me anywhere on the Dome, he'd find his way home. But he always stays close.

The Tricon road is treacherous, and since I'm alone, I take it easy on the drop. This allows Loki to pull ahead. Three quarters of the way down he turns onto another four wheeler trail, one crossing over to the quirky bedroom community of Ester. More downhill fun awaits, and a couple of brief but virtually unrideable uphills, a creek crossing, and a swamp. It's a good thing on this chilly afternoon that my shoes are waterproof. Winter is the only time in Interior Alaska that you can mountain bike with reasonable confidence you won't get wet feet. Unless you fall through the ice.

UPON MOVING NORTH I'd assumed my bike riding would be limited to summers. But soon after arrival I saw people commuting the roads around Fairbanks in winter, and before long had bought studded tires so I could join them. People here ride in any conditions and so have I, although I don't recommend riding at forty below zero unless both you and your bike are prepared. Human bodies slow down at that temperature, when simply going outdoors, much less moving in it for an extended time, can be an act of willpower and perhaps limited common sense. Bicycles don't like such extremes either. Over the years, local mechanics have figured out which lubricants do best in the deep cold, but bottom brackets, wheel hubs, shifts, and brakes resist movement when thermometers plunge.

Winter riding has become a global phenomenon since fat bikes hit the market around 2000. The large tires, operated under low air pressure, roll nicely over packed snow trails. It's a great way to explore winter pathways that traverse the swamps and rivers that present significant obstacles in summer, but become superhighways once everything freezes and routes are broken in.

Winter biking long predates fat bikes in Alaska, however. The earliest gold miners brought bikes as transportation tools. A few rode the Yukon River from Dawson to Nome when gold was discovered on Alaska's western beaches. Imagine doing that in 1899.

Recreational winter riding came later. In the seventies and eighties, as mountain bikes surged in popularity, Alaskans learned that by reducing air pressure in tires, they could travel the more solidly packed trails. Soon winter races began to be held. Inspired by a competitive winter cyclist who had welded two rims together for each of his wheels, local cycle mechanic Simon Rakower speculated that with wider rims than those that came stock on mountain bikes, tires would roll better over snow.

Thus were born Snow Cat Rims. Twice the width of a standard mountain bike rim, they could be installed on most frames. Riders, including myself, adopted the biannual ritual of swapping out their wheels. There was no longer a single mountain biking season.

Fat bikes took it up another notch, and now the winter trails around Fairbanks are plied daily by recreational riders. Two decades ago, trials were shared by skiers, mushers, and snowmachiners. These days, fat bikers seem to outnumber all others combined. It's a transition I've watched and been part of. I haven't skied in years now. Biking is faster and funner. And bikes have brakes. For an accident prone athlete like myself, this is a major selling point.

The other big change that has expanded winter riding is in lighting. Halogen bulbs were the brightest things on the market when I commuted in Seattle in the 1980s, and remained so into the early aughts. But when switched to full power they discharged their batteries quickly. And rechargeable batteries suffer in extreme cold. This hampered Alaskan night rides.

Then LEDs came online and the world opened up. A headlight ten times as bright as the halogen ones I once used can run for hours on a single charge. Cold remains a problem for batteries, but you learn tricks to insulate them. These days my biggest headlight issue comes when I get off of my bike and into my truck to go home. My high beams are dimmer than my bike lights. Suddenly I'm struggling to see where I'm going.

WE REACH THE neighborhoods above Ester and I'm forced to make more decisions. I can cut up to the Equinox Trail fairly quickly, and from there head home. I'm burning daylight, as Jack London put it. The sun is drooping low in the southern horizon. I'll soon need that headlight if I don't hurry. But I know a fun trail nearby that drops most of the way down to Ester. And from there I can hop the Eva Creek Trail and still reach the Equinox fairly soon.

A week from now the trails could be snowed in, and until that snow gets packed down, the Eva Creek Trail won't be rideable. This could be my final chance for weeks. So further we go, down one trail to climb another.

WHEN I FIRST arrived in Fairbanks, conflicts between motorized and non-motorized trail users were rampant. In those days, before online comment threads became the medium for outraged debates, the local newspaper's letters page saw endless battles over who had the right to use the trails, and in what fashion. It was especially fierce between skiers and snowmachine riders.

Then a curious thing happened. As more people took to winter cycling, trail disputes seemed to wither away. Rrelations between gas-oline-powered travelers and the self-propelled became downright cor-dial. There's a good reason for this. We fat bikers need snowmachine riders to pack our trails for us. It's a parasitic relationship perhaps, but it's produced a much needed truce between snow travelers. One I'm grateful for.

Even in my skiing days I recognized the potential for injury, and that the guy on a snowmachine could be the one to come along and render aid. That would leave me pretty embarrassed if I had devoted my efforts toward banning him from the trails (not an unfounded idea; banning snowmachines from parts of the valley was put to a vote many years ago and fortunately failed). So I always chose to share the trail. All I ask is that people—including my fellow cyclists—be safe and respectful. And overwhelmingly, this has been my experience. Oftentimes, when encountering motorized travelers, they turn off their engines and we talk for awhile, exchanging trail condition information and discussing what a fine day it is. Much better than animosity.

So fat bikes haven't just made my life better. They've been part of an easing of tensions in my community. A bike might have a human engine, but with all its interworking parts, it's still mechanical. So perhaps the bicycle itself provides the meeting ground between the two formerly warring camps.

IN ESTER, I spot a barely used four wheeler path heading in the general direction of the Eva Creek Trail. Loki is already exploring it, so I follow. We pop out on what I briefly mistake for the the trail, only to realize it's a section line. We bushwhack a bit further and find our objective.

The Eva Creek Trail runs through a subdivision near houses, even crossing a driveway at one point. The resident dog runs out to play with Loki and I pause to visit with its owner and marvel at this last shot of summer before winter sets in. It's one of the unique things about the trails near Fairbanks. They sometimes go right past people's houses, and many of the owners not only accept this gracefully, they welcome those traveling through. Despite having a strong compulsion for property rights, Fairbanks residents can be surprisingly generous when it comes to allowing people passage. Many of the trails are protected by easements, but friendliness isn't. That comes from generosity and the sense of shared life in this outpost town surrounded by vast open lands in every direction.

By now the sun is behind the hills, and it's a race with darkness. Loki and I climb back up the Dome to the the Equinox trail. From here I have several options that can get me home quickly. Alternatively, I can continue up the hill to another bandit trail I know about. One that will put me on Henderson Road near the top entrance to the Ester Dome Single track and a super fun downhill. There's some healthy climbing involved and dusk is setting in, but I have a light, and the days of summer riding are dwindling to zero. So up we go.

I ONCE RODE the fifty or so miles from Fairbanks to Nenana with a friend who had strung together a course that followed logging roads, section lines, recreational routes, trappers' trails, and more. We wove our way through moss, roots, gravel, deep puddles, and one of the steepest hills

I've ever climbed with a bike. I've ridden the pavement both ways in less time than it took us to go one way by trail. And burned far fewer calories doing it.

I couldn't retrace the route if I tried. It was too complex, too exemplary of the nature of trails in the Interior. At one time or another, one person needed to get from where they were to just over there and beyond. So they cut a pathway. Others, coming from different directions, followed. Over time, travel corridors were connected. But traffic was never heavy enough to warrant putting in public roads. They remained well-used trails and nothing more. And so the mazes of passageways became playgrounds for adults. It's one of the things that's kept me here. It's immediately accessible.

IT'S BEEN A strange summer in a strange and seemingly unending year, and I've spent much of it in the saddle. With a pandemic, political uncertainty, and postponed plans, mountain biking has been a beacon of normalcy. It's even been a relatively safe means of socializing. When riding with friends, we're generally far enough from each other that swapping viruses isn't a concern.

Today it's just Loki and I, though, and he's blissfully oblivious to a world in turmoil. All he knows is, everyone has been home a lot. That means he's been getting out even more often than usual. He's been all over these trails and knows the choices. He stops ahead of me, at the cut-off to Ester, and looks back inquisitively. "Not today, buddy," I tell him.

The climb grows steeper. We round a bend and Loki pauses again. A barely noticeable pathway leads into the woods. This is the one we're taking. I turn onto it and begin navigating a twisty single track. The trail traverses spruce roots, mud, and rocks. It threads between trees barely wide enough apart to accommodate my handlebars. It crosses a spring where Loki drinks his fill and takes what might be his final splash in open water for the season.

The sun has now set, but the sky remains illuminated by its vanishing glow. I take a few more photos with my phone, and notice the battery is nearly dead. Not from use, but from the cold. On my next ride I'll need to pack it in a pocket under a couple of layers to insulate it. I try to take a drink from my CamelBak, but can't. I forgot to blow the water back down after my last sips an hour earlier, and the liquid in the thin exposed tube has iced up. Further signs of summer's end.

I'm able to unclog the tube and drink deeply, then begin the last climb of the day. The news of the world hasn't been promising these past months, but right now none of this matters. I'm on my bike and in Alaska, and there's nowhere else I'd prefer to be. So in this corner of the world, all is just right.

RIDING HAS ALWAYS been a stress reducer for me. In grade school I'd escape my childhood frustrations by hopping on my spider bike and hitting the trails the cows had worn into our pastures and woods. I'd pedal as hard and as fast and as far as I could go and sometimes I'd crash and sometimes I'd bleed. So in a sense, I prepared myself for adult life as a mountain biker.

Long bike rides distracted me from studies in college, helped me ignore my perpetual lack of money in Seattle, and sustained me through breakups. More than once, when my kids were young and acting up, my wife would all but order me out onto the trail. By the time I got home, I was back on an even keel.

Cycling has helped me ride through the loss of family members. In early 2014 I spent several weeks in Seattle, tending to my sister during the final days of her struggle with cancer. It was made easier by her many wonderful friends. But I felt hemmed in by the city. As one of her friends told me a few days after she had died, "You need to be home now."

When I got home in late February I went riding the next morning with my friend Tom. From my house we headed down the hill and onto the winter trails crossing between Ester and Murphy Domes. It was ideal weather, a bit below zero. The winter sun had sufficiently returned to create a blinding brightness beaming down from the sky and reflecting up from the snow.

Winters in Fairbanks, I've always said, are much brighter than in Seattle. The days might be shorter, the temperatures significantly colder, but unlike the dank and gloomy Pacific Northwest, in Fairbanks, the sun can be seen most winter days. Even in December when it's so very far away, it usually puts in an appearance. By late February it's well above the horizon and stays up long enough to put plenty of hours on the trail. There's nothing like it.

And because seven minutes of direct sunlight are added each day, it's intoxicatingly energizing.

Tom and I rode through subdivisions and into a stretch of woods along the Dredge Trail, putting us near his place. By then I was sweaty and warm despite the cold, and smiling because we were having good dumb fun. It would be a long haul coming to terms with the death of my only sibling, but from a bicycle I began that process, knowing I could get through it.

In subsequent years, as first my father and then my mother died, I knew what to do. Get on my bike. Go find a trail. Ride. And in doing so, plunge into this beautiful place I've been lucky enough to make my home. This is how I've come to know it best. I can't imagine Alaska without my mountain bike.

It won't last forever. My own clock is ticking. It's been more than thirty years since I first came to Alaska. In thirty more, I'll be well into my eighties. I'd like to think I'll still be riding up steep hills and careening down steeper descents. But the reality is, should I live that long, I probably won't. Bones grow fragile. Hearts weaken. Joints quit cooperating. At some point mountain biking, which for me is completely entwined with the place I live, will become too difficult to continue, and I'll need to quit pretending I'm a kid.

NOT TODAY, THOUGH. It's downhill time. I've reached the Ester Dome Single Track, a network of loop trails and connectors that was built with volunteer labor over a decade ago. Busy with young children at the time, I wasn't involved in the construction, but try to atone for this with trail maintenance. I always carry a brush saw for clearing deadfall and other obstacles that get blown in. But is should be clear today. And since it's just about dark, I will only have my headlight to alert me if something has dropped onto the path.

It's also getting colder. What little solar gain can be had from the sun this time of year vaporized as soon as it set. And spots like this one haven't seen direct sunlight for a couple of weeks now and won't again until late winter.

I stop for a few more photographs, but Loki is impatient. I put my phone away, pull on a windbreaker, turn on my headlight full beam, and climb on my bike. It's time to turn off my brain, let instinct take over, hurl down the hill as quickly as I can, and head home. The next time I come this way, it will be covered in snow.

October 11, 2020

MELINDA MOUSTAKIS

ALASKA IS ABOUT AS FAR AS ONE CAN GET from the Deep south of Flannery O'Connor's Georgia and still be in North America. But it was appropriate that Melinda Moustakis received the 2011 Flannery O'Connor Award for her short fiction collection *Bear Down, Bear North*. Much like O'Connor's work, Moustakis' stories explore the lives and foibles of people deeply caught and sometimes trapped in the ecological and cultural landscapes of their homes. The stories are dark, sometimes darkly comic, and peopled with hardscrabble characters that readers will root for despite their deep failings.

Moustakis told me, "When I write about Alaska, I think of how important complexity and paradox are in portraying these characters and this landscape. This is a place of family stories and personal significance, but also has a fraught history. I would categorize my work as Northern Gothic for all the similarities I see it having with the Southern Gothic genre."

Moustakis was born in Fairbanks and moved to California at a young age. After living in seven other states she is presently back in California.

But her ties to the Last Frontier remain deep. "My mother's parents were homesteaders in the Point Mackenzie area outside Anchorage in the late 50's," she explained. "So I have a lot of family history in the state and I've spent a lot of time in Alaska visiting family and I usually spend my summers on the Kenai River. Nancy Lord called Alaska my heart's home after reading my work and I hold to that."

In her short stories she captures both the physical beauty of Alaska and the tolls that drawing a living from the state's land and waters can take on homesteaders, hunters, and fishermen and fisherwomen. Most of the stories in the book are interlinked and follow three generations of a homesteading family who battle each other, addictions, the elements, and the world beyond.

The stories play out in an Alaska that Moustakis beautifully summarizes in short flourishes. In the story "This One Isn't Going to be Afraid," she drops in at a small homestead in the Interior on a cold winter's night, sketching a scene that many Alaskans will instantly recognize, that moment when the northern lights whip across the frigid, star-ridden sky, illuminating the night during the darkest time of year.

She stepped outside and I went with her. She was a little tipsy, happy-tipsy. We turned to the back of the homestead, arms linked, headed toward the outhouse. The clear night strewn with ice-picked stars. We were trudging along in the snow and stopped. Above the ridge, serpentine green ribboned the sky, tangled and bright. I'd never seen them—neon streamers making love to the darkness and I couldn't stop looking.

The following selection, "They Find the Drowned," won a 2013 O. Henry Prize. Standing apart from the cycle of stories comprising much of *Bear Down, Bear North*, it's a journey along the Kenai Peninsula during salmon season, where people, animals, birds, fish, and insects face the prospect of drowning in the rushing Kenai River which, Moustakis explains in another story,

is a rope, choking off a piece of land with a slow, snaking hold.

— From *Bear Down, Bear North* —
THEY FIND THE DROWNED

Humpies
Oncorhynchus gorbuscha

A river loses strength, loses water. Scientists catch the humpies and put them into tanks and drive to the Kenai River. The humpies are released near the mouth when the reds are running. The humpies don't know where to go—they don't know the Kenai and they don't follow the reds. They don't recognize the currents of the river, or the smells, or the way the light refracts into the water and bounces off the bottom. The reds run up while the dead humpies float down. They die because they have the wrong memories.

Outhouse

A woman with long, dark hair falls asleep with throbbing shoulders from fishing all day. She sits up and rummages in the cabinets for aspirin. She can't find the bottle and she doesn't want to wake the others. But her daughter wakes up and tugs her shirt.

The woman takes the girl's hand and they tiptoe out the cabin door. The girl forgets and the door slams shut.

They wince and wait for the others to stir, but no one does. They walk the short trail to the outhouse and the girl goes first, the mother standing outside. She hears a rustle and a low, throated moan. And then nothing.

The mother looks around. The girl takes a long time so the mother raps her knuckle on the door. "Shouldn't take this long."

The rustle comes closer. She sees a large, dark creature in the woods. And then nothing.

Did her daughter think this was a game? She knocks hard on the door. "Are you in there? Answer me." She stops knocking to listen. "I said answer me."

The mother hears the rustle creep closer. "Open this door." She kicks the door in with her unlaced boot. The wood splinters from the force.

"Stop," says the girl from inside. She opens the door. Her eyes marvel at her mother.

An animal bursts out of the bushes. The mother shoves the girl behind her and the grizzly charges toward them, running as if he's going to knock them over and then he stops, sniffs the air and walks toward the river. The bear wades into the Kenai, crossing water to reach the mainland. When they see him climb the bank on the other side, they hurry back to the cabin.

She puts the girl back to bed. "What?" the mother says.

"I wanted to see what you would do," says the girl, thinking of the broken door.

The girl goes to sleep. The mother remembers the first aid kit has packets of aspirin. She swallows two tablets and lies down on her side of the bed, her husband dreaming deep, swimming dreams.

Loon
Gavia immer

A loon drifts down the current. The bird has a daggered beak and with his black, black head, red eyes and white-striped wings, he's easy to spot. The loon dives down and disappears and the scientist times him, scanning for the breach. After a minute and eleven seconds, the loon reappears upstream, shakes the water off his head. There are loons and there are ducks. Ducks are never alone.

Storm

Her husband knocks on the door. They were looking for him. He has blood soaked down the front of his shirt. They hadn't heard a gun. Maybe the axe, but there isn't a wound. A thick, familiar smell calms them.

He stumbles over the doorway and falls. Two of his buddies carry him to the boat and he's vomiting red into the river. The woman with the long, dark hair watches the boat leave her and the island and the blood behind. "This is the last time," she says. She nods as she's nodded before, lays towels over the mess and wipes the blood with the toe of her boot. Then she dips the towels into the river, wrings them out.

The woman sits on a stump near the bank. In the stillwater, the smolt move like a storm of comets. The terns swoop down with their pitchfork tails and scoop up small fish. Seagulls on the gravel bar bicker over scraps.

The Scientists

The scientists sit in a boat and dip tubes into the river.

"Turquoise," says one, noting the color of the water.
"Green," says another.
"Glacier blood."
"Crushed sky."
"Kenai Blue."
They test levels of sediment from the ice fields.

Life-Jacket

The neighbors across the river have a big family. Grandma has a whip of a cast, a fluid flick of line into the water. Grandpa wears his white underwear to swim; his barrel of belly hanging out. The grandchildren scream and splash about in their life jackets. There are five boys and their shouts echo and amplify through the spruce, scaring away the moose and the mosquitoes, if mosquitoes could be scared away. The boys swim out past the dock and let the current carry their floating heads downriver. They stay in the shallow, where they can put their feet down and climb the bank. But if their feet miss, they can grab the net rope fixed to an orange buoy. Sometimes they swim farther across and spend an afternoon on the gravel bar with the gulls.

Spruce Bark Beetle

Dendroctonus rufipennis

The scientists call it the plague—the outbreak of spruce bark beetles that has infested the forests of the Kenai Peninsula for over ten years. A couple of warm summers and the beetles became a blight. They have eaten through two million acres of white, lutz, black, and sitka spruce.

They are the length of a small bullet and they thrive in dryness and heat. The scientists hope for a summer of rain to contain them. The beetles burrow through the bark and chew a path to the cambium layer, the only part of the tree that is alive. They tunnel a gallery inside the host tree and lay eggs. The scientists set pheromone traps and watch as the forest turns into firewood, the dead outnumbering the green.

Roll

The woman hunches over the reel and her long hair falls forward. Her hip's bruised blue from fishing, but she's got to anchor down with the rod. Boats move out and make a clear path as they drift down.

"Everyone wants to be you with this big ol' fish," says her husband.

"They pass the end of the drift and he takes a side channel to avoid the backtrollers.

"Let's get this one in," he says.

She reels in slow and steady. The spinner flashes and he strikes with the net. The king thrashes. He slips to one knee, loses the handle. The king rolls, fifty pounds of fish wrestles out of the net. He steps in and grabs the handle, then grasps at the mesh. She reels but the hook springs loose.

"A hen," she says. "Could've used those eggs."

"Don't jaw me," he says. He throws down the empty net. "I know."

Moose
Alces alces gigas

The scientist has a favorite—he calls her Al and every once in a while he'll sit on the river near Bing's Landing and look for her. She has twins now and crosses to the island at night when the river is quiet. He found her on the side of the road after she'd been hit by a truck on Sterling Highway. The driver died and he didn't think she was going to pull through. The scientist visited her when she was bandaged and bruised— he'd talk to her. "Listen," he'd say. "You're the first thing I've been good to in a long time."

Yellow Patches

He and his buddies cut the trees that were turning brown from the blight, where bark beetles eat and weaken the tree from the inside. The diseased trees are yellow patches in a quilt of green. They are also dangerous. She's afraid the closer trees might fall over and crash into his cabin. But they're laughing and she calls them a bunch of idiots with axes.

One by one, the trees crack and fall away from the cabin. They splash into the Kenai and the current pushes them toward the bank. But one won't fall. His axe wedges into the diagonal cut. The tree teeters toward cabin and land, not water. Women and kids scatter. After the boom, the cabin stands untouched. They stand unharmed. He raises a bottle of beer to his good fortune.

Rainbow Trout
Oncorhynchus mykiss

Rainbows are the shimmering litmus, the indicator fish. If anything goes wrong in the Kenai, the rainbows tell the scientists. If there is pollution, they die. If the temperature changes too much, they die. If a feeder stream stops feeding, they die. Kiss a rainbow, the scientists say, and you'll know all the river's secrets.

A Sixty-Pounder

Mom and Dad and Grandma and Grandpa play rummy and drink beer from an ice chest. They don't see the boy slide out of his life jacket on a dare. There's struggling and a shout. The Dad dives in and emerges empty-fisted. Grandpa, in his white underwear, jumps into the boat and Grandma follows. They drive to the sinking boy and Grandma holds out the king net to him. When the boy doesn't grab, she scoops him with the net. He's a sixty-pounder and Grandpa has to help heave the net aboard. Grandma pinches the boy's nose, her nails making moon indents into his skin. She forces air into his icy mouth, presses his chest. The boy chokes on air and Grandma turns his head to the side. She brushes her tears away. "You little shit," she says. The boy spits the river and she pats his back.

Eagle
Halieaeetus leucocephalus

The eagle is perched up in the tree, singing. His call jumps octaves, runs with scales. The scientist records the eagle's sounds and writes down the time of day. A boat drifts down Superhole and stops near the scientist.

"Isn't that something?" says the fisherman. He and the woman both wait for an answer.

The scientist holds up his recorder and points. "Shhhh," he says.

"Well, if you knew anything, you'd know they sing all the time," says the fisherman. His boat starts downriver. "They sing opera."

The Waltz

He has sprawled in her absence. She lies on her elbow and hip in the narrow space and unbraids her long, dark hair. The bed is high—there are storage cabinets built underneath. Blankets and waders are stashed in the gap between her side of the mattress and the wall. Her husband rolls closer and gains inches of mattress.

"Move over," she says. "I don't have any room."

He moves, but he rolls toward her and knocks her off the bed.

The gap is narrow enough to be a problem. "Help me up," she says.

She pats around in the shadows and feels fur. And a snout. Teeth.

She screams and scrambles to dislodge herself. Her husband, grabbing her legs, pulls her up. She finds footing on the mattress and runs out of the room and then outside. The whole cabin wakes with the commotion.

Her husband stands on the deck with a bear head. "I was saving it for the teeth and claws." He unfolds the skin. "Harmless," he says and puts the bear head over his shoulder. He fanfares off the porch and then he waltzes, hand to paw, around the camp fire. Man and bear nod in rhythm, in step.

Half Life
Oncorhynchus nerka

The red swims a slow, stilted speed as if worming through sand. He swims outside the current, keeping to the edges with the smolt. His tail is white with rotting; layers of skin hang in silken scarves. A bite? Raked by the claw of a bear? The fish should be dead. The scientist steps closer and wades into the water, aiming with the net. The fish darts away.

Beetlekill

"We survived the oil spill and now this," says the scientist. There's division—no one agrees on how to separate the living from the dead. The canopy has thinned by seventy percent and everything under it is changing—a beetle gnaws through the bark of a tree and then the salmon count drops and then a fisherman drinks himself into a ditch.

Logging

The boys swim strapped inside the life-jackets. The jackets float up near their ears. The river brings a tree to them and they swim to the uprooted trunk lodged near the gravel bar—the amputated branches silky with moss. Three boys straddle the tree as if they were riding a horse. The other boys grab the broken-off branches and shove and push. The river catches the tree and the boys shove more. "Go," they say. "Go." The three riders wave their arms when the current takes the tree. Grandma and Grandpa clap. Mom and Dad grab the camera and start the boat. The boys are waving for the picture as they ride downriver. The fisherman starts his boat, drives fast and waits below the Mom and Dad. Naptowne rapids waits behind him.

"One snag," he yells. "And the tree will roll."

Hen

Oncorhynchus tsawytscha

The scientist hovers over the dead hen, a female king salmon, with tweezers. He pinches a scale from the head, the side, and the tail, measures the length and girth.

"Ain't she pretty?" says the fisherman.

The scientist holds one scale up to the light—the sheer skin of a pearl. Kneeling, the fisherman leans over the scientist's shoulders, puzzled about the lengthy examination. "It's a fish," he says.

"Yes," says the scientist.

Crutch

He breaks things—doors, glass, plates. He breaks bones, but only his own, and punches the walls of the cabin. Most of the time he comes home wobbly and soft and puts his arm around her and she crutches him to the couch, hoping he doesn't wake their daughter. "I love my girls," he says. "I love my girls."

Bodies

The scientists come across a body while doing research. They need to count salmon and a human disrupts the day. A human can last six minutes to six hours in the water depending on the temperature. They find the drowned don't have liquid in their lungs—they gasp in the cold water until their tracheas collapse.

CPR

The woman and her husband walk a trail along the edge of the Kenai. The husband watches her long, dark hair swoosh across her back as he follows behind with two poles and a tackle box. She stomps ahead not thinking about where they are going. He follows because he has always chased after her. This is what they do. He has not touched her hair in two months. She has not wanted him to touch her in two months. They have no children, not yet. They have a cabin and two trucks and long-standing argument about who should drive which truck. The woman trips over a root and there is a little blood on her knee.

"Are you ok?" her husband asks.

"I'm fine," she says and keeps walking. Her jade ring feels tight on her finger.

The man's hand begins to sweat around the handle of the tackle box.

"Pick a spot so we can fish," he says. He wishes that her hair wasn't beautiful, with tinges of red, in the sun.

She walks a minute to make a point, and then stops. "Here," she says.

A low-throated call makes them look upriver. A moose calf is struggling against the current. His head sinks and then pops up, then sinks again.

"He's drowning," she says.

"No he isn't," he says.

The calf gains footing for a brief moment and then falls.

"He's being swept away." She starts to walk up the trail.

"Where are you going?" he asks.

She runs. She wades out into the river. He's still holding the poles and the tackle box. The calf isn't struggling anymore. He's floating.

"Please," she says. "Bring him this way." She goes in up to her waist. She grabs the calf by the neck and finds the riverbed with her feet. "Help me," she says to her husband.

They both haul the calf to the shore.

She puts her face ear the moose's nose. "He's not breathing."

"He's dead then," her husband says.

The woman covers the moose's nostrils with her hand. She puts her lips on the moose's mouth and blows air. "Where's his heart? Where do moose put their hearts?"

"I don't know," he says. "The chest seems right."

The woman compresses the chest and tries more air. "Go get help," she says.

The man runs up the trail. If only she were willing him to live, pressing her mouth to his. Her hair falling over his face. He finds another fisherman and the fisherman gets someone to call the Rangers and Fish and Game.

The calf's mouth feels like a stubbled cheek. She cups the jaw and focuses the air stream. One. Two. She crosses her hands over the chest. The ears twitch. She pumps and hears a gurgle and water spills out. She tilts his head to allow the water to drain.

When the man returns to his wife, there is a crowd. The calf's side heaves with signs of life.

His wife looks up at him and says, "I think he might be breathing."

Fish and Game comes with oxygen. "You saved the calf's life," they say.

"We saved the calf's life." She looks directly at her husband. Then someone hands her a bottle of water and she swishes out her mouth.

The man and woman gather their gear. They walk the trail as before. But when they're away from everyone else she turns to face him. He's holding the poles and the tackle box so he stands there and she wraps one arm around his neck and puts her mouth on his. She kisses him and he kisses her and she puts one hand on his chest where his pulse quickens under her palm. This is what they do.

Degrees of North

Here, the scientists know north is eighteen degrees on a compass. Not zero. They don't wander into the woods without a map. Or directions. Walking from camp, following the trail of moose—they don't lose their way. Losing, as they say, is not scientific.

KIM HEACOX

"**D**ENALI MATTERS," KIM HEACOX TELLS US in *Rhythm of the Wild*. "It teaches and inspires; it slows me down. It opens my lungs. I love the intimate distance, the raw existence, the unexpected ravens, the furtive lynx, the stoic moose, the resilient birch, the poetry of water over stones; I love pulling my sleeping bag up to my chin and wondering: how far away is the nearest bear? The farthest star? I love sunrises and sunsets, the only gold rush I care to be a part of. I love the survival amid hardship, the warm embrace of indifferent mountains, the simple but profound freedoms; I love the dream-tossed nights when, according to comedian George Carlin, 'the wolves are silent and the moon howls.'"

Denali National Park is a place millions of people hope to see just once in their lives. Heacox is one of the fortunate ones who has lived there. He first visited as a seasonal ranger for the National Park Service in 1981, then returned in the early nineties, living nearby with his wife for several years. He was back again a decade later, absorbing the wilderness as America marched off to war in Iraq, and then in 2012 for a writer-in-residence stay at the cabin of the famed wolf researcher Adolph Murie.

Rhythm of the Wild is Heacox's memoir of those years and how his encounters with Denali have formed his thinking and continue to influence it. As he recounts his wanderings in the Park, which rests in the physical and spiritual heart of Alaska, he observes unobstructed nature unfolding, discusses the value of wilderness and the human need to have wild places to escape into, critiques consumerism and post-industrial civilization, confronts his own mortality, and argues for a slower, simpler, and more observant way of life than the one America–and most of the rest of the world–has embraced..

All of these elements come together in the selection that follows. Heacox accompanies a group of teenagers visiting Alaska on a National Geographic Student Expedition. The kids come from affluent suburban and urban families and have little wilderness exposure beyond television and the internet. Taking them into the Park, he works to transform their thinking, and in the few short days he has, prepare them to confront the challenges facing their generation. Particularly climate change, which is taking a visible toll on Denali. Heacox, a lifelong activist whose memories stretch back to the Civil Rights and Vietnam War eras, knows how insurmountable society's problems can seem. But he also knows that progress can be made, which leaves him cautiously hopeful.

Elaborating on this, Heacox told me, "In a world beset by climate change and mass extinction, I feel that it's my moral duty to be an activist writer. Yes, it can be burdensome. But mostly writing sets me free. People ask if I'm pessimistic. I say: Imagine being in a dark room, with a heavy door blocking the way. But at the bottom of the door, a sliver of light shows the way to a brighter future. That's what I write to. I write to the light. How, exactly? I do my best to tell bigger stories, better stories."

In many ways, *Rhythm of the Wild* does for Denali what Edward Abbey's *Desert Solitaire* did for Arches National Park. Like Abbey, who he cites frequently, Heacox uses his wilderness experiences as a springboard for political musings that suggest a way of organizing a society built on values rather than the value of things. He doesn't surrender to the caustic cynicism that overtook Abbey's later writings, however, making his the more optimistic voice.

Heacox is the author of over a dozen books, including memoirs, natural and human histories, and photography collections. He lives in Gustavus, near Glacier Bay National Park, where he continues to explore, write about, and advocate for Alaska's wildernesses.

— From *Rhythm of the Wild* —
Wolfing Down Pizza

ALASKA AIRLINES GETS ME TO THE TERMINAL ON TIME. I breeze through the gate, down the concourse and past security, and descend the escalator to be greeted by a dozen teenagers waving the National Geographic Society tricolor. With them are their two instructors, Em Jackson and David Estrada. We make introductions and take a few photos. At baggage claim the kids playfully compete with each other to carry my stuff.

So begins my week with National Geographic Student Expeditions.

Tomorrow, we'll drive to Denali.

At dinner that night in a Fairbanks restaurant I pose a question: "What would you rather be, a domestic dog or a wolf?"

The students look at me with saucer eyes: six boys and six girls, all fifteen to eighteen years old, impossibly fresh-faced and young. A few are college-bound that fall, most are set to begin their junior or senior years in high school. Raised in affluence in cities and suburbs from Boston to San Diego, not one of them has been to Alaska before.

They vote. Ten of the twelve would rather be a domestic dog. They have dogs at home. Dogs they love and miss. Dogs they treat with great affection and care.

I nod. Sounds like a good choice, a great life, being a dog in a house filled with love. Only two, Joey and Max, say they'd rather be a wolf.

"It's not easy being a wolf," I say.

"I know," answers Joey Abate from Brooklyn. "I'll take my chances."

Is he giving me the answer he thinks I want to hear? "Instead of the soft sofa and short leash," I add, "you'd have to hunt for all your food. You could starve to death, get kicked by a moose, run over by a snowmachine, trampled by a mastodon, shot by a redneck, robbed by a bear."

They laugh.

"There's no Purina Dog Chow or Ace Ventura Pet Detective in the wilderness of Alaska."

Joey shrugs.

The girls fiddle with their desserts.

SOUTHBOUND. THE NEXT MORNING WE ROLL DOWN the George Parks Highway through Ester, Nenana, and Anderson, half of us in one van, half in the other. Em and David discreetly keep the kids from dividing into cliques. We stop often to talk about geology, ecology, history, photography, whatever the land and light inspires.

I call the shots, being the so-called National Geographic "expert," a title that makes me uncomfortable.

I ask the students to regard me as no expert at all, but as an expatriot park ranger guitar picker in search of a new definition of the American Dream. They seem to like that. They call me "dude."

A few miles north of Healy, we stop at the turnoff to two roads: Lignite Road going east, Stampede Road going west.

"Does this spot mean anything to anybody?" I ask.

Blank stares. A few students shake their heads.

"This is the old Stampede Trail, where eighteen years ago a hitch-hiker named Chris McCandless said good-bye to the last person he ever saw and walked into the wild. It was late April, cold. He called himself Alexander Supertramp." I point west. "The abandoned bus where he died is about twenty-five miles that way."

Everybody falls silent. They know the story. They come from well-to-do families, many back East, and have a fascination with Alaska, as McCandless did at their age. A few take photos posing next to the Stampede Road sign as I walk back to the vans parked off the highway some fifty feet away. The boys join me while every girl lingers on the Stampede, some folded into each other, heavy with sadness, no doubt thinking of the idealistic young man, so handsome and full of commitment and potential, dying as he did. Recent evidence suggests he didn't starve, but that he unknowingly poisoned himself eating the seeds of a seemingly innocuous plant called wild potato. The boys tell me that while Jon Krakauer's book is good, it's the recent movie adaption by Sean Penn, starring the heartthrob Emile Hirsch as McCandless, that slammed the girls. They all fell for him.

Back in the van, a girl named Bailey tells me, "The whole thing is so sad. It hurts more when you stand where he stood and think about all the things that could have gone another way for him."

I remember Krakauer's line about "innocent mistakes" that turned out to be "pivotal and irreversible."

"How old would he be now, if he'd lived?" a student asks from the back of the van.

I do the math. "Forty-two."

"Oh gosh . . . my dad is forty-two."

PAST HEALY AND OTTO LAKE, WE DROP INTO the Nenana River Canyon and stop at Windy Bridge. Time for another diversion. We walk down a steep path and climb under the bridge to admire local graffiti; the art and love messages and political mutterings of local kids their age. Again, more photos. And this time, as I had hoped, laughter.

I tell a few stories. Always stories, or a parable at least, and if not a parable a tale with a theme, and if not a theme, a corny punchline. Back in the van, the students teach me the verses of Jason Mraz's "I'm Yours" while I teach them the melody and harmony parts to "Across the Universe." It's a fair deal.

All twelve students are keen on photography and want to know what it's like to work for the National Geographic Society. It's precious, perilous duty, I say, especially writing books, homebound, chained to a desk. Not as glamorous as working as an assignment photographer in Botswana or Bhutan for the yellow-bordered flagship magazine, but still a sweet deal. I became a writer because I like ideas. Because today's writers might not be so different from the Niaux Cave artists of fifteen thousand years ago: searching in the dark, seeking a more durable life, a better world; or at least a finer appreciation of this one, nothing more.

Back on the road, I talk to the kids about the lesson—and the burden—of history, how those who ignore it are destined to repeat it. While those who embrace it go crazy watching others ignore and repeat it. Many are worried about the cost of college tuition: fifty thousand dollars per year to attend Brown or Yale. Some parents can afford it, others cannot. The kids hope for generous scholarships. Even small state schools cost twenty times what they did thirty years ago. I tell them that total college debt today (in the United States) is higher than total credit card debt. The kids shake their heads. "How did this happen?" asks one girl.

Says another, "And we have money. Imagine the poor."

I have no simple answer. All I know is that my tuition in the 1970s was about two hundred dollars per quarter. I joined a musician's union, played in a local band three nights a week, got free beer, and graduated with money in the bank. I was lucky.

WE ARRIVE AT THE DENALI EDUCATION CENTER, have a nice dinner, and that night walk along the Nenana River. The next morning we head out the park road for the Savage River, as far west as private vehicles can travel without a special permit. Our objective: to hike up Mount Margaret, the easternmost end of Primrose Ridge. It's time to leave behind the burden of history.

The mountain slams us. Three-fourths of the way up, with another five hundred vertical feet above and a ferocious wind blasting us from the south, pelting us with rain, I call everybody together. Half the kids look strong, a few seem shaky but able to continue on, two or three appear ready to break down and cry. I've noticed several on wobbly legs, their fatigue increasing with each arduous step. The instructors, Em and David, signal me that they think we should abandon the summit.

"How's everybody doing?" I ask.

"Good," says Joey and a couple others.

A few keep their heads down to avoid eye contact. When we do talk, the wind is so fierce we can hardly hear each other.

"Huddle up, everybody," I say. "This is a nasty wind. If we push for the summit it'll be an unpleasant experience. Here's what we're going to do. We'll contour over to that ridge and take shelter behind that rocky outcrop, get a lee from the wind, have a nice lunch, rehydrate, rest up and regain our strength. How does that sound?"

"What do you mean 'contour'?"

"We'll stay at the same elevation and side-hill across, careful not to gain or lose elevation and waste valuable energy. Does that sound good?"

They nod.

An hour later things improve greatly. The rain stops. We eat lunch surrounded by wildflowers and recover our good spirits.

Back on our feet, we crest the ridge to find five Dall sheep rams bedded down in their own tundra flowers. The kids can't believe it. This is their reward: to have climbed all this way and receive these regal mountain animals with golden horns and keen eyes. The sheep remain casual yet watchful; they've had visitors before. I ask the kids to stay in a tight group, move slowly, give the rams ample room.

We find a small fold in the topography, a break from the wind, and sit to admire what I tell them is "the signature animal of Denali National Park." Not the mighty grizzly or the stately wolf; not the moose, caribou, or lynx. Noble though they are, they don't hold the place in Denali's history that the Dall sheep does.

"Why?" the kids ask.

They quietly take photos; some crawl around to get better compositions. As things settle down, I tell a story.

"ONCE THERE WAS A MAN WHO BY THE AGE OF THIRTY-FIVE had all the money he needed . . ." After making a small fortune in a Mexican silver and lead mine, he came north to see what remained of wild America. Here was Alaska, a second chance, a magnificent gift. This man would dedicate the rest of his life to the higher ideal of saving wild animals by preserving their habitat, their world. His name was Charles Sheldon. The world he campaigned to save is today called Denali National Park and Preserve.

Not a bad legacy.

It was an exciting time. In the first decade of the twentieth century, a self-described nature lover and "Audubonist" occupied the White House. America had never before had such a president. Young and vibrant, Teddy Roosevelt would burst into a cabinet meeting thrilled or angry— nobody could tell—to announce, "Gentlemen, do you know what has happened this morning?" Everybody would brace; heads might roll. "Just now I saw a chestnut-sided warbler—and this is only February."

For Roosevelt, who'd grown up an asthmatic child made well by going outdoors on grand adventures, and later working a ranch in the Dakotas, birds and other wild animals colored the world and gave it wonder and grace. The strenuous life was a good life, he said. Don't get soft sitting in padded chairs and fancy sofas. The best medicine was fresh air, hard work, and a deep appreciation for wild nature.

Go out there.

Remember Thoreau: "I'd rather sit on a pumpkin and have it all to myself than be crowded on a velvet cushion."

And Muir: "I only went out for a walk, but finally concluded to stay out till sundown, for going out, I found, was really going in."

Sheldon, like Roosevelt, was an Ivy League man with tremendous pluck and drive and a love for open space and wild places. "The words that his [Yale] classmates used over and over again to describe him," according to historian Douglas Brinkley, "were 'rugged' and 'no nonsense.'"

To illustrate this, Brinkley tells a story:

ONE AFTERNOON A SALESMAN CAME TO YALE, *banging on students' doors, offering boxes of Cuban cigars. Not long after the salesman's visit, Sheldon noticed that his flute had been stolen from his quarters. Immediately he turned detective. For a long day he visited all of Long Haven's and New York's pawnshops, hoping to find his flute. His determination paid off. At one of the Manhattan shops, Sheldon stumbled on the petty thief, the flute sticking out of his suit coat pocket. Without hesitation Sheldon, like a linebacker, tackled him to the ground. He then made a citizen's arrest. The salesman went to jail and Sheldon returned to Yale with his treasured instrument.*

BORN IN 1867, THE YEAR THE UNITED STATES purchased Alaska from Russia, Sheldon might have felt a kinship to this place. Now that we owned it, what should we do with it?

Here the Yale man could go back in time while the rest of America rushed openhanded into the future. How easy he found it to gun down seven Dall sheep rams one summer evening with only eight shots. Yes, the sheep could be hard to find, living at high elevation. But once found and approached with quiet determination, they made easy targets. Market hunters, combing these mountains for wild game to feed prospectors and railroad workers, would soon shoot them all. It was theft of another kind, and not so petty. It had to be stopped.

I look at the kids. They nod in agreement.

"Otherwise," I end the story, "future generations—such as students on National Geographic Student Expeditions—would never see the only species of wild white sheep in the world."

WE BEGIN HIKING DOWN TO THE SAVAGE RIVER. The wind has abated. Patches of blue sky appear. The kids practically fly, fleet-footed, bound for the vans parked far below; vans that will carry them back east to the park entrance for ice cream and pizza. Some hold back and hike stride for stride with the old man—me—and have questions.

"So he succeeded, right?" asks Joey. "I mean, the sheep are still here, and we have a national park."

"Yes."

But it was not an easy road. Thankfully, Sheldon had capable help from Belmore Browne, who beautifully articulated the park idea (in 1915) to friends back East, including the secretary of the interior. Both Sheldon and Browne had to tread lightly and win over the right allies in the right order. Judge James Wickersham, delegate of the Territory of Alaska, disliked the idea at first and sympathized with prospectors in Kantishna, where he himself had claims. He said he wanted to protect their mining and hunting rights, and moreover, their way of life. William T. Hornaday, director of the powerful New York Zoological Society, loved the park idea and strongly opposed such special mining and hunting privileges. Sheldon recruited his colleagues in the Boone and Crockett Club; Browne recruited his in the Camp Fire Club. Together they won the endorsement of Stephen T. Mather, assistant to the secretary of the interior, who would soon find himself as the first director of a new agency called the US National Park Service.

While the American Game Protective Association commanded the public hearings, Browne, always an artist, offered this memorable testimony:

Giant moose still stalk the timberline valleys; herds of caribou move easily across the moss-covered hills; bands of white big-horn sheep look down on the traveler from frowning mountains, while at any time the powerful form of the grizzly bear may give the crowning touch to the wilderness picture. But while the Mount McKinley region is the fountainhead from which come the herds of game that supply the huge expanse of southcentral Alaska, that fountainhead is menaced. Slowly but surely the white man's civilization is closing in, and already sled loads of dead animals from the McKinley region have reached the Fairbanks market. Unless a refuge is set aside, in which the animals that remain can breed and rear their young unmolested they will soon follow the buffalo.

Meaning they'll disappear as the buffalo did. "The great good that has come with our national expansion," Browne concluded, "has always been followed by evils. Are we a nation able to profit by our mistakes? Can these tragedies be prevented? Yes: but our last and only chance lies in the Mount McKinley region."

Congress signed the bill, and in early 1917 Charles Sheldon hand-delivered it to President Woodrow Wilson for his signature.

History shows that only a powerful centralized government can achieve this. On a local and even regional level, most people oppose the establishment of a national park; they say it infringes upon their cherished freedoms and economic opportunities.

In fact, just the opposite is true.

National parks create new economies.

AT A LOCAL PIZZA PARLOR THAT NIGHT, the kids are in a spectacular mood. For many, the hike up Mount Margaret and the discovery of five Dall sheep rams is the most difficult and rewarding outdoor adventure of their young lives. I ask one shy girl how she's doing. She says, "I feel like I could conquer the world."

"You only need to love it, Emily. Love it and honor it and change it when necessary. Find the Rachel Carson and Rosa Parks within. It's there. You are more than you think you are."

She looks at me thoughtfully.

I've told the students more than once that deep, fundamental change takes time. Some Alaskans still regard their national parks as being "locked up." They're not. They're locked *open*. Come on in. Learn to share. Be young again. Climb a mountain, run a river, sleep on the ground. Why? To reset your clock, repair your heart, rediscover what's real: the earth, your home, not a bad place to be.

The students wolf down their pizza. It's open mic night, and they dare me as perhaps I've dared them. They want me to take the stage. I grab a guitar and play Jackson Browne's "For Everyman" followed by Steve Earle's "Copperhead Road," pounding away on the offbeat— Earle does it with a mandolin and bagpipes—while the kids stomp the wooden floor and clap. Later, I tell Em and David, "This is what we do at National Geographic Student Expeditions. We invite prosperous, well-educated, well-mannered kids to Alaska and teach them moonshine songs."

THE NEXT DAY IT RAINS, AND THE KIDS HOLE UP inside the Denali Education Center to be students and write their research papers, one of the requirements of the program. Em, David, and I call them "students" when they're quiet and indoors, and "kids" when they're rambunctious and outside. Near as I can tell, it's more fun and healthy being kids.

Later, we drive north to Healy to visit the Usibelli Coal Mine. At the mine's entrance we wait for our guide and talk about the realities of coal. I'm surprised at how much the kids already know: that more than forty percent of the electricity generated in the United States comes from coal-fired power plants, and these kids have grown up in the comfort of that electricity, as have I; that China burns much more coal today than it did thirty years ago; that because of our coal addiction here and overseas, mercury exists in rivers and oceans around the world. And in all major seafood. And in us. The kids have studied this in high school. The more vocal ones tell me that atmospheric carbon dioxide (CO_2)—a planet-warming greenhouse gas produced by burning coal and other fossil fuels—will soon go above four hundred parts per million (ppm), the highest it's been in at least eight hundred thousand years, perhaps three million years, and it's increasing by about two ppm per year, and there's no sign of it stopping, even abating. They know about "methane monsters." As permafrost melts, large pockets of methane, previously trapped in the icy ground, erupt into the atmosphere. And don't forget methane hydrates (cage-like lattices of ice with molecules of methane trapped inside) everywhere beneath the ocean floor. In its first twenty years after release, methane is about eighty times more powerful than CO_2 as a greenhouse gas. They know all this; they know what it means. This is my generation's legacy, their generation's inheritance.

"So why do we keep digging up coal and burning it?" I ask them.

They pepper me with answers and comments:

"Because it's there, and easy to get."

"It's cheap."

"I'm not so sure it's cheap. If you factor in the long-term environmental costs and health costs, maybe it's a lot more expensive than we think it is."

"Our entire political system runs on money; lobbyists and all that, and the oil and coal industries have a lot of lobbyists, and a lot of money."

"My dad says the *London Guardian* reported that the Republican Party is the only major political party in the developed world that doesn't accept climate change, or that human beings are causing it."

"Can it ever turn around?" I ask them. They look at me skeptically, as if I've asked a trick question. I say, "When Doctor Martin Luther King Jr. stood on the steps of the Lincoln Memorial in the summer of 1963, he didn't say, 'I have a nightmare.' He could have. He'd seen terrible racial injustice, even death. What he said was, 'I have a dream.' He made us believe in a greater society, a better world. The next year, the Civil Rights Act was signed. And today we have a black man in the White House."

A few kids smile.

"The future belongs to you," I tell them, "with all its challenges and exciting possibilities. Don't shy away from it. Here comes the tour guide. Please be gracious and open-minded. Take a deep breath. Enjoy yourselves but don't goof off. You are guests here. Learn as much as you can. Reserve judgment. I'll ask you for a one- or two-word assessment upon your return. Think about it during the tour. The escort vehicle has just enough room for all of you but not me. That's fine. I've been here before. I'll wait in the van and see you in an hour."

Massive coal trucks the size of buildings thunder past as the students climb into the guide's vehicle and take off.

DOES EVERY GENERATION REQUIRE ITS APOCALYPSE? Its dark cloud on the horizon? My parents had theirs: global thermonuclear war. In grade school the air raid sirens would go off and I'd climb under my desk and huddle, waiting, my knees pulled to my chest like every other dutiful student. To my left, Foxy Felicity would slide over to touch me as we sat and waited for the evil Soviet Empire to nuke Fairchild Air Force Base. Ka-boom! What a way to die, in the embrace of the cutest girl in school. I might even sneak in a kiss before we melted.

Other generations had the Holocaust, the Stalin purges, the Spanish influenza, the Hundred Years' War, the Black Plague. In sixteenth, seventeenth, and eighteenth century North and South America, smallpox alone killed millions. Imagine losing ninety percent of your friends and family in one winter. In some Saxon villages, people lived their entire lives in fear of the Vikings, and for good reason. When the Vikings came, it meant death to all. In some villages, they never came; in others, they did.

I often wonder if as each of us age and fill up with bad news and its accumulated bile, and face our own mortality, do we grow fearful? Resentful? Do we assume, like the grumpy old man in front of his television, that the "world is going to hell"?

And yet, here we are. Despite tyranny, ignorance, and disease, we live on. We explore. We dream. We bring forth the unlimited power of a new youth.

I cannot tell these twelve high school kids what future awaits them. Perhaps the best I can do is offer them hope; get them to improvise and sing, suggest new pathways to creative solutions. Show them the strengths they didn't know they had, strengths they discovered in their national park.

After surviving the Holocaust, Austrian neurologist Viktor Frankl said we must turn predicament into achievement. "Our greatest freedom," he wrote, "is the freedom to choose our attitude."

Canadian journalist Naomi Klein adds, "In the hot and stormy future we have already made inevitable through our past emissions, an unshakable belief in the equal rights of all people and a capacity for deep compassion will be the only things standing between civilization and barbarism."

AN HOUR LATER, THE KIDS ARE BACK.

"In one or two words," I ask them, "what are your impressions? Take your time."

"Nice people."

"Practiced."

"Courteous, kind."

"Propaganda."

"Ostriches."

"Reclamation."

"Helmets, smiles."

"Coalca Cola."

"Dirty Paradox."

"Coalcaine."

"Sad."

"Hardworking."

Another day at the Denali Education Center. The students research and write, talk futures, tell stories. And finally, finally . . . the next day we climb aboard a shuttle bus to head deep into the park. Em, David, and I make a pact: no talking today about climate change, ocean acidification, ecosystem decay, mass extinction, the death of democracy, or Justin Bieber. The kids are burdened enough with packing their lunches and organizing gear.

The day welcomes us with sun, rain, river, cloud, wolves, and bears, the last two at a distance. We explore the new low-profile Eielson Visitor Center, artfully built into the topography where the previous visitor center used to be. With its commitment to renewable energy and sustainability, the NPS designed the center with great care. Today, it's one of only two buildings in Alaska to achieve a platinum (highest possible) level certification from the Leadership in Energy and Environmental Design (LEED).

Inside, we discover *Seasons of Denali*, a magnificent seven-by-twelve-foot quilt by Ree Nancarrow, wife of Bill Nancarrow, the park's first permanent naturalist in the 1950s, a self-effacing veteran of the 101st Army Airborne who fought in the Battle of the Bulge, was wounded twice, and awarded two bronze stars. The quilt, with its four panels and tastefully rendered mountains, braided rivers, and tundra, along with ninety-seven species of plants, birds, and mammals, is a masterpiece. It commands an entire wall and requires a long look to be fully appreciated. A few students sit before it, study it, and write poems.

Outside, near the entrance for all to see, the two moose skulls (from the battle below Mount Galen) are on display, the antlers still locked together like an Escher painting, a Mobius strip of life and death. They too command our attention, and speculation. I hear one visitor say to another, "Jesus, what a way to die."

After lunch, we head up Thorofare Ridge.

The wind is light. Rainsqualls hit us but otherwise the hiking comes easy compared to the other day on Mount Margaret. The kids breeze up, feeling feisty, laughing, talking. One thousand feet above the visitor center, they reach the top and fan out to explore. Some get down on their bellies to photograph flowers. Others climb overlooks and take landscape shots and run free, moving with fluid grace, unlike children we see everywhere today who slouch forward, walking with their heads down, slaves to their iPhones in what Em calls "the Walking Zombie Apocalypse."

In his groundbreaking book, *The Last Child in the Woods*, Richard Louv notes that kids today don't ramble and roam. They seldom go outside. When they do, they cover an area only one-ninth the size of what kids covered forty year ago. Fearful parents today, many in cities, raise clean, wrinkle-free kids, bubble-wrapped against the worst that can happen on the evening news.

That's why it's good to have these kids—any kids—set free in Alaska. Free of television, the endless drumbeat of advertising.

How did we become consumed by consumerism?

In the summer of 1929, President Hoover's Committee on Recent Economic Changes observed that the biggest challenge facing growth in America was the frugality of most Americans. Industrialists worried that production threatened to become so efficient it would soon turn out goods at a pace far greater than people's desire to have them. How to solve this? Create a new culture, one that shifted from fulfilling basic human needs to creating new ones. Transform America from a nation of producers into a nation of consumers. "Economically we have a boundless field before us," concluded Hoover's committee. A field of "wants which will make way endlessly for newer wants, as fast as they are satisfied." In other words, turn *wants* into *needs*. Turn *novelties* into *necessities*.

Years later, historian Steven Stoll would write in his compelling little book, *The Great Delusion*:

We tacitly assume—simply by the way we live—that the transfer of matter from environments into the economy is not bounded by any condition of those environments and that energy for powering our cars, dehumidifiers, leaf blowers, and iPods will always exist. We think of growth as progress. Separating these long-connected ideas is like peeling apart leaves of ancient parchment stored so long in clay jars that they have petrified into one mass. But doing the separating reveals that they are, in fact, distinct, that there can be one without the other; progress does not depend on economic growth, and economic growth does not always lead to progress.

My advice to the kids: Climb a mountain. Learn the songs of birds. Read the secret language of storms. Befriend a flower. Listen to the land.

We're on our bellies atop Thorofare Ridge, fanned out in a radial pattern, our heads together, keying out a species of saxifrage, when a caribou appears.

"Stay still," I whisper.

A full-grown female, the caribou prances directly toward us, head up, knees high. It stops only thirty feet away, and stares, unsure what we are, given that not one of us is standing. The moment stretches itself out, back to the ice age and before, when man, woman, and beast shared shamans and dreams, and men—and hopefully women and children too—painted their stories on cave walls. Then something snaps, a memory, a fear; the caribou leaps, spins in midair, and runs off in another direction.

The kids whoop and holler.

"Did you see that?"

"Whoa."

"Cool."

"Anybody get a picture?"

No. But we have it on the fine emulsion of our minds.

BACK ON THE BUS, EASTBOUND, I ASK THE DRIVER, Mona Bale, to slow down on the downhill run off Polychrome Pass so I can point out the East Fork Cabin. Mona, one of my favorite drivers, stops. She can guess what I want to talk about.

"That's where Adolph Murie lived, while doing fieldwork on the dynamics of predator and prey," I tell the kids, "primarily on wolves and Dall sheep, but also caribou, bears, and other species. He also lived in other park cabins, mostly the Igloo Cabin. He was the real deal, a keen observer and careful chronicler of what he saw and found, and later a lyrical writer in defense of wild Alaska. He proved that wolves not only create healthy populations of prey, they bring vitality to the entire ecosystem; they enrich the whole park. He's known today as 'the conscience of Denali.'"

"What's it like inside the cabin?" one of the kids asks me.

"I don't know."

THE BUS RUMBLES ON.

That night, my last with the students, we share a large dinner at the Denali Education Center and tell stories, always stories, and talk over many things: What does it mean to be a critical thinker? To challenge your own assumptions before you challenge those of others? To stand atop a mountain and find God in nature, time in a flower, perfection in a caribou, poetry in a river? To question answers rather than answer questions? What does it mean to be a radical, a liberal? What did it take to free the slaves and give women the vote? To get Social Security, Workman's Compensation, a Civil Rights Act, a Wilderness Act, the first Earth Day, the establishment of Mount McKinley National Park, and its enlargement and redesignation to Denali National Park and Preserve? It took vision, hard work, and courage. It took liberal values championed again and again, always opposed by conservatives. And it's conservatives today, their fists closed tightly around their money, who despite all scientific evidence say human-caused climate change is fiction. Let us knock the wheels off their clown car. Let us write and speak with brave self-reflection and go forth, inspired by all, intimidated by none, grateful for every day, to accept seemingly insurmountable problems as golden opportunities. "Your job," I tell the kids, "is to joyously confront the crises before you. Can you do that?"

A few nod. A few appear solemn.

"Sometimes it's overwhelming," says dark-eyed Erica, bound for Cornell. "All the serious problems in the world, the magnitude is so huge."

I tell her I feel the same way sometimes. Em and David, the two instructors, agree.

"Try this," I tell Erica. "Fall in love every day. Fall in love with a friend, a flower, a cloud, a novel, a poem, an idea, a song. Fall in love with words, with life. Open your heart to the beauty around you every day. Can you do that?"

"Yes."

"Have you fallen in love with Denali?"

"Yes, we all have."

"Good. So I have a final question for you, for all of you."

"Bring it on," says Joey, grinning.

"What would you rather be, a domestic dog or a wolf?"

They laugh and throw back their heads to raise a racket, a howl, so wild and free and pack-like. This time their answers add up to the opposite of what they were a week ago: ten kids say wolf, two say domestic dog.

"What's changed?" I ask.

"Everything," Joey says. "Everything changes in the wilderness."

"How so?"

He shakes his head.

There are no words.

Only tears.

POSTSCRIPT BY NED ROZELL

— Life at Forty Below Zero —

A FATHER WAKES, ROLLS OUT OF BED, and steps on cold carpet. He grabs a flashlight, and shines it outside the window.

The thermometer reads 40 below zero, the only point at which the Fahrenheit and Celsius scales agree. The red liquid within his thermometer is alcohol; mercury freezes at 38 below.

His little boy wakes, dresses and hands his father birch logs to add to the wood stove. The logs are heavy, cut last fall and not properly dried.

The green wood contains almost 50 percent moisture, compared to about 30 percent in cured wood. The logs hiss amid other burning logs. They give off no heat until the moisture is driven off.

Outside, the car is plugged in. The father remembered the night before to activate the heating element that warms his antifreeze, which in turn keeps his motor oil just viscous enough to allow the pistons to move.

A heat blanket, another northern adaptation, has kept the battery at about 20 degrees Fahrenheit; just warm enough to permit 50 percent of the cranking strength available in summer.

After breakfast, the mother dresses her boy so he can wait outside for the school bus. She pulls a big pile hat over his head, knowing that's where the human body loses the most heat, followed by his neck, the sides of his torso under the arms, and his groin.

Mother and son walk outside, crunching the snow on the driveway as they break the bonds between snow crystals. The dry snow is cold enough to prevent skis from gliding. The air is so cold it robs the interface between ski and snow of heat produced by friction that creates melt water on which to glide in warm temperatures.

On the road, car headlights cut through the ice fog that hangs over the road like cotton candy. Exhaust, about 250 degrees in the tailpipe, cools to minus 40 in less than 10 seconds after it comes out of the vehicle. Water cooled that fast turns into tiny particles that make up ice fog. Cars and trucks aren't the only things that make ice fog. Any source of water vapor will do, including people.

Waiting for the bus, mother and son turn to the sound of a nearby train. Though the train is more than five miles away, a temperature inversion makes it sound as if it's coming down the street. The inversion, created when warm air rests on top of colder air, acts as a tunnel in which sound waves bounce for great distances.

The boy sees a raven flying above the ice fog and points to it. Ravens often roost close to town during a cold snap.

As the black bird flies through the air, its hyper metabolism keeps its body temperature at about 107 degrees.

Through various adaptations, most animals are bothered very little by the cold, though chickadees adapted to life at bird feeders will probably die if people stop feeding them now.

School is rarely closed by cold weather in Alaska (the Fairbanks North Star Borough has no official temperature cut-off), so the bus arrives on time. The mother walks back into the house, her toes tingling as her extremities go through a normal cycle of warming and cooling. Her toe temperature rises to 68 degrees after falling to 50 while waiting for the bus.

The father starts a sluggish car engine. During the cold start, his engine spews a large amount of carbon monoxide, nitrogen oxides and a whole slew of hydrocarbons.

After five to 10 minutes, heat from the engine warms the gasoline, which changes more readily to vapor, allowing more gas to ignite and reducing the pollutants out the tailpipe.

As he pulls out of the driveway and into the fog floating above the street, his car bounces due to a tire that has retained a flat spot.

He bumps down the road slowly until the tire warms enough for the rubber to become more flexible.

Life rolls on.

ACKNOWLEDGEMENTS

THANKS FIRST AND FOREMOST GOES TO all the authors who contributed to this project. They represent just a few of the many talented voices writing about Alaska. Every single one of them was a joy to work with, and every single one of them encouraged this project from the moment I reached out to them. As a writer, I've learned from all of them.

Thanks also to the publishers who allowed excerpts to be included here. A special thank you goes to Nate Bauer and Laura Walker at University of Alaska Press, where several of these selections were first published. University presses are an underappreciated outlet for some of our finest writing.

I've worked with many fine editors over my years as a freelance writer in Alaska. In one way or another, all of them helped me improve my craft and put me in a position where this book was possible. They include Deirdre Helfferich, Jeff Richardson, Mike Campbell, Suzanna Caldwell, Victoria Barber, Susan Sommer, Rod Boyce, Julie Stricker, and Gary Black.

I met my wife, Karen Jensen, at a propane pump in 1992, the most Alaskan thing I've ever done in my life. In 1999, when our first child was born, she was well into her career at Rasmuson Library at the University of Alaska Fairbanks, where she is now the director. I quit my job at the time and stayed home. This opened up the chance for me to write, and as the kids grew up and out of the house, her career has allowed me to pursue mine. Thirty years after that meeting at the propane pump, I still feel like I won the lottery that day.

Finally, I need to thank the late Lael Morgan. She called me out of the blue one day and pitched an idea to me that evolved into this book. Then she gently but persistently kicked me in the rear after I went into a pandemic tailspin and let the project slide. She was also an enormous help in getting the permissions worked out. Several pieces contained in this collection would probably not have made it in without her dogged persistence chasing after a number of publishers and pulling strings for me. Lael has inspired and guided many of Alaska's finest authors, and her legacy in Alaskan literature and historical studies is far greater than most people realize. Her own writings are but a tiny fraction of what she contributed to Alaska, and this book is just one small example of the sort of things she spurred others to do. It would never have come together without her. Plenty of other Alaskan authors have stories of what she did to help them along their way. This book is dedicated to her memory.

CONTRIBUTORS

Dave Atcheson is the author of *Dead Reckoning: Navigating a Life on the Last Frontier, Courting Tragedies on its High Seas* and two other books and is a contributor to numerous periodicals. He can be found online at http://www.daveatcheson.com/about.html

Alexis Bunten is the author of *So, How Long Have You Been Native?: Life as an Alaska Native Tour Guide.* She can be found online at https://bioneers.org/peoples/alexis-bunten/

Zach Falcon is the author of *Cabin, Clearing, Forest.* He can be found online at https://unity.edu/about/leadership/office-of-the-president/direct-reports/zach-falcon/

Judy Ferguson is the author of the two volume series *Windows to the Land, an Alaska Native Story,* as well as seven other books ranging from histories, to memoirs, to children's books. She can be found online at https://judysoutpost.com/

Monte Francis is the author of *Ice & Bone: Tracking an Alaska Serial Killer.* He can be found online at http://www.montefrancis.com/

Lew Freedman is the author of seventy-five books, including *Yukon Quest: The Story of the World's Toughest Sled Dog Race*. He can be found on Twitter at https://twitter.com/lewfreedman?lang=gl

Paul Greci is the author of *Surviving Bear Island* and three other young adult novels. He can be found online at https://www.fantasticfiction. com/g/paul-greci/ and http://www.acsalaska.net/~paulgreci/bio. htm

Kim Heacox is the author of over a dozen books including *Rhythm of the Wild: A Life Inspired by Alaska's Denali National Park*. He can be found online at http://kimheacox.com/

Vicky Ho is a deputy editor and contributor to the Anchorage Daily News. She can be found on Twitter at https://twitter.com/hovicky

Jill Homer is the author of *Into the North Wind: A Thousand Mile Bicycle Adventure Across Frozen Alaska* and three other books. She can be found online at http://www.jilloutside.com/

Nick Jans has written twelve books including *The Giant's Hand: A Life in Arctic Alaska*. He can be found online at https://nickjans.com/

Brendan Jones is an essayist and contributor to numerous publications, as well as the author of *The Alaskan Laundry*. He can be found online at https://www.brendanisaacjones.com/books

Stan Jones is the creator of the Nathan Active detective fiction series and has written or cowritten seven volumes thus far, including *Tundra Kill*. He can be found online at http://sjbooks.com/

Seth Kantner is the author of five books including *Swallowed by the Great Land and Other Dispatches from Alaska's Frontier*. He can be found online at https://www.sethkantner.com/

Tom Kizzia is the author of three books including *Pilgrim's Wilderness: A True Story of Faith and Madness on the Alaska Frontier*. He can be found online at https://www.tomkizzia.com/

Mary Kudenov is the author of *Threadbare: Class and Crime in Urban Alaska.*

Heather Lende is the author of *Take Good Care of the Garden and Dogs: A True Story of Bad Breaks and Small Miracles.* She can be found online at https://www.heatherlende.com/

Nancy Lord is the author of eleven books including *Early Warming: Crisis and Response in the Climate-Changed North.* She can be found online at http://www.writernancylord.com/

Rob McCue is the author of *One Water.*

Kristi Mingqun McEwen is a retired school teaching raising her son while working on her writing.

Rosemary McGuire is the author of three books, including *The Creatures at the Absolute Bottom of the Sea.* She can be found online at https://rosemarymcguire.com/

Colleen Mondor is the author of *Map of My Dead Pilots: the Dangerous Game of Flying in Alaska.* She can be found on Twitter at https://twitter.com/chasingray?ref_src=twsrc%5Egoogle%7Ctwcamp%5Eserp%7Ctwgr%5Eauthor

Melinda Moustakis is the author of *Bear Down, Bear North.* She can be found online at https://www.melindamoustakis.com/

Julia O'Malley writes about about food, culture, and home. She can be found online at https://www.juliaomalley.com/about/

Tanyo Ravicz is the author of four books including *Alaskans.* He can be found online at https://www.tanyo.net/home.html

Molly Retig is the author of *Finding True North: Firsthand Stories of the Booms that Built Modern Alaska.* She can be found online at https://www.mollyrettig.com/

Ned Rozell writes the weekly Alaska Science Forum column for the Geophysical Institute at the University of Alaska Fairbanks. An archive of his columns can be found at https://www.gi.alaska.edu/alaska-science-forum

Bill Sherwonit is the author of numerous books including *Changing Paths: Travels and Meditations in Alaska's Arctic Wilderness*. He can be found online at http://www.alaskawritersdirectory.com/authors/sherwonit_bill.shtml

Sherry Simpson was the author of four books, including *The Accidental Explorer: Wayfinding in Alaska*.

Jonathan Waterman is the author of four books including *Chasing Denali: The Sourdoughs, Cheechakos and Frauds Behind the Most Unbelievable Feat in Mountaineering*. He can be found online at https://jonathanwaterman.com/books/

PERMISSIONS

DAVID A. JAMES IS A FREELANCE WRITER whose work has appeared in numerous publications including the Anchorage Daily News, The Fairbanks Daily News-Miner, the Anchorage Press, the Alaska Dispatch News, the Ester Republic, and Alaska Magazine. An avid mountain biker and longtime pubic radio volunteer, he lives with his wife Karen Jensen in Fairbanks, Alaska.